The Tearless Widow

The Lord is my Shephard, there is nothing I shall want

Grace Elvy Amullo

PublishAmerica
Baltimore

ISBN: 1-4241-6372-2
PUBLISHED BY PUBLISHAMERICA, LLLP
www.publishamerica.com
Baltimore

Printed in the United States of America

In loving memory of my beloved mother, Deodatta Aya, and siblings, Leonora Alur, Pius Otim, Christine Anyiri and Clement Okeny.

Acknowledgments

I am indebted, to my dearest late mother for emphasizing the importance of literacy, supporting my education, teaching me about the sacredness of life and the importance of treating others always with love and respect. It is the knowledge I have gained from her that has inspired me to write this book.

My heartfelt thanks to my children Michael, Henry, Sarah and Vicky and also my siblings, Lucy Alal, Magdalene Auma, Emmanuel Otto and my sister-in-law Josephine for their encouragement, support and love. My special thanks to Dr. Sabatino for her encouragement that has enabled me, to rewrite the manuscript after the first work was inadvertently deleted. I am also grateful to my dearest friends, the MacCara family, Donna MacLellan, Allison Van Diepen, Georgina Fitzgerald, Winifred Tanner, Amana Hughes and Francine Antonisse for their unconditional love and support.

I am indebted most of all to everyone at PublishAmerica, for enabling my dream to become true, as an author, by publishing this book. With profound gratitude I would like to mention by name, Jenniffer Brenneman, the Acquisitions Editor at PublishAmerica, for believing in my manuscript and recommending it to be published.

Chapter One
The Licari Village

Licari is a small village situated on a beautiful hilltop between, two shopping centres, Magwi and Loudo. Magwi is the district headquarters, for the Acoli people of southern Sudan and is north of Licari village. Loudo centre, is south of Licari, beside which is the Obbo coffee plantation. Magwi and Obbo are two of the seven Chiefdoms of the Acoli people. The others are Agoro, Pajok, Palwar, Panyikwara and Omeyo. The people of Licari village are predominantly from a clan, called Oyere, which is one of the many clans of the Obbo Chiefdom. East of Licari, is the Kinyeti ranges, with a minor peak in the Acoli part of the mountain, called Lottii. The ranges extended to the Uganda border and created very beautiful scenery in the East. The highest peak, on the Kinyeti ranges, is the Imotong Mountain, which is the highest mountain in the Sudan. When the sun rises in the morning, the rays first touched the Licari hill, while the rest of the low-lying areas are still in the shadow of the ranges. When someone stands on the Licari hill, he/she could see as far south past the Pajok Chiefdom, as the horizon on the border to Uganda. Southeast is the Catholic Parish, called Palotaka, which is about ten kilometers away and yet the Church is visible from Licari Hill. When one faces north, he/she could see as far away as the horizon beyond the Agoro Chiefdom. In the northeast stands, the beautiful Okire Mountain with its twin tower tops. Many people believed that, the base of the mountain had never been accessed by anyone because it started in a very, very deep and murky valley. The indigenous people, who are living near the mountain, have been saying that, the white explorers had attempted, many times, to access the base of the mountain but failed. Therefore, to date, no one knows the exact height of the mountain and the one documented is only an approximation. When one faces west, he/she could see as far away as the horizon beyond which is the Panyikwara Chiefdom. Many passersby liked stopping on the Licari hill while they enjoyed the picturesque view of the Acoliland.

Although the western civilization had documented that there are only two seasons in Africa, the Acoli people did not believe so because according to them, there are four seasons in a year; *Poto-kot, Cwiri, Lango and Oro.*

Poto-kot is equivalent to spring season. The rain begins to fall after the long, hot, dusty and dry season. It is the beginning of the cultivation season. During this season in Licari village, the hills, valleys and plains looked like fairyland. The grass, green and lash, the trees budded out new leaves, variety of wild flowers bloomed everywhere and the most outstanding ones were the wild lilies, on the way to Magwi because they appeared like, someone had planted them there and had been taking very good care ever since. The wonderful health of the grass, trees and flowers showed evidently, the fertility of the soil on which they were thriving. The bees buzzed and variety of other insects flew everywhere. It seemed then as if, every creature; animals and plants alike, were quite joyful and singing songs of praises to their creator.

Cwiri is equivalent to summer season. The rainfall is very heavy, with lots of thunderstorms. The torrential downpour made it hard some days, for the people to go out. Therefore, the people who did not gather enough firewood during the dry season found it hard to cook meal because everything is very wet that, even the dry wood that had been left outside in the rain, became too wet and not suitable for making fire unless, first kept in a dry place. The women cooked the smoked meat that, they had kept from the dry season, during this time of the year. Most of the people spent their time in-doors, during the downpours. The weather is wet and humid most of the time and it is the bushiest time of the year. The trees are full of foliage, the grass very long and most of the early crops by then had grown to their full capacity. However, there is a dry spell in the month of June and by then, some of the early crops were ready to be harvested and therefore, the people started harvesting the early crops, as well as cultivating the late ones.

Lango, this is equivalent to the autumn season and during this season, the people harvested most of the late crops. The rainfall is quite scarce and the grass had matured and changed their colours from green, to yellowish brown. Some of the trees' leaves changed their colours to yellowish-brown and most of the leaves would begin to fall. The scarcity of the rainfall, made the people to work on their farm, without the worry for being beaten by the rain. The people worked hard to prepare the stalls for the temporary storage of their produce and later on, stored everything into the granaries after most of the work had been completed, at the beginning of the dry season. The people did most of the final works on the farms, during this season.

Oro, this is the dry season and there is no rain or farm work because of the scorching heat and most of the trees are then without leaves. The men would go out hunting and burnt down lots of the bushes while, on the other hand, the women would go fishing almost every other day. On the days that the men did not go out to hunt and the women also did not go fishing, they enjoyed tremendously such restful moments by eating, drinking and chatting together under trees, that did not lose their leaves. During this time of the year, the people threw lots of parties and drank and danced until, the wee hours of the morning. It is the most romantic time of the year. The people, who had been having bad roofs during the rainy season, renovated their houses and those whose granaries were not good, repaired them but for most of the time, everybody rested and took it easy, as they were waiting for the beginning of the rainy season, when the whole cycle would begin again.

The people of Licari village were well known, for their hard work on the farms. They took pride in their fertile lands and grew variety of crops. Every family in Licari owned more than five large granaries and after the harvest, they would fill all of them. There has never been a history of starvation in Licari. The people worked as a community on their farms, so as to enable even the lazy people among them to double up their efforts and fully participate with others during the cultivation time. The women cooked lots of food and some of them even brewed the Acoli beers to feed their hard-working men, during the beginning of the rainy season. At weeding time, the women worked together in turns on each farm. At harvest time, most of the relatives of the people of Licari village, from the neighbouring villages, come over to help them and after the harvest, they would return to their homes with lots of food. The men in Licari village were good hunters and therefore, there was plenty of meat in the village throughout the year.

The Acoli people always gather together around the fire in the evenings and listen to all kinds of stories that the elders were telling about long time ago and therefore, in Licari village, the custom was very alive. The one place that the men of Licari did like to gather at, for most of the evenings, was the home of the Second World War Veteran nicknamed *Dikomwoi* (meaning one who has killed multitude). A celebration was held in Dikomwoi's honour, after he had returned from the war in Europe and was given the knick name, to symbolise his heroism. Dikomwoi was a very tall man, about seven feet or more and towered above everybody else in Licari village. His military training had kept him healthy, upright and fit. He fought the war on the side of the British, since the Sudan was then a colony of the British Empire.

Therefore, he told his village men about how, during the war, many soldiers had died painfully and how some of them cried like little boys, from the life threatening injuries that they had sustained. Most of his listeners, could not believe some of his gruesome tales and the fact that white men could cry because they were thinking that, the white people were too smart and civilized to cry. However, Dikomwoi refuted their ideology by telling them truthfully that, all the human beings, regardless of their colours, race or creeds, were the same whenever, they were facing ultimate danger. When his listeners, asked him to tell them about how he had managed to survive the fierce fight, he told that, "A few of us found a hole under a big rock and hid ourselves there when the Germans were attacking us quite brutally. The fight on that day was the fiercest one that, I have ever experienced. Most of the people from our group died that day. After the Germans were thinking that they had killed everyone, they started coming near the place, where we were hiding and sat down for a drink. Therefore, we started attacking and killing most of them, at their disadvantage because they did not know where the bullets were coming from. The few of them, who had survived our bullets, ran away and hid themselves for a little while, with the intention of trying to lure us out from our hiding but we did not yield to their bait. We stayed our ground and remained quiet. After a little while, they came back and started shooting randomly towards our direction. However, we took better position and gunned most of them down; the few of them, if any were at all left, might have run for their lives. We then sat where we were, for a long, long time until, all was quiet and still and thereafter, we carefully started getting out of the hole. The whole area was full of dead bodies, some of them were burnt beyond recognition, a sight that, no one would like to encounter, in a normal life's situation. We began walking eventually, for a long time before we could be rescued."

Tears formed into Dikomwoi's eyes, as he was narrating some of his stories because the memories were still very vivid in his mind, although, the whole thing had happened a long time ago. Occasionally, Dikomwoi would try to demonstrate some of his moves during the war but did not perform them well due to his age. Therefore, he would mockingly laugh at himself whenever he had failed to do the moves properly and would begin telling his audients that, "I wish that I was young again, my dear people. I would have shown you exactly what I have done to destroy those Germans (which he pronounced Jérémén)."

Dikomwoi was such an amateur storyteller that, his audience would laugh at his incredible stories and could not get enough from him.

10

Whenever the moon is full and bright, the girls would gather on Licari hill to sing *Longo* (which could be love songs to praise lovers, provocative songs to threaten rivals, praise songs to extol ones' family, satirical songs to insult and defame bad boys, etc). An opportunity is given to one girl at a time, to sing and the rest of the girls would only answer the chorus. This is the tradition that has been practiced by the Acoli girls, from the time unknown. The love songs, praised how good-looking ones' lover was, his height, might, strength, teeth, eyes, smile, the way he walked, etc. The provocative songs were sung, with the intention to humiliate, intimidate and discourage a rival who wants to takeover another girl's lover. On the other hand, a girl could choose to praise her home, brothers, sisters, uncles, aunts, strong and powerful men in her family and how well they were living. Once in a while, other girls would sing, satirical songs that insulted and reduced to ashes, the boys who had treated some of them with scorn and had caused them shame. Whenever such songs were sung, the words were quite obscene for any relative of the singer to hear. Occasionally, quarrels would break out, during the gathering because of some of the terrible languages that were being used. The girls who were rivaling for the same boy would at times end up fighting with each other; meanwhile, the boys, who usually would stand at a distant place, listened with amusement at how silly the girls were at emptying out each other in public, and therefore, they would laugh at the girls with such amusement.

The children also disliked sitting with the elders around the fire in the evening, especially, when the moon is bright and therefore, they would go out to the playground, played a lot of games until, they were quite tired and ready to go to bed. As the children were heading out to the playground, they would always sing a provocative song, which said that, anyone who was remaining with the elders and refusing to go to the playground, was weak and sick. This made all the children to start running very fast, to their gathering place. However, there were some lazy ones, who would not be intimidated by the song and therefore remained with the elders. The names of such were shouted out aloud in the playground and called weaklings. The joyful singing, rhythmic jumping and dancing in the playground, made both the children and the elders very happy. Such joyful play indicates that the village is alive, happy, and has a lot to eat. The toddlers were the only ones, who were normally staying with the elders because they slept early in the evening.

Licari was no doubt a small village, in which, everybody knew each other but the number of the boys outnumbered the girls. For some mysterious reason, the women of Licari village were producing more boys than girls. Most of the boys were quite handsome, tall and strong. Many girls from the neighbouring villages were having crushes on Licari boys. Therefore, the boys made good use of the opportunity consequently and selected the very best ones. Licari village, being in the middle of the two shopping centres, the young men took the advantages of both Magwi and Obbo market days respectively. The main purpose, why the boys were going to the markets frequently, was not necessarily to buy stuff but also to check out for the girls with whom, they could start relationships. Wednesdays and Saturdays were market days for the People of Obbo, whereas Thursdays and Sundays were for the People of Magwi.

During the dry season, the youths in Licari village threw up one party after another. A lot of people came for those parties from Loudo, Pokongo, Cama, Owinykibul, Taya, Alia, Tingili, Pambala, Lerwa, Agoro, Imolongo, Magwi and Abara villages. The news about the parties was posted on the trees on market days and sometimes by a word of mouth. The Acoli youths take great pride in their locally composed songs, which they play on *Adungu* (harp-like instruments) and dance with such vigor, when the songs were played during the party. Generally, the Acoli people profoundly love and adore their culture and tradition very much and are quite proud of who they are. During such parties, the relationships that, the Licari boys had started on market days, came to fruit eventually because the lovers had ample time to talk to each other privately and finalised the necessary plans for marriages.

The Licari boys were quite interested in marriage because they were admiring and loving profoundly the way in which, their families, married relatives and friends, were living their lives. In a year, there were more than three new brides, who were brought in Licari village. On the other hand, whenever a boy from Licari was in love with any girl from any of the surrounding villages and the girl was resisting his proposal for marriage, they would abduct the girl during a big dance or market day. The situation was a common occurrence and therefore, some of the Licari boys were, as a result, knick named, *oting kwak,* (which means, carrying away by force). However, the boys did not care about the consequences for their daring activities because they knew that they were able to meet the fines and the dowries that, the parents of the girls that they had abducted for their wives were going to demand. However, the families of the girls, who had been abducted by the boys from Licari village, upon knowing that their daughters were in Licari village, they would not complain much because they were aware that, their daughters were in good hands. Almost all, of the men in Licari village took care of their wives and children very well and were very proud of their families. However, whenever there were some misunderstandings between a husband and a wife, the elders would settle the issues peacefully until, reconciliation was achieved. Most, if not all, of the women in Licari village, were good-looking, beautiful, trustworthy, strong, hardworking, faithful and respectable because the young men selected the best girls, from the neighbouring villages.

Chapter Two
Okeny's Family

In Licari village, there was an honourable man, called Okeny, who was the youngest and only son among the daughters of his parents, hence, that is the meaning of his name. Okeny's parents and siblings loved him dearly and therefore, he grew up consequently with the confidence and determination that was, rarely found in most of his peers. Okeny was quite a tall figure, well built, walk upright with broad shoulders and very handsome. Many girls had crushes on Okeny when he was a young man but he opened his heart to only one girl, whom he dearly loved and married eventually. He had been calling his wife a blessing from on high because she was more than he had expected to find in a wife. In the society of polygamous marriages, the couple was one of the few in Acoliland, who had never broken their vows for the matrimony and were well known for their deep faith as Catholics, which they were practicing by, always helping others and telling them about the kingdom of God. Okeny was very spiritual, wise and therefore, everyone in his village respected him a lot. One glance at Okeny, would confirm that he was a man of influence and high regard in his community because he seemed so sure of himself and yet very gentle in all that he was doing. He listened to the people of his community, young and old alike, with such keen interest and spoke very little. Okeny was a hardworking man who handled every piece of work efficiently and was always available whenever his help was needed by anyone in his village. In the event that, the village elders were settling differences like quarrel between husband and wife or any other problem at all, he was the last person to say the last word, which was always unanimously accepted.

Okeny's wife was called Abongkara, who was an only child to her parents. Abongkara's parents buried nine children before her. She, therefore, was the life of her parents, who delighted a lot in all she was doing. Abongkara was approximately six feet tall, had thick dark hair, lighter complexion of skin than her husband's, good-looking face, her teeth were as white as an elephant's tusk, had dark sparkling eyes, like her mother's, had heart-warming smile that, delighted people's heart, long neck that gave her a nickname of, "Larii," meaning like a giraffe and walked upright with such sure steps. Abongkara was the most beautiful girl in her generation and when she got married, her husband loved her dearly and had never since looked at any other woman. Abongkara's parents were quite happy that, she got married to a good and honourable man.

Okeny and Abongkara had six children, three boys and girls. They loved their children dearly and sent all of them to school, including the girls. In Acoliland, the girls were rarely sent to school because only a few families were thinking that, the education of girls was important. However, Okeny, who had lived in Uganda during the first civil war in southern Sudan, saw the importance of girls' education, while he was there. Therefore, he made it his priority, to educate his sons as well as his daughters and had never looked down on his daughters or even considered them inferior to his sons because according to him, all his children were of equal importance. However, most of his colleagues had tried tirelessly to discourage him from sending his girls to school but he refused vehemently to listen to them.

The first-born son of Okeny and Abongkara was named, Bongomin. He was tall, good-looking with a smile that touched the heart of everyone who beheld him. He took most of the qualities of his father and therefore, was gentle, soft-spoken and respected people. Bongomin was the kind of a child that, every parent would wish to have. He listened to all the good advice that, his mother, father and the elders were giving him. Abongkara's heart rejoiced in all that, her son had been doing. From the time that Bongomin was sent to school, he excelled in all his undertakings, always the first in his class. He attended Rumbek secondary school and only got the Sudan School Certificate. Getting the Sudan School Certificate alone was a milestone that everyone was longing for in those days. The northern Sudan government at that time discriminated a lot against the southern Sudanese when, it came to education. It was a common thing in those days, for southern Sudanese students, not to be accepted into the university. In some years, there was not a single student from the south who, was accepted into the university. The situation, hurt a lot of young people whose dreams were to study in the university so that they could make something out of their lives. However, Bongomin got accepted eventually to the Yambio Agricultural College, in Western Equatoria Province. After graduation, he got a job as an Agriculture

Extension Officer, at Upper Talanga, Tea Project. After he had worked for two years, he got married to his one and only sweetheart, Adyero, a beautiful girl from Pokongo, one of the many clans of the Obbo Chiefdom. The couple had two sons, Logira and Akwaluka, whom they loved and adored dearly.

Okema, the second born, was a very good-looking boy. Unlike his elder brother, he liked to joke a lot and made people laughed. He was kind and would help anyone in the village who needed his assistance. Okema was the macho man of his family and his parents took pride in his strength and gentleness. Like his elder brother, he respected his parents, other people and especially, all the elders. Okema also attended the Rumbek Secondary School and graduated with the Sudan School Certificate but could not join the university. Okema liked to talk to people and it had been his lifelong dream to become a journalist. Therefore, he joined the Regional Ministry of Culture and Information and was working as a reporter. After two years on his job, he was sent for a course in Khartoum, to be trained as a journalist. The opportunity fulfilled Okema's dream, and therefore, he worked hard during his studies and graduated with honours. After graduation, Okema came back to Juba and his ministry promoted him to a senior position. Therefore, his parents and siblings were quite delighted, for his accomplishment. Okema was not yet married because his job was taking most of his time and did not have consequently, ample time for a serious courtship.

Otim, the youngest of the three boys, was a very, very quiet boy. He liked listening to what the other people were saying and spoke rarely. He was not as tall as his two older brothers but very good-looking. In school, he did very well, like his brothers. Otim liked math a lot and could sit in one place for a long time, as he was calculating all kinds of math. He attended the Juba Commercial Secondary School and got only the infamous Sudan School Certificate but wasn't able to enter into the university. As soon as Otim had graduated, he landed a good job as an accountant, with the Ministry of Health. Otim performed very well at his work that, his boss liked him a lot. Therefore, he gave his parents a lot of financial support and they were very grateful to him.

Aya was the first girl, after the boys, hence, the meaning of her name and was the apple of her parents' eyes, before the two younger girls were born. Aya was of average height and had such a sweet smile. Abongkara taught her daughter how to perform house chores at a young age. At about ten years old, Aya could do most of the routine chores in the house. She attended the Juba Girls' Senior Secondary School and, like her brothers, only got the Sudan

School Certificate. Her love and care for people who were sick made her get a job as a nurse in Juba hospital but, later on, got trained and became a medical assistant. Aya got married eventually to a man called Lony and moved with him to Torit.

The youngest child of Okeny and Abongkara was called Amyel. She was a little taller than Aya and very pretty. Okeny and his wife had the softest spots in their hearts for Amyel being the last born in the family. Consequently, Amyel grew up with such confidence and was quite stubborn. Abongkara wondered whether Amyel would one day cope well when her time came to go away to a boarding school. Amyel's older siblings left home for boarding schools when she was quite young. The only person Amyel knew very well among her older siblings was the fifth born called Ader, whom she dearly loved and adored. Amyel considered Ader as her heroine. So long as Ader was present all was well with Amyel. On the first day that Amyel had gone to the boarding school her mother thought that she would be back home by evening but that did not happen. Amyel settled well into her new environment and although she missed her mother she was equally happy to meet new friends who were of her age. Amyel, like her older sisters, completed her secondary school from Juba Girls' Senior Secondary School but did not go to the university. During her time few people from the south were able to join the Juba University but most of the chosen few were either the children or relatives of the big people in the regional government. The situation caused a lot of despair to many students from poor families that some of them completely gave up on their dreams for a better future and went to live in the rural areas. However, Amyel took some courses in teaching and eventually got a job as a teacher in Palotaka Primary School. She taught very well and her pupils liked her a lot. One thing that was a bit strange about Amyel was that she did not have any interest in boys whatsoever. She never dated anybody since she was still in school and continued to turn down the young men who had interest in her. Consequently, she was still unmarried.

Abongkara and Okeny taught their children the true teaching of the Catholic Church and therefore consolidated their deep faith in their children. In the evenings Okeny read the Bible to his children and thereafter answered their questions about some of the teachings in the Bible. After reading the Bible, the family recited the Holy Rosary. Okeny taught his children about the importance of being obedient to the commands of God, love of Jesus Christ that made him die to save all mankind and the Holy Spirit, the giver of life and guide for all to follow the will of God. Okeny also stressed to his children the importance of Mary, the mother of Jesus, in the role of Salvation. He made his children realized the risk Mary had taken to conceive out of wedlock, the fatigue and pain she went through while she gave birth to Jesus in the manger in Bethlehem, the shock she had had when the wise men visited, the fear that gripped her heart when Simeon warned her of the impending sorrow that would pierce her heart like a sword, her life in Egypt with the baby Jesus and her husband, Joseph, as refugees, the anguish she felt when Jesus got lost for three days, the tumultuous life Jesus had had with the religious people of his time, which culminated to his gruesome death, the heart-wrenching sorrow Mary felt as she saw her son died on the cross on Calvary and eventually the anguish she had experienced while holding the lifeless body of her son for the last time before he was buried. He also expressed to his children the joy that Mary felt when she found Jesus after the three days when he was lost, when Jesus turned water into wine at the wedding at Cana, when Jesus performed miracles (healed the sick, restored sight to the blind, the lame walked, the deaf heard, raised dead people to life, the hem of his cloak healed a woman whom the doctors had failed to cure, multiplied a few bread and fish to feed the multitude, the deformed restored to upright position, drove demonic spirits out of the people, etc), preached with wisdom about the kingdom of God and his resurrection from the dead. Okeny went on to tell his children, "Had the Blessed Mother been a writer, her book about the life of Jesus would have been the best seller of all ages. Jesus respected his mother very much and it is a shame to see some of the believers dishonoured her as not being of any significance. To give you a good example my dear children, in Acoli culture, people respected their mothers and mothers-in-law very much and I therefore would like you to give great respect and honour to the Mother of Jesus. She is a special mother to all mankind even those who do not believe in her Son. You must note that Jesus loves his mother a lot and we should do the same. Foremost, I would like you all to love God and put Him first in everything that you do. Remember, the fear and respect for God is the beginning of wisdom. You should also love and respect other people for no one can pretend to love only God when he does not love his fellow men. I know that there are some believers out there, who judge other people including the people of our faith for not being the true followers of Christ. Be careful my dear children and should never follow such teachings because I know that anyone who truly believes in Christ Jesus will not judge or look down on another person. Who are we to judge other people when the Holy Book clearly said that, "For all have sinned and fallen short of the glory of God?" The teachings of our church came down to us from the apostles and will last until Jesus returns. During our Saviour's lifetime here on earth, he was viciously insulted, hated, judged and eventually killed as if he were a horrible criminal notwithstanding his holy and innocent life. Our Lord did not judge anyone including the people who had committed terrible sins. He forgave and restored people's life. I would like you, my dear children, to know and follow Jesus closely for He is the Way, the Truth and Life."

When the boys reached puberty, Okeny taught them a lesson about the way they should treat girls. "I don't want you to abuse any girl at all," he admonished his sons. "You should respect girls at all times. Every girl has a family and many other relatives. As a result therefore, whenever a boy abuses a girl, the whole family of the girl is wounded and nothing will be the same in that family again. Respect all girls like you would respect your own mother and sisters. I am aware that your bodies are undergoing tremendous changes at your stage in life and with that come some feelings that you were not aware of before but that do not mean that you should act on those feelings. Those feelings are indications that you are now maturing into young men. Sons, I would like you to know that sex is very sacred and should only be practiced by married couples. Whenever anyone abuses sex, it becomes the worst curse in that person's life and the life of the other person with whom he/she has had it. Every human body is the temple of the Holy Spirit and therefore should be treated with absolute respect."

Okeny's sons therefore took their father's advice very serious and were never lured by their peers to go against whatever they had learnt from their father even after they had left home.

On the other hand Abongkara handled the girls. She taught her daughters about the importance and meaning of a woman's life. "You are now blossoming into young women," she lovingly told them, "and with that comes the twist of dealing with young men. You must respect your bodies and keep far away from boys who ask you for sex. Boys who shamelessly ask girls for sex have no respect for women. They just used girls for pleasure and not love. Love and lust are two different things. When a boy loves a girl, he cares and treats her with absolute respect but when he lusts after a girl he asks for sex and after he had gotten what he wanted from her he would abandon her. Remember, your bodies are the temples of the Holy Spirit. Have you seen anyone defecate in the place for worship or do anything shameful in it? I therefore would like you to treat your bodies with love, respect and dignity like you would treat a house of worship. Any other sin does not have a lifetime impact on you as the one you commit against your own body. Sex is holy and should be reserved for married people only. Love and respect yourself, my dear daughters, and the world will do the same. Hate and disrespect yourself and the world will even do worst things to you. In the future, some of your peers will tell you things that are contrary to what I am telling you now but please don't listen to them. Most of the happily married women are those who have abstained from sex before marriage. Some day, when any of you is faced with the temptation to give in to sexual demand from a boy, remember, there is a policeman in the sky who watches every tinsy winsy detail of your daily and secretive activities and you will answer to him at the end of time."

The girls thanked their mother for being open and honest with them about the facts of a woman's life. Not many mothers took the opportunity to speak to their daughters candidly like Abongkara had done. In the Acoli custom such advice was left for aunts and other relatives but Abongkara took it upon herself that she was a better teacher to her daughters than anyone else.

The children grew up loving and adoring Okeny and Abongkara for being forthright with them about the meaning of life. They were glad to have parents who could talk to them openly about social and spiritual life. The wonderful love and teachings that the children got at home helped them so much that no one was able to sway them from their faith even after they had left home. Wisdom, understanding, knowledge, love, kindness and compassion radiated in everything the children were doing. Okeny and Abongkara's children were the envy of all who knew them.

Chapter Three
Ader

Ader was the fifth child of Okeny and Abongkara and the tallest among her sisters, approximately six feet and very slender. She got her mother's thick black hair and lighter complexion of the skin, spotlessly white teeth, none of which crooked that awesomely attracted people's attention whenever they showed out while she beautifully smiled and shy looking eyes that delighted the hearts of all who had laid their eyes on her. Everybody who had met Ader for the first time always wanted to take a second look because of her exquisite look. Ader was as beautiful as her mother and with some added qualities from her father. She was evidently the favourite child of her parents although they would not openly admit so. One of Ader's paternal aunts once said that God had spent a little more time while he was creating Ader than the rest of the members of her family. Ader's beautiful features reminded her father a lot about his wife when she was young. Consequently, Okeny spoke to his daughter with so much love in his eyes that anyone could tell at a glance. Humility, love, obedience, meekness, hard work, respect, kindness and compassion clothed Ader with absolute beauty from inside out that made everyone liked and spoke very well of her. However, good-look did not make Ader snobbish or self-conceited because she respected everyone, especially the elders. Ader's words were very few but she liked to listen to the other people while they talked. The only time when Ader's voice could be heard aloud was whenever she was playing with her youngest sister, Amyel. They giggled and sometimes wrestled for fun. Ader was taught how to do house chores at a young age just like the rest of her sisters and therefore performed every work splendidly that her mother delighted a lot in her and secretly referred to her as, 'the joy of my heart and the sister that I have never had'. Ader was built stronger than her two sisters; consequently, she carried heavier bundle of firewood than Aya and could handle any big container whenever she went to the river to fetch some water. During weeding time,

Abongkara took Ader to the field and left Aya at home to cook most of the time because Aya got tired very quickly while she was working in the sun but Ader endured the heat without any sign of fatigue. Aya secretly admired Ader a lot and wished that she could have had the strength that Ader had. The three boys also secretly delighted in Ader's good-look and her ability to do most work very well. Ader was always readily available to help any neighbour, whenever they needed her assistance.

When Ader started school she did very well just like the rest of her siblings. Her teachers liked her a lot because of her quiet nature and hard work. Although Ader was a quiet person, she participated effectively in class discussions. She was always the best girl in her class and scored the highest marks. Ader, like her sisters Aya and Amyel, eventually attended the Juba Girls' Senior Secondary School. She never dated during her secondary school period because her mother advised her, "Boys and studies do not mix well together. Your first priority must be your education. Boys will always be available even after you have completed your secondary school. Men respect learned women and treat them better than the illiterate ones. Study hard and after you have finished the hard work a good man will come your way some day."

Based on her mother's advice, Ader avoided boys at all cost and worked very hard on all her subjects. When she finally did her Sudan School Certificate Exams, she passed and got the Certificate but missed the boxing marks for the in-take into the university by only two marks. Ader's dream of becoming a lawyer was then shattered. Consequently, she was deeply injured by the situation that she got very frustrated, depressed and went to live with her parents in the village.

Abongkara and Okeny were both saddened by their daughter's despair and therefore counseled her most of the time about the meaning of life. One day Abongkara humbly spoke to her daughter while they were working in the field, "Ader, your father and I think that it is not good for you to stay with us here in the village. We like your company a lot but we think that you could do more for yourself and us if you were working in a place like Juba. You are a young woman and have your whole life before you. Your brothers are very concerned about your stay with us in the village. Your dad and I too reciprocate their concern and would like you to go to Juba. Your brother, Okema, has expressed willingness for you to live with him. He promised that he would be very kind to you and help you to get a job in any one of the government ministries. There is a reason why you have not been accepted in the university. May be God has prepared a better future for you somewhere else rather than to study at the university. Please accept your brother's offer for you to live with him and go to Juba, my dear child. I can see a bright future awaiting for you there."

That day, Ader attentively listened to her mother and for the first time she realized that everything that her parents have been telling her was for her own good. Tears formed into her eyes as she said to her mother, "Mama, I will go and live with Okema as you have suggested and may your wishes for me come true."

Abongkara was very delighted to hear her daughter eventually accepted to go to Juba and live with her brother so that he could help her to look for a job.

After the long day in the field, Ader and her mother walked home feeling quite tired. That night, therefore, Abongkara joyfully told her husband, "I have eventually managed to convinced Ader today to go back to Juba and live with Okema."

"Did you?" delightfully said her husband, who was equally worried about the future of their beloved daughter. "This is the best night of my life. I have never thought that Ader could come to her senses and accept to go back to Juba and look for work. She is too hard on herself for having not made it to the university."

"Every hurt takes time to heal," Abongkara assured her husband. "I think that our daughter is ready to handle any challenge now that she has spent a year with us, here in the village, after finishing her secondary school."

"You are a wise woman and I love you for your wisdom," Okeny joyfully told his wife.

On the other hand, Ader deeply pondered about what her mother had told her that day and wrestled with lots of thoughts and doubts about returning to Juba. Ader had developed such low self-esteem since she had failed to enter the university. She tossed in bed with a sorrowful heart because she did not see any reason for her to return to Juba. However, Ader did not want to disappoint her parents and therefore made up her mind to travel to Juba in three days' time so as to please them.

Okeny approached her daughter the following morning with a broad smile on his face and happily told her, "Your mom and I are both very delighted to know that you have finally agreed to go back to Juba. This does not mean that we are fed up of you living with us. We dearly love you but have been quite concerned about your decision for staying with us here in the village. You are an educated girl and you have a lot to offer to the world. Here in the village you cannot utilize the knowledge you have acquired in school. The life in the village is too monotonous for a brain like yours. Do not give up hope, my dear daughter. There is always light at the end of the tunnel. You never know the kind of opportunity that is awaiting you in Juba. Please do go and may God's blessings be with you, my child."

"Thank you for being so kind and understanding, Dad," gratefully replied Ader. "I do not think that you can turn me away from this home for any bad reason at all. Anger, frustration, anguish and despair buried my hope, perception and dream for the future for a year but I have finally reclaimed my hope and could see things from your perspective. I have decided to go to Juba next tomorrow. I will wash my clothes today, pack my stuff tomorrow and travel the next day."

"Bravo!" joyfully exclaimed Okeny. "The tough daughter that I used to know is alive again. Welcome back, my dear child. You are a strong young woman. I have dreamed of this day for a long time and I am very excited that it is eventually here today. How could despair, anger, anguish and frustration defeat a kind and loving heart like yours, Ader? Love overcomes all and today you have triumphed over the monsters that have been internally devastating you for a year."

Ader was very happy to see the joy with which her father had spoken to her and therefore tenderly hugged him.

Abongkara helped her daughter washed and packed the stuff for her travel to Juba. On the day that Ader was leaving for Juba, her parents escorted her to the bus stop. The bus arrived Licari village at 11:30 AM and Ader bid her parents goodbye as she boarded the bus. Abongkara and her husband wished their daughter well on her journey and waved goodbye to her as the bus was leaving. Ader's parents stood on Licari hill and watched the bus as it sped down the hills towards Magwi until it was out of sight. They were glad that their daughter was at last going to Juba but also missed her because they were so used to living with her at home. That day, the big home was left to just Abongkara and Okeny and it seemed quite empty without Ader.

While in the bus Ader wondered what the future really held for her in Juba. Uncertainty gripped her mind and her heart was full of fear for the unknown. Ader's soul was also quite crushed with hopelessness but then she suddenly remembered her father's advice that whenever one was overcome with fear, prayer was the best weapon to kill it. Consequently, Ader quietly began to pray. "Dear God," she earnestly said, "you know everything that lies ahead of me in Juba. I am not aware of anything that would happen to me, when I get there but you, dear heavenly father, knows everything. Please, kindly remove all obstacles from my path in life and help me to daily follow you in whatever you want me to do. In all my endeavours may your holy will be done and not mine. I am an instrument of your hand, father, use me in anyway you want. Praise be your holy name forever, in Jesus' Name I pray—amen."

After the short prayer, Ader's fear for the future was instantly turned into strength and courage. An instant peace came over her and she was filled with joy and happiness. Ader did not even feel the distance between Licari and Juba as being far.

Upon arrival in Juba, Ader found her brother waiting for her at the bus station. Okema was so delighted to see his sister that he hugged her and then joyfully said, "Welcome, Ader, my dear sister. I never thought that you would make up your stubborn mind and come back to Juba."

"Well I have made it up and here I am, brother," carelessly replied Ader with a smiling face. "However, I hope that I will not wreck up your social life."

"Is that the reason why you went away to live in the village for a year?" Okema sadly questioned his sister and did seem a little hurt."

"Please, stop acting like an old man," Ader playfully teased her brother. "Since when have I become a boil in your bottom? I never meant what I have told you in the way that you have understood it. I just wanted to find out if my brother is still the senior bachelor that I used to know."

"Oh, Ader, my sister," joyfully said Okema, who felt quite relieved after comprehending that his sister was only joking. "I am still the senior bachelor that you have always been calling me but let me assure you that even if I were to have a serious relationship with a girl, there would still be a room for you in my house. Don't you know that blood is thicker than water?"

"I know that very well, brother and that is why I have decided to come and live with you," happily replied Ader.

Okema then patted his sister on the back and said, "Let us go home, you naughty girl. I know that you are tired from the journey." He then grabbed some of his sister's luggage and they walked to his house.

Okema had rented a two-bedroom house in Buluk, not far from the Yei Bus Station. He very beautifully furnished his house. Everything was immaculately clean and in proper order. Okema liked a clean environment and he worked hard on the weekends to maintain his cleanliness. Anyone who had come to visit Okema thought that he had a wife. Therefore, when they got to the house, Ader was quite amazed by what she had seen. She admirably looked her brother in his eyes and awesomely shook her head. She was overwhelmed by how neat and organized everything was. To further surprise Ader, Okema had prepared a meal before he went to pick her up from the bus station. Okema never thought that his house keeping routine was extraordinary. He therefore surprisingly asked his sister, "Ader, why do you seem so shocked and amazed to see everything in my house?"

"Brother, I have never thought that you would be such a perfect housekeeper," Ader happily told him as she continued to admire everything in the house. "Mom and Dad would be very proud of you when they see how well furnished and clean your house is."

"Well, thank you sister and welcome to my house," delightfully said Okema. "However, from today onward this house will no longer be mine alone but ours, you and I."

Ader was so overwhelmed with joy at how warmly her brother had welcomed her that she tenderly hugged him once again and said, "I am so lucky to have you, as my brother."

"Ader, I also feel so blessed to have you, as my sister," joyfully said Okema. He then showed his sister the place for taking shower because she was quite dusty from the journey

After Ader had taken shower, they settled down to a delicious meal of the sapid Nile fish and rice that Okema had cooked. The food was well prepared and tasted very nice but Ader then told her brother, "From tomorrow onward, I will not allow you to cook in this house anymore."

"May I know why I should not cook?" curiously requested Okema.

"You are getting spoiled by living such an independent life, brother," sadly replied Ader, with a look of concern in her eyes, for her brother. "This kind of life will make you a permanent bachelor. I would like you to have a room in your life for a woman. You know what, I would like to be an aunt to your children. I sincerely mean everything that I have said."

"You surely sounded serious, aren't you, sister?" amusingly asked Okema, as he laughed.

"You bet I am," assertively said Ader, like a teacher. "I think that it is time for you to have a serious relationship with a girl, who will eventually become your wife and my sister-in-law."

"Thank you for your advice, my sister," gently answered Okema. "You really are beginning to sound more and more like our mother. I will give serious thoughts to your advice."

After the meal, Okema showed his sister to the next room, which he had prepared for her bedroom. The single bed was well made and clean. Ader thanked her brother once again and then went to sleep because she was quite tired from the journey.

Ader enjoyed living with her brother a lot. Okema was very kind to Ader and provided for her needs very well. Ader cooked, cleaned the house, washed her brother's clothing and carefully ironed them. Okema was neatly dressed every day as he went to work. Life became very easy for him that he eventually understood the importance of having a woman in his life. Most of the people who did not know Ader and Okema quite well were thinking that they were husband and wife because the siblings joked, played and lived quite happily together.

After Ader had live with her brother for quite some time, he decided to pay for her training at a centre called MTC. Ader was quite adamant about the idea in the beginning because she thought that she was becoming a burden on her brother who had already done so much for her by allowing her to live with him. "Why can't you save your money as part of the dowry for your marriage in the future?" she humbly asked her brother. "You have already done so much for me and I do not want to suck your pocket dry, dear brother."

"Stop being silly and listen to me very carefully, you naughty girl," sternly said Okema. "You are my sister and I know your potential. I have not thrown my money away but invested it in your future. You are more to me than the money, Ader. If you do well at the training centre, there would be a lot of opportunity for you to work in any one of the ministries. Your success will be my pride, dear sister. Please do kindly accept my offer to you because I believe in your ability to do very well and succeed in all your endeavours."

Ader wept for joy, after listening to her brother's plea for her to join the centre. She then had realized that Okema believed so much in her and had very high hope for her future.

"Okema, dear brother," humbly said Ader, with tears streaming down her cheeks, "you have been such a blessing to me and I would like you to know that you are not only my brother but my best friend too. I will therefore attend the training, as you have suggested and trust me, brother, I will perform my very best while at the centre, as a symbol of my gratitude to you, for your selfless offer."

"I am so glad to hear that from you, little rascal," happily said Okema and Ader began to playfully chase him around the room. They played and laughed, as if they were little children. Okema felt so good after his sister had finally accepted his offer for the training.

At the MTC Centre, Ader learned the clerical duties including typing. She grasped the concept for the courses very fast and became an excellent student. The teachers liked Ader a lot and wished that all the other students were like her. Consequently, some of her colleagues, who were not doing well, took offence at her intelligence and envied her for being better than them in all subjects. Ader did not mind such attitude but continued to work hard until she graduated as the best student in her class.

Chapter Four
Luck Embraced Ader

After the graduation from the MTC, Ader got an employment as a clerk with the Regional Ministry of Public Service. Ader learnt the office routines very fast and excelled in all her work. Her record of work was so superb that her boss liked her a lot. Most of her colleagues also liked her a lot because of her hard work and gentle spirit. As was Ader's way of life, she listened to her friend's conversation and said very little. At first some of her co-workers thought that she was a proud person because she did not say much but as time went by, they understood that it was her nature to be quiet.

The director for personnel saw a potential in Ader that could make her work efficiently and effectively in the office of the minister, if she was given a formal training as a secretary. Consequently, he contacted the director for training and informed him all about Ader's excellent job performance. Ader's good record of employment automatically made the director for training to approve the proposal to send her for a secretarial course to Nairobi at once. However, Ader was not informed about the opportunity until all the necessary arrangements for her course were made.

One morning therefore, Ader went to work as usual but was called for a meeting in the office of the director for training. She did not understand why she was invited for the meeting and was quite nervous. When she entered the office, she found that the director for personnel was also there. Concerned and timid, Ader stood by the door and waited for any one of the two directors to say something. They both looked at her and perceived that, she was a bit nervous.

"Hallo and good morning, Ader," said the director for training. "Welcome to my office. Please do come and sit down," he pointed to the empty chair opposite to his.

Ader walked gracefully towards the two men, shook hands with each of them, sat down with a smiling face and humbly waited to hear what they had to tell her.

"I can tell that, you are quite surprised, as to why my colleague and I have called you for this meeting," said the director for training. "I therefore would like to get to the point for the meeting at once, so as not to waste any time. Ader, the director for personnel and I have decided to send you, for a secretarial course to Nairobi. All the necessary arrangements have been completed and money for your upkeep, while attending the course, have been approved."

Ader was so shocked by what she had heard that, she covered her face with both hands and was lost for words. She consequently, sat motionless for a few minutes before she could take off her hands from her face and eventually said, "Sirs, I am sorry for the way I have reacted."

"It is ok," simply said the director for training. "We get that all the time from the people we have chosen to send for training."

"I feel very honoured, by your decision," joyfully said Ader. "I am very happy to tell you that I have accepted your offer, with a grateful heart. I thank you both very much, sirs."

"You really do not need to thank us," answered the director for personnel. "We just wanted to show you our appreciation, for your hard and excellent work in this ministry. Your record of work is very outstanding and if everyone in your department were to work as hard as you do, this ministry would have been the best among all others."

"Thank you for your compliments, sir," humbly said Ader. "I have just been doing my work, as required of me by my job description."

"You surely have excelled in all that you have been doing," said the director for personnel. "There has never been any complaint about your work, since you have started working here. Dear daughter, your hard work, dedication and reliability in all that you have been doing have earned you this opportunity."

"Thanks, for your kind remarks, sir," gratefully replied Ader. "Would you mind to tell me, when the course would commence?"

"In a month's time," replied the director for training. "Your passport is under process and would soon be out. All that is left is for you to hand over your work to the person who would be working in your place and of course, for you to get ready."

"Sirs, I will never let you down," joyfully said Ader. "I will do my best at college, as a sign of my gratitude for your kindness in giving to me this opportunity."

"Ok then everyone, that brings us to the end of the meeting," concluded the director for training, who then handed to Ader, a formal letter pertaining to her training. Thereafter, they all got up; Ader shook hands with each of them, thanked them once again and then walked out of the office.

After Ader had left the office, the director for training told the director for personnel, "Isn't she a wonderful girl?"

"You absolutely got that right," replied the director for personnel. "There is no doubt that she has come from a good family. She is so soft-spoken, gentle and has very good command of the English language, unlike most of her colleagues."

"Such is a rare quality, these days," said the director for training. "Most girls are too loud, these days and have no respect, while talking to the elders."

"We have to accept, to live with them, don't' we?" answered the director for personnel. "The present world is quite different, from the one we grew up in."

"Well, well, well. Such is life, ever changing, eh?" replied the director for training.

There was an outburst of laughter and thereafter, they shook hands, wished each other a good day and then the director for personnel left for his office.

When Ader got back to her office, she found that her colleagues were anxiously waiting to hear about the meeting she had just attended. However, Ader did not know how to break the news to her friends because she was too excited to talk.

One of her close friends therefore broke the silence by asking her, "Are you promoted or what, girl?"

"No dear," replied Ader with a big smile on her face.

"I think that the meeting was about your transfer to another ministry, isn't it?" anxiously speculated another friend.

"Not even that," replied Ader once again.

"Could you please let the poor girl tell us about the meeting, herself?" asked a woman who was a little older than the rest of them. "Is it any wonder why men say that, all women liked the blah, blah, blah talk? Ader, would you please tell us about the meeting?"

"Well, my friends," excitedly said Ader. "I do not know how to break my wonderful news to you. I am just too thrilled to talk about it. I have never thought that such an opportunity would come my way, in life." Tears of joy began streaming down both her cheeks as she was talking. "I am nominated to go for secretarial training in Nairobi!"

"Wow girl, you deserve it!" unanimously exclaimed her colleagues.

"Your perfect and hard work has eventually paid off," said one of the ladies.

"We are all very happy for you, girl," said the older woman. "Now wipe off your tears and give us that beautiful smile of yours."

Ader therefore, gently wiped off her tears, smiled and began to hug each of them.

"When are you leaving us, oh you quiet one?" one of the girls asked.

"In three weeks, from now," softly replied Ader.

"We surely shall miss you," said the older woman. "It has been a great joy, for all of us, to knowing and having you among us. May God bless and keep you well when you go to Nairobi. Keep up your good spirit, young woman. You are such a nice person to be with. Please keep in touch with us, while there."

The rest of her friends agreed with the last speaker and thereafter, each of them went about doing her work.

When Ader got home that day, she ran straightaway to her brother, who got home from work before her and excitedly began hugging him, while trembling all over.

"Are you alright?" Okema curiously asked his sister because he was concerned about the way she was trembling. "Ader, I would like you to sit down and talk calmly. Would you mind to do that?"

Ader consequently broke away from her brother, sat down and still quite excited told him, "Okema, my brother, you will not believe what has happened to me today, at work."

"I hope that it is not something weird," said Okema, who was still anxious to know why his sister was so excited. "You better break the news or I will slap your silly head," jokingly concluded Okema.

"I don't think that you will slap me, if you get to hear what I have to tell you," hilariously replied Ader.

"You know that I was only joking, don't you?" said Okema. "I will never slap you, sister."

"Of course, I knew that you were only joking," Ader joyfully assured her brother. "You have never slapped me as a kid, why would you, now? Ok, brother, let me get to the point. God has at last answered my prayer, today. When I got to work this morning, I almost lost my mind when I was called for a meeting and surprised that I had a scholarship to go to Nairobi for a course. This is an opportunity I had never thought would cross my path, in life." Ader was still trembling, as she was pulling out of her bag, the letter that was given to her concerning the course. She then handed the letter to her brother, who was also quite excited after hearing what she had told him.

Okema read the letter very fast, then got up from his seat and tenderly hugged his sister with so much excitement and joy. Ader began to shed tears of joy but Okema controlled his emotion.

"I knew that such a wonderful opportunity would come your way some day," Okema joyfully assured his sister. "God does not forsake his children. He works on his own time when it comes to answering prayers. I am so happy for you, sister. Look at what you would have forfeited had you remained in the village. Despair is not a solution to any problem. However, I am glad that you have listened to Mom and Dad and came back to Juba."

"I owe this opportunity to especially you, my brother," said Ader with such a grateful heart. "It is you, who have paid for my training at the MTC and that has been the beginning of my road to a better future. God bless you and may you find a good wife who will dearly love you and have many children."

"Well, thank you, for your best wishes," amusingly said Okema. "May you also some day, find a wonderful husband who would make all your dreams come true. Anyway, to get back to the topic, when are you supposed to leave for the course?"

"In three week's time," replied Ader.

"Wow!" shockingly exclaimed Okema. "Not much time to get things together, is there?"

"I know, brother," said Ader as she tried to calm down. "That is why I will not be going to the village to say goodbye to Mom and Dad but only write to them. I believe that they will understand."

"You should then start packing some of your stuff, right after we have eaten supper. I have a big suitcase, which I am not using anymore, you can take it."

"Thank you so much, brother," calmly said Ader who had then composed herself and started putting things into perspective.

They then sat quietly for quite some time as if lost for word but eventually Ader broke the silence and said, "I know that we are happy but we also need some food to celebrate the occasion. I am going to start cooking right away."

"No, today I will cook," defiantly said Okema although he knew pretty well that his sister would not allow him to cook. "This is your day, dear sister and I would like you to rest."

"Not in a month of a week would I allow you to cook for me," rebelliously said Ader.

"Well then, good chef, go ahead and do your monotonous work," teasingly replied Okema.

They both laughed and then Ader told his brother to stop being silly. Shortly after, she started making fire for cooking.

On the day that Ader was leaving for Nairobi, her brother escorted her to the airport. Some of her friends from work also came to the airport to see her off. Ader was torn inside because she was happy to go to Nairobi and yet quite sad to leave behind her beloved brother, the friends she had known at work and her country. The fear of going to a foreign land among foreign people gripped Ader's heart but she controlled her emotion quite well and pretended as if nothing was bothering her. Before Ader boarded the plane, she hugged her brother in tears because that was her first time to go away from every member of her family. Okema was also quite emotional for he had already started missing his beloved sister whom he was very accustomed to live with. Thereafter, Ader hugged her friends and then walked to the airplane. Just before she entered the airplane Ader waved one last good bye to her brother and all her friends. Although everyone was happy for Ader to go for her course, somehow, each of them was missing her a lot because they love her company. Consequently, everyone walked away from the airport in a low spirit.

The flight between Juba and Nairobi was only an hour and a quarter on the Sudan Airways. Ader quietly sat and wondered how her brother might be doing because she was missing him a lot already. She prayed that God helped her to arrive safely at her destination and meet helpful people at the airport. The plane landed at the Jomo Kenyatta International Airport at three o'clock in the afternoon, Kenya time. Ader went through the immigration office, got all her papers in order and eventually got a ride to Flora Hostel. The nuns at the hostel were very kind and easy to talk to. They then showed Ader everything that she needed to know about the hostel including the rules and regulations.

Ader got used to her new place very fast and by the end of the four days before her course could start she met new friends, who showed her a lot of places including the college that she was going to attend. Ader admired the modern city of Nairobi with all the tall buildings. She thoughtfully blamed the lack of development in Juba on the seventeen years of war that had deprived the southern Sudan of any development. Ader perceived Nairobi like another world compared to Juba; the lawns were well kept, variety of flowers bloomed everywhere, paved streets, constant electricity and the people seemed full of joy as they went about their work.

As time went by Ader began to miss her family a lot and therefore wrote home frequently. In reply, the members of her family wrote back to her expressing how much they love and missed her although they were also glad to know that she was doing well. Some days on the weekends, Ader would spend a long time alone in her room while crying her heart out for her family. She missed her parents and the advice they frequently gave her while she was still at home. Furthermore, she also missed the wonderful time she had spent with her brother in Juba. Ader bought lots of gifts and sent to each member of her family whenever any Sudanese she knew was going to Juba from Nairobi. She did not buy much for herself because she put her family's needs before hers.

At college, Ader settled very well into all her classes and her remarkable intelligence was evident in everything she was doing. The teachers took special interest in Ader because of her perspicuous willingness to learn and she excelled in all her exams. Ader's good work and reputation earned her a lot of friends at the college. At the end of the course, Ader graduated with record marks and was given an award for being the best student ever in the history of the college.

The two years that Ader had spent in Nairobi went by very fast and soon after graduation she was anxious to go back home. Ader had saved some money and therefore bought gifts for everyone in her family including some of her friends and relatives. Therefore, on the day that Ader was returning to Juba, her friends from the hostel and some from the college she had attended, escorted her to the airport. Ader's friends were quite sad at the knowledge that she was going to leave them that day and they were all in tears including Ader. Consequently, Ader hugged each of her friends tenderly before she boarded the airplane. The fact that Ader was happy to go back home to her people did not ease the pain of separation from her friends, whom she had grown to love a lot in her two years away from home. Ader's friends, had then became like a family to her and therefore, she was quite sad to leave them behind. However, Ader eventually stopped crying as soon as she boarded the plane and mentally persuaded herself that all good things must come to end.

A week before Ader could return to Juba, she had written a letter to her brother telling him about the date and time of her arrival to Juba. Consequently, Okema went to the airport an hour early on the day that Ader was returning to Juba and was quite excited as he waited for his beloved sister's arrival with so much anticipation. Ader's plane touched down in Juba at 11:30 AM Sudan local time and as soon as she got out of the plane she felt the difference in weather at once. It was quite warm in Juba whereas Nairobi was quite cold when she was leaving. After Ader was done with the custom people, she saw her brother waiving and happily smiling at her. Overcome with excitement, she ran and lovingly hugged her brother with tears of joy streaming down her cheeks. Okema was also quite thrilled to see his sister, whom he loved so much. He tenderly hugged and greatly admired her. Eventually, he hired a taxi to take him and his sister to his house. On the way home, sister and brother asked each other a lot of questions as they tried to catch up on the time they had lost.

Ader showered her beloved brother with lots of magnificent gifts, which immensely delighted him and he was very grateful to her. Ader also sent home gifts for her parents and the rest of her siblings. Okema had always admired Ader and thought of her as a very good-looking girl but she was even quite prettier after she had returned from Nairobi. The good weather in Nairobi and the body products brought out the best in Ader's appearance. Her thick hair was relaxed and grew very long. She tied her hair into a ponytail most of the time and whenever she had combed it down, it was long like a wig. Ader's skin was very soft, smooth and the complexion was quite radiant. Everything about Ader then was quite modern and clean. Her dresses perfectly suited her slender figure and she seemed like a model. Everyone then, especially the young men admired Ader a lot.

On the day that Ader went back to work, she found that a lot of things had changed in the office since she had been away. Some of the people she had known before she went to Nairobi were transferred to the other ministries. There were quite a number of new faces in her ministry. When the few of her old friends who were still in her old department saw her, they all rushed to greet her with such excitement, hugged and admired the way she looked. Ader was quite delighted to see her old friends once again. After Ader had greeted her friends, she went and reported to the director for personnel.

The director for the personnel was very happy to see Ader back. He had already received the detailed information, pertaining to how excellent Ader had performed, from the college that she had attended. "Welcome back," he delightfully said, as he excitedly shook hands with Ader. "Don't you look very beautiful, my child! Please sit down."

"Thank you, sir, for your kind remarks," said Ader as she took a seat.

"You are welcome, my daughter," said the director for personnel. "The director for the training and I have read the report from the college that you have attended and are very delighted that we have sent such a good ambassador like you for the course. You have given us so much honour, by the way that you have excelled in your studies. The college further informed us that, you were the best student in the history of the college. Congratulations, Ader, on a job well done!"

"I just did what I was sent to do," humbly replied Ader.

"As a sign of our appreciation to you, for the good work that you have done," said the director for personnel, "we have promoted you to work as the secretary, in the Office of the Minister. You will consequently, start your new job, effective next week."

"Thank you so much, sir," delightfully said Ader. "This is such a great honour, for me. I will do my best in my new position and will not let you down."

"Well, I believe in your ability my daughter," said the director for personnel, as he handed to Ader the job description for her new position and her new salary scale.

Ader profoundly thanked him once again before she went back to her old office.

After work that day Ader told her brother about her new position and the best time she had had with her friends at work. Okema was overwhelmed with joy at the knowledge about his sister's new position. "We surely need a celebration for this, dear sister, don't you think so?" he excitedly told her.

"If the celebration will not include anyone from outside, it will be ok with me," carelessly said Ader. "Otherwise, I am not ready to be with people who would come in here with mix agenda in their hearts."

"How about two or three of your best friends and a few of mine?" Okema insisted.

"I can see that you are very determine to throw a party, aren't you?" amusingly said Ader. "Do what you think is right and I will stand by your side, brother."

"That is the sister that I know now talking," happily said Okema.

"Well, are you happy now?" Ader playfully questioned her brother.

"You bet that I am," delightfully said Okema. "This kind of opportunity does not come around quite often, you know. We need to thank God for his kindness, for he has truly smiled on you, sister. Can't you count your blessings? A lot of good things have recently happened to you; the training that you have just returned from, the wonderful work that you have performed while at the college and now a very senior position. Sister, you need to offer God a prayer of thanksgiving, right away."

"You are absolutely right, brother," humbly said Ader. "The Good Lord has really blessed me a lot and therefore I will indeed offer Him a special prayer for thanksgiving, just as you have suggested."

"You better do so sooner than later," joyfully said Okema, who then hugged and wished his sister a future that would forever be bright.

"Thank you, brother, and may yours be brighter than the evening and morning stars," delightfully said Ader.

That weekend therefore, Ader and her brother called over a few of their closest friends for a little party. They ate, drank and danced until the wee hours of the morning. Everyone at the party thought that Okema had thrown the party as a welcome home for Ader but his sister's new senior position was the main reason.

Ader thoroughly studied her job description over the weekend and understood exactly what was expected of her in her new job. Consequently, after the handover was finished, she settled well into the new office and performed her work to perfection. Ader had not only done well at the college but also excelled in all her tasks with the Minister, who had so much confidence in her that, he even shared with her, some of his personal problems. As such, their working rapport was so good that, Ader doubled her work output and efficiently managed the office.

Chapter Five
Ader Met Her Prospective Husband

As a young secretary, amidst the young men in the ministry, there were lots of eligible lovers who had been having their eyes on Ader and some of them, even endeavoured to have relationship with her but she never got interested, in any of them. The first priority in Ader's life then was her job, which she was loving dearly and enjoying very much. Although Ader had grown up with brothers in her family, she was finding it rather hard, to have a relationship with a man because she was afraid that, she might get a wrong one, who would ruin her life. However, Ader was occasionally praying to God, for a good man to come into her life so that, she would marry eventually and have a wonderful life with him, as her loving husband for life.

Once upon a time, God did answer Ader's prayer graciously because there was a handsome young man, called Omal, who had been admiring her from afar, ever since she had started living with her brother; that was, way before, she had even gone for her course. Omal had been seeking for an opportunity to meet, talk and intimately get to know Ader but miserably failed because he was so fascinated by the way she was looking that, he did not have courage and stamina to approach her. From the very first time that, Omal had laid his eyes on Ader, he knew and believed in his heart that, she was undoubtedly the woman for him because it was amore prima facie. Omal had been thinking of Ader as, the most beautiful girl that he had ever seen in his entire life and had been treasuring her in his heart as, one of God's most magnificent work of arts that, he must share his life eventually with.

Omal was tall, medium built, broad shoulders, walked upright, good looking, had dazzling white teeth, none of which crooked and the most wonderful smile that caught every girl's attention. However, he was very quiet, gentle, humble, simple, liked to listen to other people, as they talked and only said very little. He wasn't the kind of a boy that liked chasing after the girls. Most of the girls, found Omal quite irresistible. Some of the girls, were so determined that, they had their eyes set on him, for a possibility of relationship and Omal was very aware about the situation but tactfully, avoided all of them, as he prayed for the girl of his dream. Omal was the son of the Chief of the Magwi Chiefdom and therefore a Royal Prince. In the past, the princes only married the princesses from other Chiefdoms. However, the custom was no longer practiced and boys like Omal, were then allowed to marry the common girls, provided that they came from good families. Omal was the younger, of the two boys, after the girls, in his family. The older boy, took to drinking, at an early age, quit school, got involved into practices that were very contrary to his family's values and therefore left home for Khartoum, where he led a harum-scarum life. The Chief had given up on his older son and consequently treated Omal, as if he was the only boy, among his seven older daughters who were all married, by then. The Chief dearly loved his son and took great pride, in assisting him in his education until he had finished his secondary school. Omal, like most of the youths in the south at that time, did not go to the university but got the infamous Sudan School Certificate and eventually got trained as an accountant. Omal was the future of his family and everyone looked up to him. In the event that, the Chief suddenly died, Omal would have succeeded his father, as the next Chief of the Magwi Chiefdom. He was therefore, the Prince in wait for the Throne. Omal's parents frequently prayed to God and their ancestors, to bring a good girl into the life of their beloved son, so that he could marry, have many kids, happy life, and eventually some day, succeed his father as the next Chief of the People of Magwi.

A miraculous opportunity came for Omal to unexpectedly meet with the girl of his dream, one evening, when both of them coincidentally, attended the same party. Okema had told Ader about the party but as was usual with her, she declined to go. However that day, Okema lost his temper, for the first time with his sister, got quite angry and rebuked her as an anti-social life. Ader who did not like confrontation with anyone, therefore, opted to go to the party, so as to please her brother. At that time, Okema was dating a girl, called Auma, who came to his house and therefore the three of them, went together to the party.

While at the party, Ader sat humbly alone because she did not feel like dancing but enjoyed watching the other people, as they danced quite happily. Omal began to scrutinize quite carefully about Ader's situation and as soon as he had concluded meticulously that she was kind of lonely, he took the advantage of the opportunity, approached her when a beautiful music was playing and asked her quite humbly for a dance. Ader did not want to appear rude to Omal, although she was not feeling like dancing. Therefore, she obliged and the two danced beautifully, as if they were made naturally for each other's dance partner. As they were dancing, Omal wanted so desperately to initiate a conversation and therefore, introduced himself to Ader, by provocatively saying, "My name is Omal and I suppose that you are called Ader, aren't you?"

"How did you know my name?" inquired Ader puzzlingly, as she was looking at Omal's face astonishingly in shock. "I do not recollect if I have ever seen or met you anywhere before."

"I have known you for a long time now," softly said Omal, with a joyful smile on his face. "I went to school with your brothers, Okema and Otim, and I know them very well."

"Oh you did?" said Ader in a very polite way, as she felt a little comfortable at the knowledge that she was dancing and talking with someone who, at least, knew her brothers. "Well then, glad to meet you, Omal, and how are you?"

"I am very fine, thank you for asking," happily replied Omal, as his heart thumped very fast with excitement within him because he could not believe the chance he had finally had to talk to Ader alone and the whole situation was still like a dream for him. "And how are you doing, Ader?"

"I am doing quite well, thank you," softly said Ader. "Omal, it is one thing to know my brothers but why did you say that you have known me for a long time now?" inquired Ader curiously.

"I first saw you when you began to live with Okema. Initially, I thought that you were his girlfriend but later on found out from him that you were his sister. After a while, you disappeared and then reappeared. That is all, I know about you," gently said Omal, as he silently regretted his slip of tongue and tried to cover it up, by pretending as if he did not have any deep feelings, for Ader.

"Well, since you somehow seem to know me but I do not know you, at all," innocently said Ader, "would you kindly mind to tell me which Chiefdom of the Acoli people you come from? It is rather hard for me to guess where you are from because you do not have a distinctive dialect while you are speaking."

"I am from Magwi," humbly said Omal. He then told Ader, the names of his parents.

"Hey, you are the son of the Chief of the Chiefdom of Magwi, aren't you?" quite amazingly said Ader because Omal was so simple and humble in the way that he was speaking to her. "I really must be fortunate to dance and talk with a royalty. It is an honour for me to meet you, Your Highness!" said Ader, as she curtsied slightly to show her respect for the Prince.

"Please Ader, I do not deserve a curtsy from anyone at all and especially, not from you," said Omal, rather carelessly. "Yes, I am supposed to be the Prince in wait for the so-called Throne of the Magwi Chiefdom but it does not mean much to me, at all."

"Thank you for your humility," went on Ader, as she felt quite relaxed after realizing that Omal was not a stranger after all. "This may sound odd to you but my mother is your mother's friend."

"Is that right?" shockingly said Omal. "Small world, what a coincidence!" Omal then began to pray thoughtfully, as he was wishing that Ader's mother should never be somewhat related to his mother because it would wreck his hope and dream for wooing and marrying Ader eventually one day.

"Omal, you can't escape surely to become the next Chief, can you?" inquired Ader quite interestingly. "I think that you should not really be staying here in Juba but instead be with your father in the village in order to be groomed as the future Chief for the People of Magwi."

"Ah Ader, do you truly think so?" curiously inquired Omal, as he was amused extremely by what Ader had just suggested, to him.

"Absolutely!" predicated Ader. "You must honour and respect your heritage, you know."

"Because you have said so, I will," solemnly confessed Omal, while he was thinking quietly that 'and I pray that you would be my Queen, when I become the Chief of the People of Magwi.'

Omal and Ader had a couple of dance and then decided to just sit down and talk. They confabulated a lot about the past and contemporary news in Juba and it was the best time in Omal's entire life. Omal was quite surprise to discover that Ader was not only beautiful but very intelligent, pleasant to talk to and shared a lot of the values that he believed in. He therefore felt, as if they should sit there and talk forever. Omal was so scared, to ruin the wonderful time that he was enjoying with Ader that he failed to tell her how, he had been feeling about her.

When the party was eventually over, Omal was emotionally torn inside. He seemed helpless and rather sad, as he was saying good-bye to Ader. Ader did not understand why Omal's mood had changed instantly as soon as the party was over. She failed to pick up some of the clues, about Omal's personal interest in her, when they were having conversation because she simply thought of Omal as a nice boy to talk to. Consequently therefore, as Ader was going home with her brother and his girlfriend, she simply told Omal, "It has been nice to meet and talk with you. Goodnight, Omal."

"I have enjoyed talking to you too, Ader," softly but desperately replied Omal, as he tried to clear his throat. "I look forward to talking to you again, soon. Goodnight, Ader."

Omal sounded quite sad, as he was speaking to Ader because all kinds of feelings were stirred up within him. He had never felt that way before, whenever he was speaking to any girl. Therefore, he stood spellbound as he watched Ader, her brother and his girlfriend disappeared into the night, on their way home. Ader did not even look back, as she was walking away because she had no knowledge at all, as to how Omal was feeling, about her.

Okema had noticed the way Omal had spoken to Ader, just as they were about to leave and accurately guessed that Omal seemed to be in love with his sister. On their way home, therefore, he purposely asked his sister, "Ader, did you really enjoy the party, the way Auma and I did?"

"The party wasn't bad," replied Ader, rather carelessly. "It is just that I was a little lonely until that kind Prince of the People of Magwi came and started dancing and talking with me."

"I am glad that he had kept you company," Okema told his sister. "But don't you think that his intention of talking to you for that long time, was more than just keeping you company?"

"Now what do you exactly mean by saying that?" Ader interrogated her brother, rather angrily. "You like reading too much into things, that are not true."

"To be honest with you, sister, Omal seemed to be interested in you, from the way that I have seen him saying goodnight, to you," Okema honestly alerted his sister. "I am not a psychic but an ordinary man and I know when one is in love."

"Stop being silly!" Ader angrily stormed at her brother. "I don't like where this conversation is taking us anymore. Can we please change the topic?"

"I did not mean to hurt your feelings," her brother replied, as he amusingly laughed at the way his sister suddenly reacted to him. "I was only telling you the truth. What if some day what I have just told you came true?"

"No one is capable to predict the future, but as for now, let us not assume things that are not true," gently pointed out Ader. "However, brother, I am sorry for overreacting to you, in the way that I have done."

"I knew in my heart that you were not really angry with me, in the way that you have sounded," Okema playfully told his sister.

When they got to the house, Okema then decided to escort his girlfriend to their home, while Ader went straightaway to bed.

On the other hand, that night, when Omal got to his house, he could not put off Ader from his heart and mind. He mentally replayed over and over again the conversation he had had with her, while at the party. The sound of Ader's soft and beautiful voice kept echoing in his ears and he desperately longed for her. Omal had casually dated a girl when he was still in secondary school but she had never made him felt like the way he was feeling about Ader that night. He stayed awake until the early hours of the morning then he eventually slept and had many sweet dreams about Ader.

The days that followed the night that Omal had talked with Ader grew even tougher for him. He desperately yearned for Ader so much that his burning desire for her eventually compelled him to write a letter to her expressing how much he loved and needed her in his life. Ader was quite shocked to receive a love letter from Omal and therefore did not reply his first letter but that did not deter Omal. He wrote even more letters detailing how much he loved and sincerely longed to have Ader as his life's partner. Omal was absolutely determined to convince Ader, beyond any reasonable doubt, so that she could realize how much he dearly loved her. However, he was scared to meet Ader in person, since she had not even replied to any of his letters. The thought of probable rejection in response from Ader sometimes filled Omal's heart with fear and sorrow but he did not allow the negative thoughts to hamper him from his pursuit.

Chapter Six
Ader Fell in Love

Omal laboured to almost exhaustion as he endeavoured to win Ader's heart because his determination to have her as his life's partner was like that of a hungry lioness, which was indefatigably chasing a prey for food. He agonizingly thought that should he fail to have a relationship with Ader then his entire life would be very empty and meaningless. Omal began to pray earnestly to God to kindly soften Ader's heart so that she could respond to him and he also firmly believed in his heart that if he persevered a little while longer in writing more letters to her she would someday fall in love with him.

Ader could not believe how stubborn Omal was in sending to her the many love letters, which she had not even replied to any of them. However, she eventually realised that what her brother had previously predicted about Omal's feelings towards her was indeed true and that Omal was really serious about having a lasting relationship with her. After a long time of ignoring Omal, Ader had compassion for him, made some consideration in her heart and decided to give him a chance. She consequently one day sent to Omal a short note, stating that if he were truly serious about all the stuff that he had been writing to her, let him dare to meet with her in person then they would have a discussion, face to face. Omal was quite delighted to receive the note from Ader but felt heavily challenged to the very core of his manhood. He instantly shook off his fear of Ader and became very bold. Omal wanted to show Ader, who he really was, as a man and, therefore, decided to meet with her face to face, the very next day, after work.

Omal timed Ader, as she was walking home alone from work, quietly approached her from behind and then startled her by saluting her in a deep bold voice, "Hallo, Ader, how are you?"

Ader was caught off guard that she gasped and almost stumbled to the ground. "How dare you have made me almost fell down," she quite angrily said, as she meanly looked at Omal.

"I did not really mean to scare you," gently said Omal. "I was just greeting you, Ader."

"Well, I am fine, thank you," arrogantly replied Ader. "Next time try not to do, what you have just done to me, to anyone else. You have almost scared me to death."

"Ader, I am truly sorry," Omal apologetically confessed. "I did not know any other better way to approach and talk to you. You have made it quite impossible for me to get to you, haven't you?" went on Omal and then he paused a little bit to see whether Ader was going to reply him or not. However, Ader declined to say any word and therefore, Omal continued to pour out all he wanted to tell Ader, that day. "Ader, you have treated me like a filthy garbage for a long time now. The best thing that you have done to me, after the long time of completely ignoring to respond to any of my letters, was to challenge me in your letter and I am here today, to prove to you that I dare to talk to you, face to face. Ader, I am not scared of you anymore because I want you to understand that I am sincerely in love with you. If loving you, Ader, in the way that I do is sin then I do not think that I have any chance to go to heaven. I cannot put you off my mind and heart, since that time, when I talked with you, at the party. You don't know how long I have been waiting for this opportunity, to talk to you in person, concerning how I have been feeling about you."

Ader glanced at Omal and quickly turned her face away without responding to him. She was completely lost for words and wished that it were possible for her to vanish into the air.

"You really know how to ignore people, don't you?" Omal continued with such boldness and determination that could have intimidated even the most rascal girl. Ader, who never thought of Omal as being brave enough to face her, became very timid and could not believe how bold and serious he sounded. Omal noticed the impact of his words on Ader and provocatively asked her, "Are you still ignoring me or can I assume that you are the one, who is scared of me, now?"

Ader deeply sighed, as her heart throbbed due to the strange feelings that were awakening in her heart for Omal but stubbornly replied, "I am not scared of you, Omal, but I do not know what to tell you because you are sounding really hurt, over nothing."

"Surely, Ader, I am not hurt, over nothing," seriously said Omal, as he fixed his eyes on her. "I am hurt because I love you but you have made it quite impossible for me, to convince you that I truly love you. I do not want to pressure you into saying something you do not mean. Ader, I have expressed myself over and over again in my letters to you, that I indelibly love you and that you are the only girl, I ever needed to have relationship with and hopefully become my future wife but you have never responded to me. However, today, I would like you to honestly tell me the truth; that is, whether you love me or not. You will make my day, if you tell me that you love me otherwise I will be the most miserable man on earth but believe me, beloved Ader, I will never give up my pursuit of you, until you have decided to choose someone else over me."

"I wouldn't have sent you a letter if I did not like you," timidly said Ader, with her face down.

"Ader dear, how hard is it for you to tell me frankly that you love me too," Omal insisted, as he firmly held Ader's hand. "I will never let you go until you tell me that you love me. Ader, I would like to hear you clearly say the words."

Ader felt really awkward but then realized that there was no escape for her that day, until she had admitted to Omal the truth that she loved him. She was a little shaky out of nervousness but eventually cleared her voice and timidly said, "Omal, you have indubitably proven to me that you sincerely love me and I therefore reciprocate. There, are you happy now?"

"Ader, could you kindly tell me those three wonderful words, plainly?" seriously insisted Omal.

"Ah Omal!" replied Ader in a shaky voice, out of frustration. "You are quite stubborn and too inquisitive, aren't you? Omal, I love you and I know that you know that I love you."

"That is what I have been dying to hear from you, oh magnificent Ader!" delightfully said Omal, with such an excitement as his heart went wild with joy, while he fondly squeezed Ader's hand. Omal then wished that he was alone with Ader in his house, so that he could have cuddled her like a little baby in his arms and passionately kissed her. His hands trembled, as he gratefully whispered to Ader, "Thank you for making me the happiest man on earth today. You do not know how long I have been waiting to hear those three wonderful words from your sweet lips. Ader dear, I love you more than anything in this world and I do not want to live without you."

"Well, thank you for loving me the way you do," softly said Ader in a relaxed tone of voice because she was relieved that she had at last told Omal the truth that she also loved him.

After Ader had declared to Omal that she loved him, they walked quietly and it seemed then that each of them understood what the other heart was thinking about. Love filled their hearts with so much joy and comfort. When they got closer to Ader's place, Omal bid her goodbye and went away, feeling like a person who had just recovered from a bad and long illness. His heart was full of joy, happiness, hope, peace, dream for a wonderful future with Ader and love that no word could describe. He walked, lost in his daydream about Ader and did not even understand how fast he got to his house. In his house, Omal was overcome with tremendous joy of knowing that Ader also loved him and so he at once restfully fell asleep out of happiness.

On the other hand, when Ader got home, she felt both physically and emotionally exhausted and perspired a lot. She could not believe what had happened between her and Omal that day. She reminisced the way that Omal had approached her, the impact of his words on her and the manner he had fondly held and squeezed her hand. Omal's spoken words about love were even more powerful than those he had expressed in his letters. The sound of Omal's voice, the way he pronounced his words and repeatedly called Ader's name kept echoing in her ears. Furthermore, the way Omal had lovingly looked at Ader with such intensity until she had to turn away her face from him or faced down overwhelmed Ader with the kinds of feelings that she had never experienced before. Ader trembled all over, felt very strange and could not comprehend how Omal's words rendered her powerless to resist him that day. She replayed the whole scene in her mind many times and eventually concluded that Omal was indeed the man God had chosen for her. The power of falling in love did deprive Ader of her energy so much that she lied down until her brother came home from work. Ader kept her love for Omal secret and so Okema was oblivious of the new development in his sister's personal life.

Omal and Ader did all they could to keep their relationship secret, for a while. The first time that Ader had gone to visit Omal was when her brother had gone away for some work, in Yei. Omal was so delighted to see Ader, when she went to visit him and warmly welcomed her into his house. Ader was initially rather nervous to be alone with Omal but he made her visit so comfortable that her fear for being alone with him dissipated. Omal entertained Ader quite well and behaved more as a friend than a lover, in the way he chatted with her. He did not mention anything to do with his love for Ader because he was aware that such talk would make her nervous and ruin the wonderful time that he was having with her. They therefore instead talked about general matters including their families, until Ader said, "Omal, thank you for warmly welcoming me into your house today and giving me such a pleasant time. I have truly enjoyed my visit with you but I think that it is getting late and I would like to return home."

"Thank you so much for coming," gratefully said Omal. "This has truly been the best day of my entire life. I wish that it were possible for us to spend more quality time like this together quite often. My precious Ader, I deeply love you more and more each passing day."

Ader timidly smiled but did not respond to Omal, as she was getting up to leave the house. Omal did not want Ader to leave that day, without him first kissing her. He thought that he must kiss Ader or else it would be a long while, before he could have another opportunity to be alone with her. As the result, therefore, he quickly reached out for Ader, just before she could get to the door, tenderly held and spontaneously began kissing her. Omal took his time as he passionately kissed Ader and, at that very moment, felt like he should keep her as his wife. The kiss was Ader's first and her mind was so confused because the whole thing had happened very unexpectedly. Ader felt so dizzy and almost fell down after Omal let go of her. "How dare you?" she feebly said, as she looked away from Omal. "Why have you attacked me with such a kiss, after the wonderful visit I have enjoyed with you? Omal, you are a very, very strange person, aren't you?"

"Sweetheart, I do not think that I have done anything wrong to you, have I?" humbly said Omal, as he intensified his look at Ader, with so much love and deep desire in his eyes. "Ader dear, know that if I were to gently ask you for a kiss, you would have not obliged and so I took the short cut. There is absolutely nothing to be ashamed of because I love you and you love me. Lovers always kiss each other, don't they?" asked Omal, as he still lovingly gazed at Ader.

Ader glanced at Omal, once again and quickly looked down, without saying a word because she was frightened by the way that he was gazing at her.

"Beloved, I was only trying to express to you a little bit of how I have been feeling about you," Omal joyfully continued, "and I would like you to know that I have very much enjoyed kissing you. I have been desperately longing to do this, for a long time now and I am so happy that I have at last tasted your sweet lips, today."

Ader kept quiet, the whole time while Omal was talking to her because she was trying to regain her composure, after the long and very electrifying kiss that has rendered her quite disoriented.

Eventually, Ader hastily walked out of the house because she was too mixed up about the whole situation. Omal followed her and they walked without saying anything to each other until they got to Okema's house. Then Omal tenderly hugged Ader and humbly said, "My love, please forgive me, if the way that I have kissed you has made you felt bad but honestly speaking, on my part, I have really enjoyed it. I am aware that you are not comfortable with me right now but I would like to thank you for visiting and making me feel so wonderful today. Ader, I have tremendously enjoyed my time with you. I wish you, sweet dreams, tonight."

"I wish you the same," timidly said Ader, almost in a whisper, before Omal left.

Alone in her brother's house, Ader felt so lost but thanked God that her brother was not at home then, otherwise he would have noticed that something extraordinary, had happened to her that day. Ader could not believe how dare and stubborn Omal was to passionately kiss her that day very unexpectedly. She tried to make sense out of the whole situation but got more and more confused. "I grew up with brothers," she quietly pondered, "but I do not think that I know anything at all, about the way men think." Ader was quite exhausted from too many thoughts that she did not even eat supper but went straightaway to bed. On the other hand, as soon as Omal got to his house, he also went to bed and immediately fell asleep because he was so overwhelmed with the joy, for at last kissing the woman of his dream. That night he slept like someone who had taken an overdose of sleeping pills.

It took time for other people, including Okema, before they could find out that Ader had at last fallen in love with Omal. Okema knew the fact that Omal was writing love letters to Ader but thought that his sister would never be interested in Omal because of the way that she had been ignoring him. However, one afternoon on a weekend, Omal came to visit Ader, unaware that Okema was at home. The way that Omal and Ader looked at each other made it quite obvious that they were in love. Okema being a witty person quickly understood what was going on between the two and therefore decided to leave them alone, by going away to the next room, without saying anything. Omal kept his visit very brief because he was somehow scared of Okema.

After Omal had gone Okema asked his sister, "Wasn't I right, when I previously cautioned you that Omal seemed to be in love with you?"

Ader timidly smiled and simply nodded, to confirm what her brother had just said.

"The two of you are in love, aren't you?" seriously inquired Okema.

"Yes, I have decided to give Omal a chance," honestly replied Ader.

"And why didn't you inform me when it happened?" gently asked Okema.

"It is hard to talk about such thing, with a brother, you know," humbly said Ader.

"Ader, you have put me into an awkward situation today," sternly said Okema. "I did not know whether I should go out of the house or to the next room, after I have noticed the way that the two of you were looking at each other. Had you informed me earlier on, I would have gone away, before Omal could come in."

"I don't think that you have done anything bad," uncomfortably said Ader. "You even left us alone, to talk to each other."

"I am the reason why Omal's visit was so brief," Okema sincerely assured his sister. "Couldn't you even see how uneasy he felt while I was in the room with you? For some strange reason, the guy was quite scared of me, as if he had never known me for a long time."

"Ok, brother, our relationship is less than a month now," frankly admitted Ader. "I was eventually going to tell you about it, one of these days."

"Well, today I have known about it on my own, haven't I?" retorted Okema.

"I hope that you are not angry with me," fearfully replied Ader, as she began to feel quite uneasy.

"Are you kidding or what, my dear sister?" amusingly questioned Okema. "Why would I be angry with you for falling in love with Omal? Ader, you are now a mature young woman, with a career and I think that the time is ripened for you to love someone. Don't you think that I would love to be called an uncle by your offspring? Omal is a good boy, from a good family and I am not at all angry with you, for falling in love with him. It is just that you have kept me in dark, about the new development in your life, you little rascal."

"I am very sorry, my dear brother," humbly said Ader. "However, I am quite relieved and delighted to eventually know that you are not, after all, upset with me for falling in love with Omal. Thank you for being very understanding."

"Hey, come here," enthusiastically said Okema, as he opened his arms, to hug his sister. "I am very proud to be your brother because you are the most wonderful girl, anyone would love to have for a sister. I love you, Ader, my sister, forever."

"I love you too, Okema, my brother," joyfully said Ader, as they tenderly hugged each other. Ader was finally quite happy, to openly live her new life for being in love with Omal.

After it was quite obvious that Ader and Omal were in love, many young men wondered, as to what Omal might have done to win Ader's heart. The one thing that most of the young men had failed to understand about Omal was that his perseverance was the one that had won Ader's heart. Ader gradually learnt how to be comfortable, whenever she was alone with Omal because he was more of a friend to her than a lover. Consequently, they spent most of their weekends together, felt free with each other because sex was never mentioned in their conversation and therefore their love blossomed into a very beautiful relationship. However, most of the time whenever Omal was alone with Ader, he had a nagging desire in his mind to ask her to make love to him but dared not because she had plainly assured him, from the very beginning of their relationship that she firmly believed in abstinence from sex until marriage. Omal, therefore, did not venture to make his innermost contemplation known to Ader because he respected her so much and feared that she would instantly abandon him given her spiritual upbringing.

Chapter Seven
Ader Got Engaged

After almost a year of courting Ader, Omal eventually decided to courageously ask her to marry him. One Saturday afternoon, therefore, they went for a walk by the river Nile, as they most of the weekend had been doing but that day was different because Omal was rather exceptionally quiet. Consequently, they tarried silently among the mango trees until Omal saw a good spot to sit down and relax. Ader wondered why her boyfriend was so quiet that day but dared not ask him. Omal eventually broke the silence and told her, "Darling, would you mind if we sit down under that large mango tree, near the bank of the Nile?"

"Not at all," replied Ader as she questioningly gazed at him.

Omal saw the way Ader was looking at him but pretended as if he wasn't aware of it. "Can you feel the breeze, Ader?" he softly said, as he sweetly smiled at his girlfriend.

"Yes, it is nicer and cooler here than in Buluk," answered Ader, who was still curious about the strange way that her boyfriend was behaving, that day.

Omal and Ader restfully sat, as they watched the river Nile flowing gracefully northward. Omal suddenly cleared his throat and seriously announced, "Ader, I have something very important to ask of you today."

"Spit it out," carelessly said Ader, who was thinking that her boyfriend wasn't serious.

"Ader, please stop joking because I am very serious about what I am going to ask of you," said Omal in a tone of voice, like that of a school headmaster wanting to announce something very important to his students.

"Well if you are that serious, then could you cut to the chase and simply tell me what it is?" anxiously asked Ader in astonishment because Omal indeed seemed so serious. "You have been acting rather strange ever since we got here. What is it that is so important that you want to ask me about?"

"The matter is involving two lives," said Omal, as he drew closer to Ader, held her head with both of his hands and looked her straight into her eyes.

"You were absolutely right when you said that I was acting strange today. Ader, I have a very important issue to discuss with you and that is why I have decided to bring you out this far. I am aware that you are not quite comfortable with me whenever we are alone in my house, but out here, it is easy to talk to you about this very important matter because you are relaxed. Ader, I have been courting you for quite a long time now. I think that we have had more than ample time to know each other very well and I firmly believe that the hour has ripened for us to face the final truth about our relationship. Ader, my sweet love, would you kindly be my wife?"

Ader was so astounded by Omal's unexpected proposition that she closed her eyes and did not know what to tell him. Omal sat quietly and patiently waited for her response, as he was still holding her head. Ader suddenly broke away from him, deeply sighed and softly said, "Omal, you are full of surprises, aren't you?"

"Ader, would you kindly and plainly respond to my simple request," pleadingly replied Omal as he tried to get hold of Ader once again. "I think that it is time for you and I to get married. I can no longer bear to treat you as my girlfriend only because I desperately need you as my wife."

"Well, Omal," softly said Ader with tears in her eyes, "I will be delighted to marry you but let me first discuss the issue with my brother. He is the right person to ask my parents, whether it would be ok for me to marry you. Would you therefore mind to wait for my final answer to your proposal until after I have heard what my parents would have to say?"

Omal, who did not want to disappoint his girlfriend in any way, accepted the idea. "I will surely but anxiously wait for your parents' consent," he uncomfortably told her. "I hope that your parents would not take too long to respond because I really need you in my life, as my wife, Ader. You do not know how much I long for you every day and hate to see you leave each time whenever you have come to visit me."

Ader timidly smiled and turned her face away from her boyfriend. Omal enjoyed looking at Ader whenever she was shy and so he fixed his eyes on her as he amusingly laughed.

"Why are you laughing at me?" seriously demanded Ader, as she attempted to look at Omal's face.

"I am enjoying the way that you are lost for word and seemed quite nervous all of a sudden," Omal honestly told her. "Are you timid to look at your future husband or is there something else that you are intentionally not sharing with me?"

"Stop being silly," sternly said Ader. "I love you and how could I be scared of you? Furthermore, what are you suspecting that I am hiding from you?"

"If you are sure that there is nothing, then what is preventing you from looking at my face?" inquired Omal. "Ader, please stop being scared of me because you and I are going to spend our lives together."

Ader mockingly laughed and shook her head without saying anything. Eventually, they then got up and began to walk back home. Omal was very happy to know that Ader on her part was willing to marry him.

Ader thought about her boyfriend's proposal for a while before she could tell her brother. She wondered whether Okema and her parents would really allow her to marry Omal. Ader loved Omal so much that she prayed to God to let her parents accept Omal to marry her. Eventually, Ader approached her brother one evening and told him, "Omal has asked me to marry him but I told him that I needed to discuss the issue with my parents before I could give him my consent."

"That was an intelligent response that you have given to Omal," delightfully answered Okema.

"What is your opinion about my intention to accept to marry Omal?" Ader asked her brother.

"Well, on my part, I really do not have any objection," replied Okema. I have known your boyfriend since our days in Magwi Junior and all the way up to Rumbek Senior Secondary School. He is a good boy, humble, responsible and very respectable. The fact that he is from a royal background does not make him snobbish or self-conceited at all."

"Would you therefore mind to write a letter to our parents and tell them about Omal's proposal?" Ader humbly requested her brother. "I am shy to write to them, myself."

"Hey, what do you think brothers are for?" joyfully said Okema. "I will write the letter tonight and give it to the bus driver tomorrow morning, to drop it off at Licari for Mom and Dad."

"You are the best," Ader delightfully told her brother as she tenderly hugged him.

"You are a wonderful sister and I am quite happy that you have found the right person to love."

Okema therefore wrote a letter that night, as he had promised to his sister and sent it the following morning. When Okeny and Abongkara got Okema's letter, they were very delighted to know that Ader was in love with Omal.

Ader's parents knew Omal's family very well and had no problem to allowing their daughter to marrying a son from that home. Consequently, they replied to the letter immediately and told Okema to inform Ader that they absolutely have no objection about the proposal.

On the day that Okema got the reply from his parents, he told Ader at once, "Mom and Dad have written back, saying that they have no objection whatsoever for you to marry Omal."

Ader went wild with joy, spontaneously jumped up with such excitement and happily hugged her brother. She was so thrilled by the news that she acted like a little girl whose wildest wish had come true. Okema was so surprised to see such excitement in his sister and wondered how women felt when it came to the issue of marriage. "I am proud of you and wish you happiness in your upcoming new life," he gladly told his sister.

"Thanks a lot, my dear brother," Ader replied, still in high spirit. "I am glad that our parents have accepted that I am free to marry Omal. Otherwise, I would have not known what I could have done with my life."

Okema amusingly laughed at his sister and thereafter, teasingly said, "You would have cried, might be for a long time if necessary, but eventually, you could have found for yourself a new lover."

"It is not that easy, as you are trying to make it sound, when you love someone deeply, as the way that Omal and I love each other," assertively refuted Ader.

"Well, I haven't found that kind of love yet," carelessly said Okema. "I hope that I would some day experience your kind of love and then I will understand."

"You never know how things would turn out between you and Auma," Ader cautioned her brother. "I know that you know that she is a wonderful girl."

"We are getting serious but not yet up to your extent," Okema honestly assured his sister.

"Well, I am at least glad to hear that from you," happily said Ader. "Okema, you will be a wonderful husband. Look at how you have been taking very good care of me all these years."

"Hey, what are brothers for?" joyfully said Okema and then he told his sister that he was going to visit his girlfriend.

Ader wished her brother a wonderful visit with his girlfriend, and after Okema had left, she knelt down and said a prayer of thanksgiving to God.

The following day was a Sunday and so Ader informed her brother that after the Mass she would be going to share her good news with her fiancé.

Okema simply smiled and nodded approvingly for he did not want to spoil the excitement of the two lovers. Consequently, Ader went to the Church and after prayer she met Omal, who also attended the same Mass, and together, they slowly walked to his house. That day, Ader seemed happier than usual, which made Omal wonder as to what was happening in her life. Omal, who had been waiting for Ader's reply to his marriage proposal, for three weeks then, never suspected that the joy that Ader was having was for both of them.

When they got to his house, Omal served some cold drinks, which he and his lover sipped quietly. Therefore, after they had finished the drink, Ader softly announced, "Omal, I have something very important to share with you."

Omal instantly got alert and seemed like someone who had woken up from a frightening dream. He looked so funny that Ader started laughing at him. Ader found it hard to say, what she wanted to tell Omal but he surprisingly cut in and anxiously asked her, "Darling, does what you wanted to tell me have to do with my marriage proposal to you?"

"Are you a psychic or what?" asked Ader, in complete astonishment.

"I knew so because that is what I have been waiting to hear from you, with so much anticipation, for a long time now," delightfully said Omal.

"Hmmm," sighed Ader, as she tried to construct the sentence in her mind, before she could speak it out, to Omal. "I have received my parents' consent yesterday saying that I am free to marry you and I am really happy because I love you, young man, very much." Tears of joy streamed down Ader's cheeks, as she was emotionally speaking, while she was looking at Omal.

Omal momentarily gazed at Ader rather absentmindedly and eventually said, "Am I hallucinating or what I thought I have just heard you said is real and true? Sweetheart, could you kindly please repeat what you have just said?"

Ader smiled, ogled at her fiancé and mockingly said, "You have clearly heard me, haven't you, Mr. Repeat?"

"I am not sure whether what I thought that I have heard you said is true or not and therefore I would kindly like to hear you say it again," Omal earnestly insisted.

"Now open both of your ears well and carefully listen to me," said Ader, who sounded like a teacher who was trying to discipline a stubborn kid. "Omal, my parents have written to me that it is ok for me to accept your marriage proposal and I am happy to tell you that I will be your wife."

Omal instantly jumped up with excitement, spontaneously carried Ader into his arms and loudly said, "I am the happiest man alive! This is the greatest day in my entire life! Oh God, thank you ever so much for granting me the desire of my heart!" Omal then sat down with Ader still in his arms and began to passionately kiss her. He was so overcome with excitement that he even asked Ader for the first time in their relationship, "Would you kindly mind if we make love today?"

Ader instantly pulled away from Omal and seriously told him, "If you really love me as you have been claiming, then you should wait for me until we finally get married. I have told you from the very beginning of our relationship that I do not believe in premarital sex."

Omal desperately insisted and further said, "But why can't we make love, at least to celebrate our great news today? Sweetheart, I can't help my feelings for you, right now."

At that point, Ader threatened Omal, "Our relationship is over. I do not think that you have any respect for me. Goodbye, Omal. Please get yourself a new girlfriend."

Omal who could not dare to lose Ader, stopped his advances and apologised. "I am truly sorry for making a fool of myself in front of you," he sadly said and seemed deeply hurt, as he tried to control his feelings. "I dearly love you, Ader, and I really did not mean to violate you in anyway. I wish that you could slightly understand how much I want to be with you right now, but since you don't agree with my idea, I will not force you against your will. Please do not abandon me, my love. I absolutely cannot live without you," sincerely pleaded Omal.

Ader compassionately gazed at her fiancé and eventually changed her mind. Tears began to form into her eyes because what Omal had just said sounded really sad to her. Internally, Ader was torn between accepting to make love with Omal and maintaining her principle to remain a virgin until her wedding night but suddenly she remembered her mother's advice, "Every man needs a virgin wife on his wedding night." Consequently, she thoughtfully said to herself, *If I foolishly succumb to Omal's request now, he may eventually leave me for another girl and I will be humiliated for the rest of my life. I don't think that I am ready for such a miserable life. I will preserve my virginity, whatever the circumstance may be. If he really loves me, as he has been claiming that he does, then I see no reason why, he cannot wait for me until we are married.* "I love you, Omal," Ader eventually told him, after a while of deep thoughts. "I hate to see you talk with so much pain because it breaks my heart. Omal, please try to ask me for things that you know that I could easily give to you. That way, you can save us both from such anguish, as we are experiencing at the moment."

"I can understand what you mean," Omal humbly replied. "Ader, let me honestly disclose to you, today, my long kept secret. Every moment that I am alone with you, I have a devastating temptation to be intimate with you but controlled myself with a lot of efforts. Today, however, I thought that you would understand, since your parents have given you their consent, for you to marry me. Anyway, I am sorry for everything, I have said to you. Now can we change the topic and talk about something else?"

"That sounds much better," happily replied Ader, while she was wiping off her tears and trying to look cheerful, once again.

They then talked about, how they should start making arrangements for their upcoming marriage and travel home to meet their parents.

Omal escorted Ader, as she was returning to her brother's house, that evening. When they got to Okema's house, they found him quietly reading a book.

"Congratulation for your great news," Okema joyfully told Ader and Omal. "Should I now call you, Mr. and Mrs. Omal? You already look like, a married couple."

"This is the best day of my whole life," Omal delightfully told his would-be brother-in-law, as he looked lovingly at his fiancée.

"You all look very happy indeed and I hope that thirty years from now, you would still be in such deep love," Okema teasingly told them.

"We will definitely be," they both simultaneously replied and joyfully started laughing.

Omal did not stay long, for fear that he might say something silly to Ader, in front of her brother.

After Omal had left, Okema sternly asked his sister, "I hope that you have not done anything stupid with your fiancé, now that you know that you are free to marry him".

"I have anticipated that you would ask me such a question," Ader calmly told her brother. "I will not tarnish the name of our family and bring shame on everyone, especially you, whom I love so much. In other words, to answer your question more precisely, I did not do anything with him."

"I am so proud of you, sister. That is why I always love and adore you," joyfully said Okema

They then tenderly hugged each other, and afterward, Ader began to cook supper.

After supper, Ader decided to go to bed. Okema did not mind to let his sister go to bed early because he understood that she had a lot to think about.

In bed, Ader began to think quite nervously about her upcoming marriage, and how she would soon be a wife and eventually a mother. She also remembered her fiancé's behaviour, towards her that afternoon and wondered how he might be feeling, right then. Ader was so overwhelmed by her thoughts that tears began spontaneously to stream down her cheeks. She tossed in bed for a long time, before she could fall asleep.

The excitement and confusion of soon becoming a wife drove Ader to the brink of her sanity, for she did not know how to handle the situation well. She needed her mother's advice and reassurance that what she was about to undertake, was the right thing to do. Consequently therefore, Ader avoided her fiancé at all times for fear that she might be tempted to give in to his needs. Omal was so worried for the whole week and thought that he might have done something wrong to Ader. However, one thing that made him calm was that Ader would sweetly smile at him, whenever they met at work but avoided at all cost any situations that could leave the two of them alone. After the week of that funny behaviour from Ader, Omal gathered up his courage and decided to go and meet Ader at her brother's house and discuss the issue with her.

On the day that Omal went to visit Ader, he gently knocked at the door and Okema warmly welcomed him in. As soon as Omal entered the house, Ader, who was sitting in the living room, gave him an unwelcoming look that utterly subdued him. Omal sat on the chair adjacent to Ader's but she declined to even greet him and they both sat staring at each other rather awkwardly, without saying a word. Omal did look very heartbroken, whereas Ader's body language on the other hand, was rather haughty. Okema coincidentally saw his sister's mean look at Omal when he came in and wittingly understood that there was obviously something wrong going on between his sister and her fiancé. He felt out of place due the thick tension between the lovers and consequently told them that he was going away to visit his friend but his main reason for leaving them alone was to enable them have some private time to sort out and solve, whatever was bothering them.

There was a moment of silence, after Okema had left the house that one could even hear a pin drop. Omal and Ader were each scared, to be the first one to talk. However, eventually, Omal boldly broke the silence, by agonizingly asking his fiancée, "Ader, have I lately became an ogre or some infectious disease, to you?"

"Who said that you were an ogre or some infectious disease anyway?" retorted Ader, as she mockingly laughed and looked away from Omal.

"If not then, why have you been behaving very funny to me lately, whenever I wanted to talk to you alone? Not only that you have been avoiding me, since the last time that you have told me that your parents have accepted that we can get married. Furthermore, you have not even greeted me, when I came in here today but instead, gave me the meanest look ever. Are those the proper way for you to treat the man, you have promised to marry? Ader, do you even care, as to know how much pain that you have inflicted in my heart over the past week?" Omal sadly expressed his disappointment and frustration with his fiancée.

"I did not mean to cause you any pain, at all," humbly replied Ader. "However, I am sorry. It is just that I am getting confused, each passing day. I seemed to be causing you more pain than joy, whenever I visited you, for example, last Sunday. Consequently, I needed some time alone, so as to sort out my priorities. Omal, you know that I love you and will soon be your wife but I don't understand why all of a sudden you seemed to be doubting my love for you."

"Ader, I do not doubt your love for me at all but lately I have been confused by the way that you have been tormenting me. Anyway, thank you for your explanation. I love you dearly and right now, I just want to fondly hold you, into my arms. Am I allowed to hug you, in this house?" Omal desperately requested, with a sad and longing heart.

"I think that you are allowed," softly said Ader, as she at last started smiling sweetly at her fiancé. "Otherwise, my brother wouldn't have left us alone, would he?"

Omal then tenderly held Ader in his arms and felt like, not letting go of her. "This is my impression of heaven," he lovingly whispered to her. "I feel so much peace in my heart, right now. Ader dear, I deeply love you but please do not avoid me again, as you have done in the past week. It was such a punishment that could not be described in words. I just want to be with you every minute of my life, if it were possible."

"Omal, I deeply love you too," softly whispered Ader, as her heart beat very fast. "I have never meant to hurt you in any way by what I have done last week. I am very sorry for all the pain that I have caused you, my love."

Omal felt so comforted that he held Ader, as if she was a little baby and said, "You are my life and my world. I do not think that I can live without you in my life."

After Omal let go of Ader, they both sat down and she softly told him, "I am planning to go home next week, to visit my parents because I would like to personally talk to them, about us."

"What a coincidence!" joyfully said Omal. "I have also been planning to travel home. Consequently, beloved, you and I will travel home together."

Ader timidly smiled but did not say anything and Omal concluded that it was her way of affirming that she would travel with him. Thereafter, Omal said that he was going home and so Ader escorted him on his way. Omal seemed happier, as he was returning to his house than, when he came to visit Ader.

Chapter Eight
Ader and Omal Visited Their Parents

When Ader sent a message home to her parents that she would soon be visiting them, they were very delighted at the news. Ader had not visited her parents, ever since she had returned from Nairobi and therefore Okeny and Abongkara, looked forward with so much anticipation to meeting their beloved daughter because they were missing her a lot. Okeny saw this as an opportunity for Amyel to spend some days with her sister, whom she dearly loved. Consequently, he sent a message to Amyel, telling her about Ader's homecoming visit. Amyel went wild with joy at the knowledge that her beloved sister was coming home. She therefore asked, for some days off from her work and went home two days before Ader got home. Amyel helped her parents a lot as they were preparing for her sister's visit.

Ader took some days off her work and traveled to the village, together with her fiancé for the first time. The two did not say much on their way home. Omal was so happy, to share the same seat with Ader in the bus. The long bus ride between Juba and Magwi did not bother Omal at all on that day because he was lost in a world of fantasy. He was fantasizing about Ader agreeing to go home with him to visit his parents, for a few days, before she could go and visit her parents. The situation was so real in his mind that he closed his eyes and pretended to take a snooze. In his world of fantasy, Omal made come true all his dreams about Ader. He was so joyous and peaceful that his face shone with delight. Ader wondered as to what was happening to her fiancé that had made him feel so happy in his snooze. When Omal eventually opened his eyes, he did not seem happy, to return to the world of reality that Ader was not after all going to his parents' home with him. Ader was quite surprised to see the sudden change of mood in her fiancé. However, she did not want to bother him by asking him about what he had been dreaming about, which had made him so happy and why all of a sudden he seemed quite sad. Omal tried hard to conceal his frustration about not being able to take Ader home with him but it was quite obvious that something beyond his power was bothering him.

As soon as the bus arrived at Magwi Centre, Omal was very unhappy and felt so frustrated. Before he got off the bus, he looked at Ader with such love in his eyes and wished that he could at least kiss her. Omal therefore squeezed hard his fiancée's hand and softly but sadly whispered to her, "I am missing you so much already. How I wish that it were possible for you to come with me to our home for just a few days."

Ader disapprovingly shook her head, as she compassionately looked at her miserable fiancé. "Are you suggesting that we elope?" surprisingly whispered Ader to her fiancée.

"Why not, if you could have possibly accept," whispered Omal in reply. "Anyway, I already know, your answer. Get home safely. I love you and look forward to seeing you soon. Please convey my greetings, to your family."

"That I will do," replied Ader, with a broad and beautiful smile on her face. "Have a wonderful time, with your family and pass my warmest regards, to them."

"I surely will do that," said Omal and then he got off the bus. Omal stood spellbound, as he watched the bus sped pass the Amika hill, until it was out of sight. Then he eventually got alert once again and realised that he had to walk home.

When Omal got home, his parents were very delighted to see him. Omal had not visited his parents for quite a long time. His mother ran to welcome him, with such a yodel that was indeed fit to welcome a handsome prince home. Omal was a little embarrassed by his mother's over exaggeration of her affection and excitement for him but did not show his emotion. He thought that his mother was making a big deal out of nothing. Omal's dad heard his wife's voice as she joyfully was yodeling and wondered what might have thrilled her so much. When the Chief got out of the house and saw his son, he also began to hurry towards him but was late because his wife had already got to Omal.

"Welcome home, my child," delightfully said Omal's mom, as she took away the luggage from her son's hands and put them down, so that she could hug him. "I miss you so much and sometimes I wished that you were a little boy once again, so that I could cuddle you in my arms and keep you here at home, with me. Well, son, I love you as a grown up man too. Look at you! You are handsomer than when I last saw you. Something good has surely happened in your life that is making you seem so full of life, hasn't it, son?"

"I miss you too, Mom," gently said Omal, while he was wondering as to how accurately his mother had guessed about the love and joy that he was feeling in his heart for Ader. "It feels so good to come home and visit you," went on Omal, as he was opening his arms to reciprocate his mother's arms, which were up in the air and ready to lovingly hug him.

Omal's mother then tenderly hugged him, as she was admiringly looking at his face and joyfully smiling. Thereafter, she then carried his luggage; the heaviest one, she put on her head and hand carried the lighter one.

When the Chief got to his son, he shook hands hard with him and called him all the praise names he could remember. "Oh son, you give me so much joy," he delightfully told him, while he was holding his son's hand, as they were walking towards the house. "Welcome home, my hero. It has been such a long time since you last visited us. You rarely come home without any reason. There should be something very special that has compelled you to come home at this time of the year."

Omal's parents both spoke, as if they were psychics and there was no way that Omal could avoid their inquisitive questions about the change in his life. "You got it right, Dad," said Omal, with a big smile on his face. "But I also wanted to visit both of you. I miss you too, you know?"

As soon as Omal and his dad entered the house, his mother told him, "You are so dusty, son, please go and wash up. There is some water that I have put for you in the shower shelter."

Omal obeyed his mom and did as he was told. After Omal had taken shower, his mother cooked the dish that he liked the most and he settled down to dinner, with his dad and the other men, who had come over to see him. It was not customary for Acoli women to eat with men, especially the Chief, and so Omal's mom ate with the women, who were with her in the home. After the meal, the Chief tried to get his son to tell him the other reason for his visit but Omal tactfully avoided all the questions because he wanted to tell his parents about Ader after the rest of the people were gone. They therefore chatted, until Omal told his parents that he was tired and would like to retire for the night.

The next day in the afternoon, Omal humbly approached his mom and dad when they were alone and announced that he had something very special to discuss with them. The chief and his wife excitedly sat down and joyfully looked at their son, with so much anticipation in their eyes.

"Well, Mom and Dad," respectfully said Omal. I wrote to you about a year ago that I have met a girl, whom I dearly love."

"Yes?" anxiously said his dad, when Omal paused a little bit.

"Our relationship got serious over the time and I have eventually asked her, to marry me. I know that I should have asked for your permission first, before I had proposed to her but I am deeply in love with the girl. My fiancée's name is Ader. She is the daughter of a man, called Okeny, from Licari village. Her mother's name is, Abongkara. I went to school, with some of her brothers. Is there anything wrong in the history of our families, that could prevent me from marrying her?"

"Are you kidding son?" excitedly said his father, with such a joyful heart. "You have made the wisest choice, for your future wife, an Acoli girl, from a good family, to bout! Our ancestors have truly looked down on us favourably and answered our prayer. Look, you have made the most important decision, without first consulting us and yet, it is the best one. We know the family of your fiancée, very well. They are wonderful, spiritual and very respectable people. There is absolutely no problem at all, between our families. Son, you have made me, the proudest father, today."

"I am very happy for you, my son," delightfully said his mother, with tears of joy, running down her cheeks. "God has really smiled on us and may His Name be praised. I personally know your fiancée's mother. She is my friend, a very good woman and everyone talks very well about her and her family."

"Mom, Dad, you have today made me the happiest son and man on earth," gratefully said Omal, as his heart beat very fast with delight. I do not know how I should thank both of you."

"You have made us very happy, son," joyfully said the Chief. "There is nothing more that you could give us that is better than the news that you have just told us. Son, may God bless you in all your endeavours all the days of your life."

"There is one more thing that I need to tell you," gently continued Omal. "Ader has also come home to visit her parents and to tell them about us."

"Is that right?" excitedly asked the Chief, in very high spirit.

"Yes, father," happily replied Omal. "I was thinking that we should send her parents a message, so that you and I could visit them, before Ader and I would return to Juba."

"Surely," delightfully said the Chief. "I will send a message at once tomorrow to tell them of the date and time when we would be visiting them."

"Am I allowed to come with you people?" humbly inquired Omal's mom.

"I am sorry, dear, not this time," deniably answered the Chief. "This is supposed to be men's visit. You will come on the big day, when we will return to meet our obligation for the marriage."

"I understand," gently replied Omal's mother, but in her heart, she was hurting and wishing that it were possible for her to go too.

"Well, thank you both very much once again, for giving me your consent, for me to marrying my beloved Ader," Omal gratefully told his parents. "I am very happy to have you for my parents."

"And we are very joyful, to have you, for our son," delightfully said his parents.

Omal, shortly after, left his parents and went to his room. He was so overcome with joy that he fell asleep on the chair and was later on woken up by some of his cousins who had come to visit him.

On the other hand, when Ader got home, she found her parents and sister waiting for her. As soon as Amyel saw Ader, she ran and fondly hugged her sister with tears of joy in her eyes but without saying a word for a long time while their parents were standing and watching them in awe. Okeny and Abongkara were both deeply touched to see how their daughters were expressing their love for each other in such a tender manner.

"Hey, Amyel, would you also give us a chance to greet Ader?" Abongkara interrupted.

"Leave them alone," replied Okeny, as he delightfully continued watching his daughters while they were still lovingly hugging each other. "We will take our turns after she had done hugging her sister. You know very well that Ader has been away from Amyel for such a long time and how the two of them have always been so fond of each other, don't you?"

"Well, I am sorry," haughtily said Abongkara, as she felt a little embarrassed after what she had told Amyel. "I also love Ader and would like to greet her. My arms are longing to hold my sweet daughter. Okeny, have you forgotten that I have given birth to her?"

"It is a rivalry between you women, isn't it?" said Okeny, who was amused by what his wife had just told him. They both laughed and then momentarily left Ader alone with her sister.

After the long hug, Amyel broke the silence and said, "Ader, I have missed you so much and thought that you would never come home anymore."

"Now that was a silly thought, don't you think so?" replied Ader, as she was admiring her little sister. "I was so busy, one thing after another and that is why I did not come home. I love you a lot and have been crying sometimes from missing you too much."

"You did?" curiously asked Amyel in surprise at the knowledge that her sister had been doing the very same thing like her. "I also have been crying a lot from missing you. Whenever I missed you too much, I would come home to visit Mom and Dad and that seemed to ease some of the pain."

"Amyel, you are so precious to me," Ader lovingly assured her sister, "and I love you dearly."

"I hope so," doubtfully replied Amyel, "but aren't you going to get married pretty soon and leave me alone? However, thanks for everything that you have sent me from Nairobi. I couldn't ask God for a better sister."

"You deserved every single one of them," said Ader. "Furthermore, marriage will not make me love you less, my dear sister. Now let me go and greet Mom and Dad."

Abongkara tenderly hugged her daughter, blew a breath of blessing on her head and called her all the praise names she used to call her when she was a little girl. Tears of joy ran down on both Ader's and Abongkara's cheeks.

"Welcome home my lovely child," said Abongkara, with such a delightful heart. "I have been missing you so much over the years that you have been away from home. Child, I am very proud of you and what you have become. However, I won't hold you long because I am aware that your father would also like to greet you."

"You bet that I do," joyfully answered Okeny, as he was walking towards his daughter so as to hug her. "Oh God, praise be your holy name for bringing home my lovely daughter. Ader, your mother and I never thought this day would ever come. We have been missing you a lot. Welcome home, my dear. You are such a delight to have for a daughter. Thank you for everything that you have done for each member of the family. You are really God's gift to all of us in this family."

"Dad, you and all the members of our family are also a special gift to me," gratefully said Ader. "Thank you for loving and giving me hope for a better future. Do you remember the time when I was so depressed after I had finished secondary school? I came to live with you here and refused to ever go back to the city but you and Mom loved, advised, counseled and gave me hope for the future. I owe you a lot."

"You owe us absolutely nothing, my child," said Okeny, with so much joy in his heart. We were only carrying out our duties as your loving parents.

"Let us not keep Ader standing," interrupted Abongkara. "The poor child has been traveling since this morning. "Please come and sit down here beside me."

"I know what you are up to," jokingly said Okeny. "You want to have her all to yourself."

"And what if I do," answered Abongkara, rather arrogantly. "Have you forgotten that I have carried her in my womb for nine months before I gave birth to her?"

"And do not forget that I am her father," retorted Okeny. Everyone then burst into joyful laughter.

"This is just like the good old days again," happily said Amyel.

"Home, sweet home," said Ader, as she took in a deep breath of the clean air in the village. "There is no better place for me in the whole world than this home."

Abongkara had already cooked when Ader got home. Therefore, she gave some water to Ader so that she could bathe before they could settle down to eat. After dinner, they continued with their conversation, as they were trying to catch up on the lost time.

The following evening, when the family gathered around the fire, Ader decided to disclose the other reason why she had come home. "Mom, Dad and Amyel," she softly said. "I know that you are all aware that I am engaged to be married to Omal. However, I would like to know if there is anything about Omal's family that I need to know before I could marry him."

"There is absolutely nothing wrong in the history of the two families," joyfully answered Okeny. "Child, you have made the wisest choice for your husband and we are very proud of you."

"I am quite thrill to know that" said Ader, with such a grateful heart. "Thank you all very much. I feel so blessed to have you for my family."

"And we feel so blessed to have you as one of us, good girl," joyfully answered Abongkara. "May God's blessings be upon you always."

"I would also like you to know that Omal too has come home to visit his parents," continued Ader. "He has planned to meet with you all before he could go back to Juba. He therefore will be coming to visit us anyone of these days."

"Ader, you never told us that bit in your letter when you wrote to us that you were coming home," shockingly said Abongkara.

"I am very sorry, Mom," contritely said Ader. "I might have forgotten."

"Oh you, naughty little girl," seriously said Abongkara. "Do you think that such is a little visit? He is our future son-in-law and we need to prepare ourselves very well, in order to properly welcome him and whoever he would come with. 'They are royalty you know,'" she whispered in Ader's ear.

"Hey, Mom, what are you whispering to Ader," curiously enquired Amyel.

"It is meant to be a secret between the two of us," stubbornly replied Abongkara and then she began to funnily laugh. Ader also burst into laughter and the rest of them joined in too.

"Your mother can be very stubborn and quite funny, you know," eventually said Okeny.

"As if he is not," retorted Abongkara, as she continued to laugh.

"You both are quite funny," happily said Ader. "No wonder the two of you are joyfully living together."

"You have got that right, my dear daughter," admitted Okeny, with a smiling face. "That is how we have been surviving since none of you is living with us at home anymore."

"Ok, ok," interrupted Abongkara, like a teacher who was trying to stop noises in the classroom. "Let us get back to the serious discussion. "Ader, the fact that your fiancé and probably his father and someone else from their family would be visiting us soon is quite a big surprise. You should have told us this in advance. However, beginning tomorrow, we need to start preparing ourselves in order to welcome them."

"I am very sorry for the inconvenience that I have caused you," humbly said Ader.

"There is nothing to be sorry about," answered Abongkara, with such determination. "I think that we can handle them. A team of three women at work is no joke."

Ader smiled at her mother because Abongkara seemed so overwhelmed by the news about the visit. Okeny first looked at his wife in admiration but finally teased her, "I hope that our future in-laws would find you in one piece when they come to visit us because you seemed so worked out about the news."

"You bet I am," rascally answered Abongkara. "Visitors always blame women when they are not properly welcomed in a home. If Ader's fiancé and his people came and found us not prepared, what impression do you think that they would have about Ader and especially me as her mother?"

"I did not mean to tear you down, dear mother of my children," arrogantly replied Okeny. "It is just that you have taken the news quite significantly."

"That is the difference between a mother and a father, you know," explained Abongkara. "Okeny, I am not angry with you at all because I know that sometimes you can be very sarcastic."

"I am very sorry, my dear wife, if I have hurt your feelings," Okeny contritely said. "I know very well that you have always been a perfectionist and that is why I delight a lot in all that you have been doing over the years."

"We have not seen this side of you two when we were growing up," surprisingly said the girls.

"This kind of honest talks come with age, my dear children," said Okeny, as he mockingly laughed and everybody joined him.

The family then chatted and enjoyed each other's company until they were ready to go to sleep.

Chapter Nine
Omal Visited His Future In-laws

When Ader's parents received the message that Ader's future in-laws were soon visiting them, they were very happy. Okeny sent a message back to Magwi and told the Chief that they were welcomed for a visit to his home. Abongkara and her daughters then got to the serious business of making all the necessary preparations for soon welcoming Omal and his family. Ader's mother went up to the extent of brewing *Kwete* (a local brew) and distilling some *Waragi* (a locally distilled liquor) for the visitors. Ader was quite impressed and pleased to see her parents doing so much for her own sake and she gratefully thanked them.

The Chief, two of his advisers, Omal and his cousin called Olebe then went to meet Ader's family. When they arrived in Licari, they were warmly welcomed. Okeny had invited two of his male cousins to help him during the preliminary marriage discussions for his daughter with his future in-laws. The men first talked about all kinds of things, from hunting to the days long ago when market days were the best days for them. Eventually they got to the reason for the visit. The Chief softly cleared his voice and respectfully said, "Mr. Okeny, I would first of all like to thank you and your family very much for warmly welcoming us into your home. Furthermore, I would like to thank your daughter and my son for giving us this opportunity to meet together today. Had it not been for their love for each other, this meeting wouldn't have come to fruit. I believe that from now onward, such a visit, although not for the same reason, would be a common one. My son has already asked for your daughter's hand in marriage and from what he has told me your daughter has accepted, which has signaled to me that you have given her your permission to accept my son's marriage proposal to her. We are very delighted about what our son has done and have come to meet with you in persons, so as to discuss and agree about the time for their upcoming marriage."

"Well thank you, Chief, for everything that you have said," gently replied Okeny. "My wife and I have indeed permitted our daughter to accept the marriage proposal from your son because we believe that there is no problem in the history of our family and yours that could prevent the two of them from getting married."

"Not at all," happily said the Chief. "There is absolutely no problem between the two families."

"Well, since that is the case," said one of Okeny's cousins, "could you please tell us then, when you would be visiting us next?"

"We were planning to come and settle everything required of us in the middle of December, if that would be ok with you," respectfully replied the Chief. "However, we would soon write to you about the exact date after first discussing the detail arrangements with the rest of the members of my family.

Okeny looked at his cousins' faces as he tried to get their opinion about what Omal's father had just said and after he had noticed that they all had approved by nodding their heads, he consequently told the Chief, "We have no objection, whatsoever." Okeny then directly faced Omal and said, "I hope that you would take proper care of my dear daughter once you have married her and I also hope that you would be as good as your father, who is a God fearing man and a great Chief to the People of Magwi."

What Okeny had said challenged Omal and he boldly replied, "Ader is the best gift that God has ever given to me and I promise you in front of my dad and everybody else here present that I will take very good care of her. I also would like to assure you that I love Ader very much and could not imagine my life without her. Thank you so much for accepting me to marry your beautiful daughter."

"Congratulation son! You are quite a courageous and bold man, aren't you?" admiringly said Okeny. "In our days, we did not have the kind of courage with which you have expressed yourself to me. I am glad to hear your promise and I hope that you will keep it."

"Well done son!" said the Chief, who was equally delighted about the way in which his son had expressed his love for his fiancée boldly before everyone in the meeting. "I am proud of you and like my friend has said I hope that you will keep your promise."

"I will surely keep my promise, Father," assertively said Omal, once again.

"Well then, that brings us to the conclusion of the meeting," joyfully said Okeny.

After the discussions, Okeny sent for Ader to come and greet her future in-laws and fiancé. Consequently, Ader gracefully came into the room and humbly greeted the Chief first.

"I am very delighted for at last meeting you, my child, today," said the Chief, as he interestingly admired Ader while she was respectfully greeting him. "My son has attempted to tell me about you but I think that his vocabulary had failed to capture who you truly are and properly depict you. You are quite a beautiful lady and I welcome you with all my heart to be my future daughter-in-law."

"Thank you for being very kind to me," humbly said Ader, almost in a whisper. "I am glad to meet you too." Ader felt so nervous as she was speaking to the Chief, in the presence of her father and uncles. Therefore, after she had greeted the Chief's advisors, Omal and Olebe, she hastened out of the room. Omal could not resist looking at Ader as she was going out of the room. The older men caught the way that he was lovingly gazing at his fiancée and began to softly laugh. Omal instinctively realized that he was the subject for the laughter and therefore felt quite embarrassed. Everyone noticed Omal's change of demeanor and Okeny immediately remedied the situation by telling his future son-in-law, "My son, we did not mean to humiliate you by our laughter. No, not at all, it is just that you have reminded us about our behaviours when we were young men. Please, do not feel offended. We are sorry if we have hurt your feelings."

"Son, my friend has told you the truth," the Chief reassured his son. "It is very wonderful to see a young man in love and we are very proud of you."

Omal instantly felt quite relieved after realizing that the laughter was not meant to humiliate him. Consequently, he simply smiled at his future father-in-law and thanked him.

After the meeting, food was served and everyone enjoyed Abongkara's special dishes so much. Abongkara was well known for her sapid, delicious and appetizing meal. A little while after the meal, beer was served, both *kwete* and *waragi*. Everyone was so happy that they merrily drank. The elders started telling funny stories about the time when they were young boys and everyone laughed with tears. However, Omal and Olebe wanted to return home early and therefore were excused. The Chief had then realized that his son might probably want to say something to his fiancée, as she would be escorting him on the way and so he and his advisors opted to remain behind. They drank, chatted and joyfully talked about a lot of things. The Chief was quite delighted to find out how friendly Okeny was.

Omal and Olebe went to greet Abongkara before they could leave for Magwi. Olebe was the first one to respectfully greet Abongkara, and thereafter, he walked away, leaving Omal alone with his future mother-in-law. Abongkara was very delighted to meet her handsome future son-in-law. Omal respectfully squatted down and bowed his head as he gently shook Abongkara's hand. "I am very glad to meet you, Mother," he humbly said. "It has been very kind of you to graciously welcome us into your home today. I very much appreciated everything that you have done for us."

"I am very glad to meet you too, my son," joyfully said Abongkara, with an acknowledging smile on her face. "I hope that we will talk more next time and I wish you well on your way back home."

"Thank you very much," gratefully said Omal, "and thank you too for allowing your beautiful daughter to be my future wife. I love her a lot and she means so much to me."

"Well, I am glad to hear you say that about my beloved daughter," delightfully said Abongkara. "Let God bless you and your family."

Omal smiled at his future mother-in-law and then join Olebe on their way home.

Ader and her sister then escorted Omal and his cousin on their way home. Both Omal and Ader were quite delighted that their parents have accepted for them to get married. Omal was very happy that day to meet with his future in-laws. As they were going, Omal playfully deceived Amyel, "I am taking Ader away with me to Magwi today." He spoke with such seriousness in his eyes that Amyel almost thought that what he was saying was true.

Ader cut in and reassured her sister, "Amyel, please don't listen to him, he is simply joking."

"It is so easy to deceive you, Amyel, isn't it?" said Omal, as he amusingly laughed at how Amyel had shockingly reacted to what he was jokingly telling her. "I can tell that you almost believed me."

"I knew that you were simply joking," pretentiously replied Amyel, as she also began to laugh. "I just wanted to see how far you were going to go with your joke."

Although Omal had pretended that he was only joking about wanting to take Ader with him to Magwi, deep in his heart, he was wishing that it could be possible because he was then feeling like carrying and running away with Ader and start living with her at that very moment as his wife.

As soon as the girls said that they were returning home, Omal softly whispered to Ader, "Darling, I would like to ask you about something very important to me."

Amyel and Olebe wittingly realised that Omal wanted to privately say something to Ader and so they began to walk fast and left the two lovers alone behind them. Omal then held Ader closest to his right side and pleadingly said, "I miss you a lot and would like you to come to our home to visit me and my people tomorrow if your parents could kindly allow you."

Ader shockingly glanced her fiancé and softly said, "I know that your invitation is a sudden one but I don't want to disappoint you by turning your request down. Therefore, my sister and I will come tomorrow. I am sure that my parents will not refuse when I ask them about your request."

"Thanks a lot, my dear," joyfully said Omal, who felt extremely happy and quite relieved. "I was rather afraid that you might not accept my invitation within such a short notice. Ader, you have illuminated my life with so much joy and peace and I know that my people would be very delighted to see you tomorrow. Darling, you are such a sweet person and I love you a lot."

Ader timidly smiled and the two tenderly hugged each other. As soon as Omal had noticed that Amyel and Olebe were a little further away, he could no longer resist his overwhelming desire to at least passionately kiss Ader. Consequently, he turned his back towards the direction of Olebe and Amyel as he blocked Ader out of their view and lovingly kissed her. Ader was then used to Omal's surprised kisses and willingly submitted. Omal felt so elated after the sweet kiss but told Ader, "How I wish that it was possible for us to get married tonight. Then I would have felt quite wonderful."

Thereafter, they hastened, so as to catch up with Amyel and Olebe, who were way ahead of them. Eventually, Omal and his cousin said goodbye to Amyel and Ader and then went their way. Omal seemed so miserable as he was going home and kept on looking behind until he could no longer see Ader and Amyel. Although Omal was missing Ader so much, he was also a little comforted at the knowledge that she would be visiting him and his people the next day.

On the other hand, as the girls were walking back home, Amyel noticed the spot where they used to play when they were little girls and then asked her sister, "Ader, do you remember the good old days when we used to play on that large rock?"

"How could I forget?" interrogatively replied Ader, while she laughed at Amyel who sounded so sad. "Childhood memories never fade away and do you, Amyel, remember how we used to sing under the big *Kwoko* tree (a kind of tree that grew only on ant hill)?

"Oh dear," delightfully replied Amyel. "We were such a wonderful duet. However, what has made us to stop singing anyway?"

"I think that we grew up so fast and each of us went her separate way too early," sadly explained Ader.

"You are right, we did grow up very fast," admitted Amyel. "Look, you are now planning to get married. Do you remember the time long ago when our brothers used to tease us that no one would marry us when we grow up because we were very ugly?"

"They were only joking," said Ader, as she joyfully laughed. "Those rascal boys made us really cried a lot but they were also defensive of us."

"How wonderful were those days when we were still all at home," said Amyel with a sad face. "I am so uninterested to come home these days because there is no fun anymore. We are all grown up and everyone is thinking about his/her future and some about their families. Take for instance Aya, since she got married, she is no more fun to be with and has enormously changed as if she is a complete stranger. I wonder what changes people once they get married."

Ader deeply sighed and then tried to explain to her sister, "Loving someone out of the family is what changes people because one gets attached to the person they love so much that life seemed meaningless without that person."

"Hmmm," deeply sighed Amyel, as she shockingly stared at her sister in disbelief, "Is that how much you love Omal, eh? Sometimes I feel that you should not get married because I love you so much that imagining my life without you in our family in the future is really hurtful."

Ader smiled but her eyes were full of tears as she hugged her sister. "I will always be there for you and listen to you whenever you have something important to discuss with me."

"That is what you are saying right now, dear sister, but in December you would become a different person and even your name would be changed to Mrs. Omal. How strange! I wonder whether I would be able to call you that. To me, you will always remain my loving elder sister, Ader. I am missing the days when we used to fight at night over who should sleep by the wall. Those were the days when we used to have what is called a family but not the present one." Amyel painfully reminisced.

"Stop dwelling in the past and being a pessimist," Ader sternly scolded her sister. "I knew that you were going to be in so much pain had I written to you directly that I was planning to getting married and that is why I have instead informed Mom and Dad to tell you. However, I am glad that you have taken some days off from your work in order to come and share with me my great news. You are my very, very special young sister, Amyel and I would like you to know that you will always occupy a special and tender place in my heart."

"Well, thank you for all the wonderful things that you have said," replied Amyel. "However, there is one thing that I would like you to understand, dear sister, and that is, I am not a pessimistic person. It is only that I do not believe in marriage, especially in the kind of marriage in which a man accumulates lots of women in his home and calls them all his wives. That to me is an abomination and a very stupid idea of marriage. Ader, my beloved sister, I hope that Omal will not marry another wife after he has married you."

"I don't think that he would," confidently replied Ader. "Omal loves me so much. He has truly proven to me, beyond any reasonable doubt, that he is a unique, Acoli boy."

When the girls got home, they found that Omal's father and his advisors were just leaving. Ader respectfully said goodbye and wished them well on their way to Magwi. Okeny had then made fire in the courtyard and was sitting beside it alone, a sad sight, which brought tears into his daughters' eyes.

"Amyel, I can now clearly understand what you were trying to tell me," sadly said Ader to her sister. "School is good but also has its disadvantages. Father should not be sitting alone like that if the boys were at home. We are all scattered and the home is left to Mom and Dad. They have gone back to where they have started their life just the two of them. Anyway, such is the fact of life and we shall all be that way when our time comes."

"Well, as for me I am not getting married as I have already told you," assertively replied Amyel. I want to help my parents and be there for them whenever they needed me."

"Don't say that please," Ader sadly rebuked her sister, "Mom has Dad for a company but whom would you have when you grow old, alone? Don't also forget the fact that people will say all kinds of filthy things about you when you are living alone." Ader admonished her sister.

"Let them say whatever they want to say about me," answered Amyel, rather carelessly, "but as long as I don't do the things for which they would be accusing me of, I would not care."

After finishing their little talk, the girls went and sat down beside their father, who was smiling at them. Okeny was always very happy whenever his children visited home because he was missing them so much. They ate their supper together and sat quietly as they watched the amber glowing.

Eventually, their mother broke the silence and said, "How I wished that I could be able to make you all little children once again, so that you would be with me at home, just like it used to be. I hate working alone in the field, going alone for firewood and to the river to fetch some water. Anyway, I am proud of what you have all turned out to be."

"Our children are real blessings from our Father in heaven," Okeny delightfully told his wife. "I am glad that we have all seen the advantages and disadvantages for being grown ups. God has graciously given us our children and we have done our best by raising them up very well. I am now feeling that our parental work has been properly done, and should I die now, I will rest in peace."

"Why have you even said that Father?" sadly inquired Amyel. "Do you think that by being young adults now we do not need you anymore?"

"I did not mean to upset you girls but the fact of life is that once someone is born that person would have to die some day."

"We all know that very well, Father," humbly said Ader, "but we still need you in our lives very much. We would like you to live long enough to see our grandchildren."

"And I do not want to be a widow," stubbornly said Abongkara, "Okeny, if you are scared of living, I will discipline you to love it for the sake of our children and me."

Abongkara's sense of humour amused everyone and they all burst into laughter, including Okeny.

"I can see that all of you want me to live a long, long, life," joyfully said Okeny. God's willing, I would live a long life and all of you must accept to take care of me."

"We will take care of you," was the unanimous answer.

Thereafter, everyone decided to retire for the night

Ader was rather shy to ask for her parents' permission, so as to go and visit her fiancé and his family the following day. She thoughtfully debated the issue in her mind for quite a while but eventually decided that the best person to ask for permission from that night was her mother. Hence, she waited until her father had retired to his room while her mother was left alone outside as she was putting off the fire in the courtyard. Ader then approached her mother and humbly asked her, "Mom, Omal has requested Amyel and I to visit his family tomorrow. Could you kindly allow us to go or do you think that it is not a good idea?"

"You don't expect me to say no, do you?" stubbornly answered her mother.

"What kind of answer is that Mom?" fearfully asked Ader, as she felt rather upset and very uncomfortable by her mother's response. "Mom, have I offended you in any way?"

"Grow up girl!" said Abongkara, rather unpleasantly. "Do you want me to answer you 'yes' or 'no' as if you were still a little girl? I have indirectly told you that it is ok for you to go. I will tell your father about your visit tonight and I don't think that he would object. Behave well when you go. I hope that you will put into practice everything that I have taught you so far."

"Thanks, Mom," gratefully replied Ader. "I will behave well; don't you worry about me."

On the other side, as soon as Omal got home after his visit to Licari village, he went straight away to his room and did not come out until his father and his advisors had returned. Omal's mother wondered as to what was disturbing her son but dared not asked him. So after her husband had come home, she eventually asked him, "How was your visit with our future in-laws?"

The Chief excitedly replied, "Oh dear! How I wished that you had gone with us. We were well received and we did really enjoy our visit so much. Those people are so friendly, kind, loving and very understanding in everything that they do. They have given me the impression that our two families are already united and that is why my men and I have decided to remain behind to have friendly chat with Ader's father and his cousins. Ader's father is quite a remarkable gentleman."

Omal's mother was so happy to hear what her husband was telling her. She consequently realized that her son was missing his lover. "I am glad that your visit was a pleasant one," she happily said. "I can now understand the reason for our son's moodiness. He has never spoken to anyone since he got home but went straight to his room."

"Who could blame him for feeling low?" whispered the Chief to his wife. "His girl is a knock out. She is wonderfully beautiful, commendable and exquisitely eligible to be our future daughter-in-law. The way she sweetly smiled when she was greeting us has filled my heart with so much joy. Our son indeed has good eyes to have chosen such a beauty."

"I am so happy for our son," delightfully said Omal's mother, after learning that Ader was a very beautiful girl. "I excitedly look forward with such anticipation to meeting his wonderful girl."

After the Chief and his wife had confabulated for quite a while, Omal came to where they were and softly announced to them, "My fiancée and her sister are visiting us tomorrow."

His mother was so baffled by the announcement and disappointingly asked him, "Why did you not tell me about this as soon as you have returned from your visit?"

"I did not tell you earlier on because I don't want many people to come to our home when my fiancée visited." Omal honestly assured his mother.

"Nonsense," his mother arrogantly told him. "Such a visit is very important to all our relatives and not only to you, my son, because they would also like to meet your fiancée."

Omal did not like what his mother had just told him but there was nothing that he could do about it, so he kept quiet and sadly returned to his room.

After Omal had gone back to his room, his mother asked his father, "I hope that I have not said something that has offended our son? His way of thinking is quite contrary to ours."

"Well, I don't think that you have said anything wrong to him," the Chief assured his wife. The boy is young and has a lot to learn about our tradition and especially our heritage. I do not think that he is angry with you. He is simply missing his lover."

"I am glad to know that I have not offended him," said his wife with a sigh of relief. I was beginning to wonder that I might have hurt him by what I have told him."

"Not at all, dear," the Chief reassured his wife. "It is our tradition that all our relatives should meet his fiancée when she visited us tomorrow; otherwise, everyone of them will bitterly complain if we do things our son's way. Please send out the message as soon as possible."

Consequently, Omal's mother then sent out the message that evening to all their closest relatives, including her daughters who were married in Magwi area and told them that her future daughter-in-law would be visiting the family the following day.

Chapter Ten
Ader Visited Her Future In-laws

On the day that Ader was going to visit her fiancé's family, she got up early and did all the house chores. Ader and Amyel fetched a barrel full of water for their mother so that she would not have to go to the river while they were away. After the girls had done all the necessary chores, they took shower and then put on their best dresses. Abongkara had already told her husband about the girls' visit to Magwi and consequently Okeny admiringly smiled at his beautiful daughters as they were going. Ader then realised that her father's smile was his way for proving to them that it was ok for them to go to Magwi. Therefore, Ader and Amyel smiled back at their father and happily said, "Stay well, Father; we will see you this evening."

"Good luck, my girls," their father joyfully replied. "Have a wonderful visit."

When Ader and Amyel arrived at the Chief's home, they found that a lot of people were waiting for them. Ader felt so diffident and scared to see all the people because she had never expected that there would be that many people in her fiancé's home. Omal, who was waiting with so much anticipation for the girls' arrival, was quite delighted when he saw them from afar. He therefore joyfully approached and warmly welcomed them into his father's home. Omal then took Ader and Amyel to the room where the elders were. Both Ader and her sister knelt down and respectfully greeted all the elders, according to the Acoli custom. Thereafter, Omal introduced his fiancée to his people, "Well, my dear elders, my parents and everyone here present, this is Ader, my future wife," he said, as he lovingly pointed to Ader, "and this other one is her younger sister and her name is Amyel."

Everyone smiled at Ader and nodded their heads in approval of her. Some of the people even winked at Omal to signal their approval, for the wise choice that he had made for his future wife.

"How are your parents doing?" one of the elders asked.

"They are doing quite well, thank you for asking," softly replied Ader, with her head bowed down because she was too nervous to face the elders. "They have sent you their greetings."

"Welcome home, my dear daughter," said another elder. "You do not need to fear us at all, for this home would soon be your home. We are all very delighted to meeting you."

As the elders were still talking to Ader, one of Omal's sisters came and interrupted the conversation, "I am sorry if you, the elders, should think that I am rude," she humbly said. "Could my sisters and I also have an opportunity to talk with our future sister-in-law, please?"

The girls' request was granted and so Ader and Amyel followed the lady who was sent to ask for them to the room where the rest of the young women were.

After Ader and her sister had gone to where Omal's sisters were, the elders appreciatively congratulated Omal for choosing such a beautiful girl as his fiancée and one of them told Omal delightfully, "You are the luckiest man to win the heart of such an angelic girl. Although I do not know your fiancée that well, I think that she is everything a man needs in a woman. I really mean what I have said, my son. Your fiancée is a very, very beautiful girl; tall, brown, slender, good-looking and walks with such grace."

"Do you think that you have said it all, man," said the next elder. "I learnt that she also comes from a very, very good and respectable family."

"The two of you will make a great couple and have beautiful children," another elder continued. "Both of you are very good-looking people. Son, you have our blessings in this marriage and may you have many children, both boys and girls."

Omal felt so adulated by all the beautiful compliments from his relatives about his fiancée.

He was so full of joy that he spontaneously swayed his head from left to right, with a handsome smile on his face. After the elders had finished talking to Omal, he left them and went to his bedroom because he was so overwhelmed with joy.

Omal's sisters were also very happy to meet Ader and admired a lot how good-looking she was. They talked to her about a lot of things and furthermore cautioned her, "You must get prepared for the big responsibilities that are awaiting you in this home of ours. Our brother is the only heir to this family. When our father is gone someday, your fiancé would have to take over the responsibilities of this home and you would be his partner to help him carry out the duties effectively and efficiently. We are very proud of you and we hope that you would warmly welcome us and our children whenever we visited you in the future."

"I love your brother so much and how could I exclude you girls?" Ader humbly asked them.

The girls joyfully laughed at the knowledge that Ader loved their brother so much. They then playfully started to touch Ader here and there, so as to find out whether she could easily get annoyed. Such kind of play was always expected between sisters-in-law. Ader moved here and there, as she happily giggled. Omal's sisters also began to play with Amyel, who initially declined but eventually gave up her resistance as Omal's sisters continue to bother her and joined them.

After everyone got tired of the game they were playing, they all sat down and decided to have a conversation instead. One of Omal's sisters then playfully threatened Ader, "We will detain you here tonight for our brother, whether you like it or not."

Ader smiled, disapprovingly shook her head and calmly replied, "You can't do that to me. I have my sister with me; she will rescue me from you and then I will call off the engagement."

"You can't do that" one of them said, while the rest of them were laughing, very interestingly. "Hey, Ader, do not forget that you have told us just a while a go that you love our brother so much."

"I do, and I don't deny it," confirmed Ader, "but I do not like what you have just said."

"You are in our hands," said another sister. "Therefore, there is no escape for you today."

As they were still conversing, Omal sent a little boy to ask Ader to come to him. His sisters sent the boy back to tell Omal that they had not yet finished having conversation with Ader. Omal got angry with his sisters and sent an older boy with a message insisting that he needed to talk to Ader right away. He further instructed the boy to tell his sisters to stop being stubborn. After the women had realized that their brother was indeed very serious about calling his fiancée, one of the older sisters teasingly told Ader, "Please get up and go to where your husband is because he really needs to talk to you. We have no power to argue with him over you."

"I am not yet his wife," Ader defiantly made her point.

"We can make you his wife today if we want to," one of the sisters jokingly said.

84

"Stop all your poppycock, you girls," frustratingly said Ader, as she was getting fed up of their silly jokes. "I only came here today for a visit. Is that how you girls treat all your visitors?"

"You are a different kind of a visitor," one of the girls went on. "The kind that should not be allowed to return to their home. We will send a message to our brother to lock you up in his room as soon as you get there."

Ader speechlessly stared at her future sisters-in-law, shook her head in bewilderment, got up and followed the messenger to where her fiancé was. Amyel quietly admired her elder sister's courage in dealing with Omal's stubborn sisters.

When Ader got to where Omal was, he delightfully smiled at her without saying anything, until the boy he had sent to call Ader had left the room; then he motioned with his hand that Ader should sit down. Ader therefore went and sat adjacent to her fiancé and did not dare to ask him as to why he had sent for her to come. Omal missed Ader so much and all he wanted to do was to fondly hold her in his arms before she could return home. He therefore attempted to kiss Ader but she flatly refused and sternly told him, "I did not come in here for that, and besides, there are very many people in the home. What if one of them should walk in here and find us kissing, what impression will they have about me and my family?"

Omal initially obeyed what Ader had told him and withdrew, but after a little while of deep thoughts, he got hold of Ader into his arms, looked into her eyes with such desire and sadly questioned her, "Ader, do you really love me as you claim that you do?"

"You know very well that I do love you, don't you, Omal? Ader arrogantly replied. "If you think that I don't, could you explain to me why I took the trouble to come all the way from Licari to visit you and your people today?"

"Ader dear, I am sincerely sorry," Omal contritely apologized to his fiancée. "I really didn't mean what I have said in the way that it sounded but could you explain to me whether even kissing you here in my room is the same as making love to you?"

"I know that it is not," uncomfortably replied Ader.

"Well then," said Omal, as his voice sounded very coarse from trying to repress his hurtful feelings, "let me assure you that no one is going to enter into this room for as long as they know that I am here with you. Ader, if you leave this place today, without even kissing me, I will never forgive you."

Ader then had some compassion for his fiancé and so she accepted to kiss him. Omal was always a good kisser; therefore, he passionately kissed Ader and felt like not letting go of her. Ader still afraid that someone might walk in on them and find them kissing in the way that they were pushed Omal away and did not seem pleased.

"I am sorry if you feel bad," Omal apologized as he tried to catch his breath; "however, I wonder why you are so ambivalent about the way we have both kissed each other. It felt so right and fulfilling to me and I think that you, too, have felt something. Ader there is nothing to be shameful about because I love you and you love me. Furthermore, your family and mine are both aware that we would soon be husband and wife. I will never do anything stupid to you, especially on a wonderful day like today." Even though Omal had withdrawn from kissing his fiancée, his whole being was still yearning for her. He therefore sat down, while gazing at her with such consuming desire in his eyes.

Ader avoided her fiancé's eyes, but every time that she looked at him, she found that his eyes were still fixed on her and so she decided to diffuse the situation by angrily asking him, "Omal, what is really the matter with you today? Was it wrong of me to have accepted to come and have a little chat with you privately here in your room?"

"Oh no, dear, not at all," replied Omal, as he was still breathing heavily. "It is so hard for me to control myself today. Ader, my love, I am not ashamed to tell you that right now I feel like being with you as my wife. However, I am sorry if I have caused you any embarrassment or shame."

"You have not caused me any shame at all," carelessly said Ader. "I am sad because you are behaving very strange today and making my visit with you quite uncomfortable."

"I am sorry if I have made you felt quite uncomfortable in our home because my intention was the contrary," contritely said Omal. "Please feel at home dear. Ader, my love, you know very well that I love, adore, respect, honour and care about you deeply as my future wife, don't you, sweetheart? Surely, Ader, did you expect me to let you return to Licari today without even having a private moment with you? I have called you here to chat, kiss and fondly hold you for a little bit, before you could return home because I have been deeply missing you."

"And so your wishes have come true, haven't they?" uncomfortably inquired Ader, with a mean look at her fiancé. "Can I now return to where the young women are? I know that they are waiting for me and my sister should be wondering as to why I have spent such a long time with you."

"Not yet," stubbornly said Omal, as he drew Ader to himself and started holding her quite fondly once again. Ader did not resist him then because she knew pretty well that he would never force her to make love to him. Omal slowly and tenderly kissed Ader one last time before he could let go of her, and thereafter, Ader was short of breath and could not even bring herself to look at Omal's face anymore.

"I feel much, much better now," joyfully said Omal in a very clear voice and was seemingly quite happy. "Can we now discuss about our journey back to Juba?"

Ader only nodded and there was a moment of silence. Omal then suggested that they travel together on a Tuesday and Ader agreed again by quietly nodding. Omal then realized that Ader was very uncomfortable to talk to him and so he decided to walk with her back to where his sisters and Amyel were. Omal was quite surprised to see a smile breaking on Ader's face as they were approaching the place where the young women were. He wished that Ader could smile and freely talk with him whenever he was alone with her.

"I think that it is getting late and we are returning home now," happily said Ader as soon as they got to where Omal's sisters and Amyel were. "It has been wonderful for me to meet with all of you."

"We have also enjoyed your company, although our brother has cut short our conversation," said one of the sisters.

"I also needed to talk to her, you know," said Omal, as he was fondly holding his fiancée's hand and joyfully smiling at her. "I am sorry if you all are feeling that I was trying to be mean to you by taking Ader away from you."

"We did not feel that you were being mean to us at all," answered one of the older sisters. "We had just wanted to tease your fiancée a little more. Frankly speaking, brother, we had fun with her. She is a wonderful girl, just like her younger sister."

"Goodbye then, everybody," said Ader, with a sweet smile on her face. "I will see you next time."

"As our brother's bride by then," jokingly said the youngest of the sisters. "Otherwise, Omal, why are you simply allowing Ader to return to Licari today without any struggle on your part to immediately keep her as your wife? You seem to go so easy on this beautiful girl."

Omal thoughtfully wished that he had the stamina to boldly execute what his sister had just suggested but he did not reply to her. There was an outburst of laughter at what the last speaker had suggested, as Omal, Ader and Amyel were walking out of the house.

As soon as the trio got to where the elders were, Omal respectfully said, "My dear elders and parents, Ader and her sister are now returning home."

"Oh thank you so much for coming to visit us," said one of the elders to Ader. "We are very happy to meeting you today and we look forward to the day when you would finally come to living with us. Please convey our greetings and gratitude to your parents when you get home."

"Thank you all very much," softly said Ader. "I am also glad to meet all of you. I will surely pass your greetings and gratitude to my parents."

"I am so delighted to meet you today, my child," delightfully said Omal's mother, "From now onward, I will treasure you in my heart as a member of my family. I love you, my child."

"I am very honoured," shyly said Ader, while she was sweetly smiling. "Thank you for being kind to me, Mom."

Ader then respectfully shook hands with all the elders, including Omal's parents and timidly walked away very quickly. Everyone was amused by Ader's shyness but Omal interestingly smiled and said, "Well, she may be shy but is the love of my life."

"She is a wonderful girl!" the elders unanimously responded to him. "We are very proud about the wise choice that you have made for your future wife."

"Thank you all very much, my dear elders," delightfully said Omal and then he followed his fiancée.

Two of Omal's cousins, Ocillo and Otto, joined him as he was escorting Ader and Amyel on their way home. On the way, Omal slowly walked with Ader, while Ocillo and Otto walked with Amyel ahead of them. As they were going, Omal frustratingly told his fiancée, "If it were possible that things could be done my way, I could have even married you today and there would have been no reason for you to return to Licari as it is right now. My sister's suggestion to me was absolutely right, although she was merely joking. I am surely letting you easily go, as if I do not daily agonize with the desire, to be with you. Ader, I very much feel like kissing you one last time."

"Don't be ridiculous," shockingly replied Ader. "Why are you in such a rush to be with me? December is not all that far away. Besides, when we get married in the proper way, we shall have all the time we need for each other and we will happily live together, until death do us part."

Omal deeply sighed and fondly squeezed Ader against his side, without further saying a word. They then walked silently, while from time to time awkwardly stared at each other because Omal did not know what else to tell Ader and on the other hand, Ader felt that whatever she was saying did not give him any comfort. Therefore, as they were about to reach Licari, Omal and the boys decided to return home. Omal seemed so sad as he was saying goodbye to his fiancée because he was vehemently controlling himself from kissing her one last time out of respect for his cousins and Amyel. However, he fondled her hands, looked into her beautiful eyes and powerlessly said, "Sweetheart, I dearly love and I am painfully missing you a lot already, but if I fail to get some sleep tonight, may you also stay awake. Anyway, I will see you on Tuesday, on our way back to Juba."

"Goodbye, Omal," sadly said Ader, "I wish you a restful sleep and wonderful dreams."

On the way back to Magwi, Omal's cousins were quite concerned about the way he was looking so depressed, and therefore, Otto gently asked him, "What is disturbing you, gentleman?"

Omal stared at his cousins without saying a word but the boys insisted that Omal should tell them why he was looking so miserable. Omal hesitantly thought for a while and then decided to disclose to his cousins why he was feeling that way. "I am missing my fiancée so much that I feel like I should have not allowed her to return to her village today but to start living with me as my…ah, as my loving wife."

"And what has prevented you, anyway?" curiously but simply inquired Otto.

"Well, Ader would like us to follow the proper procedures for marriage, according to the Acoli custom and tradition, that is, my family meeting the obligations of her family first, and then, she would be officially escorted to me," Omal frustratingly told his concerned cousins.

"Hmmm," pitifully sighed Ocillo. If I were you, and knowing that the girl also loves me so much, I would have just eloped with her, to avoid the long procedures for marriage."

"My fiancée does not believe in elopement," Omal honestly assured Ocillo; "otherwise, I would have done it a long time ago but I don't want to disappoint her by taking her against her will."

"You, the so called educated guys, are so different from us who lived in the village," shockingly said Ocillo. "You take life too seriously that you end up hurting yourselves in the end. Who has lied to you that girls normally offer what we boys desperately need from them when it comes to relationship? You have to be very tough all the time in order to get anything at all from a girl, including the possibility for eloping with her. For us here in the village, most of the time, once a boy loves a girl so much, they elope and it shortened the tedious formalities for marriage. Besides, life is too short for anyone to worry about such thing."

At that point, Omal sadly asked his cousins, "Could we please change the subject of our conversation because it is taking me nowhere but instead is adding to my frustration?"

Omal and the boys then talked about other things until they got home.

After all the visitors were gone, the Chief congratulated his son once again. "You have made me a proud father today, my son," he delightfully to him. "Did you see how all the relatives were happy? Even your sisters were glad to meet your beautiful future bride. Son, your marriage would be just like the marriage of my time and I am grateful that you are following in my footstep. You are so fortunate to get a girl from a family like that of your fiancée and I would like you to take good care of your wonderful woman, when you eventually marry her until death do you part. There is one more thing that I would like you to know, my dear son, after meeting the obligation for your marriage in December, I will plan for you a big wedding in the Church. How about that my hero?"

Omal was overwhelmed with joy at sound of the news about the wedding and excitedly replied, "I am so thrilled, Father; I love Ader so much, and when I wed her in the church, then she would truly understand how much I am really committed to love her forever. She means everything to me and I cannot just imagine my life without her. Dad, I would like you to know that you are the best father in the world and that is why I am always very proud of you."

"I am very proud of you too son and will always be. You are my hope for everything. You may not know how much you mean to me. You are the future of this family."

Omal's mother, who was quietly listening to the passionate conversation between her husband and son through the window, eventually questioned them, "And why am I excluded from such important discussion?"

"We did not mean to exclude you, my dear," surprisingly replied her husband. Our conversation was meant to be a man-to-man talk and we did not know that you were eavesdropping on us. Besides, this is just a preliminary talk, but when the serious arrangements get started, you would be at the centre of everything, so don't you worry, my dear wife."

"I am sorry to have mistakenly heard what was meant to be only for men," sadly replied his wife, who sounded quite upset.

"Please come here and behave like the wife of the Chief," playfully said her husband. "I was only joking when I answered you that we were having a man-to-man talk and I see no reason why you are feeling so offended," concluded the Chief but his wife then kept quiet.

Omal did not want to get entangled into the ugly situation of argument that was almost developing between his parents and consequently requested his dad, "Could you please excuse me? I am feeling rather tired after the long day and would like to sleep early." His father therefore excused him and he went to his bedroom.

When the Chief was alone with his wife, he apologised to her for answering her back in a rude manner. "I am sincerely sorry for hurting your feelings," he contritely confessed. "I would like you to know that you are the love of my life, my very special wife and that is why I did not marry another wife. Furthermore, I would like you to know that I did not deliberately hurt you but was only joking because I was carried away by the excitement of my conversation with our son. Beloved, you should really be proud because the fruit of your womb has made everyone in our family very happy today by introducing to us his beautiful fiancée."

Omal's mother, who had been listening to her husband in silence while he was apologizing to her, eventually said, "Thanks for your apology, but next time, please do talk to me with some respect, especially when our son is around. Try not to humiliate me before him because he may do the same to his wife some day in the future."

"I definitely will, my dear wife," agreed the Chief. "Let us not ruin the joy and happiness we have experienced today. Come on here, sweetheart, this is the kind of night, which makes me feel young again and desperately need to be with you."

"You really have your way to get to my heart, haven't you?" humbly said his wife. "I could never hold any grudge against you because you are the love of my life and God's best gift to me."

The sweet talk between the Chief and his wife, coupled with the joy of the day, brought such passion into their hearts that soon they were lost in each other's love.

Alone in his room, Omal lay awake in bed as he desperately thought about Ader. He knew how truly special Ader was because he had tried several times to make love to her but ended up in argument with her and feeling ashamed. However, he started having fantasy about how he would make love to her for the first time when he married her. Omal got lost in his world of imaginations that he felt as if Ader was indeed with him in his bed, but when he finally came to his senses, he was quite sad to realise that he was alone. He wished that it were possible for Ader to spend that night with him, just that one night; then he would have been the happiest man alive. "Too bad that is not what my sweet Ader believes in," he softly whispered. "Her motto is abstinence until marriage and I must comply with it, if I really want to have her, as my loving wife. My time will come. I know that the time will soon come and I will have her anyway." Omal tossed in bed, with lots of wishful thinking for a long time, before he could asleep.

On the other hand, as Ader and her sister were going after Omal and his cousins had bid them goodbye, Ader walked rather slowly and kept looking behind at Omal until he was out of sight because she was missing and feeling quite sorry for him. Amyel got fed up of her sister's unusually weird behaviour and eventually admonished her, "We should really be walking fast because it is already beginning to get dark."

Ader quietly looked at her sister as if someone who had woken up from sleep, deeply sighed and then increased her pace. They then silently walked until Amyel said once again, "Ader, your love for your fiancé is stronger than that for me, isn't it? Sister, why don't you want to talk with me today? Furthermore, what has Omal really done to you while you were alone with him in his room that has deprived you of your power of speech?"

"Nothing!" exclaimed Ader, who sounded like someone who was awakening from a stupor.

"My heart went out for Omal today because he seemed so heartbroken and lonely as he was returning home. I love Omal as much as I love you. Amyel, you would some day understand how true love feels like when you meet the man of your dreams," painfully explained Ader.

"I don't think that I will love someone out of our family as strongly as the way that you love Omal," carelessly said Amyel. "However, today I have indeed witnessed and understood how deeply both of you are in love with each other," Amyel honestly assured her sister.

Eventually, the sisters got home when it was already dark.

Chapter Eleven
Ader Received Invaluable Advice

Abongkara did not want to ask her daughters in the evening, after they had returned from their visit to Magwi because they seemed tired, especially Ader. However, the following day after breakfast, she happily asked them, "Girls, how was your visit yesterday?"

Ader smiled but her sister was swift to answer. "Mom, you wouldn't believe this," she excitedly said. "When we got to Magwi, we found Omal waiting for us near his home, and when he saw us, he almost jumped up for joy. He was extremely excited to see us, but specifically Ader of course. When we got to the courtyard, we found a lot of people waiting for us. Mom, I was a little brave but I wish that you could have witnessed how Ader became so nervous and shy."

"Now stop there, Amyel," authoritatively interrupted Ader. "You have gone too far on me as if you were not also scared. Do you think that I did not notice your demeanor? If we had a chance to escape from those people, we would have all ran away."

"I was only shocked by the number of the people but not timid like you," stubbornly explained Amyel.

"Hey, girls, stop your nonsensical argument!" disciplinarily cut in their mother. "I just wanted to know about your visit, not how you were shy, timid, nervous or frightened."

"Mom, I think that I am the right person to truthfully tell you everything about our visit," rascally insisted Amyel.

"Go ahead then, you pig head," teasingly said Ader, as she smiled at her stubborn sister, who was very anxious to tell their mother every tinsy winsy detail about their visit to Magwi, "but don't over exaggerate the stuff that you are telling Mom."

They all laughed and Amyel continued, "Omal first took us to the elders, who all admired Ader as if she were a princess from a far off land. Before the elders could finish talking to Ader, Omal's sisters sent for her. Oh, Mom, we had fun with those girls. They were all very funny. Those people love Ader so much and I am glad to inform you that once Ader is married she will happily live thereafter. Omal's mom went up to the extent of publicly welcoming Ader as a member of her family and assuring Ader that she loves her."

"Is that true Ader?" delightfully asked Abongkara, with a broad joyful smile on her face.

"Yes she did," humbly replied Ader. "Mom, the reason why I was shy is that I never had expected that there would be that many people in the home. I was not pleased with Omal at all about the situation but he told me that his mother was the one who had invited all the people without his consent."

"Well, I do not see anything wrong with that" joyfully said Abongkara. "Ader, do not forget the fact that Omal is still the Royal Prince, although the custom has changed a lot in recent time."

Ader disapprovingly rolled her eyes to remonstrate that her fiancé was royalty, because according to her, Omal was just like any other boy, simple and common. Abongkara noticed her daughter's eyes and seriously cautioned her, "Ader, you may believe your distorted idea about who Omal really is but you will never change the fact that he is indeed the Prince of Magwi Chiefdom and you will be the future Queen of the People of Magwi when he becomes the Chief."

"I did not fall in love with Omal because he is the Prince," carelessly said Ader. "I just love him because he is a good person to talk to and very friendly."

"I think that someone is scared of the knowledge of being the future Queen of the Magwi Chiefdom," said Amyel, while she was playfully making funny faces to her sister.

"Mom, have you seen what Amyel is doing to me?" childishly said Ader.

"Amyel, please stop behaving like a boil in ones' bottom!" warned Abongkara.

They all burst into very interesting laughter, and thereafter, Abongkara concluded the conversation by saying, "I am very glad that you girls had had a good visit. And as for you, my dear Ader, you must start learning the art of accepting and living with many people in a home, for that would be your future."

Ader profoundly thanked her mother and afterwards went with her sister to collect some firewood from their field near Inapwa hill.

Amyel and Ader helped their mother a lot in the field and the chores around the house. Abongkara felt so comfortable and wished that she could keep them with her at home and not allow them to leave her anymore. Life was so beautiful in the home whenever the children visited. The piece of work that Abongkara used to do in four days, whenever she was alone, was completed in a day. Consequently therefore, there was a lot of free time that Abongkara had to talk with her children. Most of Abongkara's words to her children, especially the girls, were words of advice about the meaning of the life of a woman. She was very happy that Ader had found a good young man for her future husband. Aya's husband was also a good man and respected both Okeny and Abongkara very much. The only person whose future was worrying Abongkara was Amyel. Amyel was absolutely determined to remain single. She loved her family too much to fall in love with anyone out of her family.

Two of Ader's paternal aunts, Aloyo and Onianga, who had heard about Ader's engagement from their cousins, who had attend the preliminary meeting for the discussion for Ader's upcoming marriage, paid an abrupt visit to see Ader one afternoon and also to scold their brother, as to why he had not invited them. As they were approaching their brother's courtyard, Aloyo joyfully began yodeling. Everyone was so astounded by the sound of the unexpected yodel because they did not know who the yodeler was and the reason behind it. Ader, Amyel and Abongkara all rushed out towards the main road to find out what was happening, and after they had seen the two aunts, they all started laughing. Aloyo and her sister then began to sing an old favourite song that praised their father, Okumu, Abongkara joined in the chorus, as they all danced towards the courtyard. When they got to the courtyard, Okeny also joined in the dance. When some of Okeny's neighbours heard the singing and the little dance, they came over just out of curiosity. Soon a few of them joined the dancers and danced vigorously. After dancing two to three songs, everyone eventually sat down. Onianga and her sister brought along with them, some bottles of waragi, which they shared with their brother's neighbours, who had joined them. The neighbours chatted with Onianga and Aloyo for a little bit and then went back to their own places.

After Okeny's neighbours had left, Aloyo sternly questioned her brother, "Why did you refuse to ask at least one of us to come and be part of the discussion for our niece's upcoming marriage?"

"I did not want to pull you away from your heavy farm work at this time of the year, you know," humbly said Okeny, "and besides this was just a preliminary meeting. I was going to send you a detailed message about the exact date for the marriage one of these days."

"How is it that you have invited our male cousins?" curiously asked Onianga. "Didn't they too have farm work, like us? I think that you did exclude us because we are girls."

"I am truly sorry, my dear sisters," contritely said Okeny. "I did not really mean to offend you in any way, let alone excluding you because you are girls. I just respected your situation because I though that your husbands would complain if I were to pull you off from your work for such a tentative discussion."

"Are you afraid of our husbands or what?" Aloyo derogatively interrogated her brother.

"Absolutely not," firmly refuted Okeny. "I respect them, as my in-laws."

There was a sudden outburst of laughter and thereafter Aloyo calmly reassured her brother, "We are not angry with you at all. We just came here out of our own curiosity. Our cousins had told us all about the discussions for our niece's upcoming marriage but our main reason for coming up here this afternoon is to talk to our beloved niece, Ader, whom we were told is currently at home."

"Thank you, my dear sisters, am I glad to hear that you are not angry with me," joyfully said Okeny, as he felt quite relieved to know that his sisters were simply teasing him. "I will now leave you people alone so as to give you an opportunity to talk to Ader."

"Thank you, brother," simultaneously replied the sisters.

As soon as Okeny had gone away, Aloyo and Onianga decided to give some advice to Ader. "We are glad that we have still found you at home," happily said Aloyo. "We were a little worried on our way here because we thought that you might have left for Juba this morning. However, we are delighted about your wise choice for a husband, dear niece. It is wonderful for us to know that you are going to be the future Queen of the People of Magwi. Remember, that title comes with, a lot of responsibilities. Getting married into the royal family is not a small thing. I know that the custom has changed but not so much because there are still lots of work to be done in such a home. You have to deal with many people every day and treat all of them with absolute respect."

"Not only that," interrupted Onianga who was thinking that her sister was not going to give her a chance to talk to Ader, "you should always be in your best behaviour so that you may not give shame to the name of our family.

Listen more and talk less. Do not run your mouth unnecessarily, like the modern girls who have gone to school always do. Do your best in any piece of work given to you. Do not make faces, even when you are sad about something. Talk to your in-laws with respect at all times. Furthermore, do not nag at your husband, whatsoever the situation may be, my dear niece, or else his hair will turn gray before his time."

At the last sentence everyone burst into laughter again. The girls were especially amused by what their aunt had just said about men with gray hair because they had seen some men who were still in their prime but already with gray hair.

"I now know why your husband grayed so early," Abongkara teased Onianga. "You really are giving the poor guy a lot of hard times, aren't you?"

"He is the one who has been giving me a lot of hard times over the years," regrettably said Onianga, as she pretended to be a victim and made a sad face in self-pity. "Besides, gray hair is hereditary in his family. Moreover, he is not royalty like our future son-in-law." Onianga made everyone laugh with tears because she was such a comedian. Her sense of humour had always made everyone around her laughed, including her husband. Ader eventually thanked her aunts, after they were done giving her advice. She promised them that she would do exactly as they had advised her, once she was married.

After the aunts' advice to Ader, Abongkara served meal and they ate while they were amusingly laughing at some of the funny stories that Onianga was telling them. Onianga was such a loquacious woman that in every sentence she said, there was something very humourous in it. Ader and Amyel enjoyed the brief visit by their aunts and were rather sad to see them leave that evening. Onianga was married in Loudo village and Aloyo in Oyere, Bush School area.

After supper that evening, Abongkara called Ader and went out with her to a secluded place. She wanted to have a serious talk with her daughter and therefore told her, "My dear daughter, I would like to have a woman-to-woman talk with you today for the first time. I know that your aunts have talked to you earlier on today but I would like to elaborate more on what they have already told you. When you eventually get married, my dear daughter, you should behave like a typical Acoli bride, that is, respect your in-laws and husband absolutely at all time. You should never put your education ahead of everything else. I know you, the educated girls, are sometimes pigheaded towards your husbands. Any competition in a marriage ruins the beauty of the marriage. You should respect your husband, especially when he is in public.

Correct him only when you are alone with him in the house and accept his corrections to you too. The marriage relationship is always smooth in the beginning but somewhere in the middle, when you get to know each other's true nature more and more, you will disagree in many things and argue. That does not mean that you should not talk to each other or get separated. It is a normal thing in all marriages to argue with each other, once in a while. Sit down with your man and find out why you have disagreed and whoever is wrong, should apologise. That way, you will spare yourselves the embarrassment of calling the elders to sit down and solve your problems, as if the two of you do not have the brains to work out a solution on your own. Marriage involves two people who have been raised with different values. You have to learn to accept each other's faults, as being human. Learn to communicate and understand each other because love brought you together in the first place and no third person has forced you into having the relationship. One last thing, my dear daughter, you should always cook the food that your husband like the most and make your home a comfortable place for him to stay. That way, your man will most of the time be at home with you and not roam about and return home at midnight, as most of the men do these days. Why do you think that your dad is most of the time at home with me?" Abongkara funnily asked Ader, as she playfully nudged her.

Ader only smiled because she did not know the answer to her mother's question.

"Because everything that your father needs in life is always here in the house with me," Abongkara joyfully answered her own question.

At that last advice, Ader giggled and her mother laughed too. Ader profoundly thanked her mother, for the invaluable piece of advice and promised her that she would not let her mother down.

That night, when it was bedtime, the girls went to their house for sleeping and talked about all kind of things. Amyel asked her sister to sing with her, some of the favourite songs that they used to sing when they were kids. They sang lots of the stuff and got up to dance at certain tunes. Amyel wished that it were possible for them to go back to the good old time when they used to make loud noises in their bedroom and then their mother would come, screamed at them and told them to stop being witches. Amyel then asked her sister, "Ader, do you remember when I used to say that when I grow up I will marry far away from home and will not visit our mother because she was always stern?"

"You were such a little rascal, you, Amyel," interestingly said Ader. "Whenever I am alone and thinking about you, I still laugh at some of the things that you used to say to our mother when you were a little girl."

"I did not then understand our mother whenever she was telling us the right things to do," Amyel regrettably told her sister. "I now feel so sorry for the bad things that I have done to Mom, in the past. She is such a special mother and I love her now, more than ever. Consequently, I am not going to get married like the rest of you."

"There is beauty in marriage," Ader assured her sister. "Here in the Sudan and may be in the whole of Africa, when a woman is not married, no one respects her however much she is educated. Now tell me how many, women who are not married in Acoliland that you know of. I don't think that there is anyone, except the nuns of course. Even those who have decided, to live alone with their children, were once upon a time married at least but their marriages did not work out. You know what, my dear sister, I know your problem, you fear that when you fall in love with someone, they may one day break your heart. I have not forgotten the way you reacted, after reading that English literature, *The Wuthering Heights.* You used to cry whenever you read that book. Is that not true, dear little Amyel?" Ader stubbornly asked her sister.

"What a memory you have like the mainframe computer!" answered Amyel in dismay. "I did not know that you still remember all those silly details. I really do not fear that my heart would be broken if I fall in love with someone. I just don't feel like marrying anyone. I am comfortable with my life, status quo, and it makes me happy; besides, my parents and you my siblings dearly love me."

"We surely have spoilt you, Amyel," sadly said Ader. "We all have given you too much love that your heart is so full of it and there is no more room for romantic love. What a mess, we have made of you, darling Amyel!"

"That is an absolute bogus," deniably refuted Amyel, as she mockingly laughed at her sister's statement. "All I know is that I am differently wired from the rest of you."

After the girls had finished their little talk, they begun to pack their bags because the following day Amyel was going back to Palotaka and Ader to Juba. Ader gave her sister some of her dresses, jewelry and shoes. Amyel was deeply touched by her sister's generosity and began to shed tears of gratitude. She then hugged her sister and appreciatively told her, "I hope that this gesture will continue, even after you are married."

"I will surely give you more then," Ader joyfully reassured her sister. "Amyel, you will always be my babysister, and my dearest friend. You are so precious to me and I deeply love you. You know what, my dear sister, you are my morning star!"

"Ader, I love you more than Omal loves you," provocatively said Amyel.

"Omal is my lover and soon will be my husband but you are my sweet sister," gently explained Ader. My love for Omal is different from my love for you and I profoundly love both of you, each in a special way.

"Now let us try to catch some sleep, for tomorrow will be a long day for both of us."

"Sleep well and have wonderful dreams," lovingly said Amyel.

"And you too, my little angel," said Ader. They both laughed and eventually fell asleep.

Chapter Twelve
The Journey Back to Juba

Ader and her sister woke up early, on the Tuesday morning that they both were leaving home. They fetched barrels full of water for their mother, cleaned the courtyard and cooked breakfast. Amyel was going to walk to Palotaka and had to start early. So after breakfast at about 8:30 AM Ader escorted her sister a kilometre away from home. Amyel advised her beloved sister to be good and not mess up her life before marriage. Ader accepted her sister's advice, with a grateful heart. Eventually, they tearfully hugged, as they said goodbye to each other. Thereafter, Amyel began to walk briskly because she was aware of the long distance that she had to cover on foot. On the other hand, as Ader was walking back home, she kept looking back at her sister, until she was out of sight. When Ader arrived home, she got herself ready for travel and then her parents escorted her, to wait for the bus. The bus arrived at 11:15 AM and as soon as Ader had boarded the bus she somberly waived goodbye to her parents, who were also quite sad to see her go away and leave them alone once again.

On Omal's side, his mother made for him some breakfast, which he ate with his cousins. The Chief called Omal after breakfast and reminded him, "I hope that you will remember everything that I have told you, my son. Continue to be good and treat your girl with respect. I don't want to get shocking news from you that you have broken up with your fiancée for some reason. You have noticed how all of your relatives, including your mother and me, have been very delighted to meet your beautiful fiancée."

"Dad, I will remember and treasure everything that you have told me," gratefully said Omal. "Concerning my dear Ader, don't you worry, Dad. I will never do anything that will jeopardize our relationship. She is the love of my life and I am absolutely sure that she loves me a lot"

"That is my boy!" delightfully exclaimed the Chief and then he shook hands with his son.

At about 10:45 AM, Omal's parents and some of his relatives escorted him to the bus stop. The bus arrived in Magwi centre at 11:30 AM. As soon as Omal saw Ader, his eyes became radiant with happiness. He even momentarily forgot that his parents were beside him and awesomely watching his excitement. Omal's mother delightfully smiled and softly whispered to her husband, "Look at how elated our son is?"

"That is exactly how I used to feel whenever I have seen you," the Chief happily reminded his wife. "This is my son's turn to be in love; let him enjoy the moment."

The bus stopped in Magwi for about fifteen minutes, which gave Ader a brief opportunity to greet her fiancé's parents and relatives once more. Ader came out of the bus, patted her fiancé on his back, as she sweetly smiled at him and respectfully greeted her future parents-in-law and the rest of the relatives. Omal was completely absorbed in his gaze on Ader, until one of his cousins made a joke out of him by saying, "Hey, Omal! You seemed oblivious of almost everything around you but your fiancée. Are you really feeling well?"

"Don't be silly," Omal reprimanded his cousin because he was quite upset by his cousin's remarks. "It is none of your business who I choose to look at; besides, Ader is my girl. I dearly love her and we are traveling together. Is that a problem to you?"

Everybody was quite shocked, to witness how Omal snapped at his cousin because they had never seen him reacted so angrily to anyone before. Everyone undoubtedly then understood how much he really loved his fiancée. Omal eventually apologized to everyone for his rude reaction. As Ader and Omal were boarding the bus, they waived goodbye and everyone waived back and wished them a safe and enjoyable journey.

Ader and Omal got an opportunity to sit together in the bus. Magwi is one hundred miles away from Juba, through Captain Cook's road but Omal wished that the distance could have been doubled so that he could enjoy the company of his fiancée, as much as he could. However, Omal was quite anxious to tell Ader about his plan for their wedding. Therefore, he softly said to her, "Dear Ader, I would like you to know that I am planning for our wedding in the church, after my people have settled the obligation of your people, concerning our marriage in December."

"That is a great honour for me," delightfully said Ader. "I have now understood that you are truly committed to being with me forever. Omal, this is the greatest news for me and I am quite delighted. I love you dearly. However, I will be your wife after the wedding."

"You are kidding, aren't you," said Omal, with such disbelief on his face. "Not in a month of a week will I wait for you after the traditional marriage!"

Ader mockingly laughed at first and then earnestly told Omal, "Could you please stop joking? I will wait until after the wedding then, I will officially become your wife, before God and men. Omal, you are the one who have suggested, the idea for the wedding in the church, aren't you?"

Omal did not like, what Ader had told him. He therefore replied to her, "If that is how, you want things to be done then, start preparing for the wedding in the church because the dowry will be on a Friday and the wedding, the following day. I absolutely wouldn't be able, to wait for you after then. I hate all the formalities, pertaining to marriage."

"What!" shockingly exclaimed Ader. "Why would you want to exhaust all our people like that?"

"You call that exhaustion because you have no knowledge about what I have been going through all this time because of you," frustratingly replied Omal. "You better accept my option for combining the traditional marriage and the wedding in the church consecutively. That is the only way in which, we could resolve everything, once and for all."

Seeing the pain with which her fiancé had expressed his frustration, Ader accepted his plan by approvingly nodding her head. Omal squeezed Ader's hand and smiled for the first time, since they had started their conversation. Omal kept looking at Ader and did not even care that there were other people in the bus. Ader being sensitive of her surrounding angrily reminded Omal in a whisper, "Why are you looking at me that way, have you forgotten that we are in public?"

"Now what mistake have I done?" Omal softly whispered back. "I don't think that there is anything wrong with the way, that I am looking at you, don't you agree with me?"

Ader then pretended that she was feeling sleepy and Omal offered to let her put her head, on one of his shoulders. He felt so comfortable to have Ader's head on his body that he was surprised when they eventually arrived Juba. That day, Omal felt as if, the distance between Juba and Magwi was cut into half. He seemed rather depressed, as he was walking out of the bus and Ader quietly followed him. Omal then humbly asked his fiancée, to first come with him to his house, before she could go, to her brother's house. Ader first thought of declining her fiancé invitation but the beseeching look in his eyes compelled her, to accept his request.

A little while after Omal and his fiancée got to his house, he humbly requested her, "Would you please make for us some tea before I could escort you home?"

Ader jokingly replied, "I can't because I am only a visitor, in this house."

"A vi…sitor!" stammered Omal, who was baffled and shocked seemingly by Ader's statement. "Don't you know that in a few months' time, you would be a wife, in this house?"

"Yes indeed, in the nearest future but not now, sir," playfully answered Ader, who as she was speaking, was already lighting up the stove, in order to start making the tea.

Omal looked at Ader in disbelief for a while and eventually said, "You seemed to be enjoying, to hurt my feelings so much these days, you, woman, don't you?"

"How could I enjoy inflicting pain on the man that I have chosen to love and promised to marry?" Ader curiously questioned him. "Whatever hurts you hurts me too. I was only trying to be humorous. It has been a long journey from home, here."

Omal silently stared at Ader and only sighed, for according to him, the journey wasn't long at all. Suddenly, a sensational thought raced through his mind, *What better time than now to persuade Ader, to make love with me?* However, he quickly became alert and instantly put off the temptation, for he knew very well that if he ventured, he would lose Ader forever.

After Ader and Omal had had tea, Ader washed up the utensils and set everything at their right places. Omal fixed his eyes on Ader the whole time, as she was doing everything and Ader was aware of his gaze but pretended as if she was oblivious of it. Therefore, as soon as Ader had sat down, Omal moved closer to her and gratefully said, "Thank you very much, for making the nice tea and for washing up everything, my love. How I wished that it were possible for you, to accept your true position in this house. However, I have promised not to force you to be with me but I just want to hold and tenderly kiss you now, before I could escort you to Buluk. Dear Ader, I will not accept, no, for an answer from your sweet lips."

"How can I trust you?" Ader uncomfortably asked with a look of concern on her face. "It is very hard for me to touch you these days. As soon as I allow you to hold me now, you will become a different person and quite difficult to deal with. Omal, I am lately quite scared of your behaviour whenever I am alone with you."

"Trust me this time because I have also made a solemn vow to myself that I will abstain from asking you to making love with me, until the day that we are married," Omal sincerely assured his fiancée. However, Omal gave no time for Ader to further say anything but at once firmly held and began to passionately kissing her. Ader tried to break out of his kisses and hold but in vain. The harder she tried the firmer he held her. Ader almost fainted when Omal at last let go of her. They then sat down and awkwardly stared at each other's face without saying any word, as they were trying to catch their breath. After a few minutes, Ader got up and in tears uncomfortably said, "I am going home right now." She then had realised that, if she stayed there a little while longer, she might succumb to her fiancé's desire.

Omal humbly pleaded with her, "Please, Ader, not right now. Give me some minutes to clear off my head because I am not in a good shape to escort you now."

"I did not ask you to escort me," defiantly responded Ader, who was so determine to get out of the tensed situation at once.

"Please, I beg you, Ader," further pleaded Omal. "Stop being stubborn. Understand me for once and give me some minutes. I want to escort you home, whether you like it or not."

"You truly are silly and not trustworthy," sternly said Ader. "This is not the first time, that you have misbehaved like this to me. I am afraid that you would one day squeeze life out of me. I do not even know, why I am still in love with you but I really am and that I cannot deny."

"I love you too, Ader," humbly said Omal, as he seemed like a little boy who had been grounded for being stubborn and felt so defeated. "Ader, I am very committed to marry you but it is so hard for me these days to control myself whenever I hold you into my arms. It is not intentional that I have been lately losing my self-control whenever I am alone with you but everything changes instantly as soon as I touch you. My precious love, I do not mean to violate you in any way because I understand your ground about abstinence."

"I am glad to hear that from you, once again, Omal," doubtfully said Ader, with a bit of smile breaking on her face. "However, the next time that I will allow you to hold me in your arms again would be when I have eventually become your wife."

"Ader, I hope that you do not truly mean that, do you?" shockingly asked Omal in surprise.

"Try me," assertively said Ader, with such an absolute determination. "Since I can no longer trust you whenever I am alone with you, why would I further allow you to hold and kiss me anymore?"

"Ader, I am breaking my promise to you right now and make love to you this very minute, if that is how you have decided to mistreat me, from now onward," seriously replied Omal, in frustration and disappointment, as he got hold of Ader and firmly held her once again. "This moment is the beginning of our life together, as husband and wife because you have driven me beyond the edge of my endurance. Ader, I am going to do whatever I desire with you and I do not care anymore, what the consequence of my action, would bring on me. I am ready to pay whatever fine that your people would demand from me for taking you by force."

Omal was then completely determined to make love to Ader against her wishes because he thought that Ader was thinking of him as a wimp, who could not stand up to her. Omal consequently began to forcefully draw Ader towards his bed. Ader had then realized that Omal was very serious about whatever he was saying and going to do to her. Hence, she spontaneously began to tremble with fear, as tears were streaming down both her cheeks, at the thought that she was about to lose her virginity, out of marriage. "Please could you kindly forgive me," helplessly pleaded Ader with such a contrite heart, as she was seemingly so feeble and fragile against powerful Omal. "Omal, whatever I have said to you, was out of anger and I am truly sorry," went on Ader, as she sorrowfully sobbed. "I will always allow you to kiss me but please do not force me, to make love with you, right now. I cannot live with the consequence of the guilt. I love you so much but do not like to imagine how I would abominate you if you indeed forced me to be with you right now."

Omal compassionately looked at Ader, as she was pleading with him and felt quite sorry to see her so vulnerable. Consequently therefore, he decided to forgive her and stopped his advances. Ader was quite relieved and quietly thanked God for saving her from Omal's unimaginable cruel intention that evening. "Thank you so much for being very understanding," said Ader, with such a grateful heart and a sigh of relief, as she sobbingly stared at Omal.

"You have provoked me beyond my usual endurance this evening," sadly said Omal. "However, I have forgiven you and I am profoundly sorry for everything that I was trying to putting you through. Ader, please try not to frustrate me, by some of your very disappointing remarks, anymore. I love you and hate to see you in tears. I hope that you will not venture, before we could get married to deeply hurt my feelings once again because I very much doubt if I would be able forgive you, anymore."

"I dearly love you, Omal, and hate some of the situations that you have been lately trying to putting me through, whenever we are alone," softly said Ader, as her tears were still streaming down her cheeks. "I will try, not to say anything provocative to you anymore but you also have to give me the respect I deserve, if our relationship is to continue."

Omal sympathetically looked at Ader and finally said, "Ader, I could never disrespect you. The very fact that I have taken pity on you and gave up my determination to forcibly making you as my wife this evening, shows just how much I respect and love you, otherwise, I could have done exactly that. Anyway Ader, are you implying that you are anticipating to break up with me because of the way that I have lately been feeling about you?" purposely inquired Omal. "I hope not, otherwise, I will make you my wife this very minute."

Ader wittingly realized the gross mistake that she had made by her slip of tongue, when she told Omal, 'if our relationship is to continue', and tactfully said, "Omal, I love you too much, to anticipate such silly notion. You are my first and last love. That is how much I love you."

Omal felt so comforted by Ader's reassurance about her deep love for him that he completely forgave her and eventually escorted her to Buluk.

When Omal returned to his house, after escorting his fiancée to her brother's house, he did not have any appetite to eat supper. He was completely exhausted, from the overwhelming feelings he had had when he was holding Ader and could not believe that his yearning for her had driven him to the edge of his sanity that evening. He kind of felt sick and wondered how long he would have to restrain his feelings for Ader, whenever they were alone. Omal remembered how delicate Ader had been in his arms, when he was gripping and forcefully holding her. The guilty thoughts for almost forcing Ader to make love with him overwhelmed Omal so much that he felt weak and almost fainted, as he shamefully remembered everything. He wondered what Ader might be thinking about him that night and felt very sorry for her. Eventually, Omal gathered up his strength and began ironing his clothes for going to work the following morning, before he went to bed.

On the other hand, after Omal had gone, Okema asked his sister, "How are our parents, and is it raining in the village?"

"Our parents are quite fine," answered Ader. "But are kind of lonely, since none of us is living with them, anymore. About the weather, there is not much rain in the village but the crops are thriving fine. It is even breezier at home than here in Juba."

"I am glad to hear, that our parents are doing well," joyfully replied Okema. "However, I feel sorry for Mom and Dad. They are indeed lonely, without any of us living with them anymore. I don't know, what I can do about the situation."

"I don't think, that any of us has a solution, to change their situation?" Ader told her brother. "Such is the way of life and we must accept the fact that we shall all be like them, when our time come."

"What you have said is true," said Okema. "Life is quite strange and mysterious, isn't it?

"Life is indeed a mystery and no one will ever understand it," agreed Ader. "Is it any wonder, that the professors of the sciences in the various universities of the world, gray and become bold in their prime, due to the fatigues from their restless and tedious research, as they try to solve some of life's problems?"

"And they haven't come up with much, have they?" laughingly concluded Okema.

Shortly after their conversation, Ader started cooking supper, for there is a saying in Acoli language that '*Welo pa mon pe*,' which means that women are never visitors and must cook wherever they go. Ader ate very little and said that she was not feeling hungry.

Okema was somehow concerned, about Ader's lack of appetite but teasingly told her, "You are satisfied from the enjoyable journey, that you have shared with your fiancé, aren't you, sister?"

Ader childishly giggled and told her brother, "Stop your poppycock, you naughty boy."

Okema looked at his sister sympathetically and only shook his head.

As soon as Okema had finished eating, Ader gathered up everything they had used, put them away, cleaned the room and humbly asked her brother, "Okema, would you mind to excuse me to go to bed early? I am feeling quite exhausted."

"You are excused, Princess," teasingly said Okema. "I am aware that you are tired. Please do go to bed and have sweet dreams, about your journey."

"Why do you call me a Princess, you stubborn, boy?" inquired Ader, rather sternly.

"And what do you think, that you are soon going to be, my dear sister?" rascally replied Okema, as he made funny faces to his sister. "The wife of a Prince is a Princess, isn't she?"

"I am too tired to wrestle with you, silly brother," exhaustively replied Ader as she was going to bed.

As soon as Ader stretched out herself on the bed, the memory of the struggle she had gone through with her fiancé, prior to coming to her brother's house, clouded her mind. She replayed the scene vividly in her mind and chill ran through her spine. She could not believe, that the simple statement she had said to Omal that evening, could have seriously provoked him into being so mad at her. Ader therefore convinced herself that the next time she was alone with Omal, she would be extra careful about, what she should and should not say to him. Too many thoughts overwhelmed Ader's mind and kept her awake for a bit but eventually fell soundly asleep because she was really tired; physically, mentally, emotionally and psychologically.

Chapter Thirteen
The Preparation for the Marriage

On the day that Ader had gone back to work, after she had returned from the village, the first person who, ran and tenderly hugged her with such excitement, at the entrance to her ministry, was Hinda, her long time best friend, since secondary school. Hinda was from a tribe called Fojulu, average height, dark skin complexion, sparkling white teeth, slender figure, thick dark hair, beautiful eyes and friendly smiling face. After secondary school, Hinda got a job in Yei District but kept communication with Ader. She was transferred, to work in the same ministry where Ader worked, just before Ader went to the village. Hinda was quite happy about Ader's engagement but missed her friend a lot, while she was away. The girls were such close friends that they share all their secrets. Hinda knew all about Ader and Ader about Hinda. The friendship between the two young women was the truest kind that only a few lucky people experience in their lifetime. They were quite honest with each other and corrected one another fearlessly, whenever the other had done something wrong.

"Hey, girl, how did everything go, on both sides?" Hinda anxiously asked her friend.

"Omal's and my parents were all happy to meet each of us and they gave us their blessings for our upcoming marriage in December," Ader joyfully told her friend.

"Beautiful!" excitedly exclaimed Hinda, as she felt so happy, for her dear friend. "That is what I was expecting to hear. I am so thrilled, about your good news, girl. I think that I must start preparing presents, that I will be giving to you for your marriage."

"Well, thanks a lot my dear," gratefully answered Ader. "You have always been very loving, understanding, caring, trustworthy and kind to me and I thank God everyday, that you are my best friend."

They then talked about many things, before the other people could come to the office that morning and promised each other that they would always love one another even after they had been married.

Ader's boss missed her a lot while she was away and so as soon as he walked into the office and saw her, he warmly greeted her, "Good morning, our bride-to-be, and congratulation for your engagement, to that lucky young man! I have been missing you a lot while you were away and I think the rest of your friends did too. There was absolutely nothing that was exciting in this office, while you were away. I am so used to working with you because you are an excellent secretary."

Ader joyfully smiled and felt quite grateful to know that her boss really valued her work. In appreciation, she humbly told her boss, "Thank you very much, for your compliment. I also did miss you when I was away. You are a good person, to work with."

"Good luck, in your upcoming new life," continued her boss.

"Thank you, sir," gratefully said Ader and thereafter her boss went to his office.

Ader sorted out her work and began working on the most urgent report, which the Minister needed for a meeting at 1:00 PM, that day. The typist, who substituted in the place of Ader while she was away, did most of the work poorly and consequently the Minister wanted everything retyped. He knew that Ader would give him a perfect piece of work because she normally typed without mistakes and proof read her work, before she could hand them over to him. Ader typed at a great speed and as a result she finished the reports before noon and handed them in to the Minister, who was really happy to see the work well done and without errors.

At lunchtime, Ader gathered up her courage and went to Omal's office, so as to ask him to go out with her for lunch. She found him alone in the office and seemed quite depressed.

"What is really bothering you, boy?" sympathetically asked Ader.

"You," he snapped back at her. "I can't get you off my mind and I do not know what to do about it. You are like a plague, in my heart and mind."

Omal looked so defeated, as he was speaking to his fiancée that she consequently began shaking one of his shoulders a little bit and said, "Stop behaving like a child and be a grown up man."

Omal, amused by Ader's statement, mockingly laughed and replied, "Are you kidding, Ader? Grown up men are not happy, without the women that they love. That is why most of them are married. I too would like to have you in my life and be intimate with you."

111

Ader felt so silly but made faces to Omal because his answer to her statement was very intelligent. Omal felt so good, after he had realised that his response had created an impact on Ader. Consequently, he cheered up a little bit, as they were going out for lunch.

After lunch, as Ader and her fiancée were going back to work, he asked her, "How is your friend, Hinda, doing?"

"She is fine," replied Ader. "I talked with her this morning."

"And why didn't she come with us, for lunch?" Omal curiously inquired.

"She had told me that three is a crowd," amusingly answered Ader.

Omal and Ader both lovingly glanced at each other and laughed.

Ader then said to Omal, "I am sorry for talking carelessly to you, earlier on. I really don't enjoy seeing you hurting by some of the things that I have been jokingly telling you. Omal, you are not only my fiancé but my best friend too. I do not want, a repeat of the ugly situation that had happened between us, yesterday evening. I know that I am to blame, for my stubbornness and I am sorry."

"Oh, that is the most sensible thing, that you have told me, in a long time," gratefully said Omal. "Ader, you are my soul mate. I wish that you could understand how much, I love and care about you."

"I know very well that you love me," confirmed Ader, "but I must honestly confess that nowadays I am no longer comfortable to be alone with you, specifically in your house."

Omal gave Ader a sad look of dissatisfaction, deeply sighed and sadly said, "I like being alone with you because it is the most gratifying moment for me. However, last evening, you deeply provoked me and you let me felt, as if I had premeditated the whole situation. Anyway darling, I am sincerely sorry, for what I have put you through."

"I am glad to hear that from you, Omal," gratefully said Ader, "but I still think that you have a long way to go, when it comes to keeping your promise about, you know."

"You are quite right," confirmed Omal. "Although, naughty as you may think that I am, I still believe that I am a good man because to date, I have not done anything terrible to cause you shame, despite your frequent stubbornness and the fact that I yearn to be with you a lot."

Ader kept quiet, after Omal's last sentence. They then walked silently, to their respective places of work.

After work that day, as Omal and Ader were going home together, he asked her, "Ader, would you mind to go with me, for a show at Nyakuron, Culture Centre, tonight?"

"I will be delighted, to go with you," happily replied Ader, who had promised never to say anything negative to her fiancé, anymore.

"Ask your brother to come with us too, if he is interested," Omal joyfully went on.

"I will try," said Ader. "At what time, will the show begin?"

"Around seven o'clock," replied Omal, who was very excited, at the knowledge for spending another evening with Ader again. "Well then, see you at 6:30 PM, this evening."

"See you, when you see me," said Ader and they both lovingly smiled at each other.

Omal then proceeded home to have some rest, before he could come back to pick up Ader.

When Ader got to her brother's house, she found him lying down. "Good afternoon big, handsome, and tired-looking gentleman," she teasingly told him. "How was your day at work?"

"Same routine, as ever," carelessly replied Okema.

"Is there something that you are not telling me?" curiously asked Ader because she was quite concerned to see her brother in such low spirit. "You seemed so down today. What is really bothering you, brother?"

"Nothing much, sister," boringly replied Okema. "I have already begun to miss you, Ader. Soon you will be married and I will be left alone in this house, once again."

"How about Auma?" asked Ader, with such sympathy for her brother. "Do you mean to tell me that you are not yet ready, to commit to her?"

"Well, not now," hesitantly replied Okema. "I am not yet ready to get married. There are still a number of things that I would like to do, before I could get married."

"Would you mind to share with me, some of them?" pleaded Ader.

"Stop being inquisitive, you little rascal," said Okema, as he got out of his bed and began to playfully chasing his sister around the room. Ader joyfully ran, meanwhile both of them were laughing. She was quite delighted, to see her brother feeling cheerful once again.

Eventually, they sat down and then Ader asked her brother, "Would you mind to go with me and Omal to Nyakuron tonight, for a show?"

"Whmm, that sounds tempting, isn't it?" reluctantly said Okema, "but you know what, I am not going because I would be lonely, since Auma has gone away to Khartoum to see her brother."

"Sorry, brother, I forgot," pitifully said Ader and then she began to cook. After the meal, Ader started embroidering her bedcover, while her brother took some nap.

On the other hand, when Omal got to his house, everything seemed meaningless because nothing made sense to him. He could not understand, what was happening to him. While he was with Ader, he was excited and happy and as soon as he entered into his house, everything changed. He made a cup of tea, which he slowly sipped, as he blankly stared at the wall. He even tried to play some of the music, that he and Ader liked listening to, whenever she had visited him but that even did not cheer him up. He then decided, to lie down on his bed with the anticipation, that he might catch some sleep but to his surprise, he remained wide-awake. However, lying down was more restful than sitting up on the chair. Omal was so lost, in his wishful thoughts for Ader that time went by very fast and he soon was supposed to go and pick her up, so as to go with her to Nyakuron.

At about 6:30 PM Sudan local time, Omal arrived to pick up Ader, as he had earlier on promised and found her already dressed up as she was waiting for him.

"Stay well, brother," Ader pitifully told Okema, as they were leaving. "I am sorry, that you could not come with us. Anyway, I will tell you, all about the show afterwards."

"Good luck and enjoy yourselves," softly replied Okema. "I will come with you next time, when Auma is in town."

On their way to Nyakuron, Ader and Omal did not have much to say. The fact that they were together was enough comfort for each of them. When they got to Nyakuron, they found the place packed with people, who had come to watch the show. The show on that day was about multicultural dances and was very entertaining. Some of the dances were so funny that Omal and Ader laughed with tears. After the show, Omal saw Ader off to her brother's house and immediately left for his house. He was quite happy, for the joyful evening that they had spent together and that night, he had a good sleep.

At that time, there were rumours in Juba that there was an organization somewhere, which, was sponsoring the southern Sudanese secondary school graduates whom, the discriminatory school system of the northern Sudan did not allow to attend the university or to go to any college. Many youths, started disappearing without any trace and no one neither knew exactly where they were going nor what was happening to them. The young men, who were working in the various Government Ministries, also started vanishing. It was quite scary, to live in Juba at that time. Ader pleaded with Omal never to go, if he truly loved her. She began to spend long hours with him at his house on the weekends, without any fear, anymore. Omal understood the concern of his fiancée and refused to listen to the wonderful things, most of his colleagues were saying about the mysterious organization.

In the various, regional government ministries, at least three to four people, mostly young men, disappeared in a week. Many parents were concerned but had no power, to stop their determined children from going, to wherever they were going. Some parents were happy because they were thinking that at last there was a solution, to the lack of university opportunities for most of the southern Sudanese students. However, what many people did not know then was that the disappearing youths were joining a rebel movement, which was just beginning in Dinkaland. The reason, for the movement was to fight against the northern Sudan discrimination on the southern Sudanese and the imposition of the Sharia Law on the Sudanese people, especially in the south, where the law meant nothing for the predominantly Christian people. The situation in Juba, at that time was like a volcanic mountain, which was about to erupt. The people lived in constant fear of the unknown. Some people started sending their families to the villages with anticipation that it would be safer for them there than in Juba. The Ministries that used to be vibrant with workers joyfully moving up and down, was then bit-by-bit becoming a spooky place to work in, due to the disappearance of the young people.

In Acoliland, the young men from Agoro villages started disappearing and there were such concern among the elders, as to what they should do to curb the situation. However, whatever the elders were trying to say and do did not yield any meaningful result because the young men continued to vanish without traces. The villages were left with old men and mostly women and children, quite a sad sight. The next groups, who followed the Agoro boys, were from Panyikwara villages. Eventually the elders perceived and understood that the young people were going to be trained as rebels to fight the northern Sudan government, after they had heard the news that there was a rebel movement in Dinkaland. Fear gripped the hearts of the people because they did not want to return into exile again, since memories of their sufferings during the first civil war, were still fresh in their minds.

Ader was so concerned about her brother and fiancé that she was always around while she indefatigably tried to talk some senses into their minds and hearts. However, one day, as they were conversing, Okema thoughtlessly said, "Had it not been that you, Ader, were living with me, I would have gone with the first group of the young men who had disappeared."

Ader was terribly shocked by her brother's statement and angrily rebuked him, "Stop being foolish! I have never thought, that an intelligent person like you would have such a careless intention. Do not be carried away by the news that the people who are disappearing are going to join the universities somewhere in the blue. You will be surprised someday, to know that the disappearing people, have been lured to join the rebel movement which some people say has started in Bor."

"Ah, who would like to work as a rebel, anyway?" pretentiously said her brother.

"Well, if you don't want to be a rebel then, let us wait to hear what those boys would write back to their families about their studies, in the near future. Students, normally write back home, don't they?" Ader seriously asked her brother.

Okema kept quiet after Ader had asked him the last question. Omal, who quietly sat, as he was listening and watching how brother and sister were arguing, eventually said, "There is some sense in what Ader is saying because my father had written to me a letter saying that the young men have started disappearing from the villages in Acoliland too but specifically from Agoro and Panyikwara villages."

Ader then asked both Omal and Okema, "Could you boys then explain to me whether the village boys are also capable of attending the university?"

"Don't you think that we are aware of that?" Okema arrogantly retorted.

"Well then, my dear brother, my instinct is telling me that there is a hidden agenda about the disappearance of the young men," said Ader, as if she had all along known the exact truth.

There were also reports, that in some areas even young girls were disappearing. The uncertainty, about the disappearance of the young people, broke the hearts of most of the parents so much that some of them were seen in tears even in public places. The state of fear, panic and uncertainty continued, until the newly established rebels attacked a military convoy, which was going to a town called, Bor, in Dinkaland and it was then that some of the government soldiers who had escaped from the ambush, saw some of the boys who had earlier on disappeared from Juba. The soldiers told their families about the people that they had seen and then, the rest of the people in Juba eventually understood, the real reason behind the disappearance of the young men.

After everyone in Juba was aware that the young men who had been disappearing were simply being trained as rebels, most of the parents whose children had disappeared earlier on were quite shocked. Ader was so happy, to be on the right side all along, as she had been condemning the disappearance of the young men, from its onset. Thereafter, Omal completely changed his mind. Ader was so happy about the decision her beloved fiancé had taken not to join the rebel movement and profoundly thanked him. Okema, however, had never changed his mind, for he kept saying that what was more important in the life of a man than his ability to defending the rights of his people. Ader then knew that some day, her brother would join the movement, when his right time came. Consequently, she did not want further argument with him and whenever such situation aroused, she would ask her fiancé, to go for a walk with her, along the river Nile.

The time went by very fast despite the fact that everything seemed to be falling apart. It was soon November and Ader had not yet bought her wedding dress. Therefore, she went to Khartoum for only four days, to bring a magnificent wedding dress that one of her friends had bought for her from Nairobi. She also wanted to buy some of the stuff that she would need when she was married. In Khartoum, things were generally peaceful but when one was caught breaking the Sharia Law, their arms or legs were chopped off because the deadly law was very effectively practiced. Some southern Sudanese became the victims of the merciless law, not because they were breaking it but were stereotyped. Ader did not like life in Khartoum because most of the southern Sudanese were living in constant fear, for getting arrested or having their limbs chopped off due to their cultures, which were quite contrary to the Moslems ways of life. Ader consequently, comprehended why the rebel movement was started in the south.

Omal missed his fiancée a lot, while she was away in Khartoum. However, he was also busy, as he was trying to putting things together that he was going to take home for his marriage. Despite his busy schedule, Omal still spent most of his evenings with Okema. Okema talked about the rebel movement with such passion, since his sister was not present to oppose his views. Omal, however, kept his promise to his fiancée and doubted what the movement might eventually achieve, given the gross mistakes which were made by the southern politicians, after the first civil war.

When Ader returned to Juba from Khartoum, she found that her parents had written a letter to her saying that they were ready for her marriage and were only waiting for her arrival. Ader was very delighted about the news and worked hard to arrange everything she needed before she could travel home. Hinda helped Ader a lot, bought a golden necklace with Ader's name inscribed on the pendant and some China sets as a wedding present to her. Since Ader's wedding was going to take place in Palotaka, Hinda could not attend because she too was preparing for her marriage. That very same December, Hinda was traveling to Lanya to introduce her boyfriend to her parents.

Ader became so busy as she was absorbed in making all the detailed preparations for her marriage that she avoided her fiancé most of the time. Omal understood the situation and kept his distance. He went over once in a while, just to say hello to his fiancée. Omal was also quite busy because he was supposed to buy a lot of stuff to take home with him, both for the occasion of the dowry and the wedding. However, Omal was very happy because the moment was soon approaching for him to have the woman that he had been dying to be with for a long time. Ader and Omal both took one month of the annual leave and another month of leave without pay to, enable them finished all they wanted to do for their marriage. Ader wanted to travel home alone but Omal refused and insisted that they would be traveling together. He scolded Ader to stop avoiding him from then onward because according to him, she was already his wife, except for the formalities of marriage. Ader, who did not want any argument anymore, accepted to travel home with Omal.

Okema traveled home ahead of Ader because he was aware that his sister was a tough girl and would not do anything silly before her marriage. The next reason, why Okema had gone ahead of his sister to the village was, to help his parents with the enormous preparations, for welcoming the visitors for his sister's marriage. When Okema arrived home, his parents went wild with joy at his sight and welcomed him like a prince who had been away from his father's kingdom, for a long time. His mother shed tears of joy and his father called him all the nicknames and praise names that he could remember. There was such joy in the home that no word could describe. The young cousins were all in the home, to help with the work for the big day. In the evening, they all sat around the fire and listened to the stories from long time ago, told by the elders. Okema, like his sisters, Ader and Amyel, wished that he were a small boy once again, so that he could live with his parents and enjoy their wonderful company everyday.

Ader and Omal traveled home, a week before the marriage day. On their way home, they talked a lot about Upper Talanga, where they were going for their honeymoon. Ader had written a letter earlier on to her elder brother,

Bongomin, stating that she and her fiancé had chosen Upper Talanga for their honeymoon. Bongomin accepted his sister's request and made all the necessary arrangements. Bongomin's annual leave was normally in December. Consequently, he was not going to be in Upper Talanga, when the newlywed would be there for their honeymoon.

Ader arrived at home at 5:00 PM and found that everything looked quite different. A big shade was erected, which was going to accommodate up to one hundred people. The areas surrounding the home were all purged. When Ader's cousins saw her, they joyfully shouted, "Here comes the future Queen of the Chiefdom of Magwi!"

Ader mockingly laughed at them and said, "I am not yet a bride but will be in a week's time."

One of Ader's cousins, called Andiko, then teased her, "Our beautiful girl seems to be scared of getting married to her handsome prince. Can't you people tell, from the way that she is looking?"

"Stop your baseless nonsense, you silly girl," Ader playfully scolded her. "Please do let me sit down first, before you could tear me into pieces with your ugly jokes."

Everyone laughed at what Ader had said but the jokes continued. Ader took all the teasing very well without getting angry, even though she was tired from the journey home.

Bongomin came home with his family, three days before the marriage of his sister. He brought lots of stuff with him, to help his parents take care of the visitors who would be coming for the marriage. He gave Ader a beautiful pair of expensive white shoes and a set of beautiful china that he had bought from Uganda, as his wedding gift to her. Aya came from Torit with her two sons, Ikoradui and Arwono. She also brought lots of gifts for her sister. Okema surprised Ader by informing her that he had bought for her a double bed and its mattress and that the stuff are in his friends house in Juba. Amyel was the last one to arrive from Palotaka and she made four pairs of bedcovers and a beautiful basket for her sister. The only person among the siblings, who was missing then, was Otim because he was attending a course in Khartoum. He too sent a big suitcase with variety of gifts inside and some cosmetics for her sister, including a beautiful card, which stated that although he would not be able to physically attend his sister's marriage, he would be with her in spirit. Ader was so overwhelmed by the generosity of her siblings that she started shedding tears as she profoundly thanked all of them. She told Bongomin that she would wear the shoes he had given her on her wedding day. There was such joy and laughter in the home that no word could describe.

Most of the relatives arrived on Thursday evening. There was loud and joyful laughter in the home, for some of the relatives had not seen each other for years. Aunt Onianga was the principal entertainer because of her sense of humour. People laughed at her stories with tears and yet they couldn't get enough of her incredible tales. The female relatives talked about the moments when they were young and like Ader, were preparing for their marriages and how scared some of them were, to talk to their husbands alone for the first time. Marriage celebration was the kind of gathering that came about once upon a time and people made good use of it by talking, laughing and enjoying one another's company. Ader's marriage was in the beginning of the dry season and so most of the people slept outside but some of them talked until dawn.

Ader shared a room with her sisters and they talked about all kind of things. At certain points they were sad partly because they did not live together anymore. Aya took the opportunity to advise Ader and told her, "Portray a good image of our family at all times. Many marriages are breaking down, especially in our time, because some women liked to control their husbands and would not allow them to talk to just any female. Such situation drives men mad. Some men would start to have affairs with other women just to provoke their wives and see what they could do to stop them. Give your husband a space in his life and let him show you voluntarily that he loves you. When in doubt, sit down and ask your husband in a civilized manner. Don't befriend women who go to the witchdoctors to get love portion so that their husbands might love them more. Such women are evil and lack self-confidence. Let your husband love you because you are attractive, beautiful, trustworthy, hardworking, understanding, kind, compassionate, caring, respectful, loyal, faithful and loving. These are the qualities that cement commitment in marriage relationship but not love portion from witchdoctors and careless nagging."

Ader attentively listened to everything that her elder sister was telling her and after Aya had finished what she wanted to say, gratefully said, "Thanks a lot for your invaluable advice. You are the special elder sister that every girl would wish to have in her life. I thank God for having you as my sister. I will put into practice everything that you have taught me tonight."

On the side of Omal's family the preparations were not so intense, as in Ader's. The elders came to see Omal in the evening, when he got home from Juba. The reason for their visit was, to decide on how much cash they should take along to Licari village, just in case the demands of their in-laws would be too high. However during the meeting, Omal's father excitedly told everyone, "I am ready, to pay just any amount that would be demanded by our in-laws because according to me, my son's fiancée is priceless."

Omal was so happy to hear the wonderful remarks that his father had made about his fiancée because he, too, thought the same about Ader. Furthermore, Omal had brought some cash with him from Juba too, even though, according to the Acoli custom his father was supposed to pay for everything. The relatives also contributed some amount of money to help the Chief to settle the requirements for his son's marriage.

On the eve of Omal's traditional marriage, his relatives came and spent the night at the Chief's home. They merrily ate and drank together. The men playfully teased their wives, about how some of them were so shy, on the night of their marriage and spoke almost in whispers, when asked any question. Everybody laughed and continued to tease one another, until they slept.

Chapter Fourteen
The Traditional Marriage Day

The Friday, on which Ader's traditional marriage was going to take place in the evening, was a beautiful day and quite breezy, which made it quite comfortable for the people to work without perspiring. Everything for the occasion was ready and Ader's people were only waiting for the arrival of their in-laws from Magwi that afternoon. However, Ader lost her appetite and only ate some fruits. No one attempted to persuade Ader to eat because most of the married female relatives, relatively understood what she was going through. She laid down most of the day and did look somehow lost. Abongkara didn't like, the way her daughter looked and she therefore approached and gently told her, "Please cheer up, my child. You should look your best today because it is your day and such a day, only occurs once in a woman's lifetime. You seemed not to be sure of yourself today, is there something that is bothering you?"

"Mom, there is nothing that is bothering me," humbly replied Ader, as she tried to conceal her true feelings from her mother. "I am really fine."

"Ader, my dear daughter, I gave birth to you and watched you grew up and blossomed into a beautiful young lady," replied her concerned mother. "I know you better than you know yourself, my child."

"Ah, Mom!" said Ader, rather hesitantly. "Was it easy for you to leave your family, on the day that you were married?"

"I might have been slightly stressed out and a little nervous," honestly replied Abongkara, "but I would like you to look cheerful. I know very well that you love Omal, don't you?"

Both of them laughed and then Ader said, "Mom, I am quite torn up between leaving you, the people that I have loved all my life and joining my husband in marriage. I love all of you in my family and I love Omal too but I feel so lost today."

"It is ok, for you to love us," Abongkara gently assured her daughter, "but your life beginning tomorrow, belongs with your husband. The kind of love that you have for us is different from, the one you have for your husband and each is unique and special. You will always be, the child of this family and my dear daughter. Now give your mom, those wonderful smiles of yours."

Ader sweetly smiled and cheered up a bit. "What can I do without you, Mom?" she gratefully said. "You have made me feel better already. I love you and will miss you a lot."

"I will always be available, if you need any advice at all," joyfully replied Abongkara, "but I am sure that the time has come for you, to belong with your husband."

Ader finally realized that she had to look cheerful and beautiful for her husband and his people when they arrive. She therefore washed up, groomed and put on a beautiful long dress. Her hair was braided in a wonderful style that made her looked indeed like an Acoli princess.

A few hours before Omal and his people could arrive, Ader asked for some food, which she ate together with her sisters and cousins. During the meal, Ader thoughtlessly said, "I feel as if this shall be our last happy meal together because of the civil war that has just started in Dinkaland and who knows where each of us would run to."

"What has made you to say such a negative thing, especially on a day like today?" Aya angrily asked her sister.

"I don't know," timidly replied Ader. "I did not mean to upset you people; it is just that a thought came into my mind and I spoke it out spontaneously, without first thinking about it. I am sorry that I have upset your feelings."

Everyone was quiet for a moment, as if each of them was trying to figure out, why Ader had spoke so carelessly but soon after, they started talking with such excitement again about how, they would meet the in-laws and the dance that would follow when the requirements for the marriage are met. Ader watched everyone quietly, as she was wondering about what the future really held for each.

Omal and his family arrived in Licari at 4:30 PM Sudan local time and were welcomed into the shade, where they took their seats and shortly after, Ader's elders joined them for a discussion. The discussion was about the amount of the dowry, as demanded by Ader's family. Ader's aunts from her father's side, were involved in the discussion because such was the only time, when everyone paid close attention, to what the elder girls in the family had to say in the making of the decision. Whatever conclusion the women came up with, was absolutely obeyed by their male counterparts. After a moment of the discussion, both sides of the families agreed upon 1,500 Sudanese

Pounds, which was a lot of money then, in 1984, six goats, six rams and many other minor gifts. When the message was sent out to the rest of the relatives that the dowry had been accepted, everyone was so happy and the women began yodeling to express their joy for the occasion. Omal was then asked to stand up, for Ader's relatives to see him and they approved of him because he was what, they had expected for their daughter's husband. Ader's relatives thought that Omal was good-looking, fit and seemed responsible. Everyone congratulated Ader, for her wise choice for a husband. On the other hand, Ader was also asked to stand up, for her in-laws to have a good look at her, she consequently stood up with her face down because she was shy to look at them. Omal's relatives were all delighted, to see their exquisite bride and said that they were very proud of her.

After the payment of the dowry, variety of food was served and shortly after, the people started drinking all kinds of beers. Thereafter the food and drinks the people started dancing to celebrate their happiness. The moon was full and bright which made the night, almost as clear as daytime. The rhythmic sounds, which were produced by the women banging large saucepans top down on the ground, were heard as far away as Loudo and Amika villages respectively. The best singers led the songs and the rest of the people only answered the chorus. Everyone danced, vigorously with a joyful heart. The rhythm of foot stamps, coupled with the beautiful sounds of the jiggles around the women's ankles, produced very beautiful sounds. The best yodelers yodeled at different intervals and sounded quite lovely. It was such a moment that everyone was so merry and happy that no word could describe the joy all of them felt. Some people got drank, carelessly slept on the ground and had to be carried off to their proper places for sleeping. Omal danced with Ader's cousins and sisters and on the other, Omal's cousins danced with Ader. Omal and Ader, were deliberately kept away from each other, so that they could dance with the crowd for a while. However, Omal was quite anxious to have a private moment with his bride for the first time but controlled himself, so as to appear like a gentleman.

Eventually, Omal got an opportunity to briefly meet with his bride and he was so excited to hold Ader into his arms, as his wife, for the first time.

"I feel like the whole universe belongs to me now," he told his wife with such delight, as he was holding her quite delicately, tenderly and lovingly. How do you feel, my dear? Please, do tell me."

"I am very happy to be the wife of the future Chief, of the Chiefdom of Magwi," Ader told her husband playfully, as she was laughing joyfully.

Omal fondly hugged his wife for a long time, as if he wanted to feel her every heartbeat and eventually whispered into her ear, "Darling, I am taking you with me to Magwi right now and we will proceed from there, to the church tomorrow?"

"I don't think that is a good idea," reluctantly replied Ader. "I have a lot to do before the wedding, and besides, I will officially be your wife tomorrow, after the wedding."

Omal wanted to take Ader by force to Magwi because she was traditionally already his wife and he could do whatever he wanted with her, without anyone interfering. "Ader, stop your silly jokes," he seriously admonished her. "You have no right, whatsoever, to reject to be with me tonight. I could even take you somewhere right now and make love to you and no one will question me. I am only respecting you because I don't want you to feel that I am a domineering husband, within such a short time after our marriage and above all I dearly love you. Anyway, waiting for you for another night is not so bad, given all the time that I have been languishing, aching, wanting, needing and desperately crying to be with you."

Omal then took Ader to a secluded place and passionately kissed her. He was so overcome, with such desire to be with her right then and full of frustration warned her, "My beloved wife, tomorrow, you will pay all the price, for refusing to go with me now to Magwi."

Ader got frightened and told her husband quite humbly, "If you really love me, I see no reason why you should be mean to me tomorrow."

"I did not mention anything about being mean to you," said Omal frustratingly. "I really want you, to come with me to Magwi tonight. Ader, please, I kindly beg you, have some compassion for me. Please do not let me sleep alone again tonight, as if I am still a bachelor."

"Omal, dear husband, I, too, long to be with you but tomorrow will be our special night together," pleaded Ader. "We shall be away from everybody. Just the two of us, think about it."

"That sounds quite nice but too hard for me to swallow right now," painfully said Omal. "Well, what can I do? I will see what other excuses you will pull up tomorrow. Ader, believe me, I will never listen to anything that you will come up with. How I wish that you could imagine, what is in store for you tomorrow's night." Omal then carried his bride up in the air and danced around with her in his arms. Ader happily giggled, although she was a little scared that she might fall down and hurt herself. After Omal had put his wife down, he passionately kissed her one last time, before he could take her back, to where the people were dancing. Ader then decided to go to bed because she was so overwhelmed with uncertainty, as to whether she would be able to adequately handle her husband, the following day after the religious wedding, given the way he is so frustrated with her.

On the other hand, Omal called a few of the boys from his family, so as to go with him to Magwi and get ready for the next day. On the way, the boys vehemently complained, "Omal, something is obviously not right here. Why is Ader not coming with you to Magwi tonight? She is now officially your wife and yet you are going to spend this night alone without her?"

"Yes brothers," humbly admitted Omal, as he tried to conceal his frustration about the whole situation. "Just this one last night alone because I want to go away with Ader, where no one will interrupt us, for a whole week. It will be just the two of us."

The boys burst into mocking laugher and laughed off their head interestingly because they thought that Omal was a very funny, unrealistic, powerless and stupid man.

After Omal had arrived at home, he could not sleep but tossed in bed in tears, as he desperately longed for Ader. *The love between a man and a woman is supposed to be, one of the most wonderful things in life,* he painfully thought, *and yet, it is very complicated. Why would the other creatures, meet their opposite sex and mate immediately, whereas human beings, have to go through lots of formalities. Love life is not fair for the human being at all, especially men. Oh God, was it your intention that human beings must burn with the desire for the opposite sex for such a long time, before they could be allowed to be together or it is the human beings, who have complicated the whole thing. Dear Lord, look at how I am painfully burning up with the passion for the need to be with my beloved wife but have to comply with the formalities for proper marriage. How could I sleep tonight, when my mind, heart and body is on such consuming fire that nothing could extinguish but Ader. Please Lord, kindly give the Acoli people, the wisdom to enact a new law that could allow for marriage to be sooner, simpler and straightforward. I am deeply aching to be with my wife and it is not fair at all that she is not here with me right now. Oh God help me to get some sleep because I can't on my own.* Omal frustratingly regretted having left Ader in Licari. He struggled with his devastating desire to be with her antagonistically, for such a long time until the wee hours of the morning, before he could get some sleep eventually.

Chapter Fifteen
The Religious Marriage Day

The next day, after Ader's traditional marriage, as the people were still dancing and feasting, Ader woke up early and started preparing everything that she would be taking with her to Upper Talanga for her honeymoon, after the wedding in the church that day. Amyel watched quietly her beloved sister, as she was preparing everything for her big day. For according to Amyel, that Saturday was the final day for her, to have Ader to herself. She therefore tenderly hugged Ader and sadly said, "Sister, let me hold you for one last time, before you would completely belong to Omal."

Tears formed into Ader's eyes, as she compassionately looked at her sister. "Amyel," she sadly said, "My love for Omal, is a different kind from the one, I have for you. Mom has made me aware of this yesterday, when I was feeling down about leaving you, people, especially you, Amyel. My marriage will never separate me from you. I love you, Amyel, forever."

After Ader had done her packing, she had lunch with her sisters and cousins. During the meal, one of the cousins called Acillo, who did not like the way that everyone was so quiet, as they were eating, initiated a conversation by funnily saying, "Ah girls, on the day that I was escorted to my husband, I thought, that I would die out of nervousness."

Everyone burst into laughter because all the married cousins, including Aya, felt the same way, on the night, when they were alone with their husbands for the first time. Ader was the only person who did not laugh but deeply sighed and humbly smiled.

"And what were you afraid of, anyway?" purposely asked another cousin, called Aling and she incited the kind of laughter that all of them found hard to stop.

"As if you do not know," retorted Acillo eventually. "The very thought, of being alone with my husband for the first time, was an enormous thing for me to face."

"I think that every woman goes through that moment of panic," said another cousin called Akwir. "Ader seemed more courageous than most of us, isn't she?" deliberately concluded Akwir.

They all glanced at Ader at once and burst into laughter once again. Ader then concluded that the talk was indirectly meant, to make her aware of what every newly married woman experience, when she was alone with her husband, for the first time.

"Thank you all, for what you are indirectly trying to tell me," timidly said Ader. "It is good for me to know that every woman experience some form of nervousness when she is newly married. Otherwise, I was thinking that I am becoming insane, for feeling the way that I do today."

"Hey girl, you are doing well," said another cousin, called Laoro. "Tonight, pretend to be brave and don't you let Omal know that you are nervous and scared of him because he will tease you about it some day in the future, you know."

The last sentence generated another bout of interesting laughter because everyone was amused, by what Laoro had suggested to Ader.

After the meal, the girls then started dressing up Ader in her wedding dress and thereafter she glamourously looked so exquisite and angelic in her wedding dress that everyone clapped for her. Most of the villagers had only seen the wedding dresses in pictures but had not yet physically seen one before. They wondered, as to where Ader might have bought such a magnificent dress. The young children thought that the angel of God had given Ader the dress at night. Furthermore, the few people who had wedded in Acoliland, had attended their matrimony service in their ordinary clothes because there was no shop in Eastern Equatoria Province, where wedding dresses were made or sold.

On the other hand, when Omal woke up in the morning, one of the older women in his father's homestead, who did not go to Licari for his traditional marriage, gave him some food which he struggled to eat because he was kind of fatigued, after his tumultuous night. After eating, Omal came to his senses and instantly realized that the day was a very special one in which he must properly groom himself and look his best. Therefore, he carefully washed himself, appropriately dressed up in his dark suit and looked so handsome. Omal's knowledge, for at last having Ader all to himself that day, made him felt like the whole world belonged to him and he seemed so cheerful. He looked so wonderfully handsome that every woman who saw him that day found him quite irresistible and envied Ader, for luckily having him as her husband. Onek, Omal's best man, was also dressed up in dark suit and he too looked so handsome.

Omal had earlier on asked, one of his friends, called Olima who was working for a charitable organization called the Norwegian Church Aid, station in Magwi, for two Daihatsu pick-ups, so as to help transporting the people to Palotaka for his wedding. Olima therefore, came with another driver to the Chief's home and found Omal joyfully waiting for them. Olima was very happy, to see his friend looked his best and quite excited. He happily shook hands hard with Omal and wished him the very best, in his upcoming new life. "The hour is upon you, handsome, to enjoy the very best fruit life has to offer," he assured Omal delightfully. "I hope that you have sufficiently prepared yourself and are efficiently equipped for tonight's, you know."

"I am more than ready, man," excitedly replied Omal. "You do not know how long I have been desperately waiting for this day to dawn. I am just too excited, to talk about it."

"Good luck, gentleman," joyfully said Olima, as he was admiring his friend. "I wish you the very best, with your wonderfully beautiful bride and may all your wishes and dreams come true tonight."

That afternoon therefore, Olima and the other driver drove Omal, Onek and the rest of the boys with whom Omal had gone back to Magwi the previous night, to Licari village. When they arrived in Licari, Omal refused, to see Ader before the wedding and therefore, remained in the Daihatsu on the road with the other driver and his parents and his immediate relatives joined him there. Ader and her family, traveled in Olima's pick-up. They arrived at Palotaka at 4:00 PM Sudan time and found the Parish Priest waiting for them. Omal was swept off his feet, at the sight of his beautiful bride in her exquisite wedding dress. Ader did look so elegant that everyone who saw her admired her deeply. She sweetly smiled at everyone and seemed so happy. A mass was celebrated for the wedding. As Omal was taking his wedding vow, he was so overwhelmed with joy that he almost lost his voice. He could hardly believe that he was at last getting wedded to Ader as he joyfully looked into her beautiful eyes, while he was pronouncing every word of his marriage vow. On the other hand, Ader was a little nervous but she still afforded to smile and managed to say her marriage vow in a voice that was audible to everyone.

As Amyel heard her sister pronouncing the solemn vow of matrimony, tears began streaming down her cheeks. The tears were for despair because deep in Amyel's heart, she was already missing her beloved sister who meant a world to her. For Amyel to hear, Ader saying to a man, till death do us part, was too much for her because she did not believe in marriage. After the wedding, when Ader and her husband were walking out of the church, meanwhile they were holding each other's hands, Amyel followed them and then called out her sister's name. At the sound, of the familiar voice, Ader turned immediately around and saw her tearful sister. She understood very well what, Amyel was going through and so she stopped and waited for her sister to come near and then hugged her tenderly. Amyel's broken spirit moved Ader to tears. "I will always love you Amyel because you are my special and wonderful little sister," Ader gently, reassured her tearful sister.

"I am glad, to hear that from you once again, my dear sister," Amyel answered sobbingly. "Deep in my heart, I feel as if this would be our last day, for being close to each other. The joyful and fun-filled family life that I used to know has disappeared today, with your wedding. Anyway, my dear sister, have a wonderful honeymoon and beautiful marriage. You deserve it because you are always kindhearted, to everyone in our family and especially to me."

Omal, who was quietly listening, to the sisters' conversation, was amazed by how close they were. He eventually assured his sister-in-law, "I will take good care of your sister because I love her, as much as you love her. I would also want you to know that you are very welcome to our home, at anytime. Anyway, before we go away, I need a big tender hug from you, like the one that you have just given to my lovely wife."

Amyel wiped off her tears, smiled a little bit and tenderly hugged her brother-in-law. "I wish you the best life, with my sister," she softly, whispered to her brother-in-law.

"I wish that you find a good and loving man soon," Omal whispered back to Amyel but she simply smiled and did not further say anything.

Eventually, all the relatives from both sides of the families queued up and began greeting the newlywed. Everyone blessed the couple and wished them well in their new life together. Thereafter, they waved goodbye to the bride and the bridegroom, as Olima was driving them away to Upper Talanga.

After the bride and the bridegroom were gone for their honeymoon to Upper Talanga, Amyel walked away downheartedly to her little house, which was near Palotaka Parish. She sadly sat alone in her house, as she was trying to comprehend the meaning of life. Everything that had happened that day was too much for Amyel and therefore, she bitterly cried. Amyel did not cry when her brother, Bongomin, got married. The distance between them in age might have been the factor because by the time Amyel was born, Bongomin was already a big boy and so they were not very close. At the marriage of her sister, Aya, she felt a little bit sad but it never bothered her very much. In the case of Ader, it was different because they had been very close to each other, since childhood. They played, sang, fought, laughed, worked and danced together. Ader was always the centre of Amyel's life. Consequently, for Amyel to see Ader going away in marriage that day, was a big blow to her heart and so she cried herself to sleep.

After the wedding, the relatives and parents, from Omal and Ader's sides of the families jammed together into one pick-up, as they were returning home. Everyone was so confused, as to why the bride and bridegroom went away to Upper Talanga instead of going to Magwi. They naively asked each other, as they were expecting that there should at least be one person among them who was capable to explain to them, what the honeymoon really meant. The old folks talked with such bitterness, resentment and hatred about the bad habits, which the school had taught the younger generation. They further said that the rich and wonderful Acoli culture and tradition would not last another decade, if the disobedient behaviours of the young people continued, at the pace it was happening. What had hurt the elders the most on that day was, the fact that Omal, who should have been a good example, to the other boys in his generation, since he was the son of the Chief, was unfortunately, one of the people who were breaking the Acoli traditional custom. The elders were quite hurt and grumbled all the way to Licari and Magwi respectively. Some of Omal's relatives did not proceed to Magwi because they still wanted to continue with the celebration for the marriage and therefore, remained in Licari village. They joyfully ate, danced and drank until the next day.

After all the visitors from Magwi had left, Okeny gave part of the dowry of his daughter, to his sisters, cousins and other close relatives, according to the rules and regulations of the Oyere clan. They were all very grateful to Okeny and hoped that all their unmarried girls would follow in the footsteps of Ader. However, the relatives wanted very much to know, what the meaning of the thing called honeymoon was and so they asked Okeny, "Now that we are all alone as a family, could you explain kindly to us, what the meaning of this thing called '*honeymoon*' is all about?"

"Oh, my people, I wish that I know the correct answer," Okeny humbly replied. "All I know is that honeymoon, is the custom of the white people and the Arabs, in which, once the young people got married, the bride and bridegroom went away to be alone by themselves, for a little while."

"And since when, have we, the Acoli people, became white or Arab, so as to follow such stupid custom?" angrily asked one of Okeny's cousins, called Awalla.

"Don't forget that language and custom are intertwined," Okeny gently pointed out. "Our children are taught at school, in the white men's languages, hence, they want to follow whatever they have learn at school. However, I cannot blame my daughter because she has not done anything wrong. She has been properly married and whatever she wants to do with her life now, is up to her. She is an adult and a properly married woman."

"Thank you, for your explanation," said one of the old men, called Ocerro. "Now, at least, we have known the source, of this thing called honeymoon. However, we are terribly afraid that foreign customs are invading ours and that is our main concern. It should also concern you too, Okeny, because we don't know the next horrible thing that the young people would come up with."

Ader's relatives continued to eat, drink and danced for another day.

The people, from Omal's side of the family also did not understand, what the honeymoon was all about because according to the Acoli custom, some of the girls from Licari village should have escorted Ader to Magwi, after the dowry had been paid. Consequently, the relatives bitterly complained to the Chief, as soon as all of them returned to Magwi after the wedding.

"What your son has done, is really not proper at all," disgustingly said, the oldest of the elders, called Okwalatek. "How dare Omal has taken away the bride from our home, so as to be alone with her in a far away place! What does this really mean? You, of all the people, have enabled your son, to break our beautiful custom, by allowing him to behave in the way that is very foreign to the Acoli custom. Chief, your son should have been the one, to give a good example to the other boys of his generation by solemnly practicing the culture and tradition as required of him. Surely Chief, why did you allow your son, to disrespectfully go to Upper Talanga with his new bride, without first coming home here according to the mandate of our heritage? This is quite preposterous, awkward, insulting and horrible to all of us."

"My dear people, I made a foolish promise to my son that I would do whatever he has requested of me, before he was married," the Chief humbly explained. "He consequently then asked me that after his wedding, he would like to take his bride away from home and be alone with her for a week. I therefore, permitted my son to carry out his plan as he had chosen because I love him a lot and could not deny him, what he thinks is going to make him very happy. Omal is so dear to me, you know. However, I am sorry, if what my son has done have offended you deeply. In this modern world that we live in today, my dear people, marriages are no longer treated as in our time.

Remember, Omal was supposed traditionally to get married to a princess and not a commoner."

"We have very rich culture and tradition and we are very sad that they are vanishing away, so fast, right before our eyes," disgustingly said one of the elders called Otenno. "Foreign customs are invading ours and we are very scared of the consequences. Anyway, when will the rascal newlywed return home? "

"They will be here next Saturday," the Chief replied quite humbly.

"However, Chief, for your sake, we will prepare a ceremonious welcome for your son and his wife, next weekend," said Okwalatek after a long and very hard thoughts. "We would like to show your disrespectful son, Omal, that we are very forgiving and loving people, who adore our traditional custom very much. We will accord to him a royal treatment, although, he does not truly deserve it, so as to show him the beauty of his heritage."

The relatives then, went away with such resentments and hurt feelings. They grumbled bitterly because they were quite disappointed about, what the Chief and his son had done.

Chapter Sixteen
The Honeymoon

The bride and the bridegroom got to Upper Talanga at about 7:00 PM and found Bongomin's housekeeper waiting for them. The housekeeper welcomed them respectfully and thereafter served them graciously some dinner. Ader ate very little and said that she was satisfied. Omal smiled sympathetically and motion with his hand, to indicate to his bride to eat more but she reluctantly shook her head. He then ate what he could but was rather concerned, as to why his wife ate very little. After Omal had finished eating, the housekeeper cleared up everything and before she left the house, she showed the couple the room that was prepared specially for them.

When Ader was finally left alone with her husband for the first time, she became very nervous and could not even bring up herself to look at his face. Ader had then forgotten completely about, the invaluable advice that her cousin, Laoro, had given to her earlier on in the day that she should never be nervous of her husband. Ader's behaviour amused Omal so much that he eventually asked her, "Why do you seem so nervous all of a sudden, my dear wife? I am the same man that you have loved for a long time and got married to eventually today, am I not?"

Ader looked down and replied timidly, "Yes, you are."

"Darling, the hour has come for you and I," delightfully said Omal, as he was enjoying the way his wife seemed so lost, "to be with each other for the first time, as husband and wife."

Ader glanced at her husband and softly said almost in a whispered, "Would you please excuse me for a moment, so that I could change into something comfortable?"

"You are very welcome to do so, my dear," calmly replied Omal, in a very relaxed tone of voice, as he was still smiling amusingly, about his wife's nervousness. After Ader had gone, Omal took the opportunity to quickly change his clothes, too. He returned to the room where Ader had left him, comfortably sat down and patiently waited for her.

When Ader got to the room where her suitcase was, she took out a beautiful nightgown, which she slowly changed into. Ader did not have the courage to go back, to where her husband was, due to nervousness. 'What is he thinking about me now,' thoughts went through her mind. 'I wished that I know what to expect and how to behave to my husband. I am so naïve about everything and I hope that he is not thinking that I am very stupid. And what if he has not forgiven me, for refusing to go with him to Magwi last night? Oh Lord, give me the courage and strength that I need, in order to be with my husband, for the first time tonight. This is my wedding night and yet I do not know, what to do.' Ader stood where she was for quite some time but eventually gathered up herself and tried to return to the place, where her husband was.

Ader slowly walked towards her husband but halfway from where he was sitting, their eyes met coincidentally and she got frozen completely. She was unable to take another step, as her heart throbbed out of nervousness.

"There is no reason at all, for you to fear me, if you really love me, as much as I love you," gently explained Omal, while he was sweetly smiling and admiring how beautiful his wife was, in her nightgown. "Remember, my dear wife, there is no excuse for you, whatsoever, tonight, to avoid me as you have done last night, when I requested you humbly, to go with me to Magwi. I would like to assure you that you are now my loving wife, before God and men and I am desiring anxiously to knowing you carnally, soulfully and spiritually tonight. I have respected you throughout our courtship and instead, struggled painfully with my burning desires to be with you but tonight, you are my wife and I am your husband. Ader, please show me that you love and care about me but stop endeavouring to intimidate me with your nervousness." Omal was approaching his wife, as he was speaking to her. When he got to where she was standing, he tenderly held her and gently asked, "Have I all of a sudden, became a complete stranger to you, my darling?"

Ader did not verbally reply to her husband but only shook her head to make her point.

"If I am not then, please show me that you love me and stop being nervous."

Ader deeply sighed and softly said, "You know very well that I love you, don't you?"

"Surely, if you truly love me," said Omal amusingly, "why do you seem so frightened of me?"

"I am not frightened of you," whispered his wife, as she was trying to pretend to be brave. "I hope that you have forgiven me, for refusing to go with you to Magwi last night. Remember, you told me yesterday that I would pay the price today. Have you truly forgiven me?"

"Is that the reason why, you are so frightened of me, my dear?" surprisingly said Omal, as he began to amusingly laugh at his wife. "Ader, my dear wife, I love you too much, to hold grudges against you. I know, that I have said certain things to you in frustration yesterday but you know what sweetheart, I have forgiven you, since last night. That is how precious you are to me."

Ader's face brightened up a little bit, as she was attempting to smile. "Omal, tonight, I am your wife and any silly idea of revenge that you may be harbouring deliberately in your heart against me for the way that I have rejected to make love with you throughout our courtship, I will remember forever," Ader provocatively told her husband.

"I have, absolutely nothing of that sort in my heart against you," Omal lovingly reassured his wife. "Ader, I love you too much to hurt you and I would rather hurt myself than you. This is the most important night, unlike any other in our life together and I do not want you to spoil it, with such negative thoughts. I want you to prove to me how much you love me and I will do the same but please do not try to ruin this lovely moment, by being so nervous for nothing. Ader, my love, let me assure you that what we are about to engage in doing is a natural exercise, for expressing love between a husband and wife and it is wonderful."

The very fact that Ader was then alone with her husband who seemed knowledgeable about, what they were about to do and in full control of the moment, took away all her courage. Furthermore, Ader was still a virgin and did not know what to expect apart from the few things that she had read in books. She was also dreading the fact that being with a man for the first time, was quite uncomfortable. Lack of knowledge about the whole situation, rendered Ader inert and she therefore, did not reply to her husband.

"I don't think that conversing while standing, is the best way for us to start our life together," gently said Omal, "besides, it seems to be increasing your nervousness."

Omal eventually carried his wife and went with her to the room that was prepared for them. He then asked her for a dance, to a beautiful love music that was softly playing on the music system. All that Omal wanted to do was, to make his wife feel comfortable with him. The dance helped quite a bit because Ader felt a little relaxed. "See, there is nothing to fear after all," Omal delightfully assured his bride. "I just want us to have a happy, joyful, wonderful, peaceful and loving time."

Ader tried, to turn her face away from her husband, as he was speaking to her but he gently held her head with both hands and lovingly gazed into her eyes without saying a word, as he was admiring her beautiful eyes. Ader began to feel a little dizzy out of nervousness and deeply sighed, as she was trying hard to closing her eyes, so as to avoid Omal's loving gaze at her. She therefore, softly beseeched her husband almost in a whisper, "Omal, please, kindly stop looking into my eyes. You are making it quite hard for me, to be comfortable with you."

Omal, who was then absolutely intoxicated, with passion for making love to his beautiful bride thought that the right moment had already come for them, to consummate their marriage. He consequently carried his wife once again and danced with her in his arms, as he was walking towards the bed. As soon as he sat on the bed, with her still in his arms, he passionately started kissing her as never before because he was then free to do whatever, he wanted to indulge with her and one thing led to the next. Eventually, what Omal felt was ineffable, when he finally discovered that his bride was still a virgin. He almost exploded with excitement, as tears of joy welled into his eyes. It was the most blissful moment, beyond Omal's wildest anticipation and he felt as if, he was past the heaven that he had always fancied. The whole experience, of making love with Ader for the first time, was like a fantasy for Omal and he found it hard to believe that it was actually taking place. A comforting thought went through his mind, as he was excitedly enjoying the moment, *God must really love me so much, for him to have graciously given to me, such a beautiful, intelligent, loving and pure wife. I can now understand, why my wife absolutely believed in abstinence, otherwise, I could have missed this mysterious surprise and the indescribable pleasure that I am enjoying with her right now. Oh God, how could I thank you enough, for this celestial moment? I have never thought that anything this exhilarating existed in this world! Dear Lord, what were you thinking about, when you were creating such a deep and consuming pleasure between a husband and a wife?*

Ader's innocence and the way she softly whispered her husband's name, deepened his desire so much that his whole being was yearning for her, even more. Ader had then completely got lost in the explosion of the moment and became oblivious of her notion that being with a man for the first time was not pleasant because her husband was quite gentle, despite being very passionate with her. The couple felt, as if they were put into a new planet that was specifically designed for them and the celestial beings sang to them an original melodious love song that the other human beings had never heard the lyrics and tune before. The ecstasy, for completely submitting to each other body, soul and spirit, ushered the couple into the paradise of comfort, fulfillment, happiness, joy, love, peace and pleasure that no tongue could describe, as they were lost in each other's love.

The next morning, Ader felt so lost, exhausted and had a changed view about the meaning of her life because she was no longer a virgin. The whole new experience, for being with her husband for the first time, was quite overwhelming for her and she nervously wondered, whether she would be able that day, to hold any conversation or even look at her husband's face, given all that had taken place between them. As Ader was thinking that her husband was still sleeping, she decided to quietly sneak out of the bed in order to bathe alone and reminisced what she had experienced. However, as soon as she started bathing, her husband joined her surprisingly. Ader almost ran away from the bathroom, had her husband not held her back because she did not expect him to follow her there. Omal who was enjoying every minute that he was spending with his wife, watched quietly her nervousness in amusement, as he was lovingly holding her and eventually gently told her, "Ader, my love, stop your poppycock, about fearing me. I am no longer your boyfriend or fiancé but your husband. I want to share with you, the most romantic moment of my life while we are here and that is why I have brought you away from the crowd at home. I really wonder, whether you would have been able to survive, the scrutinizing eyes of the people at home, had we consummated our marriage at my father's home."

"You have scared me," timidly responded Ader, as she continued to feel very uncomfortable and wished that it were possible for her to run away from her husband. "I thought that you were still sleeping and did not expect you to follow me here."

"You better get used to being comfortable with me because I will follow you almost everywhere," Omal playfully told his wife, while he was lovingly admiring her, as if he had just fallen in love with her for the first time. "Ader, I deeply love and very much enjoy being with you but I don't want you out of my sight, sweetheart. Not even, for a few minutes."

Ader faintly smiled, ogled at her husband and softly said, "You are outrageous!"

They both laughed and began to bathe together but Ader avoided her husband's face, whereas he kept looking at her with so much joy and love in his eyes. Omal could not believe, that at last, Ader was his wife because everything that he was experiencing with her, was still like an illusion to him. However, he was rather sympathetic with his wife, at his knowledge that it was her first time to be with a man. "Darling, you may be shy," Omal delightfully assured his wife, "but I earnestly would like you to know that you are the sweetest woman in the whole universe. My beloved Ader, you have made me the proudest husband and I just cannot get enough of you."

Ader only sighed and continued to look down because she neither had the courage to look at her husband nor the ability to respond to him.

As the newlywed was still bathing, the housekeeper quietly came in, quickly made breakfast and went away, before they could notice her. Therefore, after taking the shower, the couple was surprised, at how quietly the housekeeper had made breakfast for them. They therefore, joyfully settled down to eat but Ader ate very little once again, as she had done in the previous night and said that she had no appetite. Omal was quite concerned about, his wife's lack of appetite and sadly told her, "If you refuse to eat enough food today, I will also leave it."

"Ah, Omal," softly said Ader, as she was struggling to look at her husband, with pleading eyes, for the first time, that day. "I wished that you could understand me because I am really not hungry."

"I do, darling," he pitifully said, "but I do not want you to starve, while we are here."

"Believe me, I am not going to starve," humbly said Ader. "I only eat whenever, I am hungry. Omal, please, do eat some more and stop worrying about me. I am really fine"

Omal quietly looked at his wife in sympathy and then excused her.

"Thank you, for your understanding," gratefully said Ader, who was then seemingly quite relieved.

"I love you, Ader," gently said Omal, "and I hope that I have not done something wrong to you since we got here, which has deprived you of your appetite."

Ader shyly smiled and refuted what her husband had just told her, by shaking her head disapprovingly. Omal then smiled at his wife, with a sigh of relief because he was glad to know that he had not done anything wrong to her.

Each passing day, Omal fell deeper and deeper in love with his wife. He admired his wife's beauty, from her hair to toes and delighted so much to being with her. Omal daily thanked God for enabling him to having the opportunity, for enjoying his life with his beautiful bride. Ader had also gradually begun to enjoying being with her husband but was quite timid, to freely express her love for him. Omal was aware about the situation and so took his time with her. He wishfully hoped that the time would someday come, when his wife would be completely free with him whenever they were making love.

Ader continued to be timid with her husband, especially whenever they were making love. However, one afternoon, as they were sitting outside the house, a man next door began to mercilessly whipping his son of about seven years old, beside his door. All the neighbours were watching the vicious man in silence, without any effort for intervention, as he was carrying out his sordid deed, because they were all aware of his ill temper and how he violently reacted, whenever someone was attempting to stop him, from carrying out the horrible things that he had been doing to his family. However, that day, Ader jumped up, sprinted, and spontaneously restrained the man's hand from beating his son. "Stop it!" she yelled out authoritatively at him, "why do you want to kill this poor handsome son of yours? Whatever mistake he might have done, I think that you have punished him more than necessary!"

"And who are you pretty face, may I ask?" mockingly inquired the man, with such arrogance. "I think that you are a new person in this place, otherwise, you would have not dared to hold my hand. Do you really know, what I do normally to an interloper, like you?"

"And who do you think that you are anyway?" boldly retorted Ader, as she was fearlessly looking at the formidable man straight into his eyes. "You are a man, like any other and I think that there is a lot of goodness in you, although, you seemed not to want to show it but only magnify the little bad temper in you. Anyway, what are you afraid of in your life, my brother?"

"Whmm," deeply sighed the ruthless man, as anger was beginning to dissipate from his face. "Do I look to you, like a man who is afraid of anything? However, no one has ever spoken to me, with such authority like you have done today and no one has ever told me that there was a lot of goodness in me or even called me a brother. Dear lady, your parents have taught you well and thank you for pointing out to me, the things about myself that I have never known." The man then walked away, like a defeated cock. All the neighbours were so astonished and shocked, at what the impact Ader's words, had created on the violent man. Ader then wiped off the tears, from the face of the boy and told him kindly, to go to his mother. The poor child, looked quietly at Ader with such grateful eyes and thereafter, limped painfully to his mother.

Omal, who had watched quietly the fiasco, could not comprehend, the strength of his wife's character. He was very prepared to attack the man, if he were to try to beat up his wife. As Ader was humbly walking back to, where her husband was sitting, he shockingly smiled at her, as he was shaking his head in wonder. Omal was quite amazed, as to why his wife was so timid around him but was very bold when she was speaking to the violent man.

"You are quite a character, darling, aren't you?" Omal softly told his wife in admiration, as she was sitting down while wiping sweat from her forehead. "I did not even realize how spontaneous and fast you got to that man. Anyway, why did you risk your life, like that?"

"How could I sit here and watch a young child being ruthlessly beaten up," softly replied Ader. "That poor man is afraid of something and is trying unfortunately to take it out on his son."

"How do you know that he is a coward?" curiously inquired Omal because he was surprised and amused by what his wife had just said about the man.

"All violent people are," said Ader assertively. "They do violent things, to hide their weakness, fear and uncertainty, my dad, once taught me."

"Ader, my precious love, you are not only beautiful but are also full of wisdom, aren't you?" admiringly said Omal as he was fondly holding his wife's hand. "However, from today onward, I will no longer accept, any timid attitude from you. I want you to talk and behave to me intrepidly, as you done to that violent man."

"Don't be silly," replied Ader, as she was stubbornly staring at her husband. "You are not a violent man and the relationship between you and I is different. I am not at all afraid of you except that my wholly new life of being your wife is quite a unique experience for me. I am trying hard to getting used to and accepting it but I think that I am a little slow. Omal, my dear, you are my loving husband and I don't want you to think that I am scared of you. I like being with you and I want you to understand that I am in the process of learning how to be a good wife to you."

"I am very happy, to hear you say that" delightfully said Omal. "However, I was already beginning to getting worried about your shyness and thought that I might be quite boring and unpleasant to you."

"Oh no, please do not say that," said Ader compassionately, as she was looking lovingly at her husband, "You are my wonderful, pleasant and loving husband. I could not ask God for a better husband. Omal, I love being with you and you make me feel so happy."

Omal could not believe his ears because he had never thought that his wife would say such wonderful things about him. Therefore, he held fondly her hand and whispered to her softly in one of her ears, before he could get up and go inside the house, "Would you mind if we go and continue with our conversation, inside the house?"

Ader happily smiled, instantly got up and obediently followed her husband inside the house. She was instinctively aware about what her husband was up to, but was quite happy to be with him.

As soon as the couple got inside the house, Omal began to fondly and passionately kissing his wife because she was no longer shy with him. "Ader dear," he joyfully said, "it is wonderful and sweet, to see you talk to me without fear, for the first time, since we got married."

"Aren't we one body now, anyway?" sensually said Ader, as she was fearlessly and lovingly looking at her husband's handsome eyes. "A lot has happened between you and I, you know."

"Is that what, you have been believing?" surprisingly but excitedly questioned Omal. "According to me, nothing much yet but I am about to introduce you, to the next dimension."

"What are you talking about!" innocently exclaimed Ader in dismay, as she was wondering what her husband was really meaning.

"Sweetheart, I haven't made love to you yet, in the way that I have been needing it to be," Omal honestly assured his wife, as he was smiling at her. "Your nervousness, has mysteriously subdued me to be quite gentle with you all the time. However, from now onward, you will notice a different side of me. I think that it is time for you, to experience the real thing, that is, the way it is naturally supposed to be."

"You are something else, aren't you?" timidly said Ader, as she was beginning to feeling powerless once again and shaking her head in bewilderment. "Just as I was thinking that I have already known you and beginning to be comfortable with you, you have come up with something else. Omal please stop, frightening me."

Omal made funny faces to his wife and she began chasing him around the room. It was their first time to play with each other since they got married and they felt really good about it. Omal was very delighted to see his wife came out of her shell of shyness at last. They childishly played about and eventually, erotically got engaged with each other, according to Omal's wildest anticipation. From then onward, the couple joyfully ate, played, chatted and fearlessly made love to each other.

Omal and Ader enjoyed the short but wonderful honeymoon in Upper Talanga, very much. Towards the end of their stay in Upper Talanga, they decided to take a long walk near the tea plantation. They slowly walked, as they were admiring the beautiful picturesque view of the area. The valleys were quite deep, the hills, each higher than the one beneath and the plains that stretched out on some of the hills, made gorgeous view. The tea plantation was wonderfully lash and green. The weather on the mountain was cooler than anywhere in the lower lying areas. The trees around the tea plantation were very huge and interlocked canopy. The wild flowers were quite large and coloured brightly. Crops like cabbages, carrots, collards, corns, pumpkins, sweet potatoes etc, were five times larger than found anywhere else. The birds sang variety of sweet tunes everywhere and all of them seemed very joyful. Different kinds of monkeys swung from one tree to another and made all kinds of sounds. Omal and Ader were very delighted, to see all that nature had to offer. They concluded that some day in the future, they would be moving, to live in Upper Talanga. The way Omal and Ader were admiring everything around them, as they were walking, made the local people they met on the way to accurately guess that they were new in the place. Most of the young men admired Ader and thought that Omal was very lucky to have married her. On the other hand, the young women also thought that Ader was a fortunate young woman, to have married such a handsome and heart-throbbing young man, like Omal.

As the time neared, for the couple to return to Magwi, Omal felt so bad. "I don't know whether we shall have any great time together anymore when we get home," Omal told his wife one evening because he was feeling quite frustrated about returning home so soon. "I feel like, we should spend a whole month, out here. I know the kind of people at home who are awaiting to tease you and I don't like such behaviour."

"I will know, how to deal with them," Ader lovingly, assured her husband. "Don't worry about me, I am an Acoli girl and I know how the custom is."

"You are too sweet, to be teased," Omal tenderly, told his wife. "However, I know that you are a strong woman and I am quite sure that you will withstand those silly teasers but should they go to the extreme, I will surely give them my piece of mind."

"Thank you, for being so defensive of me," joyfully said Ader, as she was hugging her husband. "I have now understood, how much you love and care about me."

Omal told his wife eventually, about some of his sleepless nights, when they were not yet married and how sometimes, he would sadly cry for her. He even told Ader about, his last night alone at Magwi and how he wept, tossed in bed until almost morning and regretted having left her in Licari. Ader listened, to her husband's tales with such sympathy and admired him greatly.

The week for the honeymoon flew by very fast and eventually it was time, for the couple to return to Magwi and continue to celebrate their marriage, with the rest of the family. Therefore, Omal sent a message to Olima, to come and pick them up on the Saturday that they were returning to Magwi. Olima got to Upper Talanga at about noon and without delay drove the newlywed back to Magwi.

Chapter Seventeen
The Royal Welcome for the Newlywed

On the day that Omal had brought his bride home, after the honeymoon, there was a big celebration to welcome them, especially his wife. Most of the people from Magwi Chiefdom came to the Chief's home, before the bride and bridegroom could arrive from Upper Talanga. As the Daihatsu was slowly entering into the Chief's courtyard, the people in the procession to welcome the Prince and his bride home, adoringly prostrated, as a sign, for their respect for the Royal Couple. Therefore, as soon as Omal and his wife stepped out of the car, the women began yodeling and singing a song with beautiful lyrics and melody that praised Omal, for his wise choice of the beautiful bride as his Princess. The lyrics also praised, Omal's ancestors and father as heroes, who had given the Magwi people the courage, to fight and defeat the mountain beasts, which in the past, had devastated the lives of many people in Magwi. (The beasts were locally known as *Kitikiti*. The people of the Magwi Chiefdom believe that long time ago, their enemies from a tribe in a far off land, had the ability to transform themselves into ugly mountain beasts that were able to eat the human beings. The Kitikiti killed, a lot of people from Magwi, women and children were in the majority. However, the people of the Magwi Chiefdom then, under the command and leadership of their Chief at that time, Omal's great grandfather, courageously fought and killed all the beasts. They even burnt, some of the beasts that were hiding in the mountain caves. The location, where the last beasts were baked to extinction, is still present to date.) The young men took out their spears and shields and then, vigorously began performing the war rituals by exercising a mock fight, to repudiate any evil spirit and bad luck from the Chief's home. Furthermore, they also wanted to indicate that the Magwi Chiefdom was going to continue in their generation, with Omal some day as their Chief. The ceremony was so ritually symbolic that most of the young people were amazed, to see the part of their culture and tradition that they had never witnessed before. The Royal

Families, from the other six Chiefdoms of the Acoli people, also attended the occasion.

The Chief and his wife welcomed delightfully their son and daughter-in-law. Omal's mother then, took immediately her daughter-in-law away into a private room where, only the older women with royal blood in them sat, to be adorned as the Princess. The women, carefully adorned Ader with the royal attire and she looked so elegant. Omal's mother, was overwhelmed with joy and happiness, to finally have Ader in her home as her daughter-in-law. She was also very happy for her son, who seemed satisfactorily joyful in his new life. As Ader was being dressed up, the Chief began to adorn his son delightfully with leopards' hides, put a magnificent royal headdress on his head, an armlet that was decorated colourfully; with ostrich feathers to bout on his left arm, a royal spear in his right hand, a big royal shield on his left hand and then seated his son enthusiastically on a special chair, that was made specifically for the occasion, to complement him as the future leader of the Magwi Chiefdom. Omal was transformed instantly, into the Royal Prince of the People of Magwi and seemed different completely from, the normally simple Omal. On the other hand, as soon as the royal women had adorned Ader, they blessed her and thereafter Omal's mother escorted her daughter-in-law outside, to a special seat which signified that Ader was not only a new bride in that home but the future Queen, of the Magwi Chiefdom. As Ader was taking her seat, which was next to her husband's, the young women started yodeling and singing a melodious love song to praise her, while they were joyfully dancing. The jiggles, around the women's ankles made beautiful sounds, as the women were stamping their feet on the ground rhythmically. The young men then began blowing their horns, in variety of tunes, for five minutes, none stop. A little while after, the young men had stopped blowing their horns, the oldest man among the elders, started beating the biggest drum that sounded like a thunder. A number of the elders joined him, shortly after and they drummed their best. After the drumming, the young boys and girls, then started dancing the Bwola, followed by Dingidingi and many other Acoli dances. The day was so solemn, unlike any other, in the recent memory. Everyone was full of joy and happiness that could not be described in words.

Ader was shocked extremely by, all the symbolic rituals that were performed on her and her husband. She instantly became very nervous and wondered whether she would really be able, to handle her new responsibilities as the Princess. Ader, who was used to knowing her husband as a simple man, could not reconcile in her mind that the man who was transformed completely into the Royal Prince and seated next to her, was actually her normally simple husband. Consequently, a thought of absolute wonder, went through her mind, *How could, such a royal man falls so deeply in love with me, a commoner and insignificant nobody? Look at him, powerful, strong, deeply loved by his people and very handsome in his royal costume. What good have I done in my life, to deserve such a royal husband?* Ader glanced awesomely at her husband and looked down instantly. Omal caught his wife's glance coincidentally and only smiled at her. He had wished that he were able to guess what was racing through his wife's mind, given all the solemn ceremony. Furthermore, he wished that he could have been able to whisper to her and reassure her that despite all the rituals, he was still the same man who dearly loved her.

Most of the women, from all over Magwi Chiefdom, brewed all kinds of the Acoli beers and cooked variety of food, to welcome home their Prince and his bride. Therefore, after all the initiation dances, the people settled down to eat and drink, as much as they could stomach. Everyone was filled with joy and happiness that they began the serious dances for the occasion, soon after they had eaten and drank all that they could. The Prince and Princess, danced briefly with the people but were excused, to go to bed early. The rest of the people, danced out their hearts. Food was plentiful and drinks were everywhere. There was such merriment in the hearts of the people of Magwi that they joyfully danced until morning. The festivity, to celebrate the royal marriage, continued for a whole week.

On the other hand, when Omal was eventually alone with his wife in the bedroom, he gently asked her, "Darling, I have noticed your glance at me, during the ceremony, what were you thinking about dear?"

Ader adoringly curtsied and addressed her husband with such humility, "My lord," she respectfully said, "I really did not know, who you truly are, until today. Omal, my husband, you are not an ordinary man at all and I wonder why you have decided to choose me, a girl from another Chiefdom, for your wife, when you could have chosen any one of the beautiful girls from your Chiefdom, for your wife."

"Please stop being ridiculous and silly," Omal amusingly told his wife, as he was gently holding her head in his hands. "Sweetheart, you are the purest, most beautiful and wonderful wife that God has kindly given to me. I have never met any girl, in the whole of Magwi who is better than you. You are not only my wife and my princess but also my best friend and I love you, above everything else on earth."

"Omal, you were utterly transformed, when you were wearing your royal attire," humbly said Ader. "For a moment, I thought that you were a completely different person but as soon as I recognized you, oh my God, my heart almost exploded with awe, at the knowledge that I was indeed married to, the most powerful man in Magwi, after your father. I was deeply overwhelmed by my thoughts that I could not control my eyes from glancing at you. Oh my dear, thank you, for deeply loving me in the way you do. I feel so lucky and blessed to have you, simple but very powerful man, for my husband."

"I am glad that I did catch your glance," joyfully said Omal, as he was feeling so adulated by, what his wife was saying about him. "I knew in my heart that your glance carried more weight than any other in the past. Ader, nothing will ever change my love for you, not even my position in life, as the Prince of the People of Magwi. Come on here, I want to show you that I am still the same man that dearly loves and happily married to you. Remember, our honeymoon is not yet over," excitedly concluded Omal, as he began to fondly holding and passionately kissing his wife.

Ader joyfully responded and absolutely submitted herself to her husband, body, soul and spirit. The couple felt as if, they were making love for the first time and soon were erotically lost in each other's love.

After the festivity in the Chief's home had ended, four girls were sent from Licari to Magwi, with gifts for Omal and his people and also to help Ader for one week. The girls did all the chores in the home but cooking, which they left for Ader. Ader cooked so well that all the members of the royal family were very proud of her and praised her mother for having brought her up so well. The presence, of the girls from Licari village, made life very comfortable and easy for Ader because she happily chatted with them after their day's work. The girls assured Ader that she was doing well in her new home and they gave her lots of advice, on how she should handle her new role in life as the Princess. The one-week flew by so fast that soon the girls returned to Licari and Ader greatly missed them because she was wishing that it were possible for the girls to stay with her a little bit longer. However, Ader faced, her new responsibilities with such determination, confidence and joy that her in-laws and the rest of the relatives of Omal greatly admired and delighted a lot in her.

One evening, after the girls from Licari village had gone, the Chief summoned his son to his most private room, to have a manly discussion with him. Omal was a little concern, as to why his father wanted to have such a private talk with him because he was unaware about the agenda for the meeting. However, Omal was quite anxious to hear, what his father wanted to tell him. Consequently therefore, he went and respectfully sat down quietly, beside his father.

"Welcome, my dear son," gently said the Chief. "I can tell that you are a little concerned as to why I have called you here. Son, there is nothing that you should worry about. It is just that I have some royal formalities that I have to discuss with you. I have witnessed how happy you are with your wife. I have never seen you so joyful as you are nowadays, and your mother and I are both very happy for you. However, there are certain things that our family tradition mandates that I should ask you about your wife because we are from the royal lineage. Son, I would like you to honestly tell me whether your wife has courted other boys before she met you."

"I am the first man that she has ever courted," respectfully replied Omal externally, as he was sadly, internally wondering why his father was probing deeply into his personal life. "Father, I am sorry, if what I am going to ask you about, should sound rude to you," apologetically said Omal. "But why have you waited until now, to ask me if my wife has ever dated other boys? Don't you agree with me that the right time for you to have asked me such a question, should have been, when I first introduced my wife to you, when she was only my fiancée?"

"You are not, rude at all, my son," calmly said the Chief, "I have also reacted, in the same way to my father, when he asked me the same question, a long time ago. However, there is more to the question and is a lot more personal. I wouldn't have cared, even if my daughter-in-law were to date other boys before you but the truth I am trying to ask you about is, whether you are the first man to be intimate with her. I couldn't ask you, such a question before you were married because the law of our heritage stipulates that the question be asked, after the responsible person has been with his wife. Furthermore, I have always assumed in my heart that you would keep your body chaste until marriage, as I have always been instructing you since you were a little boy."

"Father, thank you, for your explanation because it has relieved me of my disappointment," honestly said Omal, as he was beginning to feel more comfortable with his father. "To precisely answer your question, I am very delighted to truthfully tell you that I am the only man that my wife has ever known because she was a virgin on our wedding night."

Tears of joy and gratitude to God welled into the Chief's eyes, at the knowledge that his daughter-in-law was the purest woman that he had been hoping that she would be, according to the royal requisition. "Son, I am very delighted that God has blessed you with such a virtuous wife. Honour, respect, trust and faithfully love her, all the days of your life. Never look at another woman because your wife is a rare quality in this modern age of promiscuity."

"But what if, my wife were not to be a virgin, on our wedding night," Omal deliberately asked his father, "what would your reaction have been?

"Hmm, I would have yet accepted her, so long as she made you happy," hesitantly replied the Chief "but with some reservation of course because of her background."

"Then I must be very lucky, to have married, my ideal wife," Omal gladly told his father. "Father, I am very glad to tell you that I am very fulfilled in my new life with my wife. Furthermore, I will faithfully follow your advice because God has truly been very kind to me, by having graciously given Ader to me."

"This is the secret that the two of us should keep to ourselves, from the rest of the family, including your mother," the Chief cautiously advised his son. "Anyway, I do not want to keep you away for a long time, from your virtuous, beautiful, wonderful and lovely wife. Please do go and make her happiest tonight. This is a command from your father, the Chief," jokingly concluded Omal's father, as he was joyfully winking at his son.

"Please, you do not need to command me, Father," playfully said Omal. "I am a husband now and I know my duty, quite well. Anyway, I will make your daughter-in-law happiest tonight, since you have commanded me."

The Chief playfully nudged his son and they both burst into an interesting laughter. Omal eventually, thanked and said goodnight to his father, before he left.

When Omal was alone, he pondered on his father's very personal interrogations about his wife and wondered why, such a demeaning custom was still kept. However, Omal was very grateful that he had married a virgin and felt so indebted to his wife because of her stand on abstinence. He was extremely very proud of his wife that night because had it not been for her strong moral belief, he would have made love to her, before they were married. That night, therefore, Omal fell deeper in love with his wife because he had further realized, how truly special she was. Consequently, he passionately made love to his wife, as he had never before but she was quite oblivious, as to why her husband was so excited, as if, they were making love for the first time. "What has gotten, into you, tonight?" Ader curiously struggled to ask her husband, after they had made love.

"What do you, really mean?" pretentiously replied Omal, as if he wasn't aware about his explosive copulation with his wonderful wife.

"Why, do you want me to explain to you, what I very well know that you know," exhaustively said Ader, as she was trying to catch her breath, "I have never experienced this side of you."

"I am thrilled that you have felt that way because that is what I have intended for you tonight," Omal honestly assured his wife. "Ader, my sweet wife, I am so happy that you are gradually opening up to be free with me, while we are making love. To be honest with you, there are lots of things about me that you do not yet know, when it comes to making love. However, I do not want, to rush you but will bit by bit introduce you, to everything I know. Tonight, I have fallen deeper in love with you because you have relatively responded to me, as I have always needed it to be and for some inexplicable reason, I was quite overwhelmed with a consuming desire, to intensively giving up myself to you, in such a way that I have never felt before."

Ader then kept quiet because she was feeling so lost as she was wondering, whether she would ever get to know her husband at all, when it came to their sexual life. However, Ader did not know that Omal had had a private talk with his father, about her. On the other hand, Omal felt that his father's playful command that he made his wife happiest that night, was not a simple joke but carried with it some mysterious force of energy, which had driven him to go wildest with his wife.

As the time was going by, the young male relatives of Omal came every evening to tease Ader, as Omal had anticipated because it was a common practice in the Acoli custom and therefore, no one was to stop them.

"We can tell that you are scared of our brother's ability to, you know," one of the boys, called Obwoya, one evening told Ader. "You just cannot handle our brother because he is too strong for you. However, we know that you cannot resist his handsomely good look."

"Well, I absolutely love your brother," boldly answered Ader, as she was smiling to the young men. "Your brother is, my beloved husband but how do you know that I cannot handle him well? I think that it is you, who cannot handle your wife. It is quite obvious to me that you are indirectly trying to tell me, how weak you are, when you are, you know, with your wife."

After what Ader had said, there was an outburst of very interesting laughter.

"She is the kind that cannot easily be defeated," said another cousin, called Lokang. "Ader we like you and we believe that you are a wonderful wife for our brother. Omal, you have married the right woman, for our future Queen."

"I am very aware about that" arrogantly confirmed Omal, "and that is why, I dearly love her."

The young men, teased Ader in a lot of provocative ways but she took everything very well, without getting annoyed. Ader was aware that most of the new brides in Acoliland, had to go through what she was experiencing and so, she did not care about, what the boys were saying to her. Omal, did not like some of the jokes on his wife because he was thinking that his relatives were going over board, against his beloved.

The young men, continued to tease Ader every evening but one evening Omal lost his temper and told one of his cousins, called Bongwat, "Please have some respect, for my wife. You do not know how hard I have fought, to win her heart. It deeply hurts me, when I see you, people, are treating her so cheap."

"Generally, Ader is not yours alone," haughtily replied Bongwat. "You have married her, so that she could be one of us, according to the tradition and we have the right, to tease her as much as we wanted."

"That I know," disgustingly said Omal, "but don't you think that you have tormented her enough? Some of the meanest things that you have constantly been saying to her, are just not acceptable to me, anymore. I dearly love my wife and will no longer tolerate, your extremely ugly jokes, against her."

"Brother, are you implying that we should not joke with your wife anymore?" curiously asked Bongwat.

"You are all allowed to joke with her," disappointingly replied Omal. "However, today I have noticed that you have gone beyond what is acceptable."

From that day onward, the young men did not disturb Ader as much as they had been doing because they had then realised that her husband was very defensive of her.

Omal anticipated that their holiday should get finished quickly, so that he could return with his wife to Juba, where, he would have some privacy with her and no one would tease and ridicule her, as his young male relatives have been doing. Ader saw and understood, the look of concern on her husband's face, on the night that he had had an altercation with Bongwat. Consequently, she asked him, "Why are you so worried about, what the boys have been saying to me, as if I were too delicate?"

"Those boys do not have the respect that you deserved," her husband sympathetically told her.

"What I am going through is very normal, for any newly married woman, in Acoliland," carelessly replied Ader. "The boys are simply trying, to get to know my personality."

"You really are a very resilient person, my love," Omal admiringly told his wife.

"Thank you, for thinking so highly of me but I don't think that I am," humbly said Ader. "I have seen in some cases whereby, the young men would even try to wrestle with the new bride and when they succeeded to throw her down, they would make fun of her. The way that I am being teased is relatively gentle, compared to some of the very graphic situation that other brides go through."

"I am glad that you are taking everything, so well," Omal adoringly told his wife. "But, if any of the boys, should venture to wrestle with you and throw you down, I would definitely break his neck."

"Don't be so overprotective of me, my dear husband because I am quite capable of defending myself at the moment," Ader firmly assured her husband. "I don't want you, to have misunderstanding with any of your male relatives, over me. Leave them alone with me because I am sure that they will get tired in the near future and give up on me."

Omal was so happy to hear that his wife did not care, about the situation she had been facing. "What a wife, of great understanding that I have married!" he joyfully told her. "Ader, I am very proud of you."

"I am also proud to have you, as my husband," happily said Ader. "I will surely tell you, if I need any help but as for now, leave me alone with the young men."

Ader quickly got accustomed to her new home and handled the housework and every other chore up to date. Her mother-in-law was very proud of her and treated her so well, as if she were her real daughter. However, Omal did not allow his wife, to go for firewood but instead bought charcoal from the local market for her to use. He became very overprotective of his wife so much that he started taking her early to bed, in order to avoid some of the young men, who were still coming to tease her. Omal's acts of defiance angered most of his young male relatives but they did not dare to challenge him face to face. Everybody, in the Chief's homestead admired and liked Ader so much because she was very friendly and easy to get along with. They simply referred to her as *Cii Rwot,* meaning, the Queen.

The time went by very fast and soon only two days were left, before Omal and Ader could return to Juba. Consequently, the couple went to Licari, to say goodbye to Ader's family. Abongkara and Okeny were the only two people then left in the big home and as soon as they saw their daughter and son-in-law, they warmly welcomed them. Okeny chatted with Omal, while Ader and her mother were gathering together all the gifts that the relatives had brought for Ader. As they were packaging everything properly, Abongkara told her daughter, "I can tell that you are happy, in your new life. I have been missing you so much already but I would like you to be happy, in your new home. Be loyal, respectful, understanding, responsible, hardworking and loving to your husband and his people. Put into practice everything that I have taught you. Do not bring any shame, to the name of our family. I am proud, about the news that I have been hearing about you. I love you, my child and wish you a wonderful life with your husband. I am very happy to know that Omal loves you very much."

Ader promised her mother that she would do everything, as her mother had instructed her. Suddenly, they both became emotional and began hugging each other in tears. After they had finished packaging everything ready for transport, Abongkara served some food. Omal ate with his father-in-law and Ader, with her mother.

After the meal, Abongkara and Okeny blessed the couple.

"I wish you both happiness, all the days of your life together," joyfully said Okeny. "The two of you, have made everybody happy, from both sides of the families. May God's blessings, be upon you always."

"May you live a long life and bear many healthy children, both boys and girl," Abongkara delightfully, blessed the couple. "May peace and joy, abounds in your home, forever."

The couple thanked, Okeny and Abongkara and, as it was almost getting dark, they began to tie the bundles of gifts that were given to Ader, onto their two bicycles and bid goodbye to Ader's parents. Abongkara and Okeny, who had escorted the couple, on top of the Licari hill, stood for a long time while they were watching Ader and her husband, as they were riding down the hill, until they were out of sight, on their way back to Magwi.

Prior to the couple's visit to Licari, they had already told everyone, including Omal's parents that they would be returning to Juba, on the next day, after their visit to Licari. Omal's mother gave Ader, many gifts and plus the others that Ader had brought from Licari there were lots of luggage to take to Juba. The young girls and boys in the homestead helped the couple so much, while they were packaging everything properly for their journey back to Juba. At the end of the chores Ader felt so tired that she lied down flatly on the mat and did seem so exhausted. Omal was quite concerned about his wife's well being and therefore sympathetically told her, "Darling, you don't seem well at all. Could you be falling ill?"

"No, I am not sick," softly replied Ader. "I am just too exhausted."

"I have never seen you, this tired," went on Omal "I hope that you are not hiding something serious, from me."

"And why would I, anyway?" exhaustively said Ader, as she was amusingly laughing at her husband.

Omal then, had no knowledge that his wife had conceived, since their honeymoon. However, Ader did not want to inform her husband that she was already pregnant because she did not have any morning sickness. Consequently, she had then decided that it would be necessary for her to tell him about her pregnancy, once they had returned to Juba.

Chapter Eighteen
The Couple's Life in Their Own House

On the day that the couple was returning to Juba, Omal's relatives came to help them with their luggage to the bus stop. Therefore, before everybody left the home, the Chief and his wife decided to give the young couple their blessings and consequently, took them to the private room in the home.

"May you have a wonderful life together," joyfully said the Chief. "The two of you have brought so much joy and happiness not only to this family but to the people of Magwi Chiefdom at large. Son, treat your wife well, love her dearly and honour her, in all you do. Your marriage has been, the most wonderful thing that had happened to this family, in recent time. Our ancestors have greatly smiled on us and graciously enabled you, to meet your beautiful and magnificent wife. My son, I am quite sure that you know how truly special your wife is. As for you, my lovely daughter-in-law, I hope that you would continue with your sweet spirit that we have openly witnessed, during your very short stay with us. You are such a blessing, to our son and our family. You are priceless and we love you a lot. Please, do not allow outsiders, to come between you and your husband. I am very certain that you love your husband and I pray that you maintain that spirit. You have made, our son's life so wonderful, happy and peaceful that we are all happy for him. May God bless you both, in everything you would be doing."

"My blessings are, for both of you," said Omal's mother, when it was her turn to bless the couple. "You both have, made me the proudest mother in Magwi Chiefdom. I cannot remember being this happy, except on my wedding day. May you have, many children, both boys and girls and may your home be a joyful place, for you and all who visit you. May anyone who tries, to bring trouble between you, be brought to shame and disgraced. I pray that the bus you would be traveling on today, safely to takes you to Juba, without any trouble on the way. Omal, my dear son, other people may call your wife as my daughter-in-law but to me, she is my real daughter. I have, fallen deeply in love with your wife during her short stay with me. We haven't disagreed, on anything at all. Her sweet smiles, hard work, respect, humility, loyalty, caring, love and obedience to me, I will treasure in my heart, forever. Dear daughter, may God bless you abundantly, in all your endeavours."

"My wife and I are very grateful, to receive your blessings," Omal gratefully told his parents. "You have made, my wife to feel at home and she is very grateful to both of you. Mother, thanks, for accepting Ader, as if she were your own daughter. We will surely miss, both of you, a lot."

"My husband has said everything that I was going to tell you," respectfully said Ader, with a big smile on her face. "Thank you so much, for welcoming me warmly, into your family. I consider you, more like my real parents than parents-in-law. I love you dearly, as much as I love my husband. May God bless you, in everything that you would be doing."

Omal's mother then hugged her daughter-in-law, before she hugged her son. The Chief shook hands hard with his son and then, gently shook the hands of his daughter-in-law. Omal's mother was then feeling as if, she should not let her son and his wife leave home on that day. Her heart was breaking, as she was vehemently trying, to control her tears.

After the blessings, the Chief, his wife and the rest of the relatives who, had come to the Chief's home, escorted the couple to the bus stop. As the bus was leaving, everyone was waving to Omal and Ader, who also were waving to them through the bus' window. The scene was quite somber because everyone had then started missing Omal and his wonderful wife who loved everyone. The couple also was missing the relatives. Omal was quite a gentleman in that he did not show his emotion for missing his people but as for Ader, tears were streaming down her cheeks, for the people she had learned to love, so much. She especially was missing her mother-in-law with whom she had spent most of her time, while she was in the village. Omal comforted his wife by, gently rubbing one of her shoulders. After Ader had controlled her tears, she fell asleep, with her head on one of her husband's shoulders and slept most of the way to Juba. Omal was quite concerned about his wife's health and thought that she might be falling ill. However, he did not ask her, as to what was disturbing her.

The couple had sent a message earlier on, to their friends and relatives in Juba that they were arriving on that Saturday. Consequently, there were several people that were waiting for them at the bus station, when they got to Juba. Everyone was very happy, to see Omal and Ader, for the first time as husband and wife.

"Congratulations, to both of you," said one of Omal's friends, called Olanya. "You have, at last made it traditionally and at the alter, haven't you? You look so wonderful together. Otherwise, how are you both doing?"

"We are fine, thanks," replied the couple, simultaneously.

"Omal, how were your parents and relatives, while you were leaving them, this morning?" asked Okwera, one of Omal's cousins.

"They were all doing well," replied Omal, "but were kind of sad, to see us leave, especially my mother."

"Hey, our new bride," said Oketta, one of Omal's relatives, "why are you so quiet? Please tell us about home, from your point of view."

"My husband has told you everything," softly said Ader, who did not then feel like talking because she was quite exhausted, "and therefore, I have nothing left to tell you."

"I think that you are a little shy, to talk to us," said Olanya, "but we will soon teach you how to talk like one of us."

"Let us please take the tired couple home," said Arop, another one of Omal's friends, "otherwise, we'll continue to chat here until morning. I know how crazy, we all like to talk to each other, whenever we get together."

The friends and relatives, then helped the couple with the luggage.

As soon as the couple and the friends and relatives, who were helping them with their luggage, got to the once upon a time was only Omal's house, Ader went out, to fetch some water and thereafter begun making some tea. The group chatted about a lot of things that had happened in Juba, while Omal and his wife were away. They joyfully laughed, as they were taking tea and trying hard to engage Ader into their conversation but she was diffident. Omal's friends and relatives did not stay long, after they had finished taking tea, because they were quite aware that Omal and Ader were newly wed.

After all the relatives and friends had gone that night, Omal made a move, to be intimate with his wife. However, Ader declined but did not give her husband any reason. Omal gently tried to persuade his wife, "This is really our first night in our own house and I do not know why, you are letting me down quite thoughtlessly."

"How many first times, are we going to have, my dear husband?" Ader asked reluctantly. "Our wedding night was our first time together but when we got to your parents' home, you said it was another first time and yet today, according to you, is supposed to be another first time. However, I am not trying to be rude to you. It is just that I am quite fatigued and not feeling quite well."

"The last sentence, should have been your only reply, to my request," disappointingly said Omal. I saw you, while you were sleeping most of the way here but I did not know, what was happening to you. Anyway, I am going to try to being the gentleman that I have always been, when it comes to dealing with you and hope that I would succeed but if I fail, I do not know what I am going to do to you at dawn."

"I have faith in your understanding and self-control and that is why, I dearly love you," said Ader, as she was then feeling quite relieved at the knowledge that her husband was not really angry with her.

"Don't be silly and take me for granted," Omal playfully warned his wife, as he begun to fondly holding her. "I did not promise that I would not misbehave tonight."

"I do not need, a promise from you," stubbornly said Ader. "I just trust you because I know that you are my loving and very understanding husband and that is why, I adore you."

"Your words, are making me to begin feeling some relief already," happily said Omal. "Ader, you really have an easy access into my heart."

"You too have, into mine," joyfully said Ader, "and that is why, I indelibly love you."

"I am really sometimes, not quite sure about that" jokingly said Omal, "because you are very stubborn most of the time, whenever you do not like something."

"Whatever you are trying to say, will not let me relent to you tonight," calmly said Ader. "Omal, I am very exhausted from the journey and I am desperately needing a good night sleep."

"Enjoy your sleep, my darling," understandably said Omal. "I love you."

"Thanks, for your understanding, my love," gratefully said Ader. "Have sweet dreams."

The couple then had a restful sleep because Omal was also a little tired from the journey.

Ader got up early, on the following morning and was feeling quite refreshed, from the good night sleep that she had enjoyed. She therefore, fetched some water and made breakfast. Afterwards, she did all the other basic house chores and then began to rearrange everything in the house. She immaculately cleaned the living room because she was aware that most of their friends and relatives, would be visiting them that day. Omal helped his wife a lot, as she was rearranging things around the house. He was quite happy, to see his former simple house, transformed into a loving home.

"I have never thought that this house could look this magnificent," he gladly told his wife. "Ader, you are the light of my life and it is your radiant presence that has changed this house into a loving home."

"Not at all but it is the way we love each other that has changed the house," lovingly said Ader. "Omal, you too are, the light of my life. You know what, I grew up in a happy and loving home but in my heart I was always then feeling as if, something very important was missing and I now I know that the missing piece in my heart then was you."

"The very first time that I saw you, Ader, I automatically knew that you are the missing piece in my heart," Omal delightfully assured his wife, "and that was why, I made a fool of myself by arduously pursuing you like a mad man because I was indubitably convinced in my heart that God has predestined us, to belong with each other."

"Indeed, ours is a match made in heaven," Ader agreed joyfully, "and is indefeasible. Thank you, so much for enabling me to realize that you are my soul mate. Omal, I dearly love you."

"I love you too, Ader," happily said Omal. "Your words are setting me on fire right now."

"Please tell me how I should extinguish the fire, before it could get out of hand?" requested Ader humourously.

"There is only one way," lovingly replied Omal, "and it is only you, who know it."

"Can we please stop behaving like children," alertly said Ader. "We have a long day before us. Many people will be visiting us today and therefore, I need to go to the market to buy the necessary food, to entertain our visitors."

"Sweetheart, whenever I started to confab with you, I forget completely that the rest of the world exist," Omal candidly assured his wife. "However, I will go with you to the market."

"I want you to stay home," suggested Ader.

"No," refused Omal with such determination. "I do not want you, to carry the stuff from the market alone because it would be very heavy. Darling, I really want to help you."

Ader, who could not refuse such a generous offer, opted to go with her husband to the market.

After the couple had returned from the market, Ader busied herself by cooking variety of food and setting everything ready. Omal wanted so much, to help his wife in whatever she was doing but she would not allow him. However, from time to time he was contriving, to engage his wife into a loving conversation but she avoided him because she knew that such conversation, would delay her from achieving her goal for the day, entertaining the visitors. By mid afternoon, Ader had finished cooking all the meals for the day. She thereafter, took shower and changed into a beautiful outfit. Omal bought some of the local brews and the couple was ready for the day. However, they did not go to church that Sunday because they thought that if they were to go they would not be able, to prepare, welcome and entertain the visitors.

Many friends and relatives of the couple did come that Sunday, to congratulate them for their wedding. They spent the day eating, drinking, chatting, as they were trying to catch up on the news about the marriage and also the general news about life in the village.

"We are very proud about, what you have done concerning your honeymoon," said Oketta. "You know what, we have heard about the way that our elders were so disappointed with you and grumbled a lot about your honeymoon but we have really commended you, Omal, for your bravery, in standing up for what you were needing to do. I hope that you have enjoyed your honeymoon?"

"Very much," joyfully said Omal, with a delightful smile, "but it was far too short. Some of my relatives bitterly blamed me, for breaking the traditional custom. Anyway, someone has to break it, for others to be free and I am glad that I was the one."

The rest of the people burst into laughter because they understood exactly how the elders could be very angry and bitterly complain about, the things that do not belong to the Acoli culture and tradition.

"However, how did they receive you home, after your honeymoon?" asked Okwera.

"Surprisingly, ceremoniously," joyfully replied Omal. "The elders had then seemed like, they had forgotten about their grumpiness on me, as soon as we arrived home. Initially, I thought that we would be met by angry mob, who would insult, especially me, for breaking the custom but instead, there was a celebration such as, I have never anticipated and both of us felt really good."

"I hope that the elders have at last understood, the meaning of the thing called honeymoon," said Olanya, "for most of us would be having that once we are married."

"The elders will still complain and blame Omal, as the ringleader," said one of Omal's relatives, called Anywar, "because he was the first person, to dare them but eventually, when more and more couples went out for their honeymoon, the elders will give up their whining and accept it as a new reality."

"I hope so," doubtfully said Omal. "The Acoli people very much, resist changes to culture and tradition, more than any other tribe. We are very proud people, you know."

"With you, as our Chief in the future," said one of Omal's friends, called Olobbo, "there would be more accommodating changes, to the ways we would be doing things because you are, the first person to dare the elders and we are very happy to have you, as our future leader."

"I might change my mind and refuse any alteration to our custom, when I become the Chief," jokingly said Omal. "You know how power corrupts people, don't you?"

Everyone burst into a mocking laughter because they were aware that Omal did not mean anything he was saying.

"How could we respect you then, when you are the first person, who had started breaking the custom," said Oketta in a very funny way, as everyone was still laughing at Omal's contradicting statement.

"I am quite sure that all of you are aware that I was only joking, aren't you?" carelessly said Omal.

"Yes, we have understood very well that you were only joking," answered Olanya. "But you still sounded funny because you have contradicted yourself."

On the other hand, the female visitors conversed with Ader, as they were asking her lots of questions about her marriage. Ader told them about, the day when her dowry was paid, the wedding at Palotaka Church, a bit about Upper Talanga, the ceremonious welcome she and her husband were accorded after their honeymoon, the wonderful relationship she had had with her in-laws and the warm reception that the relatives of Omal had offer to her in general.

The female and male visitors were very happy for Ader and Omal and wished them, a long happy life together. As the evening was progressing, some of the visitors started dancing while others, who were only interested in the news about home, confabulated until the end of their visit. Some of the visitors were quite drunk, as they were leaving.

After all the visitors had left, Omal helped his wife, as she was cleaning and washing up the dishes, something that was unheard of, in most if not all marriages in Juba. Ader did not want her husband to do the chores but he persistently insisted that he would like to help her. Thereafter, the couple bathed together and then went to bed. Omal, who had been anxiously longing to be intimate with his wife since the previous night, wanted that night to be a special one and was quite ready for an incredibly romantic moment with her. Ader also wanted to prove to her husband that she was no longer nervous as on her wedding night but was then quite a matured wife. Consequently, she put on a beautiful nightdress, boldly walked to her husband, who was already sitting on the bed and begun looking him straight into his eyes, as she was lovingly sitting on his lap. Omal was extremely overwhelmed with joy to see, the great strength of character in his wife that night and the astonishing change in her behaviour, coupled with her absolute beauty.

"Wow, Ader, my love, you are looking very beautiful, like a queen from the fairy land!" he delightfully reassured her, as he was fondly caressing her, "and indeed, you are my lovely queen."

Without saying a word, Ader begun to passionately kissing her husband. Omal was so astounded that he for a while thought that he was simply hallucinating because since they got married, Ader had never initiated even a kiss.

Consequently, after the long and very electrifying kiss, Omal joyfully told to his wife, "Ah, my beloved Ader, you have taken away my breath and I seem not to be thinking straight, right now. However, what has really triggered, all the changes for the better in you, tonight?"

"You, you have been on the heat for me, since last night, haven't you?" Ader honestly and sensually answered, as she was still flirting with her husband. "I have been aware about, how you were quite disturbed in your sleep last night and how you have been needing to be with me, since this morning. Right now, I immensely want to show you that I am also intimately starving to be with you because I am feeling that I have excellently learnt from you, the art of how to be romantic and therefore, I would like to experience with you, the highest climax of pleasure, tonight. Furthermore, I would like that our first night together in our own house should be, the most memorable one that none of us will ever forget."

Omal went wild with excitement, at the knowledge that his bride has finally matured into the kind of wife that he had wished that she should become, ever since they got married. "Ader, my love, you are sounding like a fantasy and good enough to be eaten for food," he lovingly assured his wife with such deep love in his voice, as his whole being was stirring up with such a consuming desire to be with her. "Oh, my love, I have been longing for such a moment like this with you, ever since our honeymoon but never got one. Ader! Your love is burning me up!"

The couple then engaged in an absolute moment of ecstasy, unlike any other that they had experienced before. Omal was extremely excited and thrilled to be with his wife that night because she was very participative, inviting, welcoming, submitting, receptive and satisfying. Ader also experienced the highest realm of pleasure, unlike any other that she had felt, ever since she got married.

A little while after, the couple's steaming night game, Ader decided to break the news about her pregnancy to her husband.

"I have something very important to tell you, before we could sleep tonight," she softly whispered to her husband.

"Please darling, could you kindly tell me, tomorrow?" said Omal, who did not want to listen to anything else because of the deep and fulfilling pleasure that he had just experienced with his wife.

"It is very important that you should know about it tonight," stubbornly insisted his wife.

"You are sounding quite serious, aren't you darling?" said Omal, as he was a little surprised but equally curious to hearing the important news that his wife was wanting to telling him.

"What is it then dear?" anxiously asked Omal because he was a little concerned. "I hope that what you about to tell me is not something bad, which could instantly ruin the way that I am feeling right now."

"Hmm," amusingly sighed Ader. "Why would I want to ruin, such a wonderful moment? Do you think that I am oblivious of it? Omal, I just want you to know tonight that I am already pregnant and therefore, we are soon going to be young parents."

Omal jumped out of the bed with such excitement, "What!" he shockingly exclaimed, "but why did you not tell me the news, before we could made love? I was too excited, as we were, you know, because I did not know that you were pregnant. However, I hope that you are ok."

"Don't be silly, I am very fine," replied his wife, as she was laughing because she was quite amused about, her husband's immature reaction to the news of her pregnancy. "Hey Omal, you have been quite wild ever since that day in Talanga, when I rescued the little boy from his violent father and each time that we have been making love since then, you have been quite, well, although tonight, you were beyond anything anyone could describe."

"Beloved, tonight was unique because you also participated effectively," Omal honestly told his wife. "Ader, this is the only night that we have both made love to each other, otherwise I was the only one who have been making love to you, ever since we got married."

"Now you know why, don't you?" joyfully said Ader. "Recently, I have started having a strong desire to be with you and I long for you a lot, especially whenever you are not near me."

"Is that right?" curiously but joyfully said Omal. "And why have you kept your feelings secret from me? Ader, from now onwards, could we please have the same level of passion, whenever we are making love, like the one, we both have experienced tonight or even better?" Omal beseechingly requested his wife. "I will never again accept anything less from you because I have now known that you could give me more."

Ader simply giggled because to her, Omal was sounding quite funny. On the other hand, Omal could not contain himself out of excitement and consequently, lit the lamp and told his wife to stand up so that he could properly look at her. Ader did stand up and her husband was so surprised, to see all the early evident changes in her. However, Omal wondered, why he had been unable to notice the signs of pregnancy on his wife, until she had told him. "How could I be so blind?" he regrettably said. "A husband should be the first person to know, when his wife has conceived, before she could even tell him. How could I be so naïve? I have always thought that I was already a grown up man but now I know that I have a lot yet to learn. However, my beloved, there have been lots of indications on you, which were somehow suggesting to me that you could possibly be pregnant but I foolishly refused to believe them because I have been selfishly needing you all to myself and hoping that it should be a while before you could conceived."

"I couldn't have dodged becoming pregnant, given what took place between us but especially the frequency during our honeymoon, could I?" laughingly said Ader. "Omal, you did not give me any space, to avoid becoming pregnant but exhausted me to the point that I was feeling like escaping away from you."

"Now that is, an absolute exaggeration!" excitedly exclaimed Omal. "Sweetheart, your nervousness with me, especially on our wedding night and the few days after, was the one that was making you felt that I was wild with you but in reality, I was, according to me at least, quite gentle with you all the time. However, I wished that I could know the exact day, when I got you pregnant."

"I wouldn't be surprise, if it took place on our wedding night," happily said Ader. "I will never forget that night, due to all the mysterious experiences that I had had with you for the first time."

"It was indeed incredible, no doubt," confirmed Omal. "I am still finding it hard, to describe that adventurous night. Sweetheart, I definitely took you with me, beyond the heaven of my imagination."

Ader continued to laugh at her husband, without saying anything anymore because she thought that he had overreacted, to the news of her pregnancy. Omal then tenderly begun holding his wife into his arms and called her his baby. The wonderful news, about his wife's pregnancy did, make him too happy to sleep. He went on sweetly talking to her, as he was reminding her about, all the wonderful experiences that had been taking place between them, ever since they got married and she responded to him likewise. Love, peace, and happiness filled their hearts with joy and coupled with the knowledge that they were soon going to be young parents, sparked another moment of incredible passion, before they could eventually fall asleep.

Chapter Nineteen
The Joyful Expectant Couple

Omal was deeply touched by his wife's pregnancy that he adoringly admired her even, more than he had done before. He found it hard, to take his eyes away from Ader whenever they were together and excitedly made love with her because she was then also enjoying being with him. Furthermore, Omal was quite fascinated, by the early evident changes in his wife's body and wished that he could know how she was feeling within. Omal wondered, as to how the simple union between him and his wife during their lovely honeymoon could have started a new heartbeat and created life. He therefore, was hopefully looking forward into the future with such joy, for soon becoming a young father. On the other hand, Ader was quite delighted, to be pregnant so fast. Ader's thought, about soon becoming a mother, filled her heart with joyful hope for a wonderful future. The couple was deeply bonded, beyond understanding.

When Omal sent the news home that he and his wife were expecting a baby, his parents and all his relatives were so happy but his relatives were rather surprised because, they had not seen any sign of pregnancy on Ader, when she was with them in the village. Omal's mother, on the other hand, was the only person, who was not surprised by the news because she had already noticed some early signs of pregnancy on her daughter-in-law, before she left the village. She told her husband, after her son and his wife had returned to Juba, about her speculation. However, the Chief advised his wife, not to tell anyone yet, until Omal officially announced the news. Consequently, although the royal couple was aware that their daughter-in-law was already expecting a baby, they laid low until Omal wrote to them. Omal's mother was extremely happy, for being able to eventually live out her joy, openly. The Chief was also overwhelmed with joy but did not express it outwardly. He praised Ader in his heart, for being the most beautiful, pure, loyal, humble, loving and fertile wife to his beloved son.

Ader was so lucky, to have conceived so quickly because in a marriage in which so much was paid for the dowry, had she taken a long time to conceive, she would have been deemed as a barren woman and a curse to Omal's family. It would have been worst in her case, since she was married to the only heir of the family. The news about Ader's pregnancy therefore, brought so much joy to both sides of the families and Ader's mother was, the happiest mother alive.

On the day that Omal and his wife had gone back to work after their long holiday, their friends were quite happy to see them together, for the first time as a couple. On Ader's side, as soon as she got to the office, her former colleagues warmly welcomed her.

"You are very radiant," one of the ladies commented, as she was admiring Ader. "What has your husband done to you that is making you to glow this way?"

None of the women had then realized that Ader was already pregnant.

"He has done, nothing extraordinary," joyfully replied Ader, as she was smiling and hugging her friends.

"Can you now see, what a happy marriage can do to a woman?" pointed out the oldest lady among them, to the younger ones, who were not yet married. "I wished that all of you should follow in the footstep of our sister, Ader, so that you might all have, happy life in the future."

Ader then thanked and wished her friends a good day, before she could go to report to her boss.

Ader got to her office, before the Minister came in that morning. The lady, who had been working in Ader's place while she was away, handed over everything to her, before she could leave the office. As soon as the Minister got into the office, he was overwhelmed with joy to see Ader. "Oh Ader, am I so happy, to see you back," he joyfully said, as he was walking towards Ader, with a broad smile on his face. "Welcome back, to our world of work. I must assure you that your husband is a very lucky man, to have married a brilliant and beautiful lady like you."

"Thank you for your compliments, sir," humbly said Ader, as she was smiling while she was happily shaking hands with her boss. "You are very kind, for saying such wonderful things about me."

"I would also like you to know that since you were away, nothing was the same in this office, just like the first time when you went home," the minister enthusiastically told Ader. "I have been falling behind, in everything that I have been doing, due to lack of proper support in the office."

"I am sorry for the inconvenience that you have been experiencing while I was away," sympathetically said Ader, as she was internally feeling so adulated because of what her boss was telling her. "I have also been missing you and my work sometimes, while I was away. You are, a wonderful boss to me."

"Oh, before I forget," delightfully said the Minister, "I have something very little in my office that I would like to give you." He therefore, quickly went to his office and came back with a rather large box of beautiful China sets, as his wedding present for Ader.

"Sir, I do not have a proper word with which, I would like to express my gratitude to you, for your generosity." said Ader, with tears of joy, which was beginning to form into her eyes, as she was gratefully receiving the wonderful gift, from the hands of her boss.

"I am glad, that you like them," happily said the minister. "You deserve, a lot more than that. You, have made my life in the office very easy over the years that I have been working with you. Ader, you are indeed born, to be a secretary and the best one too. I sincerely wished you, a wonderful marriage."

"Thank you very much for everything, sir," gratefully said Ader to her boss.

After the minister had gone back to his office, Ader started working on some of the most urgent reports and finished them all by the end of the day.

On the other hand, Omal was also warmly welcome by his colleagues. They congratulated him so much, for being able to succeed to marrying Ader.

One of his friends therefore, told him that "You are such a hero, man, because of the way that you have indefatigably pursued that wonderful girl until, you have vanquished her heart and married her. I am very proud of you."

"Thanks for your compliment," replied Omal, as he was indeed feeling like a hero. "I am glad to know that you are aware about how much I have suffered, in order to win my wife's heart."

"Man, you are quite changed," commented one of his friends, called Odiyya. "You look so full of life and happier than before you were married. What is your wife doing to you?"

"She lovingly gives me all that I need in this life and much more," Omal proudly replied.

"That is, not a secret at all," said another colleague, called Lony. "It was always obvious that your wife is a good girl and that was why some of us had tried to date her but failed miserably."

Omal was very delighted, to hear the wonderful things that his colleagues were saying about his wife. "Well, thank you all very much, for making me feel like a hero," he delightfully said to them. "I pray that all of you should some day in the future, be able to get good wives, who would be like my mine."

"May your prayer for us come true," said another of his friends, called Ojok. "As for you, I think that you deserved your wife because you are not a quitter, like most of us."

They all burst into laughter and then one of them called, Opoka asked Omal, "What should I do, in order to win the heart of the girl that I love so much, when she is not really caring about me?"

"Opoka, I do not have, a professional answer to your question," humbly replied Omal, "but I will give you an answer, based on my personal experience. In order for you to win a girl, you must first of all be yourself, that is, do not pretend to be someone you are not. You must learn to patiently wait for her response, without the anxiety for easily giving up because a girl wants to know, whether you are serious about being in love with her or not. Lastly, be loving, trustworthy and understanding, at all times."

"Oh boy, you are more intelligent than most of the older men from whom, I have sought for an accurate answer, to the same question that I have asked you," Opoka gratefully said. "Man, you should be giving some lectures in the University, about dating because you know how to explain things very accurately."

The rest of Omal's friends agreed, with what Opoka had suggested. They then thanked Omal, for his invaluable advice, shook hands and went about their works.

Omal had, a lot of work to do in his department since, he had been away for two months. There were some documents, which were pending because his signature was needed in them. He therefore worked hard as he was trying to clear most of them, before the end of the day. Therefore, he even forgot about lunch. Ader patiently waited for her husband, so that they could go out together for lunch but in vain. She consequently, went to his office to find out what he was doing. When she got to her husband's office door, she quietly stood there as she was amusingly smiling at, how lost he was in his work. After a few minutes, of watching her husband in silence, she decided to interrupt him.

"Hey!" she softly called out, "don't you want to leave some of the work, until after lunch? Let us go out and have something to eat."

Omal lovingly looked at his wife, sweetly smiled and gently asked her, "Darling, how long have you been standing there? I have even forgotten that it is already time for lunch. There is a lot of work for me to do but I can continue after lunch. Thank you so much, for coming over."

They then went to Nyakuron for lunch.

A few months, after most of the people had realized that Ader was already pregnant, some of them were happy especially her close friends and relatives but others were saying that she might have conceived before her wedding. Some of the bad people started gossiping and saying all kinds of derogative things about Ader but none of what they were saying ever bothered Ader and Omal, who truthfully knew that they had never had sex before marriage. Many people had always been saying that Ader was beautiful ever since she was a little girl but with the pregnancy, she became more beautiful than ever and her skin radiantly glowed. Consequently, Omal admired and delighted a lot to be with his wonderful wife. There is something mysterious about being erotic with a pregnant woman that most husband loves the experience and so was Omal.

One evening, Omal made a joke to his wife, as they were conversing, "Ader, you are becoming more and more beautiful, each passing day. Had you been this resplendent, when we were still dating, I would have definitely made love to you, against your will."

Ader playfully pushed her husband away and mockingly told him, "You know very well that you couldn't have done that to me. I was too strong for you. What a wimp!"

"I know that you are not meaning what you have just said," Omal playfully told his wife, as he was childishly making funny faces to her. "Ader, my love, have you forgotten the evening, when you wept in my grip like a baby, begged me to kindly forgive and spare you? You know very well that I really did make your life quite uncomfortable, whenever we were alone, don't you?"

"Please do not, remind me about that horrible evening, you silly husband," said Ader, as she begun to chase her husband about and eventually engaged into childish play, until both of them were quite tired. "I have never imagined that marriage could be this gratifying," joyfully said Ader, as she was exhaustively trying to sit down and catch her breath.

"I have known, right from the very first time that I saw and fell in love with you that when I succeed to marry you, our life together would be a lot of fun," Omal delightfully told his wife, as he was happily sitting down beside her, "and that was why, I have laboured indefatigably to win your stubborn heart and patiently waited for you to fall in love with me, my sweet and beloved wife. Ader, you are my treasure, best friend, joy, happiness and restful peace that I daily need in my life and I truly love and adore you."

"How romantic!" his wife gladly said, "You too are my loving husband and best friend."

"Darling, you are such a blessing in my life," Omal adoringly reassured his wife.

A day never passed by, without the couple lovingly playing and teasing each other. Omal sung a lot of love songs to his wife who felt so wonderful, as she was attentively listening to the lyrics of her beloved husband's songs. Each new day, Omal and Ader felt, as if they were falling in love with each other for the first time and fell deeper and deeper in love with each other. The couple was favourably blessed, with the kind of relationship that only a few chosen people had experienced in their lifetime. One of their neighbours, an old gentleman, one time commented that seeing Omal and Ader in love made him felt young again. He therefore was wishing that there were more couples that were living in such deep love as Omal and Ader.

The couple continued to deeply fall in love, as they were getting to know each other better and better. As the pregnancy was progressing and the fetus begun kicking, they even bonded more. Omal would place his hand on Ader's abdomen to feel the baby and as soon as it began to kick, he would jump up with such joy and excitement. Ader delightfully enjoyed, watching her husband behaving like a little boy and laughed at him with tears. She grew bigger everyday but did not have any difficulty with her pregnancy because her husband was giving her a lot of support in the house. Omal spent, most of his time with his beloved wife, unlike most his colleagues who were spending their time at the *Andaya* (local brewing place, where people went for drinking). Some days, whenever the sun was very hot, Omal would go to the market to buy food for his wife because he did not want her to be scorched by the heat of the blazing sun.

Omal and Ader became, the envy of some of their neighbours who were saying that they had never seen a situation in which, a man went to the market while his wife was idly staying at home. Some of the men even went on to say that pregnancy was not a disease, for any woman to be treated with such great respect and consequently thought that Ader might have given Omal some love portion. Most of the men in the southern Sudan took it that a woman must work hard even when she was pregnant because pregnancy was part of a woman's life. A lot of men said, all kinds of negative things to Omal, so as to distract his attention from his wife but they failed miserably because he would not accept any of their diabolical advice. Omal thought about his wife as the most precious gift that God had ever given to him. Consequently, most of his old friends abandoned him because they could not understand how, a man, like Omal, could absolutely commit himself to his wife. Omal wasn't bothered at all by his friends' desertion because he was very happy about his life with his wonderful wife. He therefore, convinced himself that there was no point for him to miss the friends that he had never enjoyed their company in the way that he was then enjoying his wife's.

Chapter Twenty
The Births of the Boys

As Ader's pregnancy was progressing towards the last trimester, she became very tired but her husband was very supportive and sympathetic towards her. Omal was then wishing that there could have been any possibility for him, to share the weight of the baby that his wife was carrying in her womb. When Ader became extremely exhausted, which could evidently be seen from the way that she was handling most of the chores, her husband sent for his mother, to come and help his beloved wife.

Omal's mother was very pleased, to receive her son's request for her to go to Juba. She completed her farm work very fast, with the help of the women from the homestead and prepared a sack of maize (corn), half a sack of sesame, sack of groundnuts (peanuts), big boxes of smoked antelope and gazelle meat and half sack of beans, for the provision of her daughter-in-law, after she had given birth. The excitement in her heart, could be seen from the ways that she carried out her routine chores. She blessed the name of the Lord, for giving her son a good wife who was everything that he had expected in a wife and above all a fertile woman. Omal's mother frequently prayed that Ader had a not very painful labour but easily give birth to a healthy baby. When her preparations to go to Juba were done, she then called over the women in the homestead for a little get together and asked for their blessings, so that she could take their blessings with her to Juba, for the welfare of her son and his wife. The women were all very happy and willingly gave their blessings. On the other hand, the Chief was quite delighted, to see such excitement and joy in his wife. He therefore, wished her a good stay in Juba. Omal's mother then travel to Juba, with such joy and peace in her heart.

Omal's mother came to Juba in September, when Ader was about to have her baby and helped her daughter-in-law a lot. They were more of friends than mother-in-law and daughter-in-law. Many people were surprised, to see their tight relationship. Two week's before her due date, Ader took her maternity

174

leave because she was very tired. She prepared everything ready for welcoming her first born because she trusted God and was optimistic that she would have a healthy baby, unlike most families, who did not prepare for the coming of their babies out of the fear that the babies might die at birth or immediately after birth. There is even a saying in Acoli language that *"Pe ingol obeno labong latin,"* which means (do not make a carrier for your baby before it is born because you would be ashamed, if the baby did not make it). The best translation of the Acoli saying in the English equivalent would be, "Do not count your chicken, before they are hatched."

On the night that Ader had gone into labour, her husband was so scared that he was walking up and down, as he was trying to do all that he could, to help alleviate his wife's pain. However, when a woman is in labour, there is nothing anyone could do to ease her pain except, when epidural is administered and so Omal's efforts to soothe his wife's pain was in vain. Ader helplessly groaned, as she was calling out her husband's name. Omal's mother, although concerned, was amused by the way that her son was pacing to and fro. Omal eventually, called a taxi and took his wife to the Regional Hospital. A few hours after they had arrived at the hospital, Ader had her firstborn son and one of the midwives announced the birth to Omal, who was standing outside the maternity ward. In the Sudan and may be in the whole of Africa, husbands are not allowed into the maternity ward. Omal went wild with joy at the knowledge that he was a proud father of a little boy. It was about 1:00 AM on the 15th of September 1985. The boy weighed 4 kg and was a very beautiful baby. Omal thereafter, returned home while his mother remained in the hospital to take care of the baby, as Ader was taking some rest after the delivery.

On the way home from the hospital, Omal was too excited, to realise the hour of the night. He could not even remember, how fast he got home. He sat on the bed and tried to contemplate the mystery of giving birth. He was remembering, how a little while ago his wife was groaning and seemed so helpless and then suddenly, the excruciating pain was replaced by the arrival of a wonderful little human being. He joyfully thought to himself, 'and so from now onwards, I will be a father and my beloved Ader, a mother.' "Unbelievable!" he loudly exclaimed because he could not contain his excitement. Omal eventually, tried to get some sleep but did not have much due, to happiness and excitement. The night was too wonderful for him to sleep because he was aching with the deepest anticipation, to seeing how his newborn son looked like and holding him in his arms.

After Omal had prepared some tea and porridge, very early on the following day, he hastened back to the hospital. As soon as he got there, he anxiously asked his mother, through the window of the maternity ward, "Mom, could you please tell me how my wife is feeling and how the little guy is doing?"

"Your wife is generally fine but still weak from childbirth," his mother joyfully replied. "As for your son, he is doing quite well and is still sleeping at the moment."

"Oh, I thank and praise the name of the Lord my God, for keeping all of them well and healthy!" Omal delightfully exclaimed. Mom, I am so happy that I did not sleep well last night."

It is very wonderful to be a parent, isn't it?" his mother delightfully said and they both happily started laughing. "I will send a nurse to call you, as soon as your wife is awake."

"Oh thank you so much, Mom," joyfully said Omal. "I will be waiting for your message, under that tree," he pointed to, one very large mango tree.

After Ader had woken up, she was so surprised to learn that her husband was outside the maternity ward and wondered, whether he had spent the night in the hospital. Therefore, as soon as one of the nurses had notified Omal that his wife was awake, he immediately rushed to the window, where his wife's bed was situated. "Hallo sweetheart, how are you feeling?" he anxiously asked her, in a shaky but joyful voice.

"I am fine," Ader replied in a weak voice, as she was trying to softly laugh. "Actually, both of us are fine."

"I just can't wait to see you both, especially our little son." enthusiastically said Omal.

"The doctor will be coming in a few minutes' time and I will let you know at once about his decision, concerning our going home." Ader assured her husband.

"Thanks, Dear," excitedly replied Omal. "I will be waiting for your message, under the big tree in front of the maternity ward. Tell one of the nurses, to find me there after the doctor has seen you and our son, ok?"

"Surely," weakly replied Ader.

Omal therefore, waited outside the maternity ward with such anticipation to hear what, the doctor was going to say about his wife's and son's going home. His mother joined him outside, as soon as the doctor entered into the maternity ward for checkup. After the Doctor had examined Ader and her son, he therefore concluded that both of them were in good condition to go home. One of the nurses then went and told Omal after the doctor had left, that it was ok for him to take his wife home. Omal went wild with delight at the news that it was ok for him to take wife and the newborn son home. He at once rushed out to call a taxi and shortly after, joyfully took everyone home. As soon as Omal had seen his little son's handsome face, he was so overwhelmed with joy that he began to laugh like a little boy. Ader and her mother-in-law were both quite amused by Omal's childish behaviour that they also began to laugh.

While at home, Omal's mother took very good care of her daughter-in-law. Omal was very grateful to his mother for all the assistance that she had been rendering to his wife and son since they got home from the hospital. One day therefore, he gratefully told her, "Mom, I really doubted what I could have been able to do, had you not come from the village, to help me to take care of my wife and son."

"Son, what do you think mothers are for?" his mother joyfully asked him. "I am very glad, to be of assistance to you and your wonderful wife. It was such a great fun for me, to see you racing up and down, when your wife was about to have my grandson. I am very happy to see you turn out, to be such a caring, responsible and loving young husband and father. Omal, my dear son, you have truly made me proud, to be your mother."

"Thanks, Mom," delightfully said Omal. "I love you very much and I am proud to be your son."

When it was time for naming the baby, Omal said that there was no any other name better than his own name, Omal. Therefore, the baby was named, after him. The little fellow put on weight very fast for Ader was having a lot of milk in her breast. Omal carried his son all the time, whenever he was at home and spent a lot of time talking to his son, as if the baby could understand whatever he was saying. His mother watched him in silence for quite some time but eventually asked him, "Omal, my dear son, were you taught at school, to talk to an infant?"

"No, Mom," he joyfully replied as he was laughing, "I just love my dear son, who is also like a brother to me and I am looking forward to that day, when he and I would be able to converse with each other."

His mother then realized, how much Omal had been missing to have a brother in his life, since his elder brother had never been there for him. Ader had also been quite amused by the behaviour of her husband, whenever he was talking to their son and she therefore, had been laughing at him a lot too. Omal continued to talk to the baby even more, after he had started smiling.

The loving support that Omal and his mother had given to Ader, after she had had the baby, made her regained strength very fast. One afternoon therefore, Ader humbly approached her mother-in-law and gratefully said, "Thank you ever so much, for everything that you have done for me. You are like, a second mother to me. I am very lucky to have been married, into such a caring and loving family, like yours. I thank God for you and your family everyday. May God bless you always."

"Oh my child, you don't need, to thank me at all," joyfully said her mother-in-law. "You have so graciously, blessed the life of my son. I have never seen him so happy, before he had married you. Remember, you have also given to Omal, a wonderful son. It is rather I, who really need to profoundly thank you, my dear child."

"You are a wonderful mother to me and my husband," gratefully said Ader. "We feel so indebted to you, for all the assistance that you have been giving to us."

"I feel very flattered by all that you have told me, my child," gladly said her mother-in-law. "I was only doing my work, as expected of me." She then held her daughter-in-law's hand and joyfully blessed her.

The old lady stayed, with the couple for two and half months while she was carefully showing to Ader, how she should take care of the baby. Therefore, when Ader was strong enough to take charge of her home, Omal's mother told her son and daughter-in-law that "I have very much enjoyed, my stay with both of you and I would like to return home now that I am aware that my daughter-in-law is able to handle the baby well, notwithstanding her being a new mother."

"My wife and I are very grateful to you, for all the wonderful things that you have done for us," said Omal in, gratitude to his mother. "We would have been, completely lost without you."

"Thank you, for graciously taking care of me and your grandson," gratefully said Ader. "I will greatly miss you but I know that you too have a big home to take care of. May God bless and keep you well, till we meet again."

"My dear children, continue to live in the way that I have seen you live in deep love," firmly said Omal's mother. "Do not allow strangers, to come between you. Take good care of my grandson. Remember, some day, he would be the next Chief of the Chiefdom of Magwi, after Omal. He is born to be, a great person by birth."

"We shall do our very best, Mom," both Omal and his wife simultaneously responded.

The couple bought lots of gifts for Omal's mother and also gave her some money to take home. The old lady was very grateful, to her son and daughter-in-law, for their generosity. She blessed and wished them well, on the day that she was leaving for the village. Both Omal and Ader, were quite sad to see Omal's mother go away because they were so used to her staying with them.

When Omal's mother arrived at home, the people were very happy to see her again, especially her husband. The Chief had been missing his wife a lot because they had never stayed away from each other, in almost forty years of their marriage.

"I think that our son and his wife have treated you very well because you look so young to me, once again," the Chief told his wife, as he was joyfully admiring her.

Omal's mother then told her husband about the great love between her son and his wife and finally concluded, "I have never seen any other couple, in such great love..."

The Chief interrupted her by asking, "Do you want to tell me that I am not a great lover? From whom do you think that Omal has inherited his idea, for being such a lover, as you are trying to tell me?

"I absolutely do not deny that you are a great lover," humbly replied his wife, "but it is just that the way Omal loves his wife is so special and I have no word to describe it."

The Chief then wanted to show his wife that even though he was old, he was still a good lover and so, he warned her to prepare for the wild night game. Omal's mother then felt bad, after she had realized that she had some how hurt her husband's feelings, by what she was trying to tell him, about their son's love for his wife, "I am sorry, for the way I have sounded to you," she contritely apologized. "I really did not mean, to hurt your feelings in any way. I was just trying, to depict to you the way that our son dearly loves his wife."

"I am not angry with you at all," calmly answered the Chief. "I have been missing to being with you a lot, while you were away and that is the reason why, I have reacted to you in the way that I have. I am very sorry, my dear wife."

A few days, after Omal's mother had returned from Juba, she went to visit her in-laws in Licari village. Abongkara and Okeny were very happy to see her and welcomed her warmly. Omal's mother joyfully told them about Ader, the little Omal Jr. and her son. She even mentioned to Abongkara and Okeny her son's behaviour, when Ader was in labour. Ader's parents laughed with tears, at the funny stories about their son-in-law, behaviour. They were therefore, very happy to hear that the young couple and their little boy were doing well. Omal's mother then gave to Ader's parents, the gifts that she had brought from Juba for them and a letter from Ader, before she went back to Magwi.

The letter read:

> Dear Mom and Dad,
>
> I am happy to inform you that I am now a mother to a lovely little boy, called Omal, after his dad. The labour pain was severe but I went through it with some courage. My experience, have made me appreciated my mother even more. I can now understand quite clearly, why she loves us all very dearly. Mom, I love you more than ever now that I have experienced what it is to be a mother. By saying so, I do not want Dad to feel left out because he is still my special and loving dad. I miss you both very much and I would like you to know that my husband loves and cares about me so much. Omal and his mother have taken very good care of me after, I have had our son and their assistance have, enabled me to recover very fast.
>
> God bless you, till we meet again.
>
> I am, your loving daughter,
> Ader

Ader's parents tenderly hugged each other, after they had read their daughter's letter. They were very happy to know that Ader and the baby were doing fine. Abongkara cried for joy because of the wonderful things that Ader had written about her. In Abongkara's mind, Ader was still the little girl that she had given birth to a few years ago and the very knowledge that Ader was then a mother herself, was too much for Abongkara to comprehend. Okeny and his wife profoundly thanked God, for giving to them responsible children, who had all turned out to be quite successful in life.

On the other hand, Omal did not want his wife to look after the baby and do the house chores as well, after his mother had gone back to the village. Therefore, he hired a maid, to help his wife especially, when the maternity leave would be over. The girl's name was called Anyiri. She was a very good person, took proper care of the baby and adequately handled some of the house chores. Both Omal and Ader were very kind to Anyiri, which made her work quite easy. However, some of the couple's jealous neighbours, made it their duties to gossip about Ader, for having a maid, as if she were a white woman. They even asked Anyiri, whenever Ader was not at home, as to whether she was being treated well. Anyiri who was very loyal to Ader and her husband simply told the big-mouthed neighbours that they should mind their own business because Ader was a very loving and caring woman. Consequently, Anyiri became a very good friend of Ader that those who did not know them that well, thought that they were related.

After the maternity leave, Ader returned to work and as it was then the rule in southern Sudan, for working mothers who are having infants, to work only until midday, Ader was very happy to return home early everyday in order to be with her dear son. She got so involved with her baby that she did not pay much attention to her husband, anymore. Omal only kissed his wife a few times, since his mother had gone back to the village. He was also excited for being a new father but as the months were going by, he began to miss being intimate with his wife and one night humbly requested her, "Would you mind, if we resume, you know? I really miss being with you so much and cannot bear any longer, the feelings of being without you anymore."

"I am not so sure whether it would be ok for us, to be intimate with each other, since the baby is still quite young," remonstrated Ader. "However, please kindly give me some time to firstly inquire whether it would be ok or not from one of my friends who is a nurse."

"Could you do that tomorrow, if possible, my dear?" desperately pleaded Omal. "Ader, I am very anxious, to be with you once again. It has been too long, since we last had a romantic moment."

Ader consequently, asked the nurse about the issue and was told that it would be ok for her to be with her husband, so long as they practiced safe sex.

When the couple eventually, resumed marital relationship, Ader did not take any precautionary measure, to protect herself from becoming pregnant because she was assuming that since she was still breastfeeding her baby, she would not get pregnant. However, Ader's notion was absolutely wrong because she immediately conceived her second baby. When she missed her period for the first time, she ignored it and thought that might be all nursing mothers were missing their periods once in a while. However by the second month, Ader was indubitably convinced that she was pregnant once again and became so ashamed of herself because her firstborn was only five months old. Consequently therefore, she did not know what to do and became so emotional that she did not even want to share the bed with her husband anymore. Omal somehow understood why his wife was feeling that low because he was aware about the way, some of his terrible neighbours were tattling about other people. He therefore, avoided all the situations that could lead him into confrontation with his wife.

The second pregnancy gradually began to erode, the couple's wonderful relationship. Life became very hard for Omal, who did not know what to do with his wife's mood. Eventually, however, Omal made his wife came to her senses, when he one day boldly confronted and told her, "Whatever you are doing to me now cannot reverse, what had already happened. When water or oil spills on the ground, you cannot get it back into a container. Let me assure you, my dear wife, that I will always be available to assist you. Besides, you are not the first woman to conceive, when the other baby is still very small. Please know that I understand the situation and I am here for you at all times. What you are doing to me is not fair at all because you are really hurting me by your moods, especially since you have refused to even share the bed with me. You are tormenting me as if, I am not your husband. Ader, I do not want to quarrel with you at all but I desperately need you, as my wife."

Ader realised then that whatever she was doing to her husband, was not right. She began to cry and apologized to him, "I did not comprehend that I was hurting you that much by some of my activities. It is just that I am so ashamed of myself, especially in public. Please forgive me. Omal, I am sorry, for every bad thing that I have been doing to you lately."

"That is the voice of the wife that I have married," delightfully stated Omal. "Welcome back, my love! Ader, ever since you have discovered that you are pregnant again, you have been so downright rude and strange that I almost thought that you are not the same loving Ader that I have married."

From then onward, Ader resumed normal relationship with her husband and coped well.

Ader's fearful anticipation about, the gossip and malice against her by some of her tattling neighbours, did become a reality, when they found out that she was pregnant again. They viciously maligned her that she loved sex so much and did not care about her infant boy. Ader felt so offended and cried most of the time but her husband advised her over and over again to cheer up and tell the women whenever they had insulted her that she did not get pregnant in the street. Eventually, Ader accepted her husband's advice and became proud of her pregnancy. Ader's confidence and the way that her husband loved and treated her with so much respect silenced her tormentors. She then stopped breastfeeding her son and instead, put him on the formula. The change did not cause any problem because the boy continued to healthily growing up. Omal made it a point for him, to go with his wife to work and also come back home together, so as to shield her from the vicious insults by some of his female flibbertigibbets, who had made it their duties, to hurl insults at the other women, who had babies frequently.

As the second pregnancy was progressing, Ader put on a lot of weight and thought that she was going to have a baby girl. Therefore, one evening, as she was confabulating with her husband, she joyfully told him, "Omal, I think that I am going to have a baby girl this time because I have gained so much weight and the way that I am feeling this time, is quite different from the first one."

"I completely disagree with you, dear darling," refuted her husband, as he was happily smiling and admiring her beauty. "I know in my heart that you are carrying another boy. Sweetheart, I will make you have four boys, before you could have a girl."

"And yet you have been pretending all along that you did not plan for this one, when you could even precisely predict the sex of the baby before it is born," his wife provocatively told him. "Omal, I am now convinced that you knew exactly what you were up to, whenever we were making love. I should have known better and refused you to be anywhere near me, until our son was a year old."

"Ader, I am truly sorry," contritely said her husband. "I did not mean what I was telling you in the way that you are trying to make it look. I was only joking with you and trying to put some sense of humour into our conversation. Do you mean to tell me that if my prediction were to come true after you have delivered the baby that you would then hate me for deliberately getting you pregnant in the first place? Ader dear, at the moment that you conceived, we were simply enjoying each other's love, like any other couple would but then it happened that you were ovulating and consequently got pregnant. You are a very fertile woman, this I know because I am completely sure that you did conceive our first son on our wedding night, given his birthday."

"You may probably be right on that one but once I have had this baby, I will never be intimate with you for two years," sadly said Ader, with such determination.

"Ader, are you trying to threaten me or you are simply joking?" curiously asked Omal, as he was beginning to lose his temper with his wife for the first time, since they got married.

"Joking? Absolutely not," assertively said Ader. "I mean exactly, what I have told you."

"Ader, you have truly provoked my anger today," Omal frustratingly told his wife. "You know very well that I am stronger than you and if you should decide indeed to carry out your sordid plan in the future, I would first forcibly make love to you in the wildest way and then later on involve the elders to settle the issue. I would consequently be delighted, to hear what you would have to tell the elders in your defense, you who still most of the time, find it hard to look at my face, after some moments, whenever we have passionately made love. I pray and hope that you would then have the courage to discuss such private matter, with the elders. Furthermore, according to our tradition, and may be other tribes' too, it is sin for a woman, to refuse to have marital relationship with her husband, without any proper reason, you know."

Ader angrily stared at her husband, as he was speaking but as soon as he had finished to make his points, she then had realized, how horribly her statement had indeed offended him that day and eventually said, "Omal, I have never heard you spoken to me in that tone of voice, ever since I have known you. Not only that, today, you have used very strong language against me and I hate the picture that you have painted with your words against my decision in the future. Dear husband, I am sincerely sorry, for what I have said to you in anger. I would rather be intimate with you, as much as you like and have many children, than face the elders. I love you darling and am truly sorry, for what this pregnancy has let me to become," concluded Ader, while she broke down and began to weep miserably.

Omal was somehow glad, to see the impact of his angry reaction on his wife but equally felt quite compassionate, to seeing her crying. As a result therefore, he apologized and gently comforted her, by fondly rubbing her back and asking her to kindly keep quiet.

Ader did not take her maternity leave, until two days before her due date. On the day that she had gone into labour, the pain did not take a long time, like the first one. Therefore, Omal sent for a good midwife called, Alal, who was living very close to them, to come and attend to Ader because she was just about to deliver the baby. Alal was well versed in her trade and therefore, handled everything professionally. Ader was happy, to have her son at home instead of the hospital, on 10th November 1986.

"Your prediction has come true, hasn't it?" Ader weakly but joyfully asked her husband, after the midwife had gone and he had come into the room to see her and the newborn baby.

"Yes, it has indeed, darling," delightfully replied Omal. "However, I hope that you will forgive and be kind to me now that your wildly raging hormones during the pregnancy, has settled down."

"Get out of here!" jokingly said Ader. "I am quite exhausted and I need some rest."

"I will surely let you rest," Omal lovingly reassured his wife. "I love you and am very proud of you. I just came in here, to see how you are doing and also to welcome the new member of our family," joyfully said Omal, as he was delicately holding his newborn son and admiringly looking at him. "Oh dear, he is as beautiful as our first one. Ader, thank you so much, for being the wonderful wife and mother that you are, in bringing into the world such a handsome boy."

"Thank you, for putting him inside me, in the first place," playfully said Ader, "and most of all for giving me the confidence and support that I needed during my tumultuous pregnancy."

"Thanks dear," smilingly said Omal, as he was carefully giving the baby back to his wife. "Darling, please do get some rest because you deserve it and don't you worry about the baby because I will take proper care of him, when he begins to cry."

"Thank you for being so loving and caring," gratefully said Ader, as she was lying down to get some rest.

Omal was quite delighted to have another boy once again and he therefore, named him *Okene* (meaning, I am alone).

When the news, about Ader having children one after another reached the village, the relatives on both sides of the families were quite concerned that the older child might fall ill since he could not get the full care and attention that he needed from his mother. However, the Chief was very happy and supported his son and his daughter-in-law. He said that his son was an only boy and should have as many children as he could. Both Ader's and Omal's families sent lots of food from the villages for them, so that they would not buy much in Juba.

Chapter Twenty-One
The New Vicinity

After Ader had given birth to her second child, the couple moved away from their tattling neighbours, to Kator where they rented a two-bedroom house, from a young man, called Mori, who was not yet married. Mori was from a tribe, called Bari. He was, a man with an admirable face, muscularly built and a rather quiet man who rarely smiled but whenever he did, his dazzling white teeth beautifully showed out. Unfortunately, he did not seem to have any close relative in Juba. Mori gradually, grew fond of his new tenants that he ate most of his dinners with Omal. He admired a lot, the way Ader and Omal dearly loved each and wished that he would have a life like them with his wife, when he would some day in the future, get married.

One day, Mori courageously asked Omal, "How did you meet and marry your wonderful wife and still capably manage to keep, the relationship so beautiful even after marriage?"

"I did admire my wife from afar, for a very long, long time because at that time, she had made it very hard for just any man, to approach her," Omal honestly, told his friend. "Many young men had their eyes on my wife then and some even attempted wooing her but she turned everyone down, including me. My wife completely ignored me and I suffered a lot of heartaches, as I was struggling to have a chance, to even just date her. However, I persisted in my pursuit for her love, like a fool until, she gave me a chance. Eventually, she fell in love with me, we happily got married and here we are."

"Wow! The summary of your wonderful relationship indeed, sounds like a fairytale," awesomely said Mori, as he was quite overwhelmed by what Omal had told him. "Anyway, what is the secret, for a happy marriage?"

"Faithfulness, trust, care, honesty, respect, understanding, communication, forgiveness and above all love," simply replied Omal.

Mori listened attentively, to what his friend was telling him and eventually confided in Omal, "I am having a girlfriend, who is strongly believing in abstinence from sex until marriage and I am lately thinking about leaving her because I find her too difficult to deal with, when it come to, you know."

"Please do not make such a gross mistake," Omal earnestly warned his friend. "My wife was like that throughout the time while we were still courting each other. I suffered shame and humiliation from her, until we got married. Anyway, look at how happy we are now. Please do not leave your girlfriend because I think that she is an ideal girl for a wife and worth waiting for."

"Thank you very much, for your advice," Mori gratefully told his friend. "Given what you have just told me about you and your wife, I think that I will no longer leave my girlfriend, anymore."

Mori was very grateful to Omal, for all the wonderful insight that he had been giving to him.

The little talk that Mori had had with Omal, created a big impact on him and he therefore changed his wild ways. He began to go out more with his girlfriend because she was then comfortable with him, due the respect that he was giving her. Their relationship blossomed and soon they got engaged. Mori thanked Omal a lot and one time told him, "I did not know how to behave as a gentleman, especially when it comes to dealing with women, before I met you. I have erroneously, always been thinking, that a man must make love to the woman he loves, even before they could get married, which I now know is a very wrong. You are like the brother and father that I have never had in my life."

"You, too, are like a brother to me," Omal joyfully told Mori, in appreciation for his gratitude to him. "We were two boys in my family but my elder brother, left home a long time ago and had gone to live in northern Sudan. He had declined to communicate with just anyone in our family, since he left home. Therefore, I grew up alone among my sisters and did not have any closest friend like you, in my entire life."

"May be that is why, there is such a strong connection between us," gladly confirmed Mori. "Omal, from now onward, you will not only be my tenant but also my brother."

"I am very honoured, by what you have said," delightfully said Omal. "Thank you very much, Mori, my brother."

Many people, who did not know Mori and Omal very well, thought that they were related because of their tight relationship. Mori was then wishing that he could marry a wife, who would some day love him, like Ader was loving Omal. Seeing Ader and Omal in their deep love, made Mori loved life so much and looked forward with such anticipation, to the day when he would marry his fiancée and have a family.

Mori's fiancée was called, Juan, a lady of average height, according to the southern Sudanese height and very slender. She was quite shy around the people that she did not know very well, spoke softly and was gentle in all she was doing. Like the rest of the young people in southern Sudan then, Juan attended the Juba Girls' Secondary School but only got the Sudan School Certificate and later on trained as a clerk. She therefore, was working as a clerk, in the Regional Ministry of Finance. Juan came from a good family. Juan's father took very good care of his family and was a prominent person in his community. Consequently, the people of his community were respecting him a lot.

Juan got to know Ader through her fiancé and grew to like her so much that whenever she came to visit Mori, she would end up spending most of her visit with Ader. There is a weakness in men that women normally could not understand or explain because Mori attempted one evening to make love to Juan against her will, notwithstanding his promise to her that he would not ask her for sex until marriage. They struggled so much in his house but Juan eventually, broke free from him and ran to Ader's house. Part of her blouse was torn in the struggle and she was shamefully crying a lot, as she was trying very hard to tell Ader, about her ordeal with her fiancé. Ader clearly understood everything that Juan was trying to tell her quite well because she had gone through the same situation several times, while she was still dating her husband. While Ader was mending her friend's blouse, she sympathetically told her, "I would like you to cheer up, Juan. How could you go home today, while you are looking like, someone who has come out of a wrestling arena? I know that you are hurting a lot right now but please listen to me, if you want to keep secret, what has happened between you and your fiancé. Put on a brave face and pretend as if, nothing bad had happened to you, so that no one apart from you, Mori and I may know about the incident. Stop crying, wash up your face and put on some lotion. When you get home, do not tell your sisters, not even your mother, about what had happened. Talk to them, as if all is well. You can cry in your bed at night, when no one is watching. Most men are generally weak, especially when they are alone with the women that they love. I don't think that Mori was really meaning to hurt or disrespect you but I think that he just lost his self-control and his animal instinct, took the better part of his brain."

"I will break up the engagement," sobbingly said Juan. "If Mori cannot respect me now when I am not yet married to him, how would he behave to me after I had married him?"

"You will make the biggest mistake of your life, if you leave Mori," Ader honestly assured her friend. "You know what, most of the men are the same. It is easy to deal with the devil that you have known than the one you do not know, by saying so, I mean that you might even meet a worse man than Mori if you were to ditch him. You have known and loved Mori for a long time now, why not give him a second chance?"

Juan was deeply hurt and so she refused, to listen to whatever Ader was trying to tell her. Consequently, as soon as Ader had completed mending her blouse, she left.

Juan did not tell anyone in her family about, what had happened between her and her fiancé because she thought that it was such a shameful thing to talk about. Juan was quiet exceptionally after the incident that her mother became quite concerned about her. She was thinking that Juan was suffering from something but could not guess what it was. Therefore, after Juan's unusually weird mood continued for two more days, her mother got fed up and seriously asked her, "What is troubling you these days, my dear? You don't look well at all and seem to be sad about something, very terrible."

"There is really, nothing wrong with me," Juan lied to her mother. "I am only having headache, which bothers me every day."

Juan's mother did not believe her because her motherly instinct was telling her that something more than headache, was troubling her daughter. Although she had known instinctively that her daughter was disturbed about something very serious, she did not insist that Juan should tell her. Juan tried hard to conceal what was bugging her but almost every member of her family was aware that something was very wrong with her. Since Juan had refused, to tell her mother the truth about her situation, the rest of the family also, never bothered to further ask her.

On the other hand, Mori was so much overcome with shame and guilt that he did not come out of his house, until the following evening. He did look feeble and worn out. When Ader told her husband about, what had happened between Mori and his fiancée, he deeply sighed and sadly said, "You women, you like punishing and making us, men, feel so low about ourselves."

"You called that a punishment, eh?" retorted Ader, "You, men, liked all your brides to be virgins, on your wedding nights but as well want to make love with them, before marriage. I just don't understand, how you men think."

Omal attentively fixed his eyes on his wife, as she was speaking and eventually said, "Whatever you have just said is very true but honestly speaking, when a man really loves a woman so much, it does not matter whether, she is a virgin or not on their wedding …"

"Oh Lord, have mercy!" disappointingly interrupted Ader because she was feeling terribly offended, by what her husband had just said. "Omal, are you implying that my being a virgin on our wedding night, did not mean anything to you at all? You are indirectly telling me that good girls always lost their virginity before they get married, aren't you? Thank you, Omal, for insulting, my morality this deeply!"

"I am truly sorry, my dear wife," confessed Omal, with such a contrite heart. "I do not like, where this conversation is taking us. Ader, my sweetheart, I did not mean, to offend you at all. It is just that the way we men think when it comes to relationship, is very different from the way you, women think. You have seen, how many times, I have broken my promises to you about abstinence, during our courtship, haven't you? However, I am indebted to you for your strong believe in abstinence from sex, throughout our courtship. I will never forget, what I have experienced with you on our wedding night and I will never trade the sweet memory of that adventurous and wonderful night, for anything in this life. Beloved, you have made me, the proudest husband and that is why, I have been falling deeper and deeper in love with you ever since."

Ader meanly stared at her husband and disgustingly shook her head. *Do men value any woman at all or all they think about is satisfying their sexual desires, once they are alone with the women that they claim to love?* a tormenting question, went through Ader's mind.

"Hey, I know that kind of look," interrupted her husband, who was attentively watching the reactions on her face, as she was lost in her painful thoughts. "What, are you trying to analyse quietly?

"It is none of your business," sadly retorted Ader, who was still feeling quite hurt, by her husband's remarks. "Well, I am just trying to have, a mental picture of how men think."

"You will never understand us," playfully said Omal, as he was making funny faces to his wife with the intention, to diffuse the tension that his slip of tongue had built up and was about to erupt between them like an atomic bomb, "just as much as we, men, will never understand you, women."

"Hmmm," deeply and sadly sighed Ader, as she was trying to vent out some of her disgusting tension, that had built up in her chest through her deep sigh. "You, men, are mostly thoughtless and piggish. I wonder why we, women, are wasting our time and energy, in loving you with such commitments." concluded Ader, with a little bit of smile that was breaking on her face.

"You got that right, my dear wife" smilingly agreed Omal, as he was feeling relieved, after noticing the slight smile on his wife's face. "Darling, I am very sorry and I hope that you have completely forgiven me, for saying the terrible things that I have told you today. Would you therefore mind, if I go to talk to Mori right now?"

"Not at all," carelessly replied Ader, as she was shrugging her shoulders, to elaborate her feelings. "Anyway, I have forgiven you. Next time, try to think, before you could tell me such devastating statement."

"I definitely will, my dear wife," joyfully said Omal, as he was already going, to talk to Mori.

When Omal entered Mori's house, he found him lying on the bed and looking very miserable but as soon as he saw Omal, he got up and greeted him. They first talked about other things but eventually Mori told his friend the whole truth about, what had happened between him and his fiancée.

"Juan visited me and we were having a nice time, as we were joyfully talking to each other," he humbly said, "but then I began to kiss her and suddenly, I was so overcome with passion for making love to her that I could not resist my feelings any longer. I tried to make Juan understand but she vehemently refused. I then attempted, to get hold of her by force. She slapped me across my face and pushed me away but I managed to get hold of her again. We then struggled for a while before, she broke free and ran away."

"Did you know that you tore her blouse?" Omal pitifully asked his friend.

"Tore her blouse!" shockingly exclaimed Mori in surprise because he could not recollect everything that he had done to his fiancée. "I am truly sorry, if I have done that. But how will I even tell Juan that I am sorry when she left here yesterday with so much hatred for me in her eyes."

"She really does not hate you but I think that she is disgusted with you because of what you have, attempted to do to her. You better talk to her sooner than later, otherwise, she may decide to leave you, if you delay," Omal candidly advised Mori.

"I am so ashamed about what I have done to Juan that I dare not approach her," Mori regretfully said. "Could you please ask your wife instead, to go and plead to Juan, on my behalf?"

"I will surely ask her to do that. Please take care of yourself," sympathetically said Omal and thereafter, he went back to his house.

Omal told his wife about, what Mori had suggested and she accepted that she would go and attempt to persuade Juan, to reconcile with Mori. That night, Omal wanted to make love to his wife but she flatly refused because she was still feeling quite hurt by what, Omal had told her earlier on.

"Ader, please do not torment me, for talking stupidly to you earlier on," he desperately pleaded with her. "I have never meant, to hurt you at all, my dear wife. I was senselessly carried away by what, had happened between my friend, Mori, and his fiancée. Ader, please, I beseech you, I really need to be with you tonight. Both of us are going to stay awake tonight because I will not allow you to sleep, until you have relented."

Ader kept very quiet, the whole time that Omal was talking to her but said eventually, "Am I your prisoner, tonight?"

"Definitely," responded Omal with such determination, "I will nag at you until morning, unless you, you know."

"You really are a moron," disgustingly said Ader and then she eventually accepted to be with her husband.

Omal was quite delighted and excited, to be with his wife that night.

It was a breezy evening, when Ader went to visit Juan. As soon as Juan saw Ader, she immediately concluded in her heart that Mori might have sent her. However, since Juan liked Ader very much, she did not show her any sign of anger. Juan warmly welcomed Ader, with a cheerful smile. Ader, who was aware that she was sent on a delicate mission, did not tell Juan why she visited her. They talked about recent news in Juba, until Ader decided to return home.

While Juan was escorting Ader on the way therefore, Ader humbly told her, "I have something very important to tell you, Juan."

"And what is preventing you, from telling me then?" answered Juan, rather sarcastically.

"I can see that you have already guessed what I am going to tell you and I hope that you will listen to me, as your dear friend," Ader calmly told Juan. "Mori is really heartbroken and had not eaten anything, since the incident. The man is really ashamed about, what he had tried to do you and would sincerely want, to apologise to you but is afraid to even see you."

Tears began to form into Juan's eyes and she did not answer Ader.

"I am asking you, as your fellow woman, to give your fiancé a second chance. If he behaved in the same manner again in the future, which I don't think that he would, telling from the agony that he is currently undergoing, then you could leave him," Ader humbly advised Juan.

"No, Mori thinks that I am a playing thing and he just wants to violate me," disgustingly answered Juan, with tears streaming down her cheeks.

"You still love him, don't you?" candidly asked Ader.

"Yes, part of my heart, still loves him," honestly answered Juan, "but after what he had attempted to do to me, I don't think that I need him anymore."

"I definitely understand why, you are saying that" compassionately said Ader. "You are very angry with Mori right now but if your anger subsided and you started thinking clearly, I think that you will choose reconciliation rather than dumping the man that you have loved for such a long time. Remember, getting a new lover won't be easy for you because you will be afraid, to break your heart again. Think about what, I am suggesting to you. Why do you think that our marriage is working very well now? I have forgiven my husband several times, when we were still dating but now we are happy together. There are lots of trials, in every relationship."

"Thank you very much, for your advice," Juan gratefully told Ader, as she was trying to wipe off her tears. "I need some time, to calm down my anger, clear my mind and think about, the decision I would have to make. Right now, I don't think that I need Mori anymore, in my life."

"Juan, thank you, for welcoming me kindly into your home and notwithstanding everything that has happened," gratefully said Ader. "I hope that you will make a wise decision."

After Juan had returned home, she thought deeply about what, Ader had suggested to her but was still deeply torn between leaving Mori and reconciling with him once again. She begun remembering some of the wonderful moments that she had spent alone with Mori and he did behave very well. Juan therefore, wondered why, Mori had lost his self-control that fateful evening. She even started thinking about, the pain of starting a new relationship, the time that she would need to know the person and many other complications. Juan got completely confused and deeply hurt. She cried a lot that night and did not go to work the following day.

On the other hand, as soon as Ader got home, Mori rushed to her at once and curiously asked, "Ader, how is Juan and what did she say?"

"Juan is still very, very upset and she told me that she did not like you anymore," Ader honestly told Mori. "I tried to persuade her to forgive you by giving her a lot of advise but she maintained her ground and only cried. She seemed so hurt and heartbroken. However, do not give up hope because I am sure that she will eventually forgive you, when she is over her anger and frustration."

"Would she really?" desperately asked Mori. "Would she really find it in her heart, to forgive and give me one last chance, to have a relationship with her?"

"Yes, she definitely will. We women are so forgiving and that is our weakness always when it comes to relationships with men," Ader plainly assured Mori, who had bowed down his head and seemed to be in anguish that no word could describe. "Write to her a letter of apology and then she would understand that you are truly sorry for what, you have tried to put her through."

Mori profoundly thanked Ader and promised her that he would do exactly, as she had told him.

Mori therefore wrote a letter to Juan and apologised for his misbehavior. He promised that he would never hurt Juan again and that she should kindly give him a second chance. He further said that he loved her more than life itself and hated to know that she was so heartbroken. Juan read the letter in tears and hoped that her fiancé would keep his promise. After a long, deep and hard thinking, Juan eventually decided that she would forgive her fiancé and give him another opportunity. On the day that Juan had found it in her heart to forgive Mori, she had a good night sleep because she was then feeling as if, a heavy load had been lifted off her heart. However, she did not reply to tell Mori immediately that she had forgiven him. She took her time because she wanted to teach her fiancé a lesson that he would never forget.

Juan's delay in replying to Mori's letter worried him even more because he was thinking that Juan had already made up her mind to leave him. Mori was looking so miserable that he did not even want to talk to Omal, as he normally would, anymore. All that Omal was trying to do to in order to cheer up Mori failed because he was quite upset and depressed. Omal got so concerned about his friend's condition and therefore asked his wife once again, "If Juan failed to reply to Mori's letter until next Saturday, would you mind to go back and talk to her?"

"I wouldn't mind at all," willingly replied Ader. "But I will wait, until next Sunday evening."

"I do appreciate you a lot, my dear wife," Omal gratefully replied. "You are such a compassionate and understanding woman; that is why I love you very much."

"I wished that I could do more for Mori," sympathetically said Ader. "I feel so sorry for him and I think that he has learnt a lesson that he will not forget."

Omal thoughtfully wondered whether there was any hurtful pain in a man's life other than the pain to lose the woman he loved so much. He wrestled in his mind with some difficult questions, as he was endeavouring to understand why, men found it extremely hard to control their sexual urges, whenever they were alone with the women that they love. *Are we purposely created to be weak,* he deeply thought, *or we just allow ourselves to be weak. What is really behind men's sexual drive; the need to satisfy our sexual desires, need for pleasure, desire to dominate women, the pride to prove to women what, we are capable of doing to them, procreation or what? Which one of the above reasons usually, drives us to the brink? Oh how I wished that I know the correct answer. I also wished that women could understand us, men, and try to forgive us, whenever we have misbehaved because we are quite foolish by nature.* Omal therefore asked God, to help his friend reconcile with his fiancé.

A week after the incident, Juan eventually came to see Mori. When she entered his house, she found him lying on the bed with both hands over his head and seeming really miserable.

"Hallo!" Juan softly saluted her fiancé.

The familiar voice, made Mori to quickly look up but could not believe his eyes, at the sight of Juan. "Hi," he reservedly said in a soft low voice and was seemingly feeling very ashamed of himself. "I hope that I am not hallucinating, right now. Is that really you, Juan?"

"You, surely are not hallucinating," answered Juan, rather arrogantly, "Can you please get up? We need, to have a serious talk."

"I wished that you know how long I have been waiting for this moment," Mori delightfully told his fiancée. "However, I first of all, would like to thank you, for coming to see me." He then got up and sat on the chair, next to where Juan was sitting. "Before we could start talking, I would like you to know that I am sincerely sorry, for the terrible things that I have done to you last week and I am therefore, asking you to kindly forgive me and give me another chance," Mori contritely told Juan. "I acted badly and I did not know what I was doing then. I am really sorry, to have caused you so much embarrassment, shame and pain."

Mori sounded so apologetic that the powerful anger that Juan had built in her heart against him quickly softened and she said, "I have accepted your apology and hoped that such misbehaviour won't happen again. You not only embarrassed me that day but you have also humiliated me, before your neighbour, Ader. I ran to her with a torn blouse, think about that Mori."

"Omal told me about your blouse and I just cannot recall ever pulling your blouse, up to the extent of tearing it," remorsefully said Mori. "Please forgive me because I did not really mean to violate you but just lost my self-control. I love you so much dear and the last thing that I would like to do is to disrespect you. I cannot imagine my life without you, it would be meaningless."

The sincere and apologetic tone with which Mori had spoken broke Juan's heart and she begun crying. Mori got confused because he did not know what, the tears were meant for. He sat quietly, as he was watching his fiancée while she was crying because he was scared to comfort her, by holding her into his arms, given what took place between them in the previous week.

"I love you very much, Mori," Juan said eventually, after she had stopped crying. "I would like you to know that I have also suffered a lot in the past few days, when my heart was torn between leaving and reconciling with you." She then got up and begun hugging her fiancé while she was telling him that "I hope that my hug will not spark another fire of foolishness in you, like the one that had driven you crazy, the previous week."

"I promise you, my dear Juan, that," sincerely said Mori, as he was feeling quiet relieved and relaxed, at the knowledge that Juan was still in love with him, "that kind situation will never happen again between us." They both laughed and continued talking in a friendly manner, until Juan left.

Omal and Ader were very pleased, to see Mori looking quite cheerful for the first time, since the incident. They then asked him, after Juan had gone, "Would you, mind to have supper with us tonight?"

"Oh yes, I do not mind," cheerfully replied Mori. "I would be honoured. I feel like a new person today and very happy indeed. Ader dear, you have been, such a great help for me. I do not know how, I could thank you enough. I am very grateful to you too, Omal, for asking your wife, to talk to Juan. I couldn't have succeeded to talk to her, on my own. Oh my beloved true friends, I love you dearly and owe you a fortune."

"You do not, owe us anything at all," happily said Omal. "What do you think best friends are for? We are very happy, to see you in such a good spirit, once again."

"To tell you the truth," said Ader, "we were really worried about you, over the last few days. However, we are very delighted that things have worked out well, between you and your fiancée."

Ader cooked a very delicious meal for supper because she wanted to, celebrate their friend's reconciliation with his fiancée. During the supper they told Mori, "We wish you a good relationship with Juan and soon a happy marriage. You are such a wonderful person and your fiancée is too. We are very sure that you will make a good couple and have beautiful children, in the future."

"Today is, the first time for me, to breathe in some fresh air again," joyfully said Mori. "I did take Juan for granted in the past and did not know how much, she has impacted my life but now I know better. Juan is my life and my joy. I cannot live well, without her."

"The two of you, are predestined to be together," Omal honestly assured his friend. "Consequently, if you, are able to meet the obligations of your future-in-laws, please do not delay but get married sooner than later."

"Why didn't I even, think about that before?" excitedly said Mori. "However, thank you so much once again Omal, for pointing out to me, that important fact. I will therefore, prepare myself and send a message to my future in-laws, informing them about when, I would like to meet the requirements for Juan's marriage."

"May God graciously bless you, in all your endeavours," said Omal and his wife.

Mori was so happy, to have such caring and loving tenants, who were then like his own relatives. They therefore, happily chatted and laughed a lot about the foolishness of men, when it came to having relationship with women.

Mori got married to Juan, shortly after their reconciliation. It was a beautiful traditional marriage and Juan was escorted to her new home, with lots of things. People ate, danced and drank beer for a number of days, to celebrate their marriage. Mori was very delighted to finally get married to Juan and rejoiced in her a lot. Omal and his wife were also quite delighted, to see their landlord so happy. Ader was especially overjoyed because she was at last having a friendly female neighbour. The young women confided a lot in each other and were inseparable.

One evening, Mori humbly approached Omal while Ader was away and gratefully told him, "Dear brother, I have never thought that life could be so sweet, as I am lately enjoying it. I am indebted to you and your wife, for enabling me to marry my beloved wife. I owe especially you, Omal, for your invaluable advice to me. God bless you and your family, for your kindness, compassion and love for me and my beloved wife."

"You really owe me and my wife nothing," simply replied Omal. "You also are a wonderful person and my confidant. I am so delighted that you are happily married. I wish you, the very best in your new life, with your beautiful wife."

Mori learned a lot from Omal on how, to responsibly handling his marriage. He put whatever Omal had taught him into practice and his marriage was a very happy one.

Chapter Twenty-Two
The Deadly Insecurity

Ader, Omal, Juan and Mori built a wonderful relationship and lived happily, as if they were related and not only landlords and tenants. Soon after Mori got married, he was sent for a nine months course to Khartoum. He was very disheartened to leave his new wife behind but was comforted in the fact that his wonderful tenants would take good care of her, while he was away. Juan was already pregnant, when her husband was leaving for Khartoum but none of them was then aware about it. She therefore, had her firstborn daughter, when her husband was away and Ader took very good care of her. Mori was very pleased, when his wife wrote to him about, all that Omal and Ader had done for her. Mori bought consequently lots of gifts for his wife and Omal's family, when he was returning from Khartoum.

The security situation deteriorated a lot, after Mori had returned from Khartoum that he went with a convoy to his village and brought his mother to Juba. Mori loved his mother dearly and treated her with so much respect. He bought very beautiful dresses for her and whatever she liked. The old woman was grateful to God for her son and was always smiling. Mori's mother was called, Jore. She was a jolly old woman who liked playing with little children a lot, including Ader's sons. However, lack of the common language for communication did hamper her from talking to other people, who were not able to peak in the Bari language. Nevertheless, she loved people so much and would always try to communicate with them using sign language. All the neighbours loved Jore a lot because of her wonderful sense of humour. Mori spent a lot of evenings with his mother, who was sometimes treating him as if he was still a little boy. Juan consequently, teased her husband a lot about, his childish behaviour whenever he was talking with his mother.

The beautiful scene, between Mori and his mother whenever they were conversing, made both Ader and Omal missed their parents a lot because they were no longer accessible, due to the heavy fighting between the rebels and the government soldiers on the east bank of the Nile. Ader and Omal wished that there were no war, so that their parents could have also come to visit them, once in a while. As the situation further deteriorated, many people from Juba town began to go to northern Sudan, mainly Khartoum. Omal and his wife did not think that it was a wise idea for them to go to the northern Sudan and so they remained in Juba. They daily prayed, for the safety of everyone in Juba and also those in the rural areas.

At that time, there were rumours that some of the boys who had joined the movement, when it was first beginning, were visiting their families during the night, especially, those whose families were living in places like Gumbo and Munuki. The boys told their parents about, the sting of tribalism in the movement. They narrated with deep misery how, they were always put in the front line because of where they were coming from, and therefore, most of them died during the combats. Most of the people did not believe the rumour initially but it was confirmed eventually to be true when the parents of some of the boys stared confiding to their friends about, the nightly visits from their sons in the movement.

The sad stories that the young men were telling about how they were cruelly mistreated in the movement did not deter those who were determined to join the movement because many young men continued disappearing from Juba. Okema, Ader's beloved brother, also disappeared, without even informing her because he was aware that she would not approve of his departure. Ader was so heartbroken over her brother's disappearance that she fell sick out of misery and it took her a long time to get well again. She had all along thought that her brother was very close to her and would not go away, without first telling her. Therefore, Ader found it hard to believe, what her brother had done to her and wondered whether she would ever see him again. She blamed, the whole situation on the northern Sudan government, which was treating the southern Sudanese like, jerks and rubbish. Ader also cursed, the colonialists who had drawn foolishly the map of the Sudan, to include the southerners to live with the Arabs in the north, whose cultures, traditions and religion were different totally from the black people of the south. She wished that southern Sudan was a separate country or joined to either Kenya or Uganda, in which, some of the ethnic groups, in all the two countries, were speaking the same languages as some of the tribes in the southern Sudan. Ader spent a lot of time crying in anguish for her brother. Eventually, she rented another of Mori's houses and put all her brother's belonging in it. Omal took very good care of his wife and reassured her that her brother would be well and nothing bad would come his way.

A short while after Okema had disappeared, Omal received some sad news from his village that the rebels had taken his dad away and he became so devastated. All the news, that were coming into Juba at that time were about, the people who were missing or killed and therefore, there were funerals, everywhere. Life did not have any meaning anymore, even for Ader and Omal, who loved each other very dearly. The couple was quite shaken that sometimes they could not even find any word, to say to each other. The insecurity worsened so much in the rural areas where, the rebels had taken control. Therefore, most of the people from the east bank of the Nile ran to Juba, including the people who, were working for a charitable organization, called NCA (Norwegian Church Aid). The rebels attacked mercilessly the headquarters for the Norwegian Church Aid, called Hilieu, at night, after they had first abducted, one of the expatriates. They looted, the properties of all the people who were living Hilieu, including the expatriates' houses and their food store. They scattered all the files and important documents, throughout the offices and in the compounds. They also looted whatever amount of money that they were able to get, from the Company's safe. One, of the senior Sudanese officers, who was working for the NCA was forced at gun point to carry whatever the rebels had looted from his house, for approximately two kilometers into the bushes. He was terribly weighed down by the heavy load that he was carrying that he almost collapsed to death before they could let him go. Furthermore, the rebels deadly raped many women and young girls. The fall of Hilieu to the rebels made, the NCA to transfer their head office to Juba. Many of the international organizations, which were working in east bank of Eastern Equatoria then, closed down their offices and left the country. Juba became very crowded and the prices for food were sky high.

Some of the people, from Terkeka district, also ran to Juba and reported that the rebels had looted their cows and brutally raped their wives and girls, some of whom were as young as five years of age. The survivors talked, with such resentment, bitterness and hatred against the movement that many people in Juba believed their story. However, some of the people in Juba, who had not yet witnessed how terrible the rebels were in mistreating the civilians, refused to believe the stories that the Mondari people were telling. The situation created a lot of divisions among the people, even those who were from the same family. You would find, the people from the same family; one person supporting the movement and the other one condemning it, hence sudden fights. The rebels had a radio broadcast at 4:00 PM, Sudan local time. They would brag about their successes and insulted the southern Sudanese soldiers, who were fighting on the side of the government, calling them traitors and Arabs-bootlickers. The people who were siding with the rebels would daily argued, with the ones who were not agreeing with whatever the rebels were saying and doing. The constant antagonism, created a lot of hullabaloos and bitter rifts between people.

In one of the constant terrible occurrences, the rebels ambushed a bus, which was traveling from Torit to Juba and looted everything from the passengers. About thirty of the rebels, raped two young women until, they were almost dead and had to be hospitalised for two months. There was also a report from Lokoya area that the rebels brutally raped a woman and her five years old daughter, before killing them. The husband and father, of the murdered victims, was hiding in the nearby bush and witnessed what the rebels had done to his family. He consequently, shot and killed five of the rebels, before the others could eventually kill him and therefore, the whole family was extinct that day.

The fact that a lot of people were running away from, the areas that were controlled by the rebels, made most of the people in Juba wondered, as to what the true reason for the war was. In the beginning of the movement, the people from Equatoria had so much faith and hope in it because they were thinking that the rebels would liberate them from, the oppression of the Moslem government in the north. However, the influx of the displaced people from rural areas into Juba, made many people to change their mind about the movement. To make matter worst, the rebels shot down a civilian plane, with sixty people on board, over a town called Malakal, in the Upper Nile Region of southern Sudan and everyone was killed. The death of the innocent people who were predominantly from the southern Sudan, including one of the co-pilots, angered a lot of people against the rebels and their leader. On the other hand, the rebels celebrated, the deaths of the people in that fateful plane as, their victory over the Sudan government. There were funerals everywhere in Juba, for the people who had perished with the airplane.

The suffering, of the people in the southern Sudan, from the cruelty and brutality of the rebels, brought a lot of concern to the religious leaders from the southern Sudan. Consequently, the Catholic bishops and the leaders from the other Christian denominations, decided to go and meet with the leader of the rebels, in his headquarter then, in Addis Ababa, Ethiopia. When they arrived there, the leader of the rebels warmly welcomed them and during the meeting, the delegation asked him to explain to them, as to why his men were raping women, looting people's properties, driving away most of the people from their homes and killing others, especially in the rural areas. The leader of the rebels, who was known for his elocution, silenced the delegation by eloquently replying to them that; bishops, priests and pastors preached in their churches that; the people of their congregations must not steal, kill, commit adultery and so on but after the Christians had gone out of the house of worship; they would commit the very sins that they were commanded not to do. Furthermore, he told them that he too had been giving commands to his followers that they should never to do anything cruel to anybody but some of his followers had been going out and doing the reverse of whatever, he had been telling them. It was therefore, very hard to believe whether, the information that the leader of the rebels was telling the delegation could be true because in reality, the rebels had often been telling the people, whose properties they were looting that "Our leader has instructed us that we should use our guns; as our means for the provision of clothes, food and shelter that we need. Our guns are therefore, our salaries from our leader." However, the delegation was overwhelmed by the way that the leader of the rebels had spoken to them and therefore, they returned to the south Sudan with a very different view about him and the movement.

In one of the camps, for the displaced people in the outskirt of Juba in a place called Gumbo, the rebels came at night and planted the anti-personnel near the tents and in the areas surrounding the camp. In the morning, as the displaced people were trying to go out of their tents, many of them were blown up and most of the survivors, either lost their arms or legs. Among the survivors, there were deaths in every family. The incident angered most of the people a lot and since then, no one had faith in the movement any longer. The few remaining survivors were then moved to another camp near the military barracks at a place called, Lologo. The atrocious activities by the rebels against the innocent and unarmed civilian, made even some parents whose children were in the movement, to hate their own children. Some of the people who used to listen to the Radio station, which was broadcasted by the rebels, gave it up because they were quite disgusted by the horrendous deeds that were being done by the rebels. However, others said that they would listen no matter what because they wanted to know what, the rebels were planning to do next.

Another incident also occurred a few weeks later in which, one of the rebels was caught trying to plant anti-personnel near the Konyokonyo market, with the intention to killing as many people as he could. Everyone in

Juba became extremely frightened, even by his/her own shadow sometimes. The regional military government then, declared the state of emergency because of the terrible things that the rebels were doing. By six o'clock in the evening, everyone was supposed to be in the house, even those who used to like drinking beer in bars until late at night. Whenever anyone was found on the road after six o'clock by the military, he/she was arrested and imprisoned. Many people started going to church on Sunday to pray, even those who use not to go to church. Despair, made everyone started seeking help, hope and peace of mind from a higher power.

One morning, a Bari woman from a village called, Bilinyang, on the eastern bank of the river Nile, was coming to Juba market, to sell some green vegetable. On her way, she met two men who asked her, whether she was a smoker. The lady replied innocently that she was and they gave her a stick of cigarette and told her to start smoking it at once. The woman was thinking that the men were good people and she therefore, did as they told her. Unfortunately, as soon as she had smoked the cigarette, she became very disoriented because the cigarette was drugged. Under the influence of the drug, the men then asked the woman, to carry some stuff and deliver to the government soldiers at the bridge for them. She willingly accepted and told them that she could do anything for them. The rebels then, started packing some anti-personnel in her big basket and covered them up with the green vegetable that the woman was trying to take to the market and sell. The poor woman then, carried the basket on her head and went her way, while singing loudly and laughing stupidly, as soon as she had seen any fly or insect flew by. When the woman got to the bridge, her manners were quite odd that the soldier decided that her basket be checked. To their dismay consequently, they discovered that three quarters of the basket was full of the anti personnel. The woman was then taken for interrogation. She then excitedly narrated, what had happened to her. After a little while, she asked the soldiers that she was feeling very, very tired and sleepy. The soldiers gave her a place to rest and she slept for three hours. When she finally woke up, she screamed out of shock and asked, "Where am I and what am I doing here?"

After the soldiers had narrated back to her, the story she had earlier on told them, she began crying uncontrollably. The soldiers then concluded that the woman indeed had been drugged. The soldiers therefore, forgave the woman because they were sure that she was a victim in the circumstance. Finally, they told the woman to go home and warned her not, to accept anything from anyone she did not know anymore. She thanked the soldiers for being kind to her and miserably went back home.

There were many incidents, in which the rebels were trying to send out cruel messages about, their ill intention to destroy the people in Juba but the worst one was when, they planted dynamites under the only bridge on the river Nile, so as to blow off the bridge and kill as many of the residents of Juba as possible. There is always some good in every human being, however bad the person might be. To support this statement, after the rebels had finished placing the dynamites under the bridge in the stillness of the night, one of them, who was supposed to ignite the dynamites, purposely dropped the match box into the river Nile and pretended that it fell by mistake because he did not like what they were up to. His colleagues became really mad and started to yelling at him. They even forgot for a while that they were near the government soldiers, who were guarding the bridge at night. Consequently, when the soldiers heard the noises and commotion, they started to immediately search the area. The rest of the rebels escaped and fled hurriedly in their speedboats, after first tossing off their guilty companion who had foiled their mission, to drown. Fortunately, the man knew how to swim very well and kept himself afloat, until the soldiers captured him.

The news about, the monstrous attempt by the rebels to blow up the bridge and kill as many people in Juba as they could, spread like wild fire all over Juba. Most of the people in Juba, if not all, came to the bridge to witness in astonishing disbelief, as the army engineers were dismantling tactfully the ton of dynamites from under the bridge. Many people cried openly because they were feeling that the rebels, whose motive for the war had then lost its original intention, could destroy Juba at anytime. When all the dynamites were finally removed, many people jumped, shouted jubilantly for joy and called the soldiers their heroes. From then onwards, the people in Juba lived in constant fear because they were very aware that the rebels could destroy them all, at any time.

Chapter Twenty-Three
The Massacre at Obbo Chiefdom

At that time, in most parts of the Acoliland; the rebels raped brutally the women and young girls, beat up the men viciously, who did not want to join them, looted the properties of the people; including food, constantly forced the young men that they had not beaten, to carry loots on their heads for a very, very long distance and also the women and the young girl that they had not raped; to manually grind grain into flour, within a very short period of time and when they had failed to produce the required amount of flour, they would beat them up quite badly. Therefore, some of the people from Panyikwara and Magwi villages, who could no longer bear the mistreatments from the rebels, decided to run to Loudo village because there were some militiamen there, who were protecting the villagers from the rebels. In one small village called, Palwonganji, twelve of the rebels raped brutally an old woman of about seventy-five years and before she could die, she cursed bitterly, the movement and wished it, a complete failure in all its endeavours. The incident rendered, most people ineffable, very devastated, frightened and quite ashamed of the movement.

On the side of the government, they sent the antinov warplane to bomb randomly, the rural areas and in the process they killed mainly the innocent civilians in the villages. The civilians, became so confused, scared and frightened that some of them went to live in the mountains with hope that it would be safer for them there, than on the plains but their hopes, were crushed when, the rebels followed them on the mountains and took away whatever little they were left with. The government also bombed the mountains relentlessly and killed very many people. Therefore, some of the survivors who got the chance to escape ran to Juba. Upon arrival, they did not say much but they soon started telling the people in Juba about, their gruesome ordeals with the rebels and the merciless bombing by the government. The shocking stories that the displaced people were telling made, many people in Juba to weep in despair.

The people, from Licari village were also forced to move to Loudo village because of the frequent grisly disturbances by the rebels. They went back occasionally to Licari, to collect their food from their granaries and some food that were still in the fields. One weekend however, when the people got to Licari village, they were caught up there by the torrential rain. Consequently, they decided, to spend the night in Licari. After the rebels had seen the smoke from the fire that the people had made to keep themselves warm, they rushed to Licari village and abducted all the ten people.

The children and relatives, of the people who had been abducted by the rebels, waited for the return of their loves ones in vain. After two days of waiting, they decided to inform the militiamen about the case. The militiamen then escorted them at once to go and check out what had happened. After searching for the missing people for a long time, they gave up because it was obvious that the rebels had captured them. Everyone then started praying that the rebels should not kill them because some of the people had left behind, very young children who had no one to take care of them but some of the kind and compassionate neighbours. The toddlers cried for a week but eventually gave up. Although the toddlers were well fed by some of the kind people who were taking care of them, they grew really skinny because they were missing their parents.

Some of the relatives of the people who had been abducted by the rebels, wanted to make the funeral for them but the elders stopped them and said, "There is still a chance that the abducted people might be alive and therefore, the survivors might some day come back and only then would, the funeral for those who did not make it be performed. God is always merciful and would not allow everyone of them to die." The people gathered and prayed together in the evenings, for the safe return of the missing people. After the abduction, no one, from the former Licari village was daring to go back and bring some food, anymore. A few of the relatives of the people from Licari village, who were living in Loudo village, shared with them whatever little food they had. Life became very difficult, for everyone who was then living in Loudo village.

The rebels used the people that they had abducted from Licari village, as their slaves and mistreated the people ruthlessly; to carry their loots, grind grains into flour, collect wild vegetable and cook food. Therefore, the captives became so emaciated that they could not carry out their duties, as was expected of them because they were given little food only after every three days and as the result, some of them became very ill almost to the point of death but thank God, none of them perished. They were frequently beaten and tied up with strings, especially the men among them, as an amusement for their abductors. The clothes, that the people were wearing when they were abducted, were all taken away from them and instead, were given some rags to wrap around their loins, so as to cover only their private parts. The rebels kept the people for two months but to the captives, the duration of their stay with the rebels was like a decade. However, the people's luck came one day, when the rebels had heard that there was a convoy, which was traveling from Nimule to Torit. The rebels had then realised that keeping the people longer with them, would inconvenience their attack on the convoy. So they released them to go free when they heard that the convoy had reached a village called Abara, in Panyikwara Chiefdom.

After their release, the weak and emaciated people who had been abducted, walked for two days the distance that a healthy person could cover normally within three hours on foot. As they were approaching Loudo village, some of the militiamen on patrol spotted them and reported to the responsible head person that some people were coming towards the village but did not seem to carry any arm with them and whether, they should attack the people or not. The leader refused and told them that they should first of all take proper look at the people, before they could attack. After careful scrutiny therefore, the militiamen then realized that the people were those who had been abducted by the rebels, although they looked so worn out and kind of wild. The militiamen then approached and escorted them to the centre of the village and then informed their relatives and children about, the good news. People wept for joy but some of them began throwing themselves down, meanwhile the others were screaming and cursing the rebels, for causing them so much pain and despair because the people who had returned from captivity, were all seemingly old, wild and tired-looking. There was a young boy, who had become very ill out of the misery for missing his mother when she was abducted with the rest of the people. He almost died but was fortunately, cared for by his compassionate neighbours. The boy could not believe his eyes that day, when he saw his mother because she was quite skinny and looked very wild and old. However, they lovingly held each other and cried bitterly for a very, very long time, before they could walked to their little hut in which, they chatted joyfully with each other until dawn.

As for the poor people who ran to Loudo village with the hope that it would be safer for them there than anywhere else, luck did not hold out for them. One fateful morning in July of 1987, the rebels unexpectedly surrounded the village at dawn and started shooting randomly at anyone they could see, women, men, children and even domestic animals. Some of the villagers were burnt in the houses as they were sleeping and a few of them who were trying to run, were shot dead. Those who used to wake up early and work in their fields were the only few who had escaped that deadly day but some of them were also killed. A group of some men who were digging in the field tried, to hide in the trenches that were dug by the militiamen but were all killed. The militiamen, whose ultimate intention was to protect the people who were then living in Loudo from the inhuman abuse by the rebels, all perished that day, while they were defending the innocent and unarmed inhabitants of Loudo village.

In a place called, Alia, including the other areas surrounding Palotaka Catholic Parish, the rebels massacred anyone that they could find on the road and burnt to death most of the people, as they were still sleeping. They murdered Ader's sister, Amyel, with a machine gun, as she was getting out of her house so that she could find out why, there were sounds of heavy shootings everywhere. Some of the rebels, broke down the door to the parish priest's bedroom, stripped him almost naked and bounded his hands. They then marched him, to the nuns' quarters where, they did the same things to the nuns and then took all of them away. The other rebels, went into the church and blew up the tabernacle, smashed whatever vessels that were in there, while they were yelling out that if God were to come down that morning from heaven, they would shoot him too. They continued with their deadly rampage and shot most of the people in the parish, including those who were still sleeping. There were dead bodies littered everywhere, a spooky sight that could render any normal human being unconscious but the rebels danced and rejoiced about their atrocious deeds which, they called as, the victory over the government militiamen in Obbo although, there was not a single militiaman in Alia and Palotaka Parish.

The rebels carried out, the massacre at Loudo and Alia villages including the Palotaka Parish, concurrently. They planned their grisly attack in such a way that they started killing the people in all the three places, at the exact time. On that fateful day, Ader lost her dear father, beloved and precious sister Amyel, cousins, aunts, her father's cousins and most of the friends that she had grown up with. The strong Licari boys, who use to be the pride of their village, most of them were killed that day. On the other hand, Omal lost his beloved mother and two of his older sisters plus many other close relatives. The news, about the massacre at Obbo reached Pajok where, the government soldiers were stationed, through those who had escaped and ran for their lives there.

The government soldiers in Pajok, were all from the southern Sudan, and therefore, after hearing the news about the massacre, they quickly mobilised themselves and rushed out, to rescue the few people whom they thought might still be alive in Obbo but to their dismay they were met by frightening sights of corpses everywhere. The soldiers were very heartbroken, to see the heinous deeds that the rebels had done on the poor and armless people of Obbo Chiefdom. As such, they spent a long time there as they were trying to bury, as many of the dead as possible into the mass graves they had dug. When they became tired by the end of the day, they returned to Pajok and left most of the dead bodies still scattered everywhere. The Loudo village, which used to be lively, full of activities and merriment, was then reduced to a ghost town and the sight of which was really spooky.

The rebels withdrew and hid themselves, when they heard the sound of the military trucks coming towards the village. However, they returned to the villages later on that evening, after they were sure that the government soldiers had gone back to Pajok. The rebels exhumed the bodies from the mass graves and started dismembering some of the corpses, especially the ones that they were thinking were the militiamen. Some of the dead bodies were tied up on the trees and blown up with the machine guns. The rebels, made all kinds of jokes with the corpses before they could eventually, leave the villages. They even checked the pockets of the dead people for money. The few survivors, who returned to the Alia and Loudo villages after the rebels had gone, were shocked by what they had seen because they had never witnessed such beastly deeds since the dawn of time.

The news about the massacre at Obbo Chiefdom reached Juba through the Norwegian Church Aid Radio Communication station in Pajok. There was mourning everywhere in Juba. Some people, who had lost almost all the members of their families, wanted to commit suicide but were rescued by friends who kept vigil on them. Both Ader and Omal were utterly devastated that they almost went insane. Ader could not imagine her life without her father whom, she dearly loved and was always the centre of her life. She was also, severely crushed over the death of her beloved sister, Amyel, whom she dearly loved and adored. Ader sadly remembered Amyel's talks the last time that they were together at home during her marriage and tried to piece together some of the things that her beloved late sister was trying to tell her. Eventually, she concluded that somehow, Amyel was in a way, trying to say a final goodbye to her. Ader cried for five days nonstop until, she had no more tears coming from her eyes. Her whole world crumbled and crushed above and beneath her. For the first time in her entire life, Ader hated her life. The joyful world Ader used to know vanished right before her eyes then. Not even the presence of her husband whom she dearly loved, gave her any reason to continue to live. Ader called out, the names of her late love ones; father, sister, mother-in-law, sisters-in-law, cousins, the rest of the relatives and consequently, hit her head violently against the wall in despair. She was bruised everywhere and wished that she was dead, so that she could not feel the anguish that was then shredding her poor heart into dust.

There was an old woman, originally from Licari village, called Nyarata, who was living near Ader and her husband. She was a distant relative of Ader. When she heard about the news of the massacre at Obbo, she began to think immediately about Ader and came over to console her. Old Nyarata was devastated too because she had also lost nearly all her relatives but she gathered up her strength as an elder, in order to help young Ader who was devastated extremely. Nyarata never left Ader alone day and night, for two weeks. Omal appreciated the old woman's concern and compassion for his wife so much that he started treating her as if, she were a member of his family. Before the news about the massacre at Obbo Chiefdom, Nyarata distanced herself from Ader because of the close relationship that she was having with her husband but then she shook off her fear and began to carry out her role as an elder that the couple were in need of so much, in their hour of despair.

The heart-wrenching condition of grieving that the couple was experiencing, affected everyone around them so much that life became very sad and hopeless. Anyiri, who was so used to working and staying with Ader and her husband, felt out of place and could be seen from the way she was carrying out her duties. The couple did not want Anyiri to be devastated by their situation and therefore, they gave her a good pay and told her that they did not need her service anymore. Anyiri understood very well, the sorrowful condition both Ader and Omal were facing and so she accepted that it was right for her to leave them. The children cried, as Anyiri was leaving. Nothing seemed right in the house anymore.

Although men were strong normally when, it came to the news about death, Omal was devastated utterly that he began to weep sometime, openly for his sisters and mother. Each day, he was trying hard to help his wife but in the process, found himself crying just like her. Mori was always near Omal and attempted to make him understand that no one was able, to reverse what had already happened. He constantly reminded Omal, to be strong for his family's sake, especially his wife whose heart was torn to pieces. Most of Omal's friends from work came and spent their evenings with him and on weekends, they would come and spend the whole day. As time went by, the family gradually, began to heal and became stronger but their lives were changed forever.

All the news that came into Juba at that time was about, the deaths of the people in the rural areas. Government soldiers who were dying in various combats were, mostly from the southern Sudan and those who were dying on the rebels' side were also, from the southern Sudan. It was the kind of war that no one had ever anticipated, brothers against brothers. When the government authorities learnt that some of the funerals being held in Juba were, for the deaths of the rebels too, they issue a decree that any body found mourning for such deaths would be put into prison. Consequently, most of the young men, who had joined the movement when it first started, lost their lives but their wives and families were not allowed, to hold any funeral for them. Therefore, such deaths were mourned in secret, which was really very sad and tormenting for the families. No one in his/her wildest imagination had ever perceived that the rebel movement would end up causing so much pain on the very people they had said that they were fighting to liberate from the oppression of the northern Islamic government.

Chapter Twenty-Four
Omal Travelled to Torit

After the birth of the second child, Ader was seconded to work, for a non governmental Relief Organization, called CART (Combined Agencies for Relief Team), which was a contingent of the charitable organizations that had teamed up together in order to assist, the displaced people with food, materials for shelter, utensils, and many other basic necessities. Ader's new boss automatically, noticed her good work and liked her a lot because she was such a dedicated and dependable worker. Therefore, when Ader was utterly devastated by the deaths of her people, her boss gave her a long time off work because he had understood the pain that she was going through.

As time went by, Ader became stronger and eventually resumed work. However the way that she was carrying out her work both, in the office and at home was not the same as, prior to the deaths of her people because once a person had lost a member or members of a family, his/her life would never be the same anymore and so was for Ader and her husband. The couple's strong love and trust for one another kept them going but there were some days that they found it hard to even talk to each other. They occasionally visited, some of their friends and relatives who also had lost almost all the members of their families. Such visits gave Ader and Omal a bit of strength and courage because it made them realised that they were not the only ones who were grieving. There were, some people who did not have anyone left, to share their grief with, especially the widows, who had even lost their children and were living alone.

Before Ader could come to grip with the losses of her father and sister, she got another devastating news that her beloved brother, Okema, was also killed in Kapoeta, when the rebels recaptured the town from the government. Ader mourned sorrowfully, for the death of her dearly beloved brother privately because no one was allowed to hold memorial mass or funeral for such death. She missed her brother a lot and wished that he had listened to her advice and stayed in Juba. Ader's memories, took her back to the good old days, when they were still little kids and also the wonderful time that she and her brother had spent together before her marriage. "No! No," Ader would wailed in despair, as she was remembering her beloved brother, "I wanted so much for you to remain here in Juba, so that my little boys could learn to know and love you, as their dearest uncle. Okema, how could you be so cruel to go away and meet your death without even saying goodbye to me, your sister, who has always been sharing with you, her darkest secrets? Why have you, done this to me, oh brother, why? My handsome hero, how I wished that you had died of an illness then, I would have given you a decent burial and a proper requiem mass. I know in my heart that wild animals have consumed your dead body. What a way to leave this world, for such a handsome, kind, compassionate and loving person like you, my brother. Was that really how, you had wanted to depart from this world? Oh, Okema, my brother, your death has utterly crushed and devastated my life. I cannot live without you, please take me to where you have gone. The person who has started this disastrous war, is a destroyer and not a liberator, as the name of the movement is called," painfully lamented Ader in anguish and despair. She would cry uncontrollably for hours, without even listening to her husband until, she was completely exhausted. Ader could not understand why, the members of her family were almost getting finished because of the unstructured war. She bitterly cursed the leader of the rebels and the northern Islamic government, for the pain that they had inflicted on the southern Sudanese, as she lamented the losses of her dear loved ones. Despair, murk and anguish caused by the deaths of Ader's family members, engulfed her so much that she did not even know what she was going to do with her miserable life, anymore.

Ader was so much affected by the deaths of her loved ones that she gave up on her marriage life and refused to be intimate with her husband. Omal understood the devastating situation his wife was facing and therefore, did everything he could to coddle his wife's emotional breakdown back to health. It took a long time, before Ader could eventually, accept her losses and begin the healing process. Gradually, Ader started realizing that her husband was equally wounded, by the deaths of his mother and siblings. As time went by, Ader somehow resumed having marital relationship with her husband but once in a while. Omal was then greatly missing the wife that he had had before the deaths of her people and therefore tried to bring some fire back into their romantic life but nothing he had been trying produced any meaningful change to the situation. Eventually, he accepted and got adjusted, to his completely changed wife.

In Torit town, the insecurity worsened so bad that many people starved to death because the relief food could not be taken there, due to the threats by the rebels that any convoy that ventured to go to Torit, they would destroy on the way. Therefore, when all the people in Torit had ran out of food eventually, they then began to survive only on the few wild green vegetables that they could manage to get from the nearby bushes. Some women, who had dared to go a little bit further into the bushes, were abducted by the rebels and taken away for good. The few elderly women, who were allowed by the rebels to return to the town, were first brutally raped. The situation sparked fear among the people so much that they did not dare to go further into the bushes anymore, to look for the green vegetables. Consequently, half of the population in Torit starved to death and were buried into mass graves. If southern Sudan were to be like other parts of the world, where the media were allowed to take pictures, the international community would have seen the shock of their lives. To make matters worse, the rebels would go and attack the town, while killing lots of the starving survivors. The government bomber planes were also sent from Juba to Torit and randomly bombed and killed the same starving civilians. Many people in Torit then became the victims of both the rebels and the government's destructive incursions.

One of Omal's sisters, who was living in Torit, was bombed to death by the government and her husband was shot dead by the rebels. They left behind three children, who had no one in Torit to take care of them. Consequently, a friend of Omal from Torit sent him the sad message concerning the children's situation, through the radio call. The sorrowful message, prompted Omal to decide that he would be going to Torit, if any relief convoy would be going there so that he could bring the orphaned children, to live with him and his wife in Juba. Ader did not like the idea about her husband wanting to travel to Torit in a convoy because deep in her heart, she was beginning to intuitively sense that an impending danger was awaiting him. Ader tried to advice her husband and pleaded with him, "Omal, please do not go to Torit but, instead, send a message to one of your friends there, so that the children of your late sister could be brought by someone from Torit, if any convoy would be coming here from there, in the future. Do kindly listen to me, I beseech you, my love, because I do not have good feelings about your intention to travel to Torit when the convoy would be going there."

Omal politely refused to listen to his wife and, instead, stressed that "Ader, my dear wife, my late sister's children are in danger and I am the only one who could go to Torit and bring them to Juba. Look at how much the people have changed for the worse, with this war. Do you think that there is anyone out there who could accept the responsibility of traveling with someone's children on a convoy? Everyone is afraid that in the case that the convoy is attacked and something bad happened to the children, they might be held responsible. Ader, please do pray for me, to have a safe journey to Torit and back."

"I have understood what you have just explained," miserably said Ader, with a heavy heart, "but I still feel that you should not go because deep in my heart, something is warning me that I will not ever see you again, if you go to Torit. Omal, my dear husband, please kindly listen to me. I love you so much and you are the only meaningful person who, is left in my life."

"Ader, we have lost far too many family members, on both sides of our families," gently said Omal, "and I do not think that God would be so cruel enough, to take me also away from you. I adore you, Ader dear."

"It is not God who has killed, all the people that we have lost," remonstrated Ader, "but men's cruelty to each other and absolute greed for power. However, since you are so determined to go, I will allow you to go and may God be with you," heavy heartedly, accepted Ader.

Omal was quite relieved and happy, after his wife had eventually agreed that he could go to Torit.

When the military government in Juba received the news that half of the people in Torit were already dead due to the starvation, they decided to equip and assign a good number of soldiers, to escort the relief convoy to Torit. Omal was quite thrilled, after he had heard of the news about the convoy to Torit. As the time drew near, for the convoy to go to Torit, Omal began to have a strange desire to be intimate with his wife that he wanted to be with her at anytime, whenever they were alone. Ader was agitated by her husband's weird behaviour that she begun to devise ways in order to avoid him most of the time. Omal eventually knew his wife's tricks and outsmarted her. Ader bitterly complained to her husband but nothing that she was saying bothered him at all. One time, Omal told his wife that life was too short and must be enjoyed, whenever one was having the opportunity. To make matter worst, another night, a strange voice in a dream told Ader, "This is the last moments that you are spending with your husband, please enjoy it while it last and stop fighting with him anymore!" The dream was so real and it completely broke Ader's heart but she did not tell her husband about it because she was aware that he was not going to believe her. Thereafter, Ader was terribly disturbed by her husband's statement and the horrible voice that she had heard in her dream that she would cry bitterly whenever she was alone in the house. Furthermore, Ader began to have lots of nightmares at night that she would scream out loudly at times. Her husband would wake her up and reassure her that nothing was wrong and that she was only having a bad dream. However, one night, Ader dreamed that her husband was walking in the forest, when all of a sudden was attacked by the rebels, who wanted to shoot him but before they did, Ader started screaming and pleading with them, to spare her loving husband. Ader screamed the loudest that night, while she was saying that "Spare my dear husband! Please don't kill him because I cannot live without him! I love and adore my husband a lot! Please spare his life, for me and our children!"

Omal became so concerned that night and started shaking his wife rather hard, until she was fully awake. "Ader! Ader!" he loudly shouted out her name, "look into my eyes, I am alive and no one is trying to kill me! Please top crying dear! I am alive and right here beside you!"

Ader cried exhaustively even when, she was fully awake because the fear from her dream was gripping and devastating her mind, heart and soul a lot. The nightmare, Ader had had that night was so real that she concluded that something was obviously very wrong about, her husband's trip to Torit. She prayed to God, to protect her husband, when he would be traveling to Torit and back to Juba.

On the last night that the couple had spent together, Omal decided to make love to his wife for most of the night. Ader felt so exhausted, cried, complained and even ventured at some point to antagonistically struggle with her husband to leave her alone but in vain because Omal was too powerful for her to break away from.

"I wonder whether, you are still the same loving husband that I have married anymore," complained Ader quite sorrowfully, as she was crying frustratingly and feeling so helplessly defeated because of her husband's strange behaviour.

"I am the same man," happily said Omal and according to Ader, he was sounding quite strange. "Ader, I beg you, to kindly submit to me, for just this one night. Please stop resisting and fighting with me because that is not what I need from you. Give me a chance, my beloved wife, to be with you in the way that I need because I can't help the way that I am feeling about you tonight. I do not want to hurt you but just to make love to you, in a more pleasurable way. Sweetheart, please try to understand me and stop making everything too hard. I am traveling away tomorrow and it would be a long time before, we could make love to each other again."

Ader eventually, gave up the struggle against her husband because she had realized that she was fighting a losing battle against him. "I have never experienced this weird side of you yet," Ader disappointingly, frustratingly and disgustingly told her husband, as she was sobbing. "You are senselessly behaving like a total stranger to me tonight."

Whatever Ader was saying, never bothered her husband at all because he was feeling quite wonderful about, what he was enjoying with her. Omal had been sexually starving to be with his wife, since the deaths in their families, which had made his wife turned her back on him, almost completely. However, that last night before he could travel to Torit, gave him a good reason, to make love to his wife in the way that he had always wanted it to be.

The following morning, worn out as Ader was, she started preparing everything for her husband's journey and cooked breakfast. While they were eating, Ader completely avoided her husband's face and he eventually, asked her, "What is preventing you today, from looking at my face?"

"Don't try to be smart," Ader provocatively snapped back at her husband. "You know very well why, don't you? I do not know what, you have done to my wonderful husband because you are a different person. The man I got married to, was gentle, loving and did not behave to me, in the way that you have treated me last night."

After hearing his wife's complaints, Omal came to his senses and contritely told her, "Could you please pardon me?" he sincerely said. "I am sorry if I have hurt you by what had happened between us last night. Ader, it has been such a long, long time since we have had a romantic moment. I have been trying to awake your feelings for such a long time so that we could make love as we used to have before the deaths in our families but you would not relent and somehow, my yearning to be with you, built up within me and last night it exploded in such a way that I could not resist or control myself anymore. Beloved, please forgive me kindly, if I have hurt you. I am still the same man that you have loved and married and I dearly love you."

"What will I gain, by holding grudges against you, you silly husband?" Ader told her husband softly, while her tears were streaming down both her cheeks, as her heart was breaking, to hear her husband's plea for forgiveness. "I have completely forgiven you and I wished that you were not leaving for Torit today so that we could work out a solution to our marital relationship. But since you are going away, on such a delicate journey, I would like you to know that I love you despite what you have done to me last night and pray that you and all others who would be traveling with you today, have a safe journey to Torit and back to Juba respectively. Omal, my dear husband, I will continue to pray for your safety, until you come back to me and the children."

"Thank you a lot, my love," Omal told his wife gratefully. "I will also pray for you and the children everyday. Ader, I love you so much and I do not know how, I am going to cope without you by my side in Torit. Please, do not hate me for last night."

Ader lovingly gazed at her husband and still wished that he could change his mind about going to Torit. "I love you and will always do," she sadly said. "You are the only man for me and I know that you know this very well. Now come here and hug me, you silly and stubborn husband."

Omal was very delighted to know that his wife had forgiven him completely. He then tenderly hugged her and was feeling as if, they should go to Torit together. After Omal had hugged his wife, he called for his sons, who were growing up together and looking almost like twins, held and lovingly hugged them, one at a time and was feeling very proud to be their father. While Omal was hugging his children, chill ran through his spine and a weird feeling came over him that made him felt like he would never see them again. He quickly put off the spooky feelings but there was numbness in his heart that no word could explain. Ader saw the strange reaction on her husband's face, due to his horrible feelings but dared not ask him.

The boys cried miserably, as their father was leaving because he had never been away from them, since they were born. Omal was so heartbroken, to see his sons in tears. He sadly looked at them and somehow, was feeling like he should not leave them. Ader miserably, escorted her husband to the bridge where, he was supposed to get his transport. Many people came to the bridge that day, to say goodbye to their loved ones, who were traveling on that convoy. There were tears, in almost all the eyes of the women, whose husbands, or sons or brothers were traveling on that convoy. Ader stood amidst the crowd, while she was crying out her heart for her husband because since they got married, he had never traveled anywhere and left her alone. After Omal had seen his wife in anguish, he decided to get down from the truck that he was going to travel in, so as to console and hold her in his arms, for one last time.

As soon as Omal got down from the truck, he spontaneously started kissing his wife, for the first time in public, without fear. "Darling, I hate, to see you in such anguish," he desperately said. "I love you very much and seeing you in tears, really break my heart. I am not going to Torit because I want to but the circumstance, in which the children of my late sister are in, is the one that is compelling me to go. Please do not cry but rather pray that all go well with me and everyone traveling with me on the convoy."

"I will pray for all of you, day and night," Ader sadly whispered, as she was continuing to sob. "I am terribly missing you already Omal and I do not know what, I am going to do without you."

"I am missing you too dear," painfully said Omal and then he went back on the truck.

After Omal had returned on the truck, Ader suddenly realised that they had kissed in public and became so ashamed. Consequently, when the convoy started going across the Nile, Ader rushed home and did not go across the bridge, to wave her husband goodbye, as most of the women did. Kissing in public is not a common sight in the southern Sudanese society, and that was why Ader felt out of place.

When Ader got home, she straightaway went to bed because she was physically, emotionally and psychologically exhausted. She had a good rest, while she was sweetly dreaming about her husband. The dreams were so vivid and real as if, her husband had truly given up his determination about going to Torit. However, when Ader woke up at about 4:00 PM Sudan time, the actual reality struck her because the house was quite lonely and dark without her husband for the first time, since they got married. Ader looked around and wondered whether, all would be well with her husband until, he returned to Juba once again. She therefore, cooked super only for her children because she did not have any appetite. Before Ader went to bed that night, she prayed to God, to protect her husband and take him and the rest of the people with whom he was traveling, safely to Torit and later on safely back to Juba. However, there was still a deep fear lingering in her soul, the kind of fear that no word could explain. That night, Ader had lots of nightmares, about many things that she could not understand and consequently did not sleep well.

Mori and Juan did not understand, what was disturbing Ader in the last few days before her husband could go to Torit because she was seeming to be afraid of something very terrible. On the day that Omal had left for Torit Juan, was afraid to ask Ader because she was looking quite tired and worn out. Juan waited until the following day in the evening and then asked her friend, "You don't seem well at all, for a number of days now, could you kindly tell me, what is wrong with you?"

"Generally, there is nothing, wrong with me," Ader hopelessly told Juan. "It is just that I am having a deep nagging fear in my heart that I would not see my husband again. As a result, I did not really want him to go to Torit. I even told him about my fear but he won't listen to me. I am really very worried about, my husband's safety."

"Do not entertain, such bad thoughts," Juan firmly told her friend. "Let us hope that things would work out well for him and that he would return safely to you and the children."

Ader was wishing in her heart that what Juan had told her could come true. She therefore, promised Juan that she would think positively but deep inside, she was aware that nothing could eradicate the fear that was consuming her heart.

Ader missed her husband so much that she lost a lot of weight within a very short period of time and seemed quite sick all the time. To overcome the thoughts for missing her husband so much, Ader begun to keep herself busy by working overtime and when she returned home she found at least something to do like; washing clothes, bringing water from the borehole, etc. In the evenings, she would sit and chat with Mori and Juan but whenever she entered her bedroom, she would stay awake for such a long time, before she could fall asleep. Her fear for the worst grew deeper and deeper everyday. Some nights, she was having nightmares that her husband and the children he had gone to bring to Juba were burnt in the house and other times that Omal was shot on his legs and was crying for help. It was the hardest time for Ader because no one understood, how terribly devastating her fear and nightmares were. Ader also then was still grieving for the losses of her dear dad, sister, brother, mother-in-law and sisters-in-law.

Hinda knew how lonely Ader was and therefore, came from Nyakuron with her husband to spend most of their weekends with her. Whenever Hinda came for a visit, she would cook for Ader and they would eat happily together. Hinda's husband also liked Ader a lot and would joke joyfully with her, whenever him and his wife visited her. Those were the only moments that Ader seemed alive and cheerful. Some days, Ader would try to go for a walk where, she used to go with her husband but even that seemed to add on to the pain that she was feeling due to missing her husband. She would sometimes walk by the bank of the river Nile, overlooking Torit road, in tears and returned home late in the evening when, she was quite exhausted. The one thing that was enabling Ader to keep going on at that time was, her love for her children, who were reminding her a lot about her beloved husband. She consequently took very good care of them, despite the situation she was in.

On the other hand, after the convoy had traveled beyond Gumbo, Omal started thinking about his wife whom, he had last seen in tears. He was so heartbroken and prayed that he had safe journeys to Torit and back to Juba so that he could be with his wife and children once again. Omal miserably wondered about his wife and what she was going through in their house without his presence, as tears began to form into his eyes, while he was sitting with his head bowed between his knees. The sounds of his sons playing and crying filled his mind and he started missing them so much already. Most of the men, who were traveling with Omal on that truck were themselves going through the same agony as he was because none of them knew whether they ever would meet their families again. As a result therefore, no one paid any attention to Omal, as he was miserably sobbing for his family.

The soldiers who were escorting the convoy, had to clear the land mines and the anti-personnel as they were going. Under normal circumstance, Torit was only two hours drive from Juba but since the war had began, going to Torit was like traveling to Khartoum in a ship. The convoy was sporadically attacked on the way, more than three times but there was no heavy fighting. The rebels' intention to attack the convoy was just, to scare and delay it. So, after fourteen days of fear, uncertainty and fatigue on the road, the convoy eventually, made it to Torit.

The people in Torit were very overwhelmed with joy, to see the relief food arrived at last. Happiness, for the arrival of the food invigorated the starving inhabitants of Torit so much that they began to sing and dance with jubilation out the little strength left in their bodies. The severely malnourished people also, ventured to stand up on their feet for the first time, while waiving their bonny hands merrily because of the hope of life that the convoy had brought for them. Every relatively strong person, went out into the streets with screams of joy, trees' branches in hands and the women yodeled and ululated. It was such a jubilant celebration, such as had never been seen, since the war broke out. The rebels who were not very far away from Torit town, heard the celebration and were somewhat touched by, the jubilation of the people that they did not interrupt them by any attack that night. However, the inhabitants of Torit were quite surprised that the rebels did not attack and disrupt their celebration. Consequently, they thanked God on their bended knees.

Omal spent the night, in the house of one of the soldiers with whom he had traveled on the convoy and on the following day, he went out in search for his nephews and niece. After a long search he found out that the children were being kept at the Catholic feeding centre, where most of the orphans were taken care of. Omal wept at the sight of the children and tenderly hugged them. The children looked so emaciated and wild due to lack of food and missing their dead parents. Omal then introduced himself as the children's uncle, to the administrator of the feeding centre and then took the children, to live with him in his friend's house.

Omal's friend, Ohisa, was working for the cooperative department in Torit. They had gone together to the same school during their secondary school days. Ohisa was really happy to see Omal and gave him a very warm welcome. Ohisa's wife took good care of the children as if they were her own children. She told Omal not, to worry about the children, while he was staying them. Omal went to the place of the mass grave, where most of the people who had died of starvation had been buried. While there, he broke down and bitterly wept for all of them and wished that there were no war so that the surviving people could live in peace. At the grave of his sister, Omal sat down and softly mumbled, as if he was talking to someone that the other people around him could not see. His memory took him back, to the time when they were children and would play and fight with his sister. He could not bring up himself to believe that the remains that was buried in that grave, was actually his sister's. Omal spent along time at the grave every day and each day that he was there, he seemed more peaceful than, he was anywhere else.

Omal stayed in Torit for a month as he was waiting for, the return of the convoy to Juba. He tremendously missed his wife and children but could not communicate with them in any way. The one-month that Omal had spent in Torit, was like a whole year for him, without his wife. He fondly remembered, the last wonderful night that he had enjoyed with his wife and further fantasized about how, he was going to passionately make love to her once again, when he got back to Juba. As Omal also remembered his beloved sons, he would sometimes imagined so vividly in his mind as if, he had heard their voices. Omal endeavoured to ease his longing for his children by playing a lot with the children of his late sister, who were gradually growing to love him a lot. He became very fond of his niece and nephews that he began telling them a lot about his wife and sons. He also had promised the children that he would take very good care of them, once they had returned to Juba. The orphaned children were quite excited, to hear from their uncle that they would at last have someone, who would be taking care of them, as once upon a time their loving mother had done. What excited them the most was, the idea of having a home once again.

Life in Torit, at that time was like maximum-security prison, since one could not go a kilometre out of the town. Most of the suburbs of Torit that were once vibrant with life before the war had started, were not inhabited anymore. Consequently, most of the houses had fallen down, a sight quite spooky, even for grown ups. No one ventured to go to such areas because of the fear, for being abducted by the rebels. The somber moods, of the people who lived in the town, indicated quite clearly that there was no hope for a better future. Omal surveyed everything in shock and tears because he could not comprehend how, human beings could be so cruel to each other by, creating such horrific situation. However, Omal thanked God for keeping Juba relatively safe, despite the seldom ugly shelling by the rebels that killed a few people from time to time. Therefore, he concluded that the insecurity in Torit was the worst of its kind because of the deadly government bombs and the vicious attacks and abduction by the rebels that threatened devastatingly the lives of the people in the town so much. Every night, Omal prayed and pleaded with God, to kindly let him travel with the orphaned kids, safely back to his wife and children in Juba.

Chapter Twenty-Five
Ader Lost Her Beloved Husband

Before the convoy, that had gone to Torit could return to Juba, the rebels started shelling Juba relentlessly. In a place called Atlabara, a mother with her six children, who were hiding in a trench died when the shelling fell on them. Many civilians lost their lives, including Hinda's husband. Ader spent, most of her time with her grieving friend and felt such sympathy for, her friend's greatest loss. Of all the shelling that had been falling into Juba, not a single one of them had fallen into the military barracks, which made many people wondered and felt as if, the rebels were only targeting the civilians. To make the devastating situation even worst the rebels daily bragged on their radio broadcast that they had been very successful in destroying most of their enemies' targets in Juba. Many people were deeply saddened by the way that the rebels were heartlessly bragging but especially the people who had lost their loved ones to the shelling. A few of the people, whose lives had not yet been touched by the misery that the rebels were inflicting on others, still supported what the rebels were doing. Consequently, there were lots of misunderstanding among the people in Juba.

Amidst all the deaths, confusions and uncertainties in Juba, the soldiers in Torit radioed a message to the headquarters in Juba that they were preparing to return to Juba. When Ader heard about the news concerning, the return of the convoy from Torit, she was very delighted. Ader was then earnestly longing to seeing and being with her dear husband because he had stayed away from her for such a long time. Therefore, she immaculately cleaned her house and made all the necessary arrangements, for welcoming back her husband and the children of her late sister-in-law. Despite Ader's outward happiness and anxious longing to seeing and being with her husband, deep in her heart, the fear for an impending danger that had been devastating her heart ever since before, her husband had gone to Torit, was still haunting her. However, she put on a brave face.

The rebels stopped shelling Juba, as soon as they had heard the news about the convoy's return to Juba and the inhabitants of Juba were happy once again. The women began to go, for firewood without fear. There was a bit of hope in most of the people because some of them were able to say for the first time, "Tomorrow I would do and the next day, I would do that." Such was, the kind of statement that no one was able to say when the shelling was going on. The women started smearing their huts which, were looking quite awful because no work had been done on them for a long time. Furthermore, there were parties on Saturdays and the young people danced happily as if, nothing horrible had happened in the previous few weeks. When some concerned elders confronted and asked them that "Why do you, the young people, seem to be so happy when, everything is falling apart, with the ongoing war?"

They plainly replied to the elders that "Our life's spans are too short these days and therefore, whenever we are having any widow of opportunity for peace, we feel that we should be enjoying ourselves as much as we could. Consequently, we are dancing to enjoying ourselves and celebrating, the lives of our fallen friends."

What the young people were saying was so sensible that the elders did not disturb them anymore.

In Torit, the last few days before, the convoy was about to leave for Juba, Omal prayed earnestly, while he was asking God, to kindly allow him and the children of his late sister to travel safely back to Juba. However, every night, he had been having nightmares that someone bounded his hands and feet with a rope and was about to throw him into a bottomless pit, when he started calling out for help but no one came to his rescue. Omal, had initially ignored his nightmare but as soon as it had started repeating itself every night, he became quite concerned that there was obviously something wrong about, either their journey back to Juba or with his wife and children. He became so withdrawn that his friend, Ohisa, one day asked him about what was disturbing him. After Omal told Ohisa about the reason, he advised Omal not to take such thing serious but to hope for the best.

On the day that the convoy was leaving for Juba, the residents of Torit once again took to the streets, as they did when the convoy first got to Torit. They sung out loudly that everyone who was traveling on that convoy was a hero and that they wished them, a safe journey back to Juba. They further asked, those who were traveling to always remember the people in Torit. Therefore, the drivers, travelers and the soldiers who were escorting the convoy thanked, the residents of Torit and thereafter, started screaming wildly as if, they were going to war. The day was cloudy and kind of melancholy. Omal sat quietly in the truck that he and the children of his late sister were traveling in. In his heart, he was wishing that the truck could have turned into an airplane so that they could arrive in Juba within minutes. Therefore, the children sat closest to Omal and he began to assure them that they were going to travel safely to Juba and have a good life.

The convoy traveled safely until, it reached half way between Torit and Juba when, the rebels relentlessly attacked it. The soldiers and the rebels then engaged in a fierce combat in which, many people lost their lives on both sides. The survivors, then decided to proceed with their journey but a few kilometres near a place, called Liria, another group of the rebels begun attacking them once again and it was the worst of, any attack by the rebels on any convoy. Omal, the children of his late sister and the rest of the people who had children became so disoriented, confused and terrified that all of them began crying. The thunderous sounds, of the trucks being blown up, were too much for the children, who consequently, began screaming and running up and down inside the truck. Omal attempted to control his nephews and niece but eventually, relinquished after he had failed and instead, began thinking about his dearest wife and sons. As the reality, about the possibility for their deaths became clear in his mind, Omal, for the first time started wishing that he should have accepted his wife's advice. He began to clearly remembering his wife, as she was last desperately pleading with him in tears that he should not to go Torit. Omal's thoughts about his wife were so overwhelming that he got lost in the most wonderful memory land, as he was reminiscing; how he fell in love with her, the day she fell in love with him, their engagement, their lovely and memorable honeymoon in Upper Talanga, the ceremonious welcome his father and the People of Magwi had accorded to him and his wife after their honeymoon, their romantic time together before the births of their sons and when their sons were born, his last sizzling night with his wife and the last moment that he had kissed her near the bridge. Omal's mind was completely clouded with lots of sweet memories that for a while he became oblivious about the deadly danger that he and the rest of the people were in. Some travelers, who were not having children, started jumping out of the trucks because they were thinking that it would be safer for them on the ground than in the trucks. Unfortunately, most of them were killed, before they could even get to the ground, by the spraying bullets from both the rebels and the soldiers. Omal, who initially was thinking about jumping down from the truck, had then realised that the children with whom he was traveling were too young to jump down with him and so, he decided to remain aboard, with the rest of the people who were also having children. As it became obvious to Omal that he was definitely going to die on that fateful day, he quietly began asking God, to take care of his beloved wife and children. With a heartfelt gratitude, he profoundly thanked God, for the wonderful but short loving and fulfilled life that he had enjoyed with his wife. Omal contritely requested God, to kindly forgive him, for soon making his precious wife a widow and his lovely sons, orphans. He also asked God to pardon him, for the sins that he might have committed but had forgotten about and the sins of the people who were going to die with him on that day. Furthermore, he requested God in his mercy, to welcome the souls of everyone, who was going to die with him, into everlasting life. Eventually, Omal closed his eyes and impotently threw up his hands into the air, as he was helplessly waiting, with the rest of the people, for whatever would become of them. Finally, a motor from the rebels' shelling fell on their truck and blew up everyone on board. Omal and his late sister's children, lost their lives in a situation that was very, very frightening, horrifying, terrifying and eventually, deadly because they saw the ugly face of death, as it was approaching them until, it ruthlessly; deprived them of their courage, strength, hope, power, reasoning and took their lives eventually. The children were blown up into pieces and Omal's head was cut off from his body and thrown far away.

When the vicious and deadly fighting eventually ended, Ohisa, who had also been traveling on the same convoy but in a different truck, which was not blown up, unexpectedly found the dismembered head of his friend, Omal, while he was tarrying aimlessly among the debris and the dead bodies. With a heart-wrenching sorrow, he respectfully took the head of his dead friend and covered it up with a blanket, as if it was his belonging. Ohisa was very shocked, to know that his dear friend was killed. Consequently, he started acting like a crazy man, as he was mumbling to himself because he could not reconcile in his mind that his friend was indeed dead. He begun remembering Omal's nightmares and understood then that in a way God was preparing his friend, to meet his death. Ohisa sorrowfully prayed that God might rest Omal's and the children's souls in peace. As soon as Ohisa started remembering Ader and children and how devastating their loss was, he wept quite bitterly, with such broken heart because he could not imagine how cruel death might be, to separating Omal and Ader, who loved each other faithfully, deeply, dearly, selflessly, devotedly, understandably, wonderfully and adoringly. The spraying bullets, had also hit Ohisa on one shoulder and therefore, he was soaked in his own blood, which was not bothering him at all then because he was quite devastated by Omal's death.

Those who had survived the deadly fight gathered together eventually in one place but could not say any word. The whole area was littered with dead bodies, blown up trucks and some of the burning corpses were still smoldering. The whole scene was like that from a horror movie and was quite frightening and spooky. The civilians were feeling as if, they had lost their minds and did not know what to do next. Some were crying like little children, while others were speaking incoherently. However, the soldiers, who were already used to facing such encounters, although, not of the same magnitude as of that heart-wrenching day, were quite normal. They then radioed a message to Juba saying that they desperately needed emergency help, for those who have been critically injured and they also reported the heavy casualties that they had suffered. The headquarters automatically understood the danger that the survivors were facing and immediately dispatched a convoy, to quickly go and rescue the survivors back to Juba. A helicopter was also sent to bring, the critically injured people to the hospital. Consequently, Ohisa got the chance, to go to Juba in the helicopter because he was included among wounded. He therefore, took the head of his dear friend, Omal, with him, since nobody knew what he was carrying in his blanket.

On the night that Omal had died, Ader had a dream that was almost seemingly real. In her dream, her husband was dressed up in white and was playing a big harp, as he was singing joyfully in a beautiful choir. Everyone in the choir was dressed up in white and anyone who was dressed up in another colour, was not allowed to join them. Ader was dressed unfortunately, in black and so she could not join the members of the choir, as they were joyfully, happily and peacefully singing. Consequently, Ader started asking her husband, to give her a white robe so that she could join them but he vehemently refused and told her that she did not belong to the choir and should only listen to the beautiful singing. Ader sadly cried as she pleaded with her husband to kindly let her join the choir but he would not relent. The dream disturbed Ader on and off throughout the night.

The following morning, Ader was terribly horrified by the dream that somehow, according to her fearful thought, had symbolised that her husband might be dead. Ader was utterly devastated by the dream that she did not dare to share it with anyone but remained in bed with crippling fever. After Juan realized that Ader had not come out of her house since morning, she went to her and gently asked, "What is wrong with you today, my dear? I have not seen you outside since morning. Are you really, ok?

Ader only shook her head to make her point because she was burning with fever. Juan then felt her friend's forehead and concluded that she was indeed, quite ill. "Why did you not, send me one of your sons to tell me that you were not feeling well?" Juan sadly asked, her friend in sympathy.

"They have gone out to play and never came back," Ader replied, almost in a whisper.

Juan immediately started using some wet cloth, to bring down Ader's fever after, she had first given to her some febrifuge. A little while, after Ader's fever had gone down, Juan went back to her house and brought for Ader some food, which she ate very little. Juan attempted to persuade Ader to eat a little more but she flatly refused and consequently, Juan kept the remainder of the food for Ader's children. Ader thereafter, gratefully thanked her friend, for being so kind to her and her children.

When the news about, the fatal attacks on the convoy reached Juba, some of Ader's and her husband's relatives, including some of the family's friends came over to see her. Ader welcomed everyone but seemed quite weak and sad because her heart was torn apart. Instinctively, Ader was already feeling that her husband's safety was in jeopardy. One of the relatives noticed Ader's demeanour and sympathetically told her, "Please do not lose hope because I do not think that everyone on the convoy is dead. There is a likelihood that Omal may be among the few survivors."

Ader quietly gazed at her friend, as she was speaking, deeply sighed and despairingly shrugged because she was too confused, to make sense of the news about, the fate of the convoy. As Ader was listening to her visitors' conversation, someone brought the news about Omal's death and told Mori. Consequently, Mori and one of Omal's friends entered Ader's house and gently begun holding her down. Ader automatically understood then that her husband was indeed dead and did not even ask the men, as to why they were holding her down. After a moment of deadly silence, she eventually asked the two men to leave her alone. In her shredded heart, Ader could not accept that her husband had truly died and left her alone with the young children. However, there was no tear at all in Ader's eyes but her body began trembling uncontrollably and she began burning up with intense fever. Mori and the rest of the people begun to wonder, as to what was really happening to Ader and all of them became quite frightened by the situation Ader was in. Everyone wished that Ader could cry, so as to release some of the shock and anguish that she was harbouring within. All attempts, to bring down Ader's fever proved fruitless and the people did not know what do with her anymore, as they were watching her in such scare, while the pain, anguish, sorrow and despair for losing her husband so suddenly, were consuming her internally with such devastation.

When Omal's head was eventually, brought into the house, Ader immediately asked that she would like to hold and bid her husband goodbye. The people vehemently objected initially but she seriously insisted and when she was allowed to hold the head, she began kissing her dead husband's lips, as she was lovingly holding the head, closed to her heart. However, most of the elders were objecting, as to what she was doing with her late husband's head and consequently, one of them forcefully took the it away from her. Ader did not complain after the head had been taken away from her but started pacing up and down, while her eyes were burning with pain like charcoal fire. She was instantly changed and looked completely wild. Eventually, she sat on her bed and started screaming out loudly for her husband, to come and take her to wherever he had gone. The old women who had come to share in her grief, were terrified and began saying that they had never seen such a tearless widow, like Ader. They attempted to persuade Ader that it was ok for her to shed some tears, so as to relieve some of her anguish that was holding inside but it seemed then that Ader was no longer able, to communicate with the people around her because she was mumbling incoherently to herself, as her eyes were searching seemingly, for something that the other people who were around her, were not able to see. Ader's eyes were opened but it was hard to tell, whether she was looking at any specific thing and she became eventually so absentminded and quite disoriented that some of the women brought her two sons and placed them on her lap, so that she could come to her senses but that never work because Ader then seemed to have even forgotten about her children. Everyone became so concerned about Ader's situation but did not know what to do. By midnight she began calling out her husband's name, quite loudly and then unconsciously collapsed. The shock of her husband's death eventually, took toll on her. Some of the mourners quickly called a taxi and rushed her to the regional hospital where, she was admitted and remained unconscious, for a week.

Omal's head was buried, when his wife was in the hospital because it had already started to decay. It was really a sad sight during the burial because normally people buried a whole body but the devastating war in southern Sudan, had led to the burial of legs, arms, head and other parts of the body, at different times. The children were taken, to witness the burial according to the Acoli tradition but they did not understand what was taking place. They were crying not because they were missing their dad but because they were scared and wondering where, both of their parents had gone. Another reason why they were crying was because they did not understand why, the older people were sorrowfully crying, as if they were little children. Old Nyarata took good care of the children and told them that their mother had gone for a visit and would soon come back to them with, lots of goodies. There were funerals all over Juba because the number of the people who had been killed on that convoy was, the greatest ever since the war had started. The people in Juba did not know what to do anymore and lived only by faith.

While unconscious, the spirit of Ader met with that of her late husband. Omal was handsomely standing at the gate of an exquisite garden, which shone like the sun but would not allow his wife in. Ader ventured to force her way into the garden but her husband defiantly prohibited her. Consequently, they started wrestling quite viciously for a long time and eventually Omal defeated Ader. Ader then pleaded with her husband that he should kindly allow her into the great light that she was seeing in the beautiful garden but he vehemently refused to listen to her. Everyone in the light was smiling and seemed so joyful, restful, peaceful and happy. Omal told his wife that her time had not yet come, to enter where he was. Ader miserably cried because she was anxiously wanting to be, part of the joyful life that she, was seeing her husband in. Omal assertively told his wife that their sons were needing her so much and that was why he was not going to permit her in. After Ader had realised that there was nothing else that she could say or do to convince her husband so that he could let her into the beautiful garden, her spirit decided to return to her body and she therefore regained consciousness.

On the day that Ader had regained her consciousness, after staying in the hospital for a week, she began to wonder as to why she was in the hospital and therefore, asked almost in a whisper, the nurse who was sitting next to her bed, "Why am I here?" and those were her first words.

"You were very ill," the nurse gently replied. "I am very happy to see you awake and able to talk once again. How do you feel, my dear?"

"I am fine but quite weak," Ader softly told the nurse. "Where are my dear children?"

"They are at home and are doing very well," sympathetically said the nurse.

"Can I go home to my children?" humbly asked Ader. "I want to hold them in my arms."

"I can't give you the answer to that question," the nurse honestly told her.

"Would you mind to wait for the doctor on duty to come? He is the right person, who could tell you whether, you are well enough to go home or not."

"Thanks, I will wait then," weakly said Ader.

When the doctor on duty came therefore, he was very happy to find Ader fully awake and able to talk once again. The doctor then perceived that Ader would recover quickly, when allowed to go home and be with her children. Consequently, he discharged her.

The relatives and friends who were waiting on Ader in the hospital were very happy to see her walking out of the ward, supported by two nurses. They rushed to her and took hold of her from the nurses. Ader then asked them, "Where are my children and with whom have they been staying?"

One of her friends sympathetically replied, "Your children are staying with Nyarata and they are fine but missing you a lot."

Ader did not say any word but only nodded and her thoughts began wandering very far away that one could tell from the way she was looking at things.

"Are you really fit enough, to go home?" one of the women asked her.

"Yy…es ," Ader stammered, as she was trying to make sense, about her surrounding. The women then called a taxi and took Ader home because she was too weak, to walk home on foot.

The few remaining relatives who were waiting, for the recovery of Ader at her home were quite overwhelmed with relief, as soon as they have seen her, after arriving home from the hospital. Most of the women started to cry pitifully because Ader was so frail looking and sorrowful. Some of them were crying simply because they wanted Ader to also cry. Surprisingly, there was no tear in Ader's eyes. She tearlessly entered her house, grabbed her boys to her chest and lovingly looked into their eyes, which were reminding her a lot about, her dear late husband. She then deeply sighed and said, "I know that my husband is dead and can anyone tell me exactly how he had died?"

The women began to narrate to Ader what, Ohisa had told them but suddenly they realised that Ader was disoriented once again. She was staring blankly at the wall but without any tear in her eyes. Everyone started becoming scared again that Ader might lose consciousness again. However, after a moment of silence, Ader came to her senses and began to say, "Omal, is it really true that you have left us without saying goodbye? Why did you not let me go before you? You were an excellent man and I know how loving and caring you were. Our children are boys, you could have taken proper care them and be a good role model for them. I am a mere woman and cannot be a good role model for the boys. Anyway, God's will be done and not mine, may your soul rest in peace."

Everyone compassionately looked at Ader, as she was speaking and thought that she might begin to cry thereafter but they were wrong. Eventually, one of the women made some porridge for Ader and she took it very little.

Two days, after Ader had returned from the hospital, she asked the people to take her to the place where, her husband's head had been buried. Consequently, some of the people escorted her to the tomb and when they got there, Ader fell face down on the tomb and restfully closed her eyes. She seemed so peaceful as if, that was where she belonged. People could not make sense of Ader's behaviour and some of them were thinking that she was becoming insane. When the people asked her so that they could take her back to the house, she softly told them that she was still having a romantic time with her husband. Everyone started to sorrowfully weep, except for the tearless widow. The people waited for Ader in silence for a long time and then eventually, she got up and said, "We can go home now because my husband has told me that I should go home to the children."

No one was able to understand anything that Ader was trying to say or do and so they simply took her home.

After Ader and the people who had escorted her to the grave had returned to her house, she opened a suitcase that was containing, the clothes of her late husband and took out a gray suit that her he used to put on, whenever there were big occasions. She put on the suit, started walking around the house and seemed to be in such peace that no one could describe. Her eyes lingered and seemed to be looking at the things that no one else could perceive but her. Afterwards, she quietly sat down on the chair, with her head between her thighs, for over an hour. Everyone was shocked, as they were watching Ader's weird behaviour in silence because they could not comprehend her and everything that she was doing seemed so strange and unimaginable. Eventually, she got out of the chair and sat on the mat next to one of the elderly women but her eyes were still burning in anguish, which one could tell at a glance. One of the older women then advised Ader, "It is ok for you to cry because tears release some of the pain that you are going through. Please dear, do not resist to cry but let it all out."

Ader stared at the woman in silence for a while and eventually said, "Could someone give me the Bible?"

One of the women, therefore, gave her the Bible. She then asked the people, "Would you mind to listen to what I am going to read from the Bible?"

"We don't really mind to listen to you, dear," they replied, with such anticipation.

Before Ader could start reading the verses she had selected, she told them, "I know that most of you are thinking that I am becoming insane because I have never wept for the death of my husband. However, one thing that you do not know is that tears cannot express the mountain of pain, misery, sorrow, anguish, anxiety, and torment that I am going through right now. My husband was my last hope left, to live a good life on this earth but he too, is now gone. Therefore, the verses that I am about to read to you, will tell you exactly why, I have not cried for my husband."

Ader took her reading from 2 Samuel 12:15–23. The verses are as follows, for the readers who do not have the time, to refer to the Bible:

> The LORD caused the child that Uriah's wife had borne to David to become very sick. David prayed to God that the child would get well. He refused to eat anything, and every night he went into his room and spent the night lying on the floor. His court officials went to him and tried to make him get up, but he refused and would not eat anything with them. A week later the child died, and David's officials were afraid to tell him the news. They said, "While the child was living, David wouldn't answer us when we spoke to him. How can we tell him that his child is dead? He might do himself some harm!"
>
> When David noticed them whispering to each other, he realized that the child had died. So he asked them, "Is the child dead?"
>
> "Yes, he is," they answered.
>
> David got up from the floor, took a bath, combed his hair, and changed his clothes. Then he went and worshiped in the house of the LORD. When he returned to the palace, he asked for food and ate it as soon as it was served. "We don't understand this," his officials said to him. "While the child was alive, you wept for him and would not eat; but as soon as he died, you got up and ate!"
>
> "Yes," David answered, "I did fast and weep while he was still alive. I thought that the LORD might be merciful to me and not let the child die. But now that he is dead, why should I fast? Could I bring the child back to life? I will some day go to where he is, but he can never come back to me."

After the reading, Ader looked at everyone's eyes one by one and then humbly asked them, "Have you all understood, what I have just read?"

Most of her listeners did not even know that such verses existed in the Bible and were quite amazed to hear about, the great courage of King David. However, they replied, "We have understood the reading very well but could not relate it to your behaviour."

"I will try to explained it to you then," softly said Ader. "I have been having a terrible fear that had rifted my heart and soul apart, before my husband could go to Torit. I cried and prayed every night for my dear husband, while asking God to protect and keep him safe from just any danger. I pleaded with God every day but the more I prayed the deeper the fear penetrated the depth of my heart, mind and soul. Eventually, I resorted to fasting and praying but that did not help me, to get rid of my terrifying fear. You all have noticed how, I had lost weight within a very short period of time, after my husband left for Torit and many people ridiculed me about it. I did not care about what they were saying because my main concern was my husband's safety. Eventually, I had a dream that my husband was dressed in white and was seemingly very happy, while I was dressed in black and very miserable. I knew then that God needed my husband in heaven more than, I do here on earth. Therefore, now that he is gone to that beautiful home above, even if I were to cry, my dear people, would my tears bring him back to me and the children?" I do not think so. If I were to cry, I would instead, be depriving my husband of the peace that he is now enjoying but that I do not want to do. He, like David's son, will not ever come back to this world, which is heavily stricken with hatred, pain, killing, stereotyping, jealousy, envy, destruction, rejection, intimidation, misery, etc but my children and I would one day, join him above and live happily ever after."

Everyone was amazed by, what Ader had explained to them. They admired her faith, courage and strength. After her explanation, she asked for some food and ate very well for the first time since, the news of her husband's death. Later on that evening, Ader led prayer, people joined her and together they sang hymns of praise and thanksgiving to God.

Most of the people were confused, as to how Ader who loved her husband so much, could not shed any tear at his death. However, those who had known about the horrible tragedies that had afflicted Ader's life prior to the death of her dearly beloved husband realised that she had eventually, surrendered her terrible losses and sorrow to Jesus, whom she loved so much. Ader spent most of her time in prayer and asked God to give her more strength and courage, so that she could overcome all the pain that she was going through. She constantly prayed for her dear late husband so that he could find peace with God in heaven and on the other hand, intercede to God for her and the children, so that they could live well, here below. Ader also prayed for her dear father, beloved brother Okema, sweet sister Amyel, cousins, her three sisters-in-law, nieces, nephews and her dear mother-in-law. She envied all her departed loved ones because they were already living in peace with God, while she was still struggling in this torturous world. Any other normal person, given the life of Ader, would have crushed into pieces.

Nyarata was thinking erroneously that Ader's behaviour might someday let her to commit suicide, and therefore, she began to keep a vigilant watch over Ader and talked to her a lot, as she was trying to comfort her in every way possible. One day she sympathetically told Ader, "My dear child, you must learn to cry in order to cope with your sorrowful life and start the process for healing. You cannot go on for a long time, while burning with pain and not shedding any tear at all."

"There are, still many years ahead of me, for weeping," Ader carelessly told Nyarata, "but as for now, I believe that I can do well, without shedding tears."

"I think that you should start drinking some beer, in order to numb your anguish and sorrow," one of the elderly women, suggested to Ader

Ader vehemently refused and said, "I did not drink, as a young girl and when my husband was still alive. Therefore, why should I start drinking after, their very painful deaths? If I start drinking now, it would be like insulting the sweet memories that I am having, for my dearly departed loved ones."

The rest of the women were thinking that it was still early for Ader to say what she had said and that in the future, Ader might one day begin drinking and her lifestyle would be changed completely. However, the women did not understand that Ader had already accepted her greatest losses and had placed tenaciously her trust in God.

Chapter Twenty-Six
Ader's Sorrowful Life

When the guests, who had come for the funeral eventually, went back to their own places, Ader was left alone to face her sorrowful life and she became quite confused in every thing that she was trying to do. The death of Omal, took a big chunk out of Ader's life in that she felt like a stranger in her own house and everything became so meaningless to her. Ader then realised that all the changes, pains, sorrow, anguish, anxiety and misery she was undergoing, could easily break her down if, she did not ask for the intervention of a higher power. Consequently, she devoted her time to prayer and asked God in the Name of Jesus Christ, to help her overcome all the impossibilities that she was facing in her life and especially, to give her strength and courage in order for her, to go on living for the sake of her two sons. Ader's tears, came out spontaneously whenever she was praying because such was the only moment when, she was feeling that she was talking to a caring, loving friend, brother, father, Saviour and Lord who would never let her down but rather shared in her sorrow. Ader was rarely seen outside except, when she was going to work, fetch some water or go to the market.

A few months after Omal's death, Jokal, his older brother, out of the blue, showed up in Juba and claimed that he had come for the funeral of his brother. His relatives in Juba were really surprised to see him. Jokal appeared older than his real age and seemed quite ugly because he was drinking like a fish. He did not show any sign, for grieving the death of his late brother. He went out everyday, came back drank and smelled like a warthog's fart. Not many days after his arrival, Jokal authoritatively started to commanding Ader around with absolute power, while he was telling her, "do this, do that and you should ask for my permission, whenever you want to go anywhere."

Whenever Ader greeted or talked, to any man at all, Jokal would immediately get angry and demand, "Who was that man that you were talking to and how long have you known him?"

Life became so difficult and unbearable for Ader that she asked Nyarata to move in with them.

Jokal did not like the reality about, Nyarata sharing a house with them because he had his ill intention about one day, raping Ader at night. After Jokal had realized that there was no opportunity for him whatsoever, to carry our his sordid plan, he therefore, gathered some elders one evening and started asking for their permission, "I would like, to inherit my brother's widow right away. I think that it is time for Ader to start having more babies and I am the right man, to be with her according to our custom."

Before Ader could say anything, one of the elders replied to Jokal, "According to the Acoli tradition, a widow is only inherited after the last funeral rite, which in the case of your late brother, has not yet been performed, due to the ongoing insecurity. Even if the last funeral rite was already done, the decision rests entirely with Ader, who could accept or reject the idea of being with you. Remember, young man, in this modern time and age the inheritance of a widow is no longer automatic and compulsory as it used to be in the past."

Jokal was annoyed by what the old man had told him that he stormed out of the chair that he was sitting on in fury and angrily announced, "I will do whatever, I want with the widow of my late brother and none of you has the right to stop me whatsoever!"

Ader, who was then extremely disgusted by Jokal's misbehaviour, boldly stood up before everyone and said assertively "I do not want any man in my life anymore because my late husband was, the only man that I have ever loved and known. Dear elders, who has give Jokal the right to decide, as to whatever he wants to do with me? Has Jokal forgotten that I am a whole human being, with every right and freedom like him? I have got brain and I know exactly what kind of a man Jokal is. He is a vagrant, who has never been there for anyone in his family, never written to anyone since he had left home, never came for our wedding, never came for the funeral of his mother and sisters and just does not care about anybody, including himself. I even do not understand the reason why, he has come to Juba now."

Jokal became so furious with Ader that he almost beat her up, had the elders not been there, to stop him. He vehemently blamed Ader, for the death of his brother, "You are a witch, who was not supposed to have been married, into a noble family like ours. Do you think that I did not hear about your diabolical activities, when my brother was still alive? I have heard that you were giving love portion to him and fooling him around like a child, until his death. Furthermore, I am very aware about the fact that my brother used to wash even your underwear. Now that he is dead, you do not want me, to take his place and bear more children in his name. You just don't care, you wicked devil do you? You woman whose whole being is covered with curses, misfortune and smell of death!"

"Well, if I am then the woman whose whole being is covered with misfortune and smell of death, why have you brought all these elders, to give you permission to inherit me, you loser?" Ader arrogantly interrogated her brother-in-law. "Did you even understand how stupidly you have contradicted yourself, pseudo man? I am the daughter of a respectable man, although, my father was not a Chief, like yours. Jokal, your people, including my beloved late husband, your brother, did love me so much. I was the beauty of my husband's eyes and he dearly loved me until his death. I still indelibly love my late husband because he was no jerk like you, beast. You are an ignominy and execration, to the name of your lovely family. Look at you! You who could not even, find your buttocks with both hands!"

Ader's reply further infuriated Jokal so much that he fumed and threatened her in front of everyone who was there, as he was charging about, like a mad bull, while he was screaming, "Adeeeeer! Hand to me immediately, the bankbook and everything that belonged to my late brother or else I will squeeze life out of you, you idiot and big mouth!"

Ader rushed into her house in anger and took out the bankbook, other stuff, the suitcases full of her late husband belongings and threw everything at Jokal, while she was furiously telling him, "What are you waiting for, you freaky-looking and monstrous loser, take all the stuff but if you feel that you want to enter the house yourself and check out for more, suit yourself because I do not want to argue with a fool like you! My late husband hated every memory he had had of you when he was still alive and now I have understood why! I love my husband so much even if he is dead! Do not think that your stupid actions will let me regret as to why I have ever married my sweet late husband, your brother! Omal was the pride of his family and not you! No one, including your father, had ever spoken well of you! Take those material things but I don't think that you have the power to deprive me of my husband's love and the sweet memories that I have shared with him from my heart and mind!"

Jokal gathered everything that he wanted and immediately left. He went to spend the night with, one of his friends.

The elders, who had been watching the fiasco in silence, eventually told

Ader, after Jokal had left, "You should have not handed the bankbook, to that ruthless Jokal."

"I do not want any further argument with that loser and grabber, Jokal, whose heart is wilder than that of a hungry lion," Ader carelessly told the elders. "My life and that of my children, will be peaceful without Jokal around. As for the money, let me assure you, my dear elders that God will provide for me and my children, in a special way as He did for the Israelites in the desert."

The elders were amazed, to hear everything that Ader was telling them and they admired and praised her courage and strength. However, they were wishing that they could have some money, so that they could have contributed some and give to Ader and her children.

Old Nyarata spent that night with Ader because she was worried that Ader might harm herself due to all the insults that her brother-in-law had hurled at her and all the money that he had taken away.

"What your brother-in-law has done to you tonight, is very humiliating and horrendous," sadly said Nyarata. "Now what are you going to raise your children with?"

"Do not worry about me and my children," carelessly replied Ader. "Our future is in God's hands. It is up to God, to let us suffer to death or live well."

"Life is not easy at all for widows, especially with the cruel ongoing war," Nyarata sympathetically told Ader, with such a look of concern on her face.

"The divine providence, will provide," Ader faithfully told Nyarata.

Nyarata then realised that Ader was a very, very strong young widow, who had already accepted her miserable position in life. She admired Ader's courage and believed that Ader would live well with her children, without any need for a man.

As soon as Jokal got to his friend's house, his friend was surprised to see him, with lots of things in his hands. "What has happened to you that has made you to come here at night, with lots of stuff?" he curiously asked Jokal. "You do not, seem well at all."

"My sister-in-law, has just chased me out of her house," Jokal shamelessly lied to his friend. "She had brought a man in the house for the night and did not want me around. I was angry with her and we had a big fight. She therefore, threw away all the stuff that were belonging to my late brother and forced me out of the house at once."

His friend, who did not know Ader at all, believed him and started saying, "Oh my God! What a horrible woman, your late brother was married to! How could the woman, be so heartless to you? Furthermore, your late brother is not yet even a year in his grave and the woman is messing around with men already? What a shame! I do not think that your sister-in-law had even loved your late brother, when he was still alive, otherwise, she would have been kind to you. You can live with me, until you have decided to go back to Khartoum."

Jokal was very grateful to his friend.

After a few days of getting all the legal papers in order, Jokal and his friend went to the bank, to cash money from the late Omal's account. His friend was quite surprised, to learn that the money Jokal was cashing was from his late brother's account. Consequently, on their way to a drinking place, he therefore asked Jokal, "I wonder whether, what you have told me about your sister-in-law, is true."

Jokal first beat around the bush but finally, his guilty conscience caught up with him and he honestly confessed, "I had wanted to inherit my late brother's widow but after she had rejected me, I became furious and took everything that belonged to my late brother, away from her."

Jokal's friend, who was a responsible person, became very annoyed with him and sternly told him, "If you are a real man, please take the money back to the widow and her children. What you have done to your brother's widow and the orphans, is very sacrilegious indeed. For the sake of the house of your father and his name, take the money back to the poor widow."

Jokal greedily refused to listen to the advice that his friend had given him. He instead went and bought an airplane ticket and returned to Khartoum the following day, taking with him everything that he could carry and all the money.

Ader was so relieved, after she had heard that Jokal had already gone back to northern Sudan. As the result therefore, she invited all her neighbours for a dinner and cooked a lot of food for them. The neighbours did not understand, why Ader threw such a big dinner for them. Juan was very concerned and eventually, asked Ader, "Why have you decided, to cook meal for all of us?"

"I did so because I am celebrating my poverty and freedom from my insane brother-in-law," Ader triumphantly told Juan. "He was trying to take me by force, to be his wife and when I rejected him, he viciously insulted me, in front of the elders and took all my late husband's stuff, including, the money from the bank, before he could leave for northern Sudan. I don't care about anything anymore because everything in my life has been, tested to the fullest capacity. The one thing that I needed the most in my sorrowful life is, my freedom from my ruthless brother-in-law and that I have finally gotten. Blessed be, the name of the Lord."

Juan was so touched by the incredible story that she began to cry as she was hugging Ader. "Please do not worry because God will always bless a tender hearted person like you and give you your daily bread," Juan told Ader, as her tears were streaming down her cheeks. "I deeply admire, your courage and strength."

After the neighbours, had eaten and returned to their houses, Juan remained to talk and console her friend. They chatted that night until 9:00 PM.

Ader used, the little amount of money that was left in her account economically and was always cheerful. The people who did not know Ader that well, could not tell whether she was a widow because she was always smiling and freely and joyfully talking to everyone she knew. Ader never mentioned the name of Jokal at all because she was pleased that such an arrogant, horrible, terrible, rude, ruthless and greedy person was out of her life and her children for good. The elders, who had witnessed, the terrible things that Jokal had done to Ader, told the other people about it. Most of the people pitied Ader so much and wondered how she was going to survive with her children, on her little salary.

Ader gradually started enjoying her life with her two sons so much because no one was bothering them anymore. However, many people eventually, started thinking that Ader had become abnormal, since she did not want to love again. Ader had noticed, how some of the widows who had decided to remarry, were having hard time to cope with the stress and troubles in their marriages. In some of the situations, the new husbands hated the children from the first marriages so much that they told their wives to let the children go and live with relatives, while in others, the children were sometimes badly beaten up by their stepfathers. Ader did not want, such situations, to happen to her beloved children, who were born as a result of deep true love and faithful marriage. She further thought to herself, *If I make a mistake, to fall in love with another man, it will be an insult, to the beautiful memories that I am having for my dearly beloved late husband. Omal was my only soul mate and I do not think that there is another man out there, who could give me the kind of love that I have experienced with my beloved late husband. Lightning does not strike twice, in the same place.* Consequently, Ader absolutely decided, to live alone with her children and trusted God for, whatever the future was holding for them.

A time came when there was no relief food in Juba, due to the threats by the rebels that any plane that attempted to come to Juba they would shoot down. Many people suffered, especially the displaced people who did not have any source of income. A lot of people became malnourished that they could not even walk. Ader was having some food that she had been storing for emergency, since when her husband was still alive. Consequently, she started giving some of the food to the people that she knew were almost dying. Eventually, she was left with very little food. Most of the people whom Ader had helped started calling her a munificent woman and further nicknamed her, "The Angel of Good Hope." Ader did not like her nickname because she had a strong conviction that people should help one another in times of need and that was why, she shared her food with those who were in dire need.

The hunger situation worsened so much that there was nothing eventually left anymore for most people to eat. Ader used the little food that was left in her house economically, by some days not eating but cooking only for her children. The situation went on for a long time that most people gave up the hope for going to be alive anymore. The people in Juba began gathering together quite often for prayer, while they were asking God to have mercy on them. They also prayed that God should touched the stubborn heart of the leader of the rebel, so that he could agree that the relief food be airlifted to Juba. After weeks of the devastating suffering from starvation, an agreement was reached and the relief food began to be flown to Juba. On the day that the first relief airplane had touched down in Juba, everyone went wild with joy and even those who were severely malnourished, stood up for the first time, so as to celebrate the good news. The people who were a bit stronger; sang, danced for joy and praised the name of God, for answering their prayer. There were noises in Juba, for the first time, since the hunger had begun.

As for poor Ader, the good news about the relief food did not make any difference in her life at all because she could not receive the relief food, since she was classified as a working person. The little food she had been having in her house, got finished eventually. Therefore, Ader started buying food from the local market, at an alarming price. As the months were going by, her little savings dwindled and finally got finished. Ader then started depending entirely on her salary, which could not take her up to the end of the month. Unlike most women in Juba, Ader did not believe, in brewing beer for sale, in order to support her life and that of her children because she just could not handle, the way that the men who were drinking in those brewing places behaved to the women, who were brewing and selling the local beer, for their living. Ader carried on her miserable life, with such strength and courage that she often was smiling as if, nothing devastating was going on in her life. She trusted God each day for the meal that they were going to eat. However, her miserable situation was continuing to deteriorate and eventually, Ader gave up any hope for being alive and became so depressed. She hated, the idea of begging things from the neighbours so much because she had never begged in her whole life. Ader sat up most of the nights and cried to God for help but each day was the same as the previous one, as everything continued to worsen in her life. After there was nothing completely left for her children to eat the following morning, after Ader had already stayed without food for more than a couple of days, she begun pouring out her heart to God in prayer but there was no answer and therefore, she became so confused that nothing made sense to her anymore. It seemed then as if God, her only protector, had also abandoned her already. Therefore, Ader convinced herself that she would cry until she was dead and started crying as soon as her sons went to bed and wept bitterly in anguish for the whole night. The following morning, her face was swollen completely but she was not yet dead.

Chapter Twenty-Seven
Ader in Despair

It was a beautiful Sunday morning and many people were already up by 7:00 AM but Ader was still in her house, with her door closed. Ader was always the first, to wake up in the morning, especially on Sundays. She never missed to go for mass but that exceptional Sunday everything had fallen apart in her life that even going for prayer, did not mean anything to her anymore. Normally, Ader liked to do all her chores early in the morning but that particular Sunday morning was not the case. Most of Ader's neighbours wondered, as to what was wrong with her and her children but no one dared to find out. By about 8:30 AM, Mori, concerned and worried, went and started knocking at Ader's door with an intention to inquire whether, something was wrong with her or any one of her children. However, Ader did not answer the door for quite a while but Mori knocked persistently until, she eventually, opened the door, for him to come in.

When Mori entered Ader's house, he found her sitting on the floor near the bed and the areas around her eyes were quite swollen, from too much crying. Mori's mind went blank because he did not know how to construct the question that he was intending to ask Ader. He therefore, moved closer to her, squatted beside her and then gently asked her, "Would you kindly mind, to tell me what you are suffering from?"

After a moment of silence, Ader cleared her voice and honestly told him, "I am not sick. It is just that I don't have any more courage left in me, to face another day." Tears were still streaming down her cheeks as she was speaking.

Mori was almost moved to tears because he was finding it hard to believe that a strong woman like Ader was finally broken down, by her sorrowful and miserable life. He wondered why, only good people suffered a lot of misfortunes in this world. Without saying another word to Ader, Mori walked out of the house at once, so as to go and tell his wife about Ader's situation.

Juan saw the serious look of concern on her husband's face, when he was coming out of Ader's house and curiously asked him, "Is there something wrong with Ader today?"

Mori did not answer his wife for a moment because he was lost in deep thoughts, as he was trying to piece together why, such an enormous misfortune, could struck a wonderful family like that of Ader. He sadly remembered, the beautiful time they used to have when Ader's husband was still alive and how joyful and loving the couple was. *Why, why, why, would such a wonderful woman suffer so bad, a painful thought went through his mind. I can't blame, Ader for breaking down at last. She has been tested beyond, the understanding of any human being. Only God knows why.*

"Hallo!" Juan interrupted her husband's thought, "Could you kindly share with me, what you are thinking about, especially, what is wrong with our neighbour, Ader? You seem so lost, in a world far away. What is happening to you?"

"Hmmm", Mori sighed deeply, as he was endeavouring to clear up his mind and putting things into perspective. "I am very sorry, Juan," he eventually said. "I have even forgotten for a moment that you are here. Our friend, Ader, is in a very bad shape and it seems that she has been crying for the whole night. She really does not look well and I would like you to go to her and have a woman-to-woman talk. May be she will confide in you, as to what is bothering her. She really seems deeply disturbed. The woman, has been very strong since the death of her husband that if one did not know about what had happened to her, one would think that she was not a widow but I think that she has eventually broken down."

Juan did not say a word to her husband but rushed out straightaway to Ader's house and was bewildered to see, how Ader seemed, so worn out. Ader was still sitting, where Mori had found and left her. She then asked Juan, rather angrily, "Why have you come to my house, did your husband tell you that I was crying, ah?"

"No," Juan humbly replied in sympathy, "he did not actually tell me that you were crying but instead, had told me that you didn't seem well and he is worried that something terrible is affecting your life. Ader, I have come to you, as a sister and your usual trustworthy friend. I would be pleased, if you could share with me, what is breaking your heart. I have known you for a long time, as a strong and courageous woman, who could not be compared to, any other woman that I have known, especially the widows. To see you in tears, clearly indicate to that you are terribly affected by something, beyond your endurance."

Ader did not answer Juan for quite a while but was only staring blankly at her. Juan was then wondering whether, she had offended Ader in some way, by what she had just told her. She got frightened and therefore, decided to go out of the house but then Ader motioned with her hand that Juan should not go out. Juan consequently, sat down once again and was fearfully looking at Ader in silence. She did not know what to expect from Ader anymore.

"Well, well, well," said the poor and tired-looking Ader eventually, after the long pause. "It seems that I cannot get away, without answering you, can I? I am only going to tell you the truth because you and your husband have always been, like a brother and a sister to me my children and ignoring your concerns for me, is really a stupid thing for me to do. You know what, the last corn flour that I was having for food I have used up yesterday and I do not know, where the meal for today will come from. I do not even have, any penny left in this house. If I were to be by myself, I will not mind but because of my two little boys, I just do not know what to do next. I feel, so lost and devastated." With the last sentence, Ader's voice started growing faint and more tears began streaming down her cheeks again. At that point, both of her children woke up and began to look at their tearful mother with such frightful eyes. Ader did not, want the boys to see her in tears and therefore, she gathered up her strength and wiped off her tears.

Juan then walked out of Ader's house without saying any word and returned quickly with; a bucketful of corn flour, some bread and a kettle of tea. Ader stubbornly refused, everything that Juan had brought to her and her children but Juan insisted that she accepted for the sake of the children. After a moment of deep thoughts, Ader let go of her pride and accepted gratefully everything that Juan had kindly brought to them. The boys then began taking some of the tea with the bread. Ader stared quietly at her children, as they were eating and started eventually to shaking hopelessly her head. Juan saw what Ader was doing and started formulating a mental picture of what Ader could be thinking about.

Therefore, she told Ader compassionately," Please do not feel shy to ask me, whenever you needed something. What do you think friends are for? For a moment like this."

Ader accepted her friend's advice, by just nodding her head approvingly but deep in her heart, she was thinking that "Now where is my dignity as a normal person, if I have to beg others whenever, I have nothing to eat with my children. How long will this go on? Oh God, are you really listening to me? You have promised in your Holy Book that you would not leave orphans and widows alone but I don't seem to feel your presence in this house anymore. Father! Where are you? I need you most now. Please have mercy on me and my children"

Juan became frightened again, when she saw that Ader was lost in her thoughts. She therefore, asked Ader, "Are you really, ok?"

"Why do you ask me whether I am ok", angrily retorted Ader, "Do I look crazy already?"

"No", replied Juan frightfully. "I am just worried that you are hiding something terrible from me. All I want to do is to help you, my dear sister. You seemed completely lost in your thoughts and I am sorry to tell you this but you kind of look quite strange and wild," Juan bluntly told Ader.

"I like your honesty, you little rascal and inquisitive woman," joyfully said Ader, with a bit of smile breaking on her face, "that is why, I have opened up my heart to you. I love you, Juan, and your husband like my own family. Your generosity and compassion have all these time given me a reason to continue to live and above all, today you have rescued me, from my bottomless pit of despair. I pray that God's blessing be upon you always."

Juan was quite happy that she had done something good for her dear friend that day. She therefore tenderly hugged Ader and gently told her, "I am glad that I have been of an assistance to you. I would like you to remember that you too are a generous and compassionate woman. I have learnt some of the qualities from you, Ader. My advice to you is that be strong always for the sake of your children, no matter what the situation may be. I know that it is easy for me to say so because I have not yet been tested, like you have, however, please try, my dear girlfriend. Ader, beloved, thank you very much, for confiding in me, by telling me everything."

Ader did not answer Juan but simply nodded her head and seemingly looked calmer than, the moment before Juan had started talking to her.

"I know that this is not a good time for us to have conversation but I am convinced that you will be well," compassionately said Juan.

"I will," softly replied Ader. "Juan, thank you for being such a wonderful friend."

Thereafter, Juan left Ader and went back to her husband.

Mori was anxiously waiting for his wife's return from Ader's house, so that he could hear what Ader had told his wife. Therefore, as soon as Juan entered her house, her husband immediately asked her that "Has Ader by any chance, calmed down a little bit?"

Juan only nodded and did seem quite disturbed. Mori was shocked, by the look on his wife's face and loudly told her, "Juan, you look terrible!

However, could you kindly share with me, what your friend has told you? It seems, it is worst than I had expected."

"Life can be very unfair to some people, while others painlessly enjoy all kind of things," replied his wife, who was sounding like she was about to cry. "I just don't know what I would do, if you pass away before me. Look at Ader, she was always smiling and cooking for a number of visitors that her late husband used to bring home all the time. What bothers me the most is that where are all those so-called friends of her late husband now? Did they even love the late man, when he was alive at all or all they wanted to do was, to abuse his generosity by always taking from him all they could? Ader is a strong woman, I must say. I can understand why, she has eventually broken down. I am so heartbroken, to have seen her in so much pain and tears."

Mori attentively gazed at his wife, like a congregation listening to a priest saying a eulogy about a saintly person, who had just passed away. After Juan had eventually, stopped talking, her husband told her, "I absolutely know that you are quite concerned about your friend but I have not understood the point that you were trying to make."

"What do you really mean, Mori?" replied his wife, who had thought that she had precisely answered her husband's question. "I am sorry, Mori. However, what I was really meaning to say is that if only death could understand me, I would like to die before you, so that you with your good job and wonderful personality, would be able to raising our children very well. I don't think that I have the kind of strength that Ader is having, as she is bravely withstanding her very sorrowful life."

Mori instantly pulled, held and started lovingly looking into his wife's eyes, while he was assuring her that "None of us will die until, we are very, very old. Sweetheart, stop being pessimistic about life. God has a plan, for everyone on earth."

"It is not, a matter of being pessimistic or optimistic about life nowadays," sadly answered Juan, as she was trying to turn her head away from her husband. "This ongoing war has created a lot of sorrow and uncertainty, in the lives of so many people. How I wished that peace could come today!"

"There is an end to everything that happens in this world," replied Mori, as he was still holding his wife. "This war will also come to an end some day and surely, peace will prevail again in southern Sudan."

"I hope so dear," hopelessly said Juan, as she was attempting to get away from her husband's hold, so as to sit down and try to make sense out of, the devastating situation Ader was facing.

Mori did not insist that his wife should tell him about Ader's problem. He had then resolved that the best time for him to ask his wife would be at bedtime, when she had calmed down. He therefore, ate his breakfast and later on went out, to have a chat with his friend, who was living across the road from his house.

After Juan had gone back to her house, Ader knelt down and started praying before, she could lie down and take some nap, "Thank you God, for your bountiful mercy and love on an unworthy, doubtful, wretched and heartbroken sinner, that is me. Thank you also, for sending Mori and his wife, to rescue me from the pit of despair that I have fallen in helplessly. Dear Father, it is quite difficult for me, to understand your ways, after all the painful experiences that I am have been going through, in my life. My doubtful heart, has led me astray and I have been feeling as if, you have also forgotten about me, like everyone else has done. I am sorry, for letting you down, by crying in the way I have done. Please give me more strength, courage, faith, hope and love that I need so that I may persevere in my life of hardship. Thank you also, for your deep love for me that you have shown by sending your only son, Jesus, to die a shameful death so that I may have eternal life. I ask all these, in the Name of my Lord and Saviour, Jesus Christ, Amen." After the prayer, Ader sent her children out to play and lied down to rest her weary mind.

After Ader had woken up, she felt a little better but was quite weak due to lack of energy. She then decided to cook some food, which she ate very little and started having a very severe abdominal pain, due to lack of food in her system for a number of days. Omal Jr. sympathetically asked his mother, "Mama, why have you not been eating with us and only ate today?"

Ader deceived him by saying, "I was not feeling well, my dear child, and had no appetite to eat just anything, but today, I am feeling much better and that is why I have eaten some food."

"Mama, could you tell me what you have been suffering from?" the boy innocently asked.

"I have been having a bad stomach pain," Ader gently told her son.

Omal Jr. then ran, tenderly hugged his mother and assured her that, "Mama, when I grow up, I will take proper care of you."

"Thank you very much for your concern for me, my sweet boy," Ader delightfully told her beloved son, for the beautiful assurance that he had given to her. "I am very proud of you and your brother and I am very sure that some day, when both of you have grown up, you will take very good care of me. I dearly love you both. God bless you."

After the children had finished eating, they ran out to play again because they were too young to understand the misery that their mother had been going through.

On that fateful Sunday, Ader did not come outside until late in the evening, when she was going to fetch some water. She slowly and weakly walked, with her head bowed down as if someone who, had just recovered from a long illness. After fetching the water, she loving bathed and put her children to bed. She then made herself a cup of porridge and thereafter, she began to sweat heavily. Eventually, she started wiping the sweat away, as she was saying to herself, 'the daughter of a respectable man and wife of the son of the Chief of the people of Magwi Chiefdom, is now reduced to a beggar. Who could understand, what the meaning of life is? I grew up in a loving home and knew no pain or hunger at all but surrounded by the people who dearly love me as much as I love them but look at what my life has become, I am the loneliest and heartbroken soul on earth. I have never thought, in my wildest dream that my life would be this horrible and miserable. However, I need to learn, how to accept my new life, just as it has turn out to be and God, please help me!'

Thereafter, Ader begun to wash up, everything that she had used, prayed for all her loved ones who have passed away, the living members of her family, wherever they were, her sons, self and Mori and his family. After prayer, she was engulfed in the restful peace that only God could give and soundly fell asleep, for the first time in weeks.

On the other hand, that evening, when Mori was then alone with his wife, after the baby was asleep, he decided to ask her about what was, the matter with Ader that day, "I hope that this is the best time, for you to tell me about Ader's problem. Did she tell you precisely, what was bothering her?"

"Yes, she did, after a long and hard thinking," calmly replied Juan. "The woman has been starving herself for the past few days, without wanting anyone to know about it. The last food that she was having in her house, she had cooked it yesterday for her children and, hopelessly, neither knew what to do nor where to go for help anymore. Consequently, she despaired."

"How could Ader do that when she knows very well that we could help her?" sadly said Mori, as he was feeling really hurt about what Ader had done.

"Ader really did not want, anyone to know about her situation," answered Juan. "She could not bear the thought, for her to rely on others, for her survival. I can tell at a glance that Ader has come from a family that had plenty of love and food all the time. A person with such background would rather die with her pride and dignity intact than beg. I could have done the very same thing, if I were to be in her situation. You know what, she was even trying to refuse the few stuff that I had taken to help her children. I had to persuade her to accept."

"What a strange woman," awesomely said Mori, as he was trying hard to comprehend, why Ader was so different from most of the women that he had known. "I am glad that you have done a great job, to help our friend today."

"It is rather you, who have the greater part by first knocking persistently on her door, when the rest of us were just wondering as to what we could do," Juan appreciatively told her husband. "Mori, my dear husband, I very much, admire your compassion for others."

"We are a great couple, aren't we?" Mori delightfully assured his wife. They then tenderly hugged each other before they could sleep.

Chapter Twenty-Eight
Jore's Concern for Ader

Jore had seen when her son was persistently knocking at Ader's door the previous day and then eventually, entered in but thereafter, instantly came out, while looking quite sad and then later on, her daughter-in-law also went to Ader's house but a little while later, returned to her house and took something in a container to Ader. Jore had wanted so much, to know the reason for her children's movements, to and from and to and from Ader's house and the reason for the sign of concern, which was on their faces that day. However, she did not want to appear inquisitive and therefore, she waited until the following day before, she could ask her daughter-in-law.

It was a beautiful Monday morning but Juan's daughter was having a fever and was crying a lot. Keji's illness, had kept Juan up for most of the night, as she had been trying to bring down the fever, by putting some cold wet towel on her, after she had first given her some painkiller but the child hardly had any relief. Mori had also tried to stay up, so that he could help his wife, as she was taking take care of their sick daughter but Juan refused because she did not want both of them, to miss going to work the following day. That morning, consequently, instead of going to work, Juan took her daughter to a nearby clinic. Fortunately, there were only a few people at clinic and therefore, Juan's daughter was attended to very quickly.

When Juan got back from the clinic, she found her mother-in-law anxiously waiting, to know about, how her granddaughter was doing. After Jore had noticed that the child's fever had subsided quite a bit, due to the injection that she had received at the clinic, she was somehow relieved of her worry. However, there was something else in Jore's mind that morning because she was interested to know about what, had happened to Ader the previous day. Jore had been having a very soft place in her heart for Ader, right from the very first day that she had come to Juba. She, since then, had been thinking of Ader as, a very wonderful woman, whom one could be proud to have for a daughter, sister or a wife. Jore admired the way Ader had been doing all her work with smiling face and never picking up an argument with anyone. Jore was also a widow like Ader and had lost her first husband when, she was very young and a mother to only one child. Jore's brother-in-law later inherited her and from her second marriage, she had only two children, Poni and Mori. Therefore, she decided eventually to raise her children alone. She had an ample knowledge about the hardships that most of the widows were facing in life and greatly admired the courage with which, Ader was carrying on with her difficult life.

That morning, therefore, Jore brought out her mat and sat beside her daughter-in-law, who, after she had put her daughter to bed, began making the breakfast.

"Would you mind, if I ask you about something?" Jore humbly asked her daughter-in-law.

"You know very well that you are always free to ask me about anything," Juan happily answered.

"That is one of the reasons why, I love you so much," gratefully said Jore. "You have always given me the freedom that I need, as an old woman, to ask you about anything that I wanted to know. Ok, let me get to the point. You know what, I have been concerned about your movements, you and your husband, yesterday, to and from, to and from that Acoli woman's house. Hmmm, what is her name again? "

"Ader," Juan helped her mother-in-law.

"Thank you. Ader is her name," Jore went on. "Was she or any of her sons sick?"

"None of them is sick but Ader, as you know is a widow and the life of a widow these days is quite difficult," sadly said Juan.

"Hmm," deeply sighed Jore. "I am aware that she is a widow and the life of a widow is not only difficult now but has been even in my younger days and will always be, for as long as human beings shall live on this earth. I wonder why the fate of this world is only after good, beautiful and wonderful people. However, why is she not, getting another man anyway? It is a waste of time, to grieve for such a long time. Besides, the dead person has already rested from the tribulations of this life and will never come back again, to help her raise her kids. How I wished that I was young again and if I lost my husband, I would pack up my things, return to my family home, meet and marry another man sooner than later and start a new life."

"I hate, to ask you a question, that is going to sounds a little rude but you have left me no choice," Juan apologetically, told her mother-in-law. "Why do you talk insensibly, is it your life's experiences which have made you, to lose your respect for the dead? You did not know, the life of Ader with her husband very well, when he was still alive. They deeply loved one another so much that most of the neighbours were envying them, especially those, whose marriages are not happy. Everywhere Omal had gone, he would come back with a gift for his wife and hand it to her as if, he was falling in love with her for the first time. He was so faithful to his wife that people were thinking that Ader had given him some love portion. The couple took strolls most of the evenings, while they were holding each other's hand and laughing at every joke that they were making. On weekends' afternoons, they would sit outside, in the shadow of their house and sweetly chatted with each other. Their relationship was like a fairytale. It was like a dreamland that every woman would want to experience, before she died. I can go on and on and on but I don't think that you would like to hear everything about them. Now, with all these few things that I have tried to tell you, Mom, do you think that Ader really wants to get involve with another man very soon?" Juan seriously, asked her mother-in-law.

"Well, well, well, what you have just said has not swayed me at all from my stand that a widow should get another man sooner than later. Besides, life is too short and one should really make good use of it, when the opportunity is still there. We live in the present moment and not the past, for it has gone forever and the future is out of our grasp and should not worry anyone. Whenever a person concerns herself/himself so much, about past or the future, he/she may end up living a very, very miserable life. Past experiences, should only teach one to be wise because of the lessons learned and knowledge gained but one should always remember that no one is able to go back in the past and change things. Now, to get back to the point of our discussion, every relationship is beautiful in a special way. The one of your friend, as you have just told me, was beautiful and yours with my son too, is like a fairytale, my dear daughter-in-law. I always have been hearing how you are giggling, whenever your husband is at home in the evenings, isn't that a lot of fun?" Jore honestly, told her daughter-in-law, with a big smile on her face.

"You are very right, Mom," Juan replied, as she was laughing at what, her mother-in-law had just said about her and her husband. "I love my husband so much and he loves me too. I am praying that nothing should separate us until, we are very old. I just do not know what, I would do without him."

"Let me tell you more about life, my dear daughter-in-law," calmly said Jore. "Do you know of a man whose wife has died and he has stayed without a woman for a long time? Maybe there are a few out there, if any at all. Some men would start having another relationships quite secretly, immediately after the death of their wives, while others, remarry even within three to four months, after the deaths of their wives. No one says anything about such behaviour because tradition dictates that it is not normal for a man to live alone. However, whenever any woman does the same thing, she would be called all kind of names. Women, most of the time, grieved, for the losses of their husbands for years before, they could even think about moving on with their lives. We are cheated a lot in this world. I am not a cold and insensitive woman, as you may be thinking about me, my dear daughter-in-law. Everything that I am telling you is because of the experiences that I have been through in my miserable life."

Juan could no longer argue after listening to all the wise things that her mother-in-law had told her. She gratefully replied, "Mom, thank you for your wisdom."

"Now, could you tell me about what had happened yesterday morning, my dear daughter," inquisitively, insisted Jore.

"I hate to tell you what Ader told me but since you have insisted, I will tell you on condition that you are not going not tell anyone," answered Juan, as she was beginning to wash her husband's clothes.

"I am too old to gossip and you must remember that I have gone through very hard times in my life and the last thing that I would want to do is, to tattle about other people. Please tell me about your friend's problem, may be, I could help to advice her," Jore insisted.

"Ok then," eventually obliged Juan and then she narrated to her mother-in-law what took place the previous day. In conclusion she elaborated, "The whole situation, had been caused by what, Ader's beastly brother-in-law had done to her. Do you remember the night, when the elders gathered in Ader's courtyard and there was a fight? That night, her brother-in-law took away even the money that his late brother had left in the bank, for his wife and children and that was the major cause, for Ader's breakdown yesterday."

"Hmmm," deeply sighed Jore, as she was sadly shaking her head, in sympathy for Ader's situation. "Was it that bad, eh? I can relate to all of that. Being young is good but is also foolish. Crying does not take away ones' life and is not an answer to this world's problem. I once did the same thing but eventually learnt that it does not help at all. God has planned, all our ways differently. Some people enjoy life until death, others enjoy so much but briefly, like your friend Ader, whereas some have to suffer for a short time, before they could find joy and happiness but others are born to suffer, from birth till death. These are all the will of God. No one seems, to have an explanation for these things. However, I do not know whether, those of you who have gone to school, have learned how to solve some of these life's problems. Anyway, if you have learned anything in the school that could have helped but why is it that your friend is having, the very same situations that I had gone through a long time ago? My conclusion is that no human being seemed to have any answer, only God knows. We should always flow with the current of life because when you try to swim against it, you will surely not make it. Ader must learn, to be very strong for the sake of her two sons and trust God completely for food, clothes, shelter and happiness. That way, she will eventually, find some meaning in her life and gradually start to heal. I hope that Ader would some day start another relationship, once again. My dear daughter-in-law, would you mind if, I talk to your friend and tell her about my life's history? You, Juan, will be my interpreter of course, since I do not know how to speak in her language and can't also speak any Arabic. Ask your friend about, what I have told you and let me know her reply."

"You surely care a lot, about everyone, don't you?" Juan assured her mother-in-law, as she was admiring her deep insight about the meaning of life in general and compassion for Ader. "You speak with such wisdom that some of us who have gone to school, do not have. I love listening to you so much and probably a lot more than, I listen to my husband, your son. I feel so blessed for having you, as my mother-in-law. I have a lot of lessons, to learn from you about, the meaning of life. I will let Ader know that you would like to have a conversation with her and I am sure that she will not refuse. Ader likes you a lot and loves listening to some of the tunes that you sometimes have been singing in the evenings."

"I am glad to know that Ader likes me too," gratefully said Jore, in surprise, "because I dearly love the woman and her children. I do not want Ader to make, the same mistake that I have made, by refusing to have more children. My son, Mori, should have had a brother but I have deprived him of the opportunity. I could sometimes tell from his speech to me that he wished that he could have had a brother. In this world, the people who are surrounded by many brothers and sisters are always joyful and happy. No one messes with them unnecessarily but lonely people, are always taunted by everyone, bullied, carelessly pushed around and most of the people say, all kinds of demeaning things, that are not true about them because no one cares about their feelings in any way. I do not want Ader, to give up on life and only raise those two boys. She is still quite young and has a lot of living to do. She should bear, more brothers and sisters to be with her children so that some day, they would happily live together."

When Jore and Juan had finished their passionate conversation, they began to eat breakfast.

After the breakfast, Juan continued to wash her husband's clothes. Thereafter, left her sick daughter with her mother-in-law and went to the market, to buy some fresh beef and green vegetable for lunch. That day, Juan wanted to fix a really delicious meal for her family, since she had not gone to work. The Sudanese women liked to cook so much and talked a lot about it. They take such pride in their ability, to cook variety of sapid dishes. Therefore, since Juan had come from a very respectable family, she was very good at cooking because her mother had taught her very well. Mori was always very proud about the way that his wife had been cooking. He liked his wife's food so much that he had never eaten in a *Mataam* (restaurant) since he got married. When Juan got back from the market, she began cooking the food at once. The noonday sun was already quite hot, and consequently, she moved to the *Rokuba* (a shade, specifically made for cooking or having a nap whenever it was hot), where she started making *Kisira (*a thin bread made from fermented wheat flour). After she had finished doing all her chores, she took a cold shower and felt a bit of relief from the scorching heat.

Mori came home at 3:30 PM Sudan local time, with three of his colleagues from work. Shortly after they had arrived, Juan served them and then went to eat with her mother-in-law. Mori's friends were not yet married. As they were eating therefore, one of them told Mori that "I wished that I would be lucky in the future and get married to a beautiful wife, who could cook so well like yours."

"Not only is she beautiful and a good cook," answered the other friend, "she also seemed to be a very good-mannered wife."

Mori was quite pleased, to hear his friends' compliments about his wife and he then told them that "I am always very proud of my wife. She is the best gift that God has ever given to me."

"I can now understand, why you are always neatly dressed and quite happy," said the third friend.

They happily chatted and laughed, as they were eating.

On the other hand, Jore enjoyed very much, the delicious meal that her daughter-in-law had cooked and told her in admiration, "It is good to be old because one does not have to overwork oneself so tired, like you, the young people are doing. Look, I have been idle since morning, doing apparently nothing but you took your baby to the clinic, cooked breakfast, washed your husband's clothes, went to the market and cooked dinner. My God, I would suddenly die, if I were to be told, to do all that in a day."

Juan diffidently smiled at Jore and felt good about all that she was able to do that day.

After the meal, Mori's friends gratefully, told Juan that "Thank you a lot, for the delicious meal that you have so kindly served for us. Mori, your husband, is a very fortunate man, to have a wonderful chef like you, for his wife."

Mori joyfully smiled, as he was lovingly looking at his wife. Juan was feeling so adulated by what, her husband's friends had told her but she only smiled at them, without saying any word and walked out of the house as quickly as she could because she was shy.

"Your wife is quite shy, isn't she?" said one of Mori's friend.

"Yes, she only talks to the people that she knows very well," proudly said her husband.

"Such kind of women, are quite rare in our generation," said the next friend. "The women these days, talk too much once they are married. It is very wonderful to see a married woman, who is quite shy like your wife. You are a very lucky and happy husband."

"I truly think that I am lucky," delightfully said Mori. "God has been so gracious to me, a nobody, by giving to me, my dear Juan."

"We wish you a long and happy life together," gladly said Mori's friends.

Thereafter they began to play the domino until 5:30 PM, then, Mori's friends left.

When Juan and her mother-in-law were done eating, she started washing all the utensils and after, started ironing her husband's clothes. After Juan had completed ironing the clothes, she went to fetch some water from the well. By the end of the evening, she was quite exhausted. Juan was wishing that her sick daughter could sleep well that night, so that she could also have some rest because she had hardly slept, the previous night. Mori did noticed how tired his wife was that day and therefore, did not bother to ask her to be with him that night.

Chpter Twenty-Nine
The Divine Providence Provided for Ader

Ader woke up early on the Monday morning that followed the Sunday that she was in despair. The good sleep she had enjoyed, made her felt rested, refreshed and ready to face that day with the courage of a lioness. That morning, everything seemed different and full of life in Ader's eyes than the past previous days when, she had given up on life. After Ader had returned from fetching some water, she made breakfast, fed her kids, dressed them up and took them to Nyarata, who had been volunteering to take care of the children, while Ader was at work.

When Ader and her children got to Nyarata's courtyard, they found her basking in the warm morning sun as she was making her mat. As soon as Nyarata saw them, she shouted out delightfully, "Look! Who are these, young people, coming to be with old Nyarata but my two best friends, Omal Jr. and Okene? I love you boys. Now come and tell old Nyarata what, your mom had cooked for you yesterday and the folk stories that she had told you guys last night."

The children only smiled at Nyarata, without saying any word. Ader knelt down and respectfully greeted old Nyarata.

"Come on boys, do not look at your mother like that" Nyarata playfully told Ader's boys. "Let her go because we do not need her, do we? Good bye office lady, leave us alone."

"Ok, I am glad that you people do not need me," jokingly replied Ader, as she was joyfully smiling at them. "Goodbye, all of you and have fun. I will see you this afternoon."

"Please, don't forget to bring for us, those fat and big beef sandwiches that many people say that the office workers eat, while they are at work," jokingly said Nyarata, while she was joyfully laughing.

"I will surely bring some, for you," spontaneously promised Ader. However, she did not even have a penny in her pocket and wondered why she had foolishly promised Nyarata that she would buy for them some sandwiches.

On the way to work, Ader continued to think about, what the future really was holding for her and her children because in her mind, everything was seemingly bleak. Her mind kept wandering far away, as she was walking because it could not contain the uncertainties that she was facing. She then suddenly began thinking that 'The loving God in heaven will see me through every hurdle that I am now facing because I am his child, whom He has bought with the precious blood of his son, Jesus Christ. Besides, the previous day I was thinking that we were going to starve to death but God sent Mori and his wife yesterday, to rescue us. That same kind, loving and merciful God, will provide for us in his special and mighty way.' With that positive thinking, Ader cheered up and was looking quite beautiful once again.

When Ader got to the office, most of the people were not yet in. She then started working on some of the reports that she had not had time to finish, the previous week. She completed the reports before her boss arrived at the office. Ader was really happy with her work because she was aware that the first thing that her boss would ask for upon arrival would be the reports.

"Good morning Ader, you just look beautiful as usual," her boss said, as he was walking into the office. "How was your weekend, my dear?"

" Fine, sir, and thank you for asking," humbly replied Ader, "and how about yours, sir?"

"I have had a lovely weekend," happily answered her boss. "However, are some of the urgent reports really ready today?"

"Yes, sir," confidently replied Ader, as she was respectfully handing the accurately and neatly typed reports to her boss.

The boss browsed through the report and then excitedly put his right hand thumb up, meaning perfect work. He therefore, put his left hand into his pocket and pulled out 100 Sudanese Pounds note, which was then, good money. "This is how, I would like to express to you my appreciation, for the work well done and on time," he gratefully said. "Please take it because I will not accept a 'no', for an answer."

Ader hesitantly accepted the money but in her heart, she started thanking God for answering her prayers because she was then able to fulfill her promise to Nyarata by, buying the sandwiches that she had promised for them. "Sir, thank you very much, for your generosity," said Ader with such a grateful heart. "I just did what I am supposed to do and you should have not really given me the money. Therefore, next time, I will not accept such act of appreciation from you."

"It is such fun for me, to work with you," her boss delightfully, assured her. "You have always been making my day at work very easy because of your thoughtful actions when doing your work. I owe you a lot."

"Thank you, for your compliments, sir," gratefully said Ader. "I wished that there were many bosses like you." They all started laughing and thereafter, went about their work for the day.

Late that afternoon, CART passed out a circular that they have decided to give a special treatment to all the widows that were working for their organization, so that they could receive part of the relief food, that were being given to the displaced people. Each widow was going to receive three *keila* (a container used for measuring grain, in the markets in the Sudan) of corn, three litres of cooking oil and 10 kg of beans monthly, so that they could raise their orphaned children without much worry. After Ader had read the circular, she thought that she was hallucinating. The whole thing was too surreal for her to comprehend alone and too good to be true. She therefore, rushed to her friend, Hinda, who was also seconded to work with the CART. Ader found Hinda, as she was also reading the circular with tears streaming down her cheeks.

"Wipe out those silly tears girl and let us praise God, for the wonderful things he has done for us and our children by, touching the hearts of the big people in this organization, to come up with such a God-sent circular," Ader joyfully, told her friend.

"I am completely confused and cannot comprehend whether, what I am reading is real or some kind of daytime dream," said Hinda with such an excitement.

"That is the reason why I have rushed out here to you, so that the two of us could read the circular together and be convinced that it is not just our wild imaginations but a reality and a blessing, from the Most High God," Ader delightfully told her friend.

Overcome with joy, they started hugging each other and giggling like teenagers.

"So we are not going to die, as we were thinking that we would last week," they simultaneously said.

"How did you know what, I was going to say?" Hinda asked her friend, as she was joyfully laughing.

"I was going to ask you the same question, girlfriend," surprisingly replied Ader.

The widows were so overcome with joy that they started crying together, the tears were, for the joy of their relief from despair. Ader said goodbye to her friend and returned to her office, shortly after.

When Ader got to her office, it was about time to go home and consequently, she started clearing out her desk and putting things in order, before she could go home.

Therefore, on her way home, Ader bought for Nyarata and her sons, the big fat beef sandwiches that she had promised them.

At home, Old Nyarata spent her time playing with the boys and telling them stories about a time long ago when, life was beautiful in the village and there was no war. She also told them folk stories about Ogre, Hare, Leopard and many other animals. The children attentively listened to Nyarata but it was hard to tell whether, they had been understanding and enjoying all that the old lady was telling them because they were too young.

In the early afternoon, Nyarata put the boys to sleep and continued making her mat, which she was always selling for her living. Nyarata's neighbours liked her a lot because of her sense of humour. She never complained about anything. Nyarata was even funnier whenever she was sick. For example, some days when she was having a headache, she would say, "Would it not be good, if old Nyarata took all the headaches in Juba and die with it, so that no one else would ever have a headache again?" Then all of a sudden she would say, "Oh, my dear people, you know what, the headache is asking me to marry him and I am telling him that I am too old to get married. I am sixty years or more and have not enough energy for; running to the river to fetch water, going to bring firewood for cooking and warming water for bath to my husband, washing his clothes etc. Give me a break, headache, I can't marry you because you are too unfriendly and ugly. Please leave me alone. I just need to make jokes and laugh with my young friends."

Nyarata's neighbours would always laugh with tears, at all her jokes.

That afternoon, after Ader had returned from work, she found her two sons sleeping peacefully under the tamarind tree and Nyarata was sitting beside them, while she was softly singing a love song which, praised the war hero of long ago. The lyrics, went as follows:

> Look at the son of my mother-in-law, my dear husband.
> Look at his headdress, it has fitted him so well that he is really looking like the Chief of a powerful Chiefdom.
> Indeed he is the Chief of my heart, and the leader of his clansmen.
> He bravely leads his clansmen to war, while he confidently blows his horn.

The love of my heart kills only the men, who are his enemies.

However, he lets go all the women and children because they are not part of the quarrel, which has brought about the war.

He chairs the meetings that discuss the end for the war, which had been going on between his village and the enemies'.

He forgives, whenever it is necessary

What a man, I have for my lover and husband

I will love you forever, my dear.

You are a hero, a hero that every woman would want to be her own.

I am so lucky to be the wife of such a hero. Oh, my true love...

Nyarata was singing the song with such a passion that caused Ader to momentarily stand behind a tree, as she was enjoying the way Nyarata was singing. Therefore, Ader did not want to interrupt Nyarata until, she had finished singing the sweet song. Unfortunately, when Nyarata raised her head up, she saw Ader and immediately stopped singing. Consequently, she shockingly asked Ader that "Why are you standing behind the tree and not talking to me, you naughty girl?"

"I am sorry but the song that you were singing was too good, to be interrupted," replied Ader, as she was joyfully smiling at Nyarata. "I was happily enjoying the song that you were singing, quietly behind the tree because I was thinking that you would not find me out this soon."

They both laughed and then Ader gave Nyarata the sandwiches.

"Here are the sandwiches that you have asked for this morning," she happily said.

"Hey, my child, I did not mean it at all, when I told you this morning that you should bring for us some sandwiches," Nyarata said, with such a look of concern on her face. "It was part of my usual jokes and I was thinking that by now, you have already known what kind of a woman that I am. Do not spoil, your money on old Nyarata. Your priorities should always be your two sons. Don't you know that you are now both a mother and father, to your children?"

"I do," replied Ader, as she was feeling quite flattered by, what Nyarata had just told her, "but you are also part of my family. You are the reason why I am still alive today and going on relatively strong. I love you Nyarata. Please accept the sandwiches, including the ones for my sons. I will return to take the boys later on, when they are awake."

"Thanks a lot dear daughter," gratefully said Nyarata. "What would my life be like, without you around, my dear?"

Nyarata then, took a big bite of the sandwich and began chewing it, while she was twisting her mouth from left to right, in a very funny way. Ader was quite amused by Nyarata's funny way for chewing that she burst into an interesting laughter, as she was running away.

Nyarata had not had enough to eat the previous night. Therefore, she was really hungry but she was also aware that her young friend, Ader, did not have any food either. After finishing her sandwich, she drank a mug of water and began to heavily perspiring. Nyarata could not believe that she was the one that was then reduced to nothing because of the ongoing war. She vividly remembered the good old time when, she used to live in the village, self-reliant and surrounded by loving relatives. The very fact then that most of those relatives had already lost their lives in the war, brought tears to her eyes but she quickly changed her line of thoughts and began to focus on the present and positive things. The old woman had such a wonderful personality that she did not want any situation to bring her down. Her optimistic spirit had always made her a friend, to all who knew her. Nyarata therefore, lied down beside the sleeping children of Ader, while she was trying to get some restful nap too.

On the other hand, when Ader entered her house, after she had been at Nyarata's, everything in the house seemed different to her that day because she was in high spirit. She thanked God once again, for taking care of her and her children and looked into the future with the hope of being alive and not starving to death anymore. Ader therefore, ran to the market to buy some fresh beef and some green vegetables, so that she could cook her first delicious meal in weeks. While at the market, she also bought some laundry soap for washing the dirty clothes, which had piled up under the bed. After she had returned home from the market, Ader could once again feel the presence of God in her house. Ader even started realising that the troubles that she had gone through in the previous week, God did allow it to happen purposely, so that she could understand His power, care, mercy, grace, compassion, kindness, generosity, glory and above all, His deep love for her.

When Ader went back that evening to take her children from Nyarata, she took along some supper for the old lady. Nyarata profoundly thanked Ader and gratefully told her, "Generosity runs in your blood, you daughter of a wonderful man. How could I ever thank you, for this delicious meal which, I really do not deserve and all the wonderful things that you have been pampering me with notwithstanding your greatest losses?"

"I wonder, why you are under estimating how tremendously helpful you have been to me and my children, since the deaths in my family but especially, after the death of my beloved late husband." Ader tearfully, reassured Nyarata. "You are the reason, why I have been going to work every morning, without any worry and care about the welfare of my sons. Nyarata, you are the mother that I do not have here in Juba and I love you a lot."

"Thank you for thinking that way about me, my child," gratefully said Nyarata. "It is such a joy for me, as I am taking care of your children, while you are at work. They have been making my life meaningful and worth living. Ader, I love you and your handsome sons a lot because you are all I have left in this life."

When Ader and her children were leaving, Nyarata decided to retire to her little hut, to eat her God-sent delicious meal and sing herself to sleep and that was the routine that she had been doing every night. On Ader's side, as soon as she got to her house, she bathed her boys, gave them their supper and put them to sleep. Thereafter, she started reading the Bible and shortly after prayed to God, while she was profoundly thanking him, for opening the window of heaven and showering down all the wonderful things that she had generously received from the loving hands of God that day. That night, Ader had peace in her heart, as she was going to bed and slept like a small child, for the first time, in a very long time.

Chapter Thirty
Mori Rescued Ader

On Saturday morning, as Ader was going to fetch some water, Juan joined her and on the way told Ader that "My mother-in-law, would like to talk to you this evening, if you are free."

"Of course, I am free," joyfully replied Ader but she was looking rather surprised because she was wondering about, what Jore would like to talk to her about. "Please tell your mother-in-law that I would be honoured to listen to what she has to tell me."

"I knew that you would not turn down, my mother-in-law's request," excitedly said Juan. "The old woman, has a wonderful place in her heart for you. She speaks so well of you, all the time."

"I like her a lot too," joyfully said Ader. "The only barrier between us is, a common language for communication. I wished that I knew how to speak in Bari language; then I would have been spending most of my time with old Jore. She has such a wonderful personality."

"Well then," happily said Juan. "I will convey your reply to her and then this evening, you and I will hear, what she has in mind to tell you."

After fetching the water, Ader and Juan each went their different ways, as they were carrying out their routine chores.

After breakfast, Ader spent her time washing clothes and cleaning the house. Saturday was the only day that she got to do most of her cleaning. Unfortunately, that Saturday, as Ader was sweeping around her house, one of her neighbours, whose house was behind Ader's fence, started hurling insults at her as he was calling her a moron and careless woman because he was feeling that the dust from her sweeping was inconveniencing his breathing. He was heartlessly yelling, as he was threatening Ader that she should stop her sweeping immediately or else he would slap her silly. However, Ader never answered the man but simply continued with her cleaning. The ruthless neighbour was enraged, after he had concluded that Ader was being rude to him. He consequently came over to Ader and started slapping her hard across her face. Ader was quite hurt but never shed any tear. She simply covered her face with both hands, as she was painfully falling down.

Mori was cleaning his shoes outside his house, when he saw what the man had done to Ader. He therefore, spontaneously jumped up, sprinted towards the man and began boxing him on his head until the man had started bleeding from his nose. Ader sorrowfully stood up, as soon as Mori began boxing her attacker in defense of her and watched the fight with such a grateful heart. The man was too weak to withstand Mori and as a result, ran away in shame and was not seen outside for three days. After the fight, which lasted less than two minutes, Ader then tremblingly started hugging Mori, as she was gratefully telling him, "Mori, you are now the brother that I do not have in Juba. Thank you so much, for defending me from that crazy man, today. May God bless you and your family always."

Jore and Juan were in the house, when they saw Mori racing very fast towards Ader's house. They were anxious to know, the reason why Mori had ran that fast and therefore, they came outside to find out why. To their dismay, they saw Mori, as he was powerfully punching the man, who had assaulted Ader and immediately realized that Mori was rescuing and defending Ader. "What has the man done to you Ader," sympathetically asked Juan, with such a look of concern in her face.

"He has slapped me across my face, for stirring up dust as I was sweeping," humbly said Ader.

"How bad has the fool hurt you dear?" questioned Juan, as tears for sympathy for Ader, began to form into her eyes.

"I am fine, thank you for asking," gratefully said Ader. "The only pain that I am feeling is in the area where, he has hit me. However, I am glad that he has experienced more pain from Mori's powerful blows than, the light ones I have received from him."

"Some people, just don't think or care," said Mori, as he was still trembling out of anger, for what the man had done to Ader. "How dare was that stupid man, to have walked in here shamelessly and start assaulting carelessly, a very gentle widow like you, Ader? You have been doing the same cleaning, when your husband was still alive and why didn't the loser slap you like he has done today? If he has had a bad night in his house, he has no right to take it out on a vulnerable woman, like you. For as long as you shall be living here, with us, I will not allow anyone to abuse you. Your late husband was my best friend and was more like a brother to me."

Juan lovingly began hugging her husband and delightfully told him, "You have made all of us in this home very proud today by, what you have done to that beast. You are my hero and I am so glad that you have boldly defended our disadvantaged friend. I do not always condone violence but today, I think that your violent response to that man's justified the end. I am very proud, to have you as my husband. I love you, Mori."

Jore was also overwhelmed with joy, for what her son had done to defend Ader. She held her beloved son's hands and told him joyfully, "For a long time I have been thinking that I have failed completely in life but after seeing the noble deed that you have done today, I feel so blessed, to have you as my son. You have filled my heart with joy, oh my hero."

Mori was almost moved to tears by, what his mother was telling him. It was, a very, very emotional moment for him. He then told his mother, "I love you, Mom and I am very proud to be your son. It was you, who have taught me, a long time ago when I was young that I should defend the defenseless, when I grow up. I have not forgotten all, the good lessons about life that you have taught me, when I was a young boy."

"Hey! I did not know that you were still remembering most of the things that I have taught you when you were little," delightfully replied, the surprised looking Jore. "I have been thinking that the boys only valued, whatever their fathers had taught them and not what their mothers said. God be praised, for allowing me to learned a new lesson today, at such an old age."

Mori looked at his mother in admiration and humbly smiled.

The rest of the neighbours came running, to inquire about what had happened and after learning the truth they also began praising Mori and calling him a hero because of what he had done. Some of them started hurling all kinds of insults and cursed at the wicked man, for the cruelest thing he had done to Ader. All the women in the neighbourhood were quite delighted, except for the man's wife of course and wished that there were many men like Mori, who could be able stand up for justice. Mori was feeling quite flattered by the many compliments that he had received from the people that day and therefore, he went and spent his day indoors. As Mori was reminiscing what he had done that day, he could not believe the fact that he had jumped and sprinted from where he was sitting, to where the man was assaulting Ader and instantly began boxing the cruel man. Mori was a man, who did not believe in violence. He firmly believed, in settling differences in peaceful manner but that morning he violated his own principle because he had feeling that violence was the only solution to the situation.

After the fight, Ader entered her house and remained inside, as she was pondering in her heart as to what could have happened to her that day, had Mori not intervened in the fight. She cried, but the tears were for joy, as she was feeling quite secure about her safety because of a good, caring, compassionate and loving neighbour, like Mori, around to help her. As soon as Ader heard her children's voices, as they were coming back to the house, from where they had gone to play, she quickly washed her face and put on a cheerful smile. Ader was glad that her children had not witnessed, what the cruel man had done to her. She therefore, started playing with her children indoors, for the rest of the day.

When Nyarata heard about the incident, from the people who had witnessed what had taken place, she immediately rushed to console her friend but to her surprise, she found that Ader was looking cheerful.

"You are becoming quite mature, aren't you, Ader? On my way here, I was thinking that I would find you already preparing a rope to hang yourself." she jokingly told Ader.

"You know very well that I could not do that," laughingly answered Ader. "It is time for me to be strong, as you once taught me, my dear Nyarata. Consequently, I do not want, to let any cruel person to have power over me, by crying every time that someone had done something stupid to me because I would like to be a good example to my sons, so that they would grow up into strong, confident, courageous and bold men, like their father used to be. However, thank you for coming over, Nyarata. It is really very thoughtful of you. Do you know what, the bull who had attacked me is bleeding from his nose, in his house because he had met a tougher bull than himself."

"Who has kindly defended you, from the cruel man, Ader?" curiously asked Nyarata. "I must make a beautiful mat, for that person. How thoughtful of him! Is he your, you know?"

"No, he is not what you are trying to guess but rather the husband of my dear friend, Juan. The good deed that he had done in my defense today was quite brave and truly noble. I am really honoured and proud to be a friend of Mori and his wife."

"I will make him a mat, I, Nyarata, have said it. Can I go and thank him personally in his house?"

"Please do so, if you want to," amusingly answered Ader, as she was laughing at the way that Nyarata seemed so excited.

Nyarata therefore, quickly went and started knocking at Mori's door. Mori answered the door and respectfully asked Nyarata to enter in.

Therefore, Nyarata entered Mori's house and at once introduced herself, as a relative of Ader. She knelt down, as she was humbly telling Mori that "Son, I have come to thank you, for the wonderful thing that you have done in defense of Ader today."

Mori gently held Nyarata's hands, as he was humbly telling her, to kindly get up from her kneeling position. "Mom, it is really not necessary for you, to thank me while you are kneeling down." He respectfully told her. "It is rather I, who should be talking to you, while kneeling down."

"You are like the men of my time who, would not stand and watch a poor widow being beaten up," Nyarata gratefully told Mori. "You are a hero, a true gentleman and a true child of God."

Mori felt quite flattered by, all that Nyarata was telling him and eventually, he then said to her, "Thank you very much for your compliments but I think that what I have done today could have been done by just any man, who cares about others."

"There are a few men of your caliber, if any at all, left in the wild world that we are living in today," Nyarata assured Mori admiringly. "If you don't mind, my son, I will compose a song in your praise."

Mori could not contain his amusement about what Nyarata had just suggested to him and therefore, he started laughing quite interestingly. "Please, do not compose a song for me because I do not deserve such a great honour," he told Nyarata appreciatively. "However, thank you very much for all the wonderful things that you have said about me."

"You are indeed the son of a noble person," Nyarata went on. "Your mother should always count herself lucky for having a son like you."

Eventually, she thanked Mori graciously once again and then returned to Ader's house.

Mori had been listening casually to his wife, whenever she was attempting to tell him, with such an amusement, about Nyarata's sense of humour but he did not then understand how truly funny the old woman was, until that day. After Nyarata had left, Mori began laughing with tears, at the idea of Nyarata wanting to compose a song in his praise. The way that Nyarata had spoken to him with a lot of sense of humour, reminded Mori a lot about his own mother. He therefore, concluded that the older folks were fun to be with and wiser, than his own generation.

When Nyarata got back to Ader's house, after she had spoken to Mori, she told Ader everything that she had told Mori and Ader began to laugh interestingly until tears began to run down her cheeks.

"Good men like Mori are not common these days, "said Nyarata, like a teacher who was trying to convince his pupils about a new theory. "Our society has changed for the worst and the people nowadays passed each other quite carelessly even when, someone is being assaulted in front of them, without any need for intervention to stop the fighting party. In my day, the people cared a lot about each other and it was everyone's duty, to take care of a neighbour. Mori has made me very proud of him today and I pray that he lives a long life."

"Mori is surely a good man," agreed Ader, as she was beginning to remember all the wonderful things that Mori had been doing for her and her children since her husband's death. "I sometimes feel as if, Mori were my real brother. Actually, I do not look at Mori as if he were my landlord only but rather as a very good friend. His wife and mother are both wonderful people too. I am not going to move away from here unless, Mori someday would need this house that I am now renting from him."

"Are you kidding, my child?" asked Nyarata, with such serious facial expression, as she was trying to disapprove what Ader had just said. "A good man like Mori, would never turn you away from here, not in a month of a week. God has kindly, given you this nice place to live in and therefore, my dear child, chill here with your children and try to make the best of your life, with your wonderful neighbours."

"I feel very blessed to live with Mori, Juan and Jore," said Ader with such a grateful heart.

As the time was going by after Ader's incident with his cruel neighbour, the wife of the man, who had assaulted Ader, started eventually to spread juicy canard that Mori was having an affair with Ader but many people did not believe the rumour and it died down as quickly as it had started. Juan laughed carelessly and called everyone who might have believed the silly gossip a fool because she knew what type of a woman Ader was and that her relationship with Mori was simply friendship and neighbourliness.

"Do not worry about the preposterous rumour because I do not support it," Juan told Ader one day with such sympathy. You are like a sister to me and I know you better than the people who are trying to defile your reputation. Please feel free to talk to my husband, at any time you want to."

"Thank you, Juan, for being so understanding," Ader told her best friend, with such a grateful heart. "Juan, you are an angel. I cannot thank God enough for, making you as my best friend. Girlfriend, I owe you a lot for, your solid trust in me. However, I will only talk to your husband, when you are present, so that the bad people would find no opportunity, to bring up something ugly between you and I"

"If what you have just said, makes you happy, then it is ok with me," Juan said sadly, "otherwise, you are free to talk with my husband even, when I am not present. Ader, my husband, mother-in-law and I consider you fondly, as a family."

Ader wondered deeply, what her life would have been, had Juan's attitude towards her been sour, given the nature of the rumour.

Chapter Thirty-One
Jore's Life History

Juan and her mother-in-law went to visit Ader, as they had planned, in the evening of the day that Mori had defended Ader. When they entered Ader's house, they found her waiting for them eagerly, as she was quite anxious to hear what Jore had to tell her. Juan only went as an interpreter; otherwise, Jore would have gone alone.

"Greetings, my child, I have liked you ever since your husband was still alive," said Jore with a sympathetic look at Ader.

"I also like you a lot," Ader told Jore joyfully, while Juan was translating to Jore everything that Ader was saying in Arabic. "Mom, I am honoured to have you as my visitor tonight and to listen to what you have to tell me," Ader told Jore, respectfully.

"My child, I am quite concerned that you have decided to raise your children alone, without the need for remarrying. Therefore, I would like, to share with you my life's history so that you could think about it, learn from it and eventually, make a wise decision, as to how you would like to live your life in the future. I do not want you, to waste your life away like I did mine. I lost my first husband after I had just had one child. In our time girls were given away in marriage, when they were quite young. I was afraid of my husband in the beginning of our life together but eventually, accepted him and we began to love each other dearly. Life was full of hope and very beautiful. However, fate did not want our great life to last long. Therefore, when my daughter was just crawling, my husband went hunting with other men in the village. H.h.eeee never came back," stammered Jore, with so much pain in her voice, as she was trying to control the tears that were beginning to well in her eyes. "I am sorry, young women, the memory is still very fresh in my mind and whenever I have started talking about it, I still become very emotional. My husband was killed by a buffalo, which ripped his stomach apart and tore his body into two parts. I cried, while asking his clansmen to bury me alive with my husband. I refused to eat until there was hardly milk in my breast for the baby.

"My mother was still alive then and she became quite angry with me that she started slapping some senses into my mind. She therefore, asked me to tell her whether, I would like to murder my little daughter, Keji, by starving her to death. I answered my mother sorrowfully that I did not want to kill my little girl. Mom then told me to eat, for the sake of my innocent daughter. I would eat very little but cried day and night. I became very thin that I was looking like a skeleton, except, for the dark skin that covered the bones. Whenever the wind was blowing hard, I would sit down immediately because of my fear for being thrown down by the wind. As the result of my poor health, due to lack of eating but too much grieving, my in-laws allowed me to go and live with my mother for sometimes until, I was strong again. My mother was really thrilled to hear the news that I was returning home. Besides, I was her only girl among her boys. Consequently, after the funeral, I gathered a few of my stuff and my mother came and took me home.

"When my mother and I arrived at our home, everything looked so different to me from the last time that I had left home when I was getting married. None of the girls that I have grown up with were at home anymore. They were all married and I really felt lonely. My mother took good care of me and made me feel as if I were her little girl once again. My daughter grew to love my mother a lot and spent most the time with her during the day but night. After a few months, my daughter began to walk. She liked dancing around so much and the wives of my brothers grew very fond of her. Keji resembled her late dad completely. There were times when, I would look into her eyes, while I was remembering my husband and would start crying. Whenever my mother had seen me crying, she would give me an ugly look and said I quote, 'Life goes on by the way even, after our loved ones have passed away. No one has ever died because of the death of a loved one. Be strong and move on with your life.'

"At first, I was so mad at my mother for her insensitivity to my pain. I even I told her that she was lucky, to have lived with my dad for such a long time and that was why she could not understand what, I was going through. My mother never gave up on me, she kept repeating that I have my whole life before me and it was up to me, whether I wanted to waste it or make good use of it. As the time was going by, I started to see some sense, in what she had been telling me. I did stop crying eventually and got stronger and stronger every passing day. My mother and I were doing all the chores together, as we used to do before I was married. I got so used to living with my mother that I did not want, to return to my in-laws home anymore.

"After a year, of living with my mother, my elder brother-in-law sent a message that they would want me to return to their village. I became very sad that I started crying everyday. Unfortunately, my tears never drew any sympathy for me, neither from my mother nor my brothers. As a married woman, I did not belong with them anymore. My home was where, the relatives of my late husband were. Consequently, I started packing up my stuff again as I was preparing, to return to my so-called home, a home without a husband, weird, isn't it?" Jore asked quite sadly. Jore's sorrowful personal story made, Ader and Juan listened to her in tears.

"It was a dry season morning when my elder-brother-in-law showed up to come and take me with him. I looked at my mother hopefully, as I was expecting her to say something to stop my brother-in-law from taking me back to my late husband's home but she was as quiet as a dead person. Eventually, I asked her whether she was my real mother or not. My provocative question brought Mom to her senses and she told me that I belonged to the relatives of my late husband. Therefore, she packed for us some food that we would eat on the way and wished us all well. I was so angry that I did not say goodbye to any of them but just walked away sadly. We walked the whole day to get to the village. When we finally arrived in the evening, I was so tired that I went to bed without eating or bathing. My daughter cried a lot at night because she was tired and consequently, I did not have enough sleep. The following morning therefore, I was really fatigued and felt sick.

"There was no one, in the village that I could trust enough to tell that I was not feeling well. My elder brother-in-law, the one who had gone to bring me from my mother's home, came to greet me in the morning and told me, to stop pretending that I was ill. After he had spoken to me and gone away, he sent a little girl, of about seven years old, to take care of my daughter and told the little girl, to tell me that I should go to the field with the rest of the women in the home and help to harvest sorghum. Oh my God! The headache was pounding my head like a mortar and I did not know what to do. However, I gathered up my strength and went with the women to the field. As we were going, I walked slowly behind them, as they were making all kinds of jokes about the women, who could not work well in their home for marriage and humiliated their parents a lot. Some of the jokes were making me teary but I controlled my tears very hard and kept quiet. One of the elderly women, called Kharija, asked me whether I was not able to talk. I just made my point by nodding, which made her quite angry that she began jeering and telling me that I was a jerk. The rest of the women laughed loudly, as if that was what they had been waiting to hear for a long time. I never, said anything to Kharija in my defense but maintained my cool and kept going.

"We arrived in the field at 8:00 AM and started harvesting the sorghum. My headache got better for a little bit but I was continuing to feel weaker and weaker. Whenever I looked up, I felt so dizzy and it seemed as if, there were many stars twinkling in my eyes. By about 10:30 AM, my body gave up and I could no longer work. I fainted but most of the women were thinking that I was joking. However, one of them got frightened by the condition I was in and therefore, she brought some water and started sprinkling it over me and forced some through my throat. After the rest of the women had seen the danger I was in, they ran and informed the men about the condition that I was in. Consequently, they started making hurriedly, a stretcher out of some bamboos in order to carry me home immediately.

"At home, I was given some sour porridge, which I took and vomited all out. After little while, I was given some porridge again and I took very little but did not vomit anymore. Thereafter, I was given some bitter herbal medicine, which I took and then slept until dark. When I woke up in the evening, everything was like a dream for me I could not even remember how I had returned to the home of my in-laws. The headache was gone but I was too weak even to stand up. A woman called, Kiden, cooked some food and brought to me. She offered to spend the night with me so that she could help me with my daughter during the night. Tears, of appreciation started streaming down my cheeks. She hugged me and told me to stop crying because tears were signs for weakness. Furthermore, she advised me, to always be strong no matter what the circumstance may be. I slept well that night but in the morning, I started having diarrhea, which Kiden said was a good sign that I was beginning to get healed. Kiden kindly took care of me until, I was able to walk again then she returned to her house.

"After I had recovered from whatever the disease that almost killed me, a council of the elders was convened one evening to discuss, as to who should inherit me, among my brothers-in-law. I began to tremble instantly with fear and my tears started streaming down spontaneously. However, no one paid attention, to my tears. After, the rather very short discussion, they resolved that my elder brother-in-law, Jada, the one who had brought me back from our home, should be the one responsible me. Jada was already married to two women; Emba and Poni. Unfortunately, the women had never liked me even, when my late husband was still alive. My mind went blank. I was lost for word, got confused and stopped shedding tears immediately. I just wished then that I could have fallen down dead. However, I was called to stand up and accept my new husband. I stood up but said nothing. The men and the older women started laughing interestingly and said that I was only shy to speak but that Jada and I would make a good couple.

"After the meeting, I went to my little house and started crying helplessly. Therefore, I cried until I fell asleep. My sleep was interrupted sadly by a rather Wagnerian knock at my door. As soon as I opened the door, I was quite shocked to see my brother-in-law standing there. He therefore, entered in and sat by the door. He seemed rather frightened because he was aware that I did not like him at all. The unwelcoming look on my face was enough to subdue him for a while.

"'You are mine now,' he said gently, 'and if you really did loved my late brother, you will not chase me from this house tonight because I am here to represent him.'

"I kept quiet and did not answer him.

"'Are you dumb?" he asked me quite angrily. 'I don't want, to begin our first night together with a slap and I hope that you will co-operate.'

"With that last word, he moved closer and began to fondle me. My blood became so frigid and almost got frozen in my veins. I felt chilly all over. He made his advances and eventually, you know. I felt so horrible because I was very angry about the whole situation. I hated life but there was no way for me, to get out the mess.

"The next day, as I was going to the river early in the morning, I cried all the way there. Whenever I saw someone coming, I would wipe out my tears. After I had returned from the river, Jada's wives were awake and they all gave me a sinister look. I avoided having any argument with them the whole day and continued to work on whatever piece of work that I was doing. Jada's younger wife, called Poni, followed me when I was going to collect some firewood from a nearby bush that evening and told me that 'You, Jore, have had enough of my husband last night. Don't get comfortable that you will have him again tonight because he would be mine. Remember, I was not the one who has killed your husband.'

"I answered her, for the first time, 'I really don't want your husband and if he were to sleep in your house tonight I would be the happiest woman alive.' My sarcastic answer silenced the stupid woman, who was thinking errorneously that I might have liked her husband.

"When we returned home from the bushes, Poni went straightaway and told Jada that I have been telling her that Jada smelled so filthy that the odour from his body could kill all the houseflies. However, although I did not like Jada as a husband, he was a man of integrity and understanding and I couldn't have said anything so vulgar about him. Consequently, Jada began to ask Ponis rather sorrowfully, to explain to him in detail as to what might have provoked me in the first place, so that I could say such derogative things about him. Poni replied to him falsely that she was only joking with me when, she had told me simply that the previous night might have been the best night for me because it was the first for me to have man since my husband had died. Jada then walked away from Poni disgustingly and decided to go hunting overnight with some of the older men from the village. Jada's behaviour surprised the elders so much because, they did not understand why, he had decided to go away and leave me alone, after they had just given me to him.

"Jada spent two nights in the forest, as he was hunting with the rest of the men that he had gone with and came back home on the third day with lots of meat. He selected the best part of the meat and gave to me. His provocative action angered his wives so much that their faces were looking so terrible like a horrible thunderstorm. Jada was never bothered by his wives' behaviours and kept calm. That same night, he came to my house again and asked me whether, I have said that he was a filthy person. After, I had told him the truth that I have told Poni, he was quiet for quite a while and finally told me, 'I respect you, Jore, a lot and would not allow any of my wives to play around with you. However, you must always remember that the elders have given you to me, so that I could take good care of you and my little niece properly. Please accept me, just as I am, will you?'

"I sighed deeply but kept quiet. We spent the night together and I did not cry as I have done on the first night. Therefore, he continued to spend nights in my house for a week, which made Poni almost to commit suicide. She tried to vent out her anger on me but I ignored all her nonsense. Poni therefore, started slapping her husband even in public but that was something that the women of my time had never done. One afternoon, Jada went to Poni's house, so that he could pick up some of his clothes from there and was quite shocked to find that Poni was trying to hang herself. Poni's action infuriated her husband so much that he beat her up badly. A meeting was called immediately and the elders decided that Poni should be sent back to her father's home and she should remain there until, she had improved her weird behaviour.

"With Poni gone for a while, I was left to deal with Emba, Jada's eldest wife. I maintained my cool and avoided all the situations that could, lead to confrontation with her. She eventually, gave up trying to provoke me because she had then concluded that I was a coward and a wimp, who could not stand up to anything. I went about my work without asking anyone for help, even when I really needed help. Days turned into weeks and weeks into months. I kept behaving like a wimp indeed and that saved me from having a quarrel or a fight with Emba.

"Poni returned, at the beginning of the rainy season and the villagers drank and danced to celebrate her return. I was already two months pregnant then but never told anyone and moreover, I was never sick. Jada went to Poni that night and she was very happy the following morning that one could tell from the way she was smiling excitedly at everything. Most of the elders then concluded that Poni had indeed changed a little bit for the better, after spending time with her family because she was then able to smile quite often and seemed friendlier. Whenever the people were around us, Poni would pretend to talk to me respectfully but as soon as the two of us were alone, she would call me terrible names and make ugly faces to me. However, I did ignored, all her attempts to find faults with me.

"One morning, I made a large pot of porridge and called all the children in the homestead to come and drink it. Poni had then gone to fetch water from the river when, I called her children to come and share the porridge with rest of the children. Therefore, after she had returned and found that her children were playing with full stomachs, she asked them quite angrily, as to where they had eaten and after they had told her that in my house, Poni almost exploded with anger. As the result, she marched straightaway to me with such a stormy face for a serious quarrel and fierce fight. However, I was quite amused by her weird behaviour and asked her simply, whether she was not feeling well. My question infuriated her so much that she jumped on me viciously like a hungry a lioness. That day, for the first time since I was a girl, I fought with all my strength as I threw down the silly woman and began holding her neck quite tightly, with the intention of choking her unconscious but Jada intervened and separated us. That fight, gave me a new position of power, dignity and self-confidence in that home because even Emba started talking to me with some respect thereafter. Therefore, I wished that I had started fighting with the women earlier. Poni stopped troubling me but would not even answer my greetings.

"Shortly after the incident, when Jada had found out that I was pregnant but fought as if I were not, he started becoming very protective of me.

However, I did not like his idea for protecting me and I therefore, told him that he should rather be protecting his arrogant wives because I was going to beat them up at any time, if any of them should bother me once again. From that time onward, whenever it was time for Jada to come and sleep in my house, I would pretend that I was sick or give him some very groundbreaking excuses. I continued to avoid him until, I had my baby girl who was named, Poni, the name I abhorred so much because of the ugly behaviour of my co-wife but since it was customary for the Bari people to name the second born girl after the first girl, Poni, there was nothing that I could have done about it. Life went on and I did conceive again and gave birth to Mori, Juan's husband.

"After the birth of Mori, Jada started wooing another young girl. He married her the following dry season, with a celebration fit for a chief or a queen. The girl was very good-looking that everyone acknowledged her beauty, including me. She did look like a person of mix race with the Middle Eastern blood in her; average height, lighter than most people's complexion of the skin, very long dark hair, her teeth were as white as pearl and in good order, the girl had such a beautiful body that everyone was admiring her, she walked gracefully and quite aware of her beauty. The young woman really, swept Jada off his feet. He began ignoring all us and I was very happy about the situation. However, my co-wife, Poni, grew so thin out of jealousy and envy that she was looking like some wild kind of animal, that was walking on its two feet. The village women gossiped and ridiculed Poni a lot about her ugly behaviour."

At that point of Jore's story, it was already 10:00 PM and most of the families were already asleep. Jore therefore, bid Ader goodnight and then assured her that she would continue with her story the following evening.

After Juan and her mother-in-law had left, Ader stayed awake until midnight as she was pondering about Jore's incredible story. Given Jore's life history, Ader then understood why Nyarata had been persuading her, to find a man who would bring some meaning back into her life. 'Well,' she thought deeply to herself, 'That was their time, this is a new time and I think that I can take care of my boys without, the need of assistance from another man, who is not their real dad. Besides, Mori and his wife are like family to me. I do not think that anyone would dare to come and mess up with me again, after what Mori had done to that pigheaded idiot. Furthermore, my great protector and saviour, Jesus Christ, will not leave me alone. Therefore, I am safe, happy and don't need any man in my life at the moment or may be forever. The few friends that I have are good enough for me.' Ader then said her night prayer and fell asleep shortly after.

When Juan entered into their bedroom, her husband was about to sleep and as soon as he saw her, he did not seemed please at all.

Juan saw the dirty look that her husband had given to her when, she enter into the house and therefore asked him rather angrily, "What's wrong with you, Mori, and what mistake have I done to you, to deserve such a horrible look from you?

"How dare you ask me," replied Mori quite angrily. " What time, do you think it is now?"

"Is that the reason, why your face is looking like a thunderstorm or there is something else?" curiously inquired Juan because she was feeling quite upset by her husband's misdemeanor.

"You should have known that you are a married woman and that your time in bed is also my time," sternly answered Mori.

"What has really, prevented you from sleeping, anyway," retorted Juan. "I did not carry the bed with me to Ader's house, did I?"

"Hey, did you stay out that long so as, to find a reason to avoid me again?" inquired Mori rather seriously.

"Was it I who have started giving a dirty look at you?" asked Juan quite disappointingly because she was quite upset.

"Now, are we having a quarrel or what?" requested Mori, with such a look of surprise on his face. "I was missing to have you with me in bed so much and that is why I have asked you those stupid questions. Juan, my dear wife, I am sorry if, I have offended you in any way. I love you very much and hate such situation that lead us to bitter arguments. Please come to me and do not turn your back at me again tonight."

With that last sentence Mori got out of the bed, began holding his wife fondly as well as kissing her quite passionately. However, Juan was still quite upset and did not like all that her husband was trying to do, in order to console her. She therefore, broke away from him and then told him that "Don't think that those smooth talks and kisses of yours have calmed down my anger against you. Mori, the question that you have asked me, was quite pathetic because you have made me felt as if I have been out with another man."

Mori felt very sorry, about what he had said to his wife but did not know any other way for him to further ask for pardon. He therefore, knelt down and began begging his wife contritely to forgive him. "Juan, my sweet wife, I will never speak to you harshly again," he apologized humbly. "Darling, I must tell you that I would not be able, to close my eyes tonight if you refuse to, you know."

Juan kept quiet for a moment and eventually, told her husband while a bit of smile was breaking on her face, "I have forgiven you, big rascal, and hope that you would behave well to me, when I come to bed late, next time."

"I am sorry for everything that I have said to you," Mori told his wife again, "but I am happy that you have forgiven me. Thanks for being so understanding."

"I could not hold your ugly words against you because of the wonderful thing that you have done to defend Ader today," said Juan in a more relaxed tone of voice.

"Hey, Juan, my dear wife, are you implying that had I not beaten up that cruel neighbour, you were not going to accept my sincere apology to you, on bended knees? Mori asked his wife quite puzzlingly.

"Who knows?" replied Juan, rather carelessly because she was very amused by the impact that she had created on her husband.

"Please, stop your nonsense and come here," said Mori more seriously and he began to hold his wife quite tightly. "Sweetheart, the trick that you have been using on me for the past few nights, is not going to work tonight because I am not, going to listen to any more of your excuses. I would like to tell you assertively that tonight, I am in full control and there is nothing that you are going to say or do that would make me change my determination to be with you."

Juan stared at her husband quietly because she had realized then that it was impossible for her to avoid him that night. Therefore, she got into bed with him, without any further argument.

Chapter Thirty-Two
The Conclusion of Jore's Life History

On the Sunday that followed Ader's tumultuous week she woke up early in the morning, cleaned the house and made breakfast. After Ader and her children had had breakfast, she bathed and dressed them up in their best clothes and took them to church with her. They got early in the church, for the 10:00 AM mass and sat at the front pew because Ader wanted to hear the mass clearly.

The Cathedral where Ader had been attending her Sunday mass was called St Theresa of the Child Jesus, which was quite famous for its choir that sang beautifully and pronounced out the lyrics quite clearly. One old man, one time commented that "Whenever I attended the 10 o'clock mass, the beautiful singing by the choir, sweeps away my sorrows. I feel so peaceful in my heart and mind. If it were possible, I would have told the choir to sing every day, for me."

The choir drew many people to church, including those who had not been going to church before the choir was established.

That Sunday, the choir sang the song, *"The Lord's Our Rock in whom we hide, a Shelter in the time of storm"* as an introit. The song was, Ader's favourite and therefore, it comforted her very much and touched the very core of her miserable life. She closed her eyes and began thinking lovingly about Jesus, as her only shelter in the very stormy life that she was then living with her children. Ader felt such weakness on her knees, as the priest was approaching the altar and therefore, knelt down as tears were beginning to well in her eyes. Eventually, she wiped off her tears and gathered up her strength to stand once again. Ader's heart was full of gratitude to God, for all the wonderful things that He had done for her during the week. Therefore, she lifted up her heart to God in thanksgiving and thereafter paid, close attention to every word of the prayer that the priest was saying.

The first reading that Sunday was taken from **Prophet Isaiah 55:1-3**, which said:

The Lord says this: "Everyone who thirsts, come to the waters; and you that have no money, come, buy and eat! Come, buy wine and milk without money and without price. Why do you spend money for that which is not bread, and your labour for that which does not satisfy? Listen carefully to me, and eat what is good, and delight yourselves in rich food. Incline your ears, and come to me; listen, so that you may live. I will make with you an everlasting covenant, my steadfast, sure love for David."

The second reading was taken from **St Paul's letter to the Romans 8:35, 37-39** which was as follows:

Who will separate us from the love of Christ? Will hardship, or distress, or persecution, or famine, or nakedness, or peril, or sword? No, in all these things we are more than conquerors through him who loved us. For I am convinced that neither death, nor life, nor angels, nor rulers, nor things present, nor things to come, nor powers, nor height, nor depth, nor anything else in all creation, will be able to separate us from the love of God in Christ Jesus our Lord.

The Gospel was according to Matthew 14:13-21:

When Jesus heard that Herod had beheaded John the Baptist, he withdrew in a boat to a deserted place by himself. But when the crowds heard it, they followed him on foot from the towns. When he went ashore, Jesus saw a great crowd; and he had compassion for them and cured their sick. When it was evening, the disciples came to him and said, "This is a desert place, and the hour is now late; send the crowds away that they may go into the villages and buy food for themselves." Jesus said to them, "They need not go away; you give them something to eat." They replied, "We have nothing here but five loaves and two fish." And he said, "Bring them here to me." Then Jesus ordered the crowds to sit down on the grass. Taking the five loaves and the two fish, he looked up to heaven, and blessed and broke the loaves, and gave them to the disciples, and the disciples gave them to the crowds. And all ate and were filled; and took up what was left over of the broken pieces, twelve baskets full. And those who ate were five thousand men, besides women and children.

During the homily, the priest talked about God's great love and care for his people and further elaborated that "Our doubtful hearts are the cause, for most of the pains and troubles that we have in life. Human beings have refused to follow God's command, from the time when Adam and Eve disobeyed God in the Garden of Eden to date. We only trust in God when things are going well in our lives and doubt His providence when we are faced with life's challenges. The behaviours of the human beings are really quite sad because we normally find it quite hard to trust in God. However, when we do things according to God's commands, miracles happen in our lives, for the glory of the Lord. I hope that most of you have not forgotten the situation of starvation that we have gone through last week, when there was hardly any food in the city. Quite a number of you were going around, while they were crying that the end of life for the people living in Juba town had come because God has forsaken us. That my dear people, was a very, very sad way of behaving, especially from Christians, like you and me. Our God is always kind and merciful and he has shown you his power by the way that he has touched the stubborn hearts of the people in power, both the Sudan government and the leader of the rebel, to allow for the relief food to be flown from Kenya here. However, how many people among you who have fallen down on their knees and given thanks to God? There may be only a few, if any among you and that shows just how we have always been taking God for granted. I am therefore, urging everyone present here today, to put God, first, in everything and trust him completely, even though it may sometimes feels quite hard to do so. If you do so, you would be amazed at how many wonderful miracles that God will do to your lives, regardless of the ongoing war."

Ader felt, as if the priest had known about her despair on the previous Sunday, when she had decided to cry until she was dead. Therefore, she was really ashamed of herself and sat down with her head bowed between her knees, while she was quietly asking God to forgive and give her more strength, so that she could be able to overcome her temptations, especially, the kind that she had succumbed to, in the previous week. Ader even wondered, why she had not remembered that Sunday's beautiful readings from the Bible, when she was in despair. She was quite angry with herself, for allowing Satan to carry her far away from the loving hands of God and testing her to the extreme that had made her to doubt God's love. The readings, preaching and the whole mass on that Sunday, touched Ader quite deeply and brought a new beginning for her. Consequently, she promised that she would never doubt God's love again.

After Ader and her children got home from the church therefore, she cooked before they could go to spend the afternoon with old Nyarata. Ader was full of peace that day and decided to share her joy with Nyarata. She therefore, told Nyarata quite excitedly that "God has personally spoken to me in the Church today."

Nyarata gave out a loud mocking laughter and after asked Ader rather teasingly that "How does God looked like? Is He young or old? Please tell me, my dear child because I have been anxious to know what God might look like, since I was a little girl."

Ader was not amused, by Nyarata's laughter but notwithstanding she tried to explain to her what she meant, when she said that God had spoken to her that day. "I believe in Jesus Christ but sometimes my doubting heart, makes me sin against God's love for me," she told Nyarata, with such a humble spirit. "I hope that you have not forgotten, the story of my foolishness last Sunday when I had decided to cry until I die. Well, today God has spoken to me in the church, through three readings from different parts of the bible. In all the three readings, God's words were addressed to me specifically. He wanted me to listen, understand and put into practice that he is the God who loves and cares about the needs of his children always."

The way that Ader was trying to explain everything was too much for old Nyarata, who believed that only the dead people could speak with God because they were out of this world. She therefore, replied to Ader, "I don't believe that God could speak with the living here on earth but only speaks with people who have gone ahead of us to be with him in heaven, you know, the dead folks."

"Our God is the God of the living and not of the dead," Ader reassured old Nyarata but she refused completely to accept whatever point, Ader was trying make.

"Everything that you are telling me is sounding like a riddle, my dear child" Nyarata told Ader because she was full of doubts about Ader's explanation. "However, I am glad that God has decided to come down from heaven today, so that he could put some sense into that big silly head of yours. Please do not repeat, what you have done last Sunday no matter what the circumstance may be, my child."

They both laughed and then Ader said, "Thank you very much, for what you have said. I have learnt my lesson the hard way and will never repeat what I have done last Sunday."

Ader had taken along with her some sugar, tea and *lagemat* (a kind of fried cake), and therefore, she began preparing some tea. While they were taking tea, Nyarata told Ader lots of stories about life and Ader stayed with her until about 5:00 PM, before she could return to her house. After Ader had put her children to bed, she started waiting with such anticipation for Jore to come and finish the story she had started the previous night.

Juan had told her mother-in-law that her husband had complained about her delay in Ader's house the previous night, and therefore, before they could go over to Ader, Jore went to ask for permission from her son, so that she could take Juan with her as a translator. Mori accepted willingly but felt ashamed because his wife had exposed his bad behaviour to his mother. He therefore, apologized to his mother, "I am very sorry about, what I have said to my wife last night and I promise you, Mom, that I will never repeat it again. However, I did not know what you, people, were doing in Ader's house. Please Mom, my wife is your daughter-in-law and you are free to use her assistance, whenever you wish. Therefore, if you want to stay and tell your story until 11:00 PM tonight, I will not complain."

Jore was quite pleased to hear her son talked responsibly and therefore, began rubbing his hair, as if he were still her little stubborn boy. "Thank you, for your apology, my dear son," she said appreciatively. "I knew that you were not aware about the reason why we were in Ader's house so late last night. Mori, you have grown and matured into a very responsible young man. I am very proud of you, my dear son. However, I won't keep your wife long today because I am just going to conclude the story that I have started since yesterday."

"Thanks, Mom," said Mori, almost in tears, "I am very proud of you too."

Thereafter, Jore went to Ader's house and her daughter-in-law followed her shortly after.

Ader joyfully welcomed her friends into her house and was very anxious to hear the conclusion of Jore's incredible story. Jore therefore, asked the young women, "Where exactly, have I left the story last night."

"When Jada got married to another woman and his second wife, Poni, grew so thin out of jealousy and envy," answered Ader quite precisely and after Juan had translated what Ader had said to her mother-in-law, she was quite amazed by how accurate and sound Ader's memory was.

"Your memory is very good, my child," Jore told Ader in admiration and then began to laugh. "I envy you, the young people, for such wonderful and clear memory. Mine is so clouded and empty nowadays."

"How could one forget such an incredible story," Ader told old Jore humbly.

"Now let me continue, my dear ladies," Jore went on. "After the birth of Mori, Jada had nothing to do with me anymore. He was with his new wife, all the time because he delighted a lot in her. The time went by very fast and before I could mature into a fully-grown up woman, my first daughter became of age and I had to prepare her for marriage. However, I did not really want my daughter to leave home so early and therefore, I turned down lots of proposals for her until she was quite mature. She got married eventually to a tall and handsome young man, called, Tombe, who came from a good family. The young man and his family loved my daughter so much that they treated her as if she were their own daughter. Well, I became a mother-in-law when I was quite young.

"Jada's youngest wife, over the years, gave birth to only girls and all of them were beautiful like their mother. Jada was very proud of his beautiful daughters and treated them with such respect and love. Nobody complained, as they would normally do, whenever a woman was giving birth to only girls. After I had had Mori, my co-wives, each had a boy and those were their last children too because Jada had nothing to do with them also anymore, as his life was centred on his young and beautiful wife.

"A year after my daughter Keji got married she had a baby girl who was named after me, Jore. I loved my granddaughter so much that I kept visiting her and her parents quite frequently. Mori was also proud to be an uncle. He carried his niece around and joyfully played with her, whenever Keji visited us. For the first time in my life, I was full of happiness and joy. Keji's husband helped us a lot. Whenever he went hunting, he would bring to me some meat. I loved my son-in-law, as if he were my birth son because he was treating me with a lot of respect.

"At that time, most of the boys from the village came to Juba because they needed a different life style from the monotonous one in the village. They saw that those who used to go to the village for a visit from Juba looked so clean, civilized and especially, the ones who had gone to school seemed to know everything about life. Mori was dreaming, to become like one of those clean young men from the city, some day. I cried sorrowfully because of my helplessness and inability to provide for my son, so that his dreams might some day come true. I struggled over the years and managed to save some money to give to Mori so that he could come to Juba. Eventually, Mori left me in the village and came here to Juba, to work for the soldiers as a servant. I was left with my daughter Poni, only. We dug together in the field, fetched water from the river together, went for firewood together and did all kind of chores together. I got used to the monotonous routines so much that I did not care about meeting another man, as some older women were suggesting to me. I was so comfortable with my life, status quo.

"One cold morning, Tombe, my son-in-law, came knocking at my door and was seemingly in great fear. Therefore, I asked him, as to what was wrong. He told me that his wife had fallen ill at night and the fever was getting worst. I got up immediately and went with him to his village. When we arrived there, I found my daughter throwing herself about in pain. I got hold of her, held her in my arms and began to put cold wet cloth on her body, so as to bring the fever down because her body was burning like fire. She painfully looked at me but could not say anything. I continued putting the wet cloth over her until she calmed down a little bit. She vomited all the herbal medications that were being given to her. After a while, she began looking at me again and asked dizzily, 'Is that you Mom, and where is my sister, Poni?'

"I then knew that my daughter was really in a serious condition. She rested for a little while and then the fever struck again. There was nothing anyone could do to save my daughter. Her uncle, Jada, tried all that he could do by, bringing different kinds of febrifuge but none of which helped. In the evening at about 7:00 PM, she passed away. Initially, I did not cry because I could not understand why, the same God who had taken away my husband from me, could also take my beloved daughter who had been reminding me a lot about him. I held my dead girl in my arms until morning. No one dared to take her away from my arms. My eyes were burning with pain but not a single tear came out. It is good to shed some tears, whenever someone we love very dearly had died but at that time there was hardly any tear in my eyes. After my daughter was buried the following evening, I came to my senses and realize that I have lost her and would never be able to see her again. Therefore, I started screaming out quite loudly for the first time, threw myself over her grave and cried there the whole night. I had tried to kill myself many times but before I could do so each time, someone would find me. After many attempts for trying to take my own life, I gave up on the idea and instead started taking care of my granddaughter, Jore. Whenever she started crying, I would also cry and she would stop and shockingly stared at my face.

"Gradually, I accepted my loss and concentrated my energy into bringing up my granddaughter who was then the centre of my life. Mori came for the funeral of his sister and stayed with us for a short time but later on went back to Juba. Poni helped me a lot in my most trying time but was eventually, married to a man who was already having another wife. She came to Juba with her husband and I was left with my little Jore, who was growing up looking like her late mother. Jore and I became best of friends. Her father was the one digging for us and would also go hunt and bring for us some meat. Mori also began sending for us some money and sugar for our tea. Mori was then working for the soldiers as well as going to school. Eventually, after he had graduated from Juba Commercial School, he got a job and would buy for little Jore and I, beautiful dresses and shoes. He was also sending us some money so that we could buy anything that we needed in the village. Eventually, we became the envy of most of the villagers.

"My son-in-law, Tombe, eventually got married to another woman and, therefore, was not helping us as he used to do. Who could blame such a wonderful son-in-law? He was an exceptional widower, who had grieved for the death of his wife like a woman would for the death of her husband and that is, for a very long time. By saying so I mean that I have never seen a young man, who had stayed alone for a long time after the death of his wife, like my son-in-law had done. His new wife was very understanding and loving and therefore, frequently came to visit my granddaughter, while she brought along with her, some gifts from her husband. I still respect my son-in-law up to now. He is so special to me and will remain dear in my heart until I die.

"When the insecurity got worst in our village, due to the on-going war, Mori decided to bring me to Juba. It is good to have a son with a dream, like my son's. Look at me now! I have never expected to live in a place like Juba, to put on shoes on my old ugly feet or nice dresses like the ones that I am wearing now. What I regretted the most in my life now is that I wished that I had married another man, had more children then, Mori might have had a brother with whom, he could now be sharing his feelings or secrets. Mori grew up without a father or a brother and no one knows exactly what, he is missing and feeling inside his heart. He worked so hard, to be where he is now in life. Therefore, my dear daughter, Ader, my reason for sharing with you my darkest life's history is, to give you an insight into your own future. However, I am glad that you have refused to be inherited by your mad brother-in-law.

Inheritance is worth nothing to a poor widow let me assure you. If you need a man, marry someone else and start a new life with, otherwise, a brother-in-law would take you and desert you as mine did. The two children, whom I have had with him, did not mean anything to him at all and he was never there for them until he died. Mori never called him a dad. Could you imagine how much, I have hurt my children? Anyway, I thank God because he has made my two children all, turned out to be responsible adults."

Ader and Juan were both moved to tears, after Jore had concluded her sad history finally but Jore stubbornly asked them, "Why are you, young women, crying, especially, you, Ader? Take care, deep thoughts and make wise decision so that you would not live a life of regret in future, the way I am living now. Learn from the story, I have just told you if you can. Life is too short and must be lived wisely. However, you must remember that one day your little boys would wish that they were having a sister or sisters when they grow up. You better think, about a solution to such situation sooner, than later. A woman's productive life is very short and once it is over, there is nothing you could do about it."

Jore finished her story at about 9:00 PM and wished Ader, a good night with her children, before she could leave.

After Jore and Juan had left, Ader sat up as she was reminiscing Jore's advice. 'My boys would surely need a male figure in their life some day, someone who could help give them, answers to difficult questions concerning a man's life,' she thought. 'That is the one thing that I would never be able to give my boys. But where would, that good man come from, anyway? Hmmm,' sighed Ader quite doubtfully. 'God will provide, in his own good time if it is his will that I should remarry, otherwise, I am happy with my life, status quo.' Ader concluded her thoughts.

Mori was quite surprised, to see his wife returned so early that night from Ader's house and in a humble way inquired, "Has my mother really, finished telling her story to Ader?"

"Yes she did," replied Juan, as she was smiling joyfully at her husband.

"Mom is quite a remarkable woman, isn't she?" said Mori. "I did not know that my mother was such a compassionate woman, who could share with Ader, her life's history. She seemed to connect, very well with Ader and I do not know, why."

"You do not, know why?" Juan asked her husband because she was quite surprised at his thoughtlessness. "Your mom and Ader are both widows and have experienced widowhood at a very young age, when, in normal cases, most of the young women just start to get to know their husbands better. Is it clear, to you now, man?"

"Yes, it is plainly clear, after your explanation, my lovely woman," answered Mori, who was quite amazed at the intelligent manner, in which his wife had explained the whole thing to him. "You are such a genius, my dear, and that is why I love you more and more each passing day."

"I am no genius," answered Juan rather rebelliously. "I am a little thoughtful than you are."

"Then I admire your thoughtfulness," said Mori in such a sexy way, "but sometimes, you are such a rebel, Juan, and you make me feel so defeated."

"Whom are you calling a rebel?" asked Juan, as she began to playfully chasing her husband around the bedroom. They played until they got tired. Mori was quite delighted to see his wife so happy because it had been quite a while, since they last had joyfully played together. He therefore had a wonderful night with his wife.

On the other hand, Jore was quite happy that she had shared her life's history with her young fellow widow. She hoped that Ader would learn some lesson from her story because she did not want to see Ader, wasting her entire life, as she, Jore, had done. Jore had then realised for the first time that every young widow was rather silly because she allowed herself to be consumed by sorrow. Furthermore, she had found out that the young widows didn't care about their future until, after they have reached their menopausal stage then, they would realize that they had wasted their life in vain. Jore reached such conclusion because of what she had gone through in her life.

Chapter Thirty-Three
Mori's Sudden Death

Juan, Mori and Jore continued, to be very kind and compassionate to Ader that anyone who did not know them properly would think that they were not only tenant and landlord but from the same family. Mori reduced, the rent for the house so that Ader could afford and continue to live with him and his family. Ader's children started liking Mori and grew very fond of him. Mori and the boys would go out for a walk in the evenings, whenever he was at home. At that time, there were some hunters, who used to sell smoked meat in Juba. Mori would buy the smoked meat, for his family, as well as for Ader but whenever Ader had given him the money to cover for, whatever he had spent to buy the meat, he would refuse and tell her that the reason for his happy marriage was Ader and her late husband and that the type of kindness, love and compassion that the couple had given him that had enable him to marry his wife, no amount of money could repay. Ader got used eventually, to receiving things from Mori because Juan also did have a clean heart towards her. On the other hand, whenever Ader got her monthly food supply from her work, she would give some to Juan but she was accepting initially, whatever Ader had been giving to her with a heavy heart and told Ader that it did not seem proper for her to help them but vice versa. Juan started to accept gradually, whatever Ader was giving to her with a willing hear and that made Ader quite pleased.

As time was going by, Juan conceived again but became so ashamed about it that she could not even talk to Ader. She began to argue with her husband frequently but he was quite pleased that she was pregnant. Ader assumed accurately that something extraordinary might be disturbing Juan and her husband. However, she kept her distance and greeted Juan only, whenever she saw her outside. After a couple of month, Ader noticed some changes in her friend and speculated thoughtfully that she was indeed pregnant.

One afternoon, as Ader was mending her boys' shirts outside her house, Juan joined her and said with such humility, "Ader, I am sorry about the distance that has begun to widen lately between us and I accept the responsibility that I am to blame for it. However, I hope that you can now understand, the reason why I have been keeping away from you," said Juan as she pointed to her abdomen shamefully.

"Don't you look wonderful and glowing!" said Ader as she was admiring her friend joyfully. "However, why have you sounded so ashamed of your pregnancy? Juan, my dear friend, you are not the first woman to get pregnant while the first baby is still young. In your case, it is much, much better because your daughter is a little older. I did conceive my son, Okene, when my first was only five months. I became so emotional and aggressive towards my late husband that I challenged him for a fight many times. It took me time, to accept my pregnancy. See, you are not the only woman, after all."

"Thank you for sharing your story with me," said Juan with such a grateful heart. "I am really ashamed of myself and to make the situation even worst, quite a number of our neighbours have started to give me very dirty look whenever they see me outside."

"Do not worry about their leer," Ader assured her friend. "You are a married woman and such situation occur to most married women. After I had conceived my second boy, many people, including some of my relatives called me very terrible names. My late husband defended me and warned them to leave me alone or else he would fight with them. Thereafter, no one said any negative thing about my pregnancy."

"You, have made me started feeling good already," said Juan. "Ader, thank you so much, my dear. You are such a jewel of a friend. However, I do not know why I did not tell you this from the very first moment after I had realized that I was pregnant. Girlfriend, you have helped me to marry Mori and now you have given me the confidence that I need to feel good about this pregnancy. Oh Ader, you really are my guardian angel."

"Not at all, that is what best friends are for, isn't it?" gladly said Ader.

From that moment onward therefore, Juan felt good about her pregnancy and went about with such full confidence, which made her husband very proud of her.

Jore was quite happy, to know that her daughter-in-law was expecting again and praised God for giving her son, a good and productive woman. However, she was rather concerned about little Keji but trusted God to keep her well. Juan's pregnancy made Jore to become very supportive of her and began doing some of the house chores that she had never been doing before. Jore carried her granddaughter on her back most of the time and sang to her lots of the folk songs. Keji became so fond of her grandmother that she sometimes slept in her house.

As was the routine with Ader every Sunday, she got up early one Sunday morning and after breakfast, started preparing to go to church with her children. However, that Sunday as Ader and her children were going to Church, Mori asked her that "Could you please kindly pray for me and my family because we do not have enough time to go to Church?"

Ader answered him that "I will pray for all of you but only this Sunday. However, next Sunday, I would like you, Mori and your family, to come to church with us. You need to learn how, to know and worship God who is loving, forgiving, caring, kind, compassionate and all powerful."

"After you have returned from Church today, would you kindly mind to teach me more about the God, whom you love and trust in so much," said Mori with such humility.

"I would be delighted, to tell you all about the love of God today, after I have returned from Church," accepted Ader quite willingly, with a smiling face and thereafter their brief conversation, she went to Church with her children.

That Sunday, Ader prayed for Mori and his family, as he had requested and all the suffering people in the world, including the widows and the orphans, who were suffering everywhere in southern Sudan. During the homily, the priest exhorted his congregation that "Seek first the kingdom of God and everything else that you need, you will get. The knowledge of and respect for God, as our creator and father, is the beginning of wisdom. When we put God second in all that we do, it is the worst mistake because we do not know the hour, when God could easily call us to go to him. I would like to emphasize to you that despite the terrible suffering that we are experiencing at the moment, let us learn to thank and bless the name of the Lord. I know that it is very difficult to do so, even for me as a priest sometimes but God's grace is sufficient for all of us to do so. When you are faced with lots of doubts, at the moments when everything seems so bleak, you should remember that Jesus Christ has promised us that he would not leave us alone and that is why he had suffered so much, for the salvation of all mankind although He was sinless. Whenever any one of you feels completely crushed by life's trial, call on the Holy name of Jesus and offer your sufferings to Him. Christ will surely lift off the burden from your heart and give you peace, instead. Remember, His sacrifice on Calvary, is not in vain."

Ader thanked God, for the priest's beautiful preaching and wished that her neighbours had come with her to church that Sunday, so that they could have heard what the priest had said.

On the other hand, after breakfast, Mori informed his wife that "My dear Juan, I would like to go and visit one of my friends, whom I have not seen for a long time. I just would like to find out how, he and his family are doing."

"Good luck with your visit," his wife told him, "but remember to return home early."

"I will surely do, as you have told, my dear teacher," replied Mori mockingly and they began to play, while chasing each other around the room.

Thereafter, Mori put on his best *Kaunda suit* and asked his wife, "How do I look, my dear?"

"Marvelous, you handsome devil," Juan replied, as she was admiring her husband's good look joyfully.

Thereafter, Mori then kissed his wife rather passionately before he left the house.

While Mori was going, Juan followed him outside and stood by the door, as she was watching him go until he was out of sight. She then went back inside the house and wondered why her husband had kissed her that day, as if in a way, he was saying a final goodbye. A funny feeling of panic, gripped Juan's heart. She started wondering suddenly, what the future held for her, daughter Keji, her husband and the unborn child, as chill was running through her blood and spine and she started feeling as if, something was very wrong but could not tell exactly what it was. However, Juan refused to dwell on the spooky feeling that there was an impending disaster coming her way and therefore, she went about her chores as usual but was trembling occasionally, on and off.

When Mori arrived at his friend's house, they greeted each other with an excitement for a long lost friend. "I greatly miss the days when we used to visit each other more frequently and had lots of fun," said Mori's friend joyfully. "However, I am sorry that I do not visit you as I used to do anymore. I just wanted, to give you time with your wife, you know."

"You are welcome at anytime to visit me and my family," Mori assured his friend. "My wife and I all love your company because you are such a wonderful friend."

They all laughed joyfully and began to pat each other on the back. Shortly after, Mori's friend bought some *Lacoi* (a local brew that is sipped through a long tube) and they sat outside his friend's house, as they were enjoying their sip because it was hot inside the house. All of a sudden, Mori and his friend heard a whistling sound out of nowhere and before they could make sense of what was happening, both of them were hit hard by the debris from the rebel's shelling that exploded, just two feet from where they were sitting. Mori's friend died instantly but Mori stayed alive until he was taken to the hospital. The shelling were only shot twice towards Juba that Sunday. The first one hit Mori and his friend and the second one fell into the river Nile.

On the other hand, after prayer, a few of Ader's friend came to visit her and therefore, Ader cooked lunch and ate with them. As they were conversing after the meal, they heard a loud wailing outside the house and ran to find out what was the problem. To everyone's dismay, Juan was the one wailing and somersaulting in anguish, after she had heard the news about her husband's critical injury, from the shelling. Two strong men took hold of Juan and were trying to subdue her but it was such a struggle for them. A neighbour, who was having a car then, volunteered to drive Juan to the hospital where her husband was taken for treatment. When Juan got to the hospital, she found that her husband was fatally injured that he could not even talk to her. Mori gazed at his beloved wife painfully and helplessly for a few minutes, as if he was trying to tell her about something very important and then breathed his last finally.

Before the news about Mori's death could get home, his mother instinctively knew that her son was already dead. She ripped off her dress in anguish and was left only with some wrapping around her waist, as she was putting ashes on her head and body despairingly. However, she did not cry. As soon as Ader saw Jore's sorrowful action, she went to console and keep her company, since there was no other person left in the home but Ader. Jore sang lots of dirges in Bari language. Her songs moved Ader to tears, although, she did not understand the meaning of the words. While Ader was trying to move closer to Jore, so as to comfort her, she motioned to Ader not to come close to her. At that moment, Jore was feeling as if, she was the source of all pains and sorrows here on earth. Ader threw herself down in anguish consequently and cried bitterly, as she was questioning God thoughtfully, *Dear Lord, why do you send so much pain to some people, while others enjoy life till old age, without experiencing the situations like Jore's.* However, Ader could not then imagine, the strength and resilience that God had given Jore, to endure all her sorrows since she was young until then. As Ader continued to sit with old and sorrowful Jore, one of Jore's relatives came from the hospital and announced tearfully that Mori was already dead. Jore was not surprised at all at the news because she had known all along in her

299

heart that her beloved son had already departed from this cruel and sorrowful world. Ader had wanted to pray, for Mori's soul to rest in peace and his grief-stricken mother to find some solace but she could not because she was very angry with God for allowing Mori to die.

After quite a number of Jore's relatives arrived eventually to share in her grief, Ader left them and went back to her house. There, she cried resentfully, as she was trying to understand why, she had lived to feel all the heart-wrenching pain in her life and Jore's. She began asking God quite angrily, as to why He had taken away Mori who was very dear to his mother and also then was like a brother to her and her children. Ader was wishing that God should answer all her questions instantly because she was very mad at God. After a little while of burning with anger against God, Ader decided to read the Bible eventually because it was her habit, to find answers to difficult questions in the Bible. Therefore, she reached out for the Bible and randomly opened it. God indeed answered her by allowing her to read from the book of Job Chapter 38:1–11.

> Then out of the storm the Lord spoke to Job. Who are you to question my wisdom with your ignorant, empty words? Stand up now like a man and answer the questions I ask you. Were you there when I made the world? If you know so much tell me about it. Who decided how large it would be? Who stretched the measuring line over it? Do you know all the answers? What holds up the pillars that support the earth? Who laid the cornerstone to the world? In the dawn of the day the stars sang together, and the heavenly beings shouted for joy. Who closed the gates to hold back the Sea when it burst from the womb of the earth? It was I who covered the sea with clouds and wrapped it in darkness. I marked a boundary for the sea and kept it behind bolted gates. I told it, "So far and no further! Here your powerful waves must stop."

After reading the above verses, Ader was quite overwhelmed by the awesomeness of the Lord God and his mighty deeds that she knelt down and began to ask God, to forgive her for questioning His wisdom. Furthermore, she prayed tearfully that God might give strength to Juan who was very vulnerable in withstanding the situation she was in because of her pregnancy and also to give strength and courage to Jore. Ader spent her time in prayer, with tears running down her cheeks until, Mori's corpse was brought home from the hospital at about 4:00 PM, Sudan local time.

As soon as Mori's body was brought home from the hospital and taken into the house, Juan overpowered those who were holding her down and threw herself violently to the ground, while she was asking God to take her also. Everyone was afraid that Juan would lose her pregnancy. Ader sprinted from her door, got hold of Juan and said, "Look into my eyes."

Juan stopped and stood momentarily, like someone who has been struck by lightening. Her heart missed a beat and she sighed deeply, as she was looking at Ader's eyes. Then in a deep coarse voice that sounded so strange and not like Juan at all, she said eventually, "I am not strong, brave, courageous and spiritual like you, Ader. My heart is so crushed and I wished that I were dead together with my dear husband today. I just cannot live without him in my life. Please pray for me."

"I have already prayed for you and will continue to pray." Ader assured her grief-stricken friend compassionately.

After the brief but mysterious conversation between Ader and Juan, Juan lost her violent strength, collapsed and lied motionless on the ground. Most of the people were quite surprised to see, what had happened between the two women. Some women rushed, to the rescue of Juan with some salty water because they were thinking that she might have fainted. However, Ader advised them to leave Juan alone, for a while. After a long time of lying down, Juan got up, entered the house where her husband's body was laid and mourned without ever throwing herself down anymore. Ader quietly, watched her friend and understood that God had indeed answered her prayer by calming down Juan. Therefore, she praised the name of the Lord and gave Him profound thanks.

Mori's body was put on the family's bed, after the older women had washed and dressed it up. It seemed then as if, Mori was just sleeping. Everyone, including the men wept for Mori but poor old Jore. Ader went and sat beside her grief-stricken friend, while she was remembering what Mori had asked her to do for him and his family before he died. As the result, Ader began thinking that 'Mori, you did ask me to pray for you this morning and I did, may you therefore, find peace with your creator and in turn pray for those of us, who are left here below in such great sorrow.' Shortly after, Ader began holding Juan tenderly and together they cried sorrowfully. Ader advised Juan thereafter that "My dear friend, you must remember that you are carrying another life within you. Cry but do not hurt yourself and the fetus because the condition you are in is very delicate."

Juan gazed quietly at Ader but did not say anything because she was too crushed to talk anymore. However, she heeded her best friend's advice and never threw about herself anymore.

Poni, mourned for the death of her brother, in such despair. She kissed his dead body and cried out sorrowfully in a loud voice as she lamented, "I should have been the one to die. How could you all leave me alone, in this dangerous world? What have I done dear God, so that I should be left alone like this, without a brother or a sister? To whom will I turn to, whenever I am in need of help? No! No! No," she screamed in anguish, while she was hitting her head on the ground. Poni violently shook her mother, who was covered with ashes and asked her quite angrily in despair, "Why did you not die instead of my hero, you old woman?"

Jore threw her hands in the air helplessly because she could not understand why death was so mean and cruel to take her beloved son, who was quite young and very responsible, but left her, poor and ugly-looking, old Jore.

"I am too ugly, even for death, to take me away from this world, oh my dear daughter," she told her daughter in such despair. "I think that I am a witch who will live in this world until the end of the world."

According to the Bari custom, as soon as someone had died, they would start beating the drum quite loudly and therefore, they brought some drums and started beating them, while Mori's dead body was still lying in the house. Darkness and gloom enveloped, the once upon a time, very peaceful and loving home. No one could describe the pain, anguish and sorrow that everyone was feeling then due to Mori's sudden death. Jore danced miserably and sorrowfully around her son's dead body and sang all the lullabies that she had composed, when Mori was still a baby. She would kneel down occasionally and kiss her son but never shed any tear.

At dusk, the corpse was brought outside and put on the bed. Most of the relatives, by then had heard about the death of Mori and came over. Therefore, the courtyard was filled to the brink with people crying, some of them dancing quite sorrowfully and meanwhile, others were singing all kinds of dirges. Jore went and lied down on the bed, next to her son's dead body and then spoke out loudly, "I am spending my last night with, my hero and my precious son. Tomorrow, after he is buried, I will be left alone, to face this cruel world, just like I have done when my husband and my daughter died a long time ago."

As Jore was lying down beside her dead son, she sang all kinds of songs from lullabies to dirges until dawn, when she was quiet for a short while but started all over as soon as she was able to start singing once more.

At daybreak, the young men were sent to dig the grave and they finished at around 4:00 PM. While the grave was being dug, Jore continued to lie down beside her beloved dead son, without even the need for drinking some water. She looked so frail and deeply hurt. On the other hand, Juan's eyes were all swollen up from too much crying that she could not see well. She sat indefatigably, by her husband's body until morning, while swinging her head sorrowfully from left to right in anguish but there were no more tears coming from her eyes. Juan's mother asked her to lie down a bit but she refused to listen to her mother completely, while the memories of the wonderful time that she had had with her husband was flooding her mind. Juan could not even then understand, whatever anyone was trying to tell her.

Before the body was taken for burial at 4:30 PM, a priest was called to pray and bless it. While the body was being lowered into the grave eventually, Juan jumped and almost fell into the grave. She asked the people, to bury her alive with her husband because she could not bear the anguish, for being alive without him in her life. Two strong young men pulled her away and firmly held her down. After the burial, it was a tag of war to take Juan home. A number of the young men held and forced her into the truck, then drove her home quickly. While at home, Jore watched Juan in silence, for quite some time, as Juan was refusing to listen to whatever anyone was trying to tell her but Jore scolded Juan eventually, "Hey, my dear daughter, please spare the life that my son has left in your womb, if you really love him. Do you think that what you have been doing would bring back your husband to you? "

Jore's statement was so powerful that Juan calmed down at once.

After Jore had noticed that most of the people were wondering why she did not weep for her son's death, she told everyone gently, "Those of you who are crying, have just experienced the sting of death, for the first time but as for me, I am now immune to death's sting because it has no victory but cruelty and I hate cruelty. Furthermore, why would I cry? My husband died when I was very young, thereafter, my daughter who was reminding me quite a lot about him also died and now, my only son and saviour who had delivered me from the life of pain, poverty and despair also died. Therefore, why should I surely cry anymore? If weeping for the dead was an answer to prevent further deaths, then the tears I have shed for the deaths of my husband and daughter would have prevented the death of my dearly beloved son but it did not. Could you people now understand, the reason why I have not been crying? On the day I will die, if ever I would, I will have no one to give me a decent burial and dogs would surely eat my corpse. I thank God that you, my dear people, have given my son a decent burial today and so were my late husband and daughter, long time ago. I am happy for all of them and I hope that they would soon call me to join them to where they have gone, so that the family might be complete."

What Jore had said made most of the people, to begin crying with such sympathy for her, including the men. The mourners could not comprehend how resilient Jore was, to withstand all the calamities that had been afflicting her life.

The people danced at the funeral for nine days. Thereafter, the big place was left to just Ader, Juan and Jore. Mori's death changed the home completely forever and the whole place became so desolate. There was hardly any joyful conversation in the home, even between, Juan and Ader who were best of friends. They were feeling, as if, there was nothing left in their life that was worth talking about. The only time when their voices could be heard was, whenever they were talking to the three children, Omal Jr., Okene and little Keji. Juan began to gradually love prayer and started joining Ader, whenever she was reciting the Holy Rosary and reading the Bible in the evenings because in return, she was getting consolation, solace and peace. However, Jore did not join the young women because of the language barrier. She was most of the time remaining indoors unless Juan had called her outside.

Jore was feeling so lost by the death of her dearly beloved and only son that she did not know where to go to anymore because in the village where she was used to living, the rebels were torturing the people and were even killing some of the people, who failed to comply with their rules and regulations. Furthermore, she could not even go to live with her daughter, Poni, because Poni's husband was quite ruthless and could beat her up any time. Therefore Jore then decided eventually that she would live in the desolate home of her late son until she died. She also accepted the fact that her daughter-in-law who was still very young, would someday leave the home and get married to another man. Jore did not care about anything anymore and lived her sorrowful life day by day.

Chapter Thirty-Four
Ader's Cousins Visited Her

It took Ader a long time to accept Mori's death. She prayed to God for protection since, Mori was no longer available to stand up for her and her children, in any case that any one of her heartless neighbours should attack her. However, Ader spent much of her time with Juan, who was so heartbroken and advised her to stop crying but instead, to start handling the enormous responsibilities that her late husband had left behind for raising little Keji and the upcoming baby. She would cook food and insist that Juan eat enough for two. Ader' efforts seemed fruitless initially but as the time was going by, Juan began to listen to her appreciatively and was not crying that much anymore.

Juan gave birth eventually to a beautiful baby girl but the relatives of her late husband were not happy at all because according to them, the name of Mori would no longer live on, since, all his children were mere girls who would one day be married away from home. Jore was also not amused by the birth of the second child but she did not show her disapproval openly because she was thinking that if the child were to be a boy, it would suffer alone in the world because it would not have any male relative for a role model. Juan was humbled extremely, by the birth of her second baby girl but she said that the God who had made the child to be a girl knows why. Ader helped Juan a lot and would sometimes spend the night in Juan's house, while taking care of the older girl, so that Juan could have a restful sleep. The two women were bonded by their fate in life so much that they were inseparable. The little that they had, they were sharing together and whenever any one of them was feeling very low, the other one would console and cheer her up.

Juan's baby grew bigger and healthy, as the time was going by. However, Juan's parents realized eventually that their daughter needed some rest away from the sorrowful home and therefore, they took her and her daughters away to stay with them, for a while. Jore was then left alone in the big home, with only her granddaughter, from her late daughter, Keji. She missed Juan and the children so much that while they were away she became very thin. However, she was very aware about the fact that Juan would some day leave that home for good and go back to her parents. Sometimes, in the evening, Jore would come and sit outside for a little bit but she seemed very frail and miserable and her thoughts wandered very far away that one could tell at a glance. Ader, who had always been so fond of the old woman, would make some tea and go to her for some conversation, through an interpreter. Jore enjoyed very much, every brief moment of conversation that was able to have with Ader and continued to persuade Ader that she should get married, at least, for protection since, Mori was no longer alive to protect her. Ader completely rejected Jore's notion and told her repeatedly that she was comfortable with her life, status quo because she did not believe in marriage anymore.

While Juan was away, Ader greatly missed her friendship. She would sometimes remember fondly, the time when, her beloved husband and Mori were still alive and the home was full of joy, happiness, romance, peace and jokes. Such memories, crushed Ader's heart, with such anguish that she would sometimes cry especially, whenever her children were away with old Nyarata. Ader prayed a lot, as she was asking God, to grant peace to the suffering people of the southern Sudan. However, there were moments when, Ader was crushed down with heart-wrenching sorrow and wondered whether, God even listened to her prayer but she would not dwell on such negative thoughts long because she understood clearly that God was in control of whatever was happening in his creation.

On the other hand, Juan found it rather hard to stay with her parents because she was so used to staying in her own home. She missed her mother-in-law and felt so heartbroken over the fact that she had left her alone. Juan cried a lot whenever, she was by herself because most of the girls with whom she had grown up, were having joyful life with their husbands. She wondered, why misfortune had deprived her of her loving husband, at such a young age. Whenever, Juan saw her mother was chatting joyfully with her dad, she would walk away from their presence to a secluded place and began to cry. Juan fondly remembered her dear friend, Ader, and realised then how strong she was because she was handling her widowhood, with such courage and strength that most of the widows didn't have. Juan's mother did all the cooking and would sometimes take care of her grandchildren, whenever Juan had gone out with some of her friends. Juan's parents were very understanding, kind and compassionate to her and that eased Juan's grief a little bit. Juan stayed with her parents for a month, before she could return to her home.

At that time, the insecurity worsened in Juba again because the rebels had been attacking frequently, the women who were going to the bushes to collect some firewood. The rebels took way some of the women for good and their children were left to suffer alone in Juba. Therefore, everyone became so scared to death and most of the people gave up the idea, for going into the bushes for firewood. The few brave men, who had been venturing to go into the bushes and burned some charcoal, sold them at exorbitant prices that only the rich people could afford. The poor people therefore, started eventually, to dig the roots of the trees that had been cut down long time ago within the town and using them for cooking. It was a very, very sad experience for survival.

When the Military overthrew the democratically elected Government of Khartoum, in the coup of 1989, the two, rebels' groups; one as the government of the day and the other as a guerilla, reached an agreement with each other, for a cease-fire. Therefore, the people in Juba became so happy because they were once again able to go into the bushes without fear. The women began to bring lots of firewood home, from very far away bushes, just in case, the situation might worsen again. Ader and Juan also went for the firewood on weekends and brought home lots of bundles, which they kept only for emergency because they were using charcoal for cooking.

The people in Juba enjoyed the relative freedom of movement brought about by the cease-fire so much that they could go as far away as twenty miles from Juba, for the first time in years. There were lots of food in the markets and the prices were affordable because the flights between Juba and Khartoum were quite frequent. The relief airplanes also continued to bring food from Kenya to Juba and the displaced people were having enough food. The tentative agreement for the peace, made the people from various villages in rural areas, to begin coming to Juba on foot. Most of the people, met their loved ones, for the first time, in a very long time. Therefore, they cried with such emotion, as they were greeting each other and some of them even danced for joy. The people from as far away as Acoliland also, came to Juba to visit their relatives and loved ones and especially to ask for clothing and beddings because whatever they had been having before the war, the rebels looted all, when they took hold of the villages. Some of the people, arrived in Juba in rags that they had wrapped only, to cover their private parts. The relatives in Juba were so heartbroken to see their folks from the villages looked, so wild and old because of the situation they were living in. The visitors from villages, told their relatives in Juba about their ordeals with the rebels, as they narrated with such misery how, the rebels were forcing the young girls and single women into unwanted marriages and beating those who did not, adhered to their rules and regulations. Furthermore, they said that the rebels were often killing some of the villagers whom, they were thinking about as a threat, to whatever cruel activities that they had been doing. They also talked with such hatred about, the government in Khartoum for sending warplanes, to bomb the innocent civilians in the rural areas, as they described in tears, some of the gruesome deaths, which were caused by the bombings.

As the people from the rural areas continued to come to Juba, some of Ader's cousins also came from the village. Therefore, as soon as they had seen her, they started weeping in sympathy for the death of her husband and Ader cried with them sorrowfully. "Why should a wonderful girl like you, be deprived of her handsome husband, so early in life?" one of the cousins called Akec, lamented as she was crying. "Your husband has left you, far too soon, my dear. This world is so cruel, truly cruel for some of us."

"How could one person deal with so many deaths in the family, all occurring at about the same time?" another cousin called Aringo, lamented. "Ader, you have suffered more than the rest of us, in this life. Not only that, you have been grieving for the death of your beloved husband alone, as if, you have no members of your family left alive."

The women wept together very bitterly and sorrowfully, for a long time but eventually, calmed down. Thereafter, Ader gave them some water for bathing and later on cooked food for them.

After Ader's cousins had had a good rest, they started telling her about the news in the village. "Your mother has sent you her condolence and greetings," said one of her cousins, called Limango, "and she wished that she were able to walk to Juba and see you in person. We would also like you to know that your mother escaped the massacre at Obbo narrowly because on that day, she had gone out to weed in the field, very early in the morning. When she heard the sounds from the spraying bullets in Loudo village, she ran away to Iyire village, where she had stayed for three days but then returned to Loudo village to search for your father. Your father, was killed on his way to the field and therefore, when your mother found his decomposed body, she was quite devastated that she almost went insane. Worst of all, your mother had been injured badly, on one of her legs because she threw herself down violently, after she had learned about the death of your sister, Amyel. Therefore, she now walks with the help of a cane and limps so much that she cannot walk quite far."

Ader was overcome with sorrow so much, after she had heard that her mother could not even walk well and began to hit her head against the wall, in anguish. Her cousins stopped her sympathetically and then Limango said, "If you are going to behave that way, we will no longer tell you all the horrible stories about home anymore. We know very well that you are hurting but please you must understand that hitting your head against the wall, won't ease, remove, or changed the devastating facts, that have occurred. This ongoing war has already wounded you and your family more than word could say."

Ader then stopped hitting her head against the wall and told her cousins, with such spirit of despair that "Please, stop telling me the terrible stories because I think that what I have heard is enough for today. My heart is breaking and I am feeling so hurt."

Nyarata, who heard about the coming of Ader's cousins, from some people, came to Ader's house in such high spirit like a tornado and began scolding her, at once, "Why have you not send someone to call me, after your cousins have arrived, you naughty girl?"

"I am very sorry, Nyarata, for having forgotten about you," Ader apologized remorsefully. I was caught up in the news about home and have been quite overwhelmed that I have almost lost my mind and that is why I did not send for you."

Nyarata being a very understanding old lady, that she had always been told Ader, "You know what my dear, had these ladies came as my visitors, I would have done exactly, what you have done. Therefore, I am not really mad at you as I have sounded because I am quite aware that you don't have anyone here to send." Turning to the visitors, Nyarata asked them humbly, "Young women, would you mind to tell me whether, our people are still living in Licari village."

"What?" asked one of the cousins called, Alur shockingly. "Do you mean to say that you, the people, who are here in Juba, have not heard that no one, from the village, is living near the main road anymore? All the people have moved deeper into the bushes and started new villages. The people, who used to live in the Licari village, are now living in an area, near Ayii stream and they have called the name of the new village, "*Adag-daa*" (which means, I don't want to quarrel).

"Who, don't you people want to quarrel with, anyway?" Ader asked her cousins curiously.

"We do not want to quarrel with both the rebels and the government soldiers," answered a cousin called, Cecek. "We would like the two lunatics to leave us alone because we are fed up with their stupidity, which is fueling the on-going war. Both groups have destroyed so many lives carelessly and have deprived us of the peace and joy that we need so much in our life. We very much doubt, whether anything meaningful would some day come out of the struggle, eventually."

Ader, who was listening attentively to Cecek, sighed deeply and then said eventually, "Your perception about this war is the same like mine. The war has lost its original purpose and no one is going to win in the end unless the need for peace and the rights of the southern Sudanese are negotiated with the northerners, through the intervention of the international community. It is the poor civilians who will continue to lose their lives until the warlords are tired and decided to give up on the antagonism eventually. I sense in my heart that some day in the future, when the leader of the rebel is quite tired of fighting, he will sign a peace pact with the northerners that we should stay together with the Arabs, again, just like the Anyanya One leader had done, during the Addis Ababa agreement, after the first civil war."

Ader's cousins, agreed with her views. Nyarata, who had intuitively sensed that most of the people from the former villages might have already died, asked the young women quite carefully, "Would you mind to tell me, my dear ladies, the names of the elders, who are still alive, from the former Licari village?

The ladies laughed amusingly and then one of them called, Kassara replied, "You are a very, very intelligent person because you have constructed your question quite logically. Mom, most of the elders are now dead and half of them were killed by the bullets."

Kassara then announced the names, of the few elderly people who were still alive. Tears formed into Nyarata's eyes, as she was listening to the names of most of her age mates, who were already dead. She was overcome with such emotion that she hastened outside for a moment in order to clear her mind and later on, returned into the house. The women, therefore, chatted joyfully until, late at night and thereafter, Nyarata went back to her place.

The following day, Ader took her cousins to Konyokonyo market where, some second hand clothes were sold and she bought a number of beautiful dresses for all of them. The women were very happy with Ader but were equally sad that they were bothering a widow who, in the normal situation, they should be the one helping.

"Under normal circumstance, you were not supposed to buy for us anything because you are a widow. However, this cruel, on-going war has reversed every moral law," Cecek told Ader sympathetically.

"Do not worry about me," said Ader, as she was trying to comfort her tearful cousins. "I am working and the little money that I am making, I am very happy to share with you."

"You, Ader, have started to clothe all of us before you were even married," a cousin called Layat said with such a grateful heart. "All of us were wishing you a happy marriage but look at how miserable your life has turned out to be."

"Stop saying that," said Ader rather authoritatively, as she was beginning to feel the reality that her cousins were talking about. "There are many widows out there like me. This ugly and bloody war, has really devastated the lives of, so many women and their children. However, thank you all for your compassionate concern for me. It means a lot."

After the women had returned from the market, Ader's cousins began putting on their new dresses that Ader had just bought for them and therefore, started dancing for joy because of the way that they were all looking quite pretty.

"Hey, girls, you are all looking very young and beautiful once again, just as I used to know you," said Ader, as she was admiring her cousins with such a delightful heart.

"You got that right, girl," confirmed Kassara joyfully. "We are quite aware about the way that we are looking so beautiful, right now. Don't you agree with me, my dear sisters?"

"Who could dispute the plain fact, anyway," said Limango quit proudly, as she was dancing like a little girl who has just received the most precious gift.

There was an outburst of joyful laughter, as all of them continued to dance, while wiggling their buttocks, in a very, very funny way that made Ader to begin laughing with tears running down her cheeks.

"None of you have really lost any of your sense of humour, notwithstanding the horrible situations that you have been going through all these years," Ader told her funny cousins, as she continued to laugh at them amusingly.

"Hey, the Queen of the Magwi Chiefdom," Alur told Ader playfully, "are you kidding, my dear sister, we have been quite miserable that none of us has been joking anymore. However, these new dresses have resurrected our sense of humour today. You know what, our usual sense of humour flew off our heads since the war had intensified in the villages. The rebels looted most our properties, the government soldiers burnt down whatever little we were left

GRACE ELVY AMULLO

with and therefore, we had virtually nothing good to wear. Today is our first time to wear full and beautiful dresses in three years. In the village, we only wear rags and no one is caring about, the way he/she looks, anymore."

Ader listened to her cousins' tale in bewilderment and only shook her head in despair.

Ader's life greatly changed for the better, when her cousins were with her because she had known them since childhood. They talked, joked and laughed about all kind of things. Ader wished that the devastating war was never started at all and instead, the southern Sudanese politicians could have negotiated with the northern Sudanese for, the possibility for a referendum for the separation of the south from the north. She remembered, her time in Kenya, how those people were enjoying the freedom of their country, as they were living in such joy and peace. Furthermore, Ader wished that someday, God could kindly give the southern Sudanese the kind of joy and peace that the rest of the peaceful countries of the world are enjoying, so that her generation might taste, the thing that the rest of the world call peace. Every time, that Ader was lost in her thoughts about the miseries of the people of the south Sudan, she would conclude that God had foretold the whole thing vividly in Prophet Isaiah Chapter 18, which said that "God Would Punish the Sudan." Therefore, she envisaged that everything that God had predicted in Bible must, happen exactly as He had said. Ader firmly believed consequently that the Prophesy of Isaiah 18 was then being fulfilled and that was why, the vultures had been eating the dead people until, they could eat no more and the wild animals are also fed up of the human flesh.

Juan saw, Ader's cousins when they had first arrived but did not want to intrude into their reunion for both happiness and sorrow. Therefore, she waited until, they had all calmed down and rested quite well then, she went to greet them the following day in the evening, after they had returned from the market. Ader introduced Juan to her cousins, as soon as she had come to visit them.

"Juan, these are my cousins and cousins, this is my very best friend, Juan," said Ader joyfully. "Juan has also lost her husband to the cruel war and is living with her two kids and her mother-in-law. She is, my landlady. We have been good friends ever since, our husbands were still alive."

Ader's cousins were so moved by Juan's tragedy that some of them began holding her hands compassionately and wept sorrowfully, in sympathy for her. However, Juan told them humbly that "Please, do not to cry. The deaths caused by the devastating ongoing war, have touched so many people. There

312

are very many widows, like Ader and I, out there. It is very hard for us some days to even get out of the bed but we are trying to cope, for the sake of our children."

Ader's cousins did not speak Arabic quite well and so Ader translated to them whatever Juan had said. Jore also came, to greet Ader's cousins but did not stay long with them because of the language barrier and age difference.

After Jore and Juan were gone, Ader's cousins continued to tell her, a lot of stories about home.

"You must be wondering about, where your elder brother, Bongomin is, don't you?" Alur gently told Ader. "He, his wife and children have ran to Uganda when, the rebels first arrived in Upper Talanga and attacked the people there. Your sister, Aya, and her family, have also gone to Uganda and are now living in one of the refugee camps."

Ader was quite happy, to hear about her sister and brother, for the first time in years and the fact that they had escaped to safety. "I am quite delighted, to hear the news about Bongomin and Aya today," said Ader excitedly. I was afraid, that they might have also been killed because I have never heard anything about any of them all these years. May God graciously bless them, wherever they are until, we would some day meet hopefully."

"Concerning your father-in-law," went on Alur, "no one knows where he is, not even the Magwi boys, who had returned from their training for the rebels. Therefore, no one is sure whether the Chief is alive or dead."

Ader was quite sad to hear about her dear father-in-law who had loved her as if she were his own daughter. She shook her head in anguish, bit her lower lips in despair and sighed deeply.

"As for your mother," said Kassara, "she is not alone. Our cousin Aballo is living with her and is helping her a lot. Despite all the deaths in your family, your mother is doing relatively well."

"I am glad to know that my mother is living well with her disability," said Ader, as she was feeling quite relieved, to know that her mother was having a helper.

"However, there are lots of foods at home," said Cecek. In the village, sometimes we forget that there is a war going on except, for the sound of the horrible bomber planes from the government that scared people to death and the silly fights among the rebels, over women. Those are the only situations that make people ran for their lives."

"I am so happy, to at last, hear the story about home," said Ader delightfully. "For a long time, I have been thinking that I would neither see anyone from home nor hear any news about home again until I die. My dear sisters, I would like to go home with you to see my mother because I missing her a lot. It has been too long since, we have both seen each other. My mother has not even seen my children yet."

"Do not even, think about going home because we know very well that you would not return to Juba," rejected Layat vehemently and the rest of the cousins unanimously agreed with her. "You know what, in the village, young women and girls are taken by force for marriages by the rebels and even the widows. The principle of the rebels is that the women in their childbearing age should give birth to, as many children as they could, to replace the dead people."

"If that is the case then," said Ader reluctantly, "I will wait for peace to come and later go home to see my mother. I hope, that God will keep us all alive until we meet again. My life here is quite sad and lonely but I am not ready, to risk my life to go home and be forced to marry those ruthless people, the rebels because they have deprived me of my beloved and handsome husband at such young age and I vehemently abhor them."

"You have every right to hate them because they have really robed you badly. However, Ader, you are a strong person," said Limango admiringly. "You have been very strong ever since, you were a little girl as if, you somehow, foresaw the worst experiences that were awaiting you in your future. Stay here in Juba, as you are raising your children until, peace comes someday, God's willing, then you will see your mother."

"I will do that definitely," agreed Ader. "Thank you all very much, you have indeed enlightened my mind. Today, I am feeling as if it were the good old days when we use to enjoy each other's company in Licari village."

The stories that Ader had heard from her cousins about forced marriages were quite true because there were some girls who had been studying and living with their relatives in Juba after the war had separated them from their parents, and therefore, when some of them went home to visit their parents, during the tentative ceasefire, none of them returned to Juba. The rebels forced all the girls into marriages and the men who had married them treated them quite wonderfully as if they were royalties, and therefore, they forget completely about their studies in Juba. The situation then made the few girls who had remained in Juba to give up their idea for wanting to go and see their parents in the villages because they had then realized that, if they were to go, they too would end up like those who had gone ahead of them.

After one month of stay in Juba, Ader's cousins decided to return to the village. Ader gave them lots of stuff and some for her mother and cousin,

Aballo, who was taking care of her mother. The cousins were very grateful to Ader for her generosity.

"We will send you some food from the village, whenever someone from our village would be coming to Juba," they said. "We feel very sorry to leave you alone again in your sorrowful life."

"Don't you worry about me," bravely said Ader, as she was trying to conceal her sadness about, her cousins return to the village and being left alone, once again. "I will manage just fine."

"Life, as a single parent is not easy," Aringo told Ader quite sympathetically. "Please, try to find some good man and get married."

"I do not, have the heart to love any man again," said Ader sadly. "The horrible death of my beloved husband has crushed my heart into pieces completely. When you get home, please inform my mother about the decision that I have taken never to marry again."

Ader's cousins respected her decision and therefore, did not insist that she must remarry, "May God bless the choice that you have made and may you live securely, with your children here in Juba."

After their final conversation, Ader escorted her cousins across the river Nile, up to Gumbo, before she could return home.

The day after, Ader's cousins had left for the village was Saturday and therefore, Ader and Juan decided to go to the bushes for some firewood. They went so far away that on their way back, with the heavy bundles of firewood that they were carrying on their heads, they rested many times on the way, before they could get home. As they were resting at the last station before they could get home, Juan broke the silence and said in such a state of despair, "If my husband was alive, I would not have been carrying such a heavy load of firewood, like this, on my head."

"Why do you reduce yourself to a loser by such ludicrous wishes?" Ader scolded her friend sternly. "Wake up, my dear friend and face life's challenges boldly. Remember, you are not alone because God is always with you."

"I wished that I were as strong as you are then, my life would have been a bit easy for me," Juan said sadly.

"All widows, are strong in different ways, including you," Ader pointed out to her friend, "and that is why, God has taken away our husbands. God knows, that we can depend on Him for everything and face each day with such courage and strength."

Juan sat quietly and gazed at Ader admiringly, as she was wondering, what kind of a woman Ader was. She could not comprehend why Ader was so strong in the face of all her trials and tribulations and yet continued to be so faithful to God. Ader noticed eventually, that Juan was gazing intently at her and so she asked Juan, "Girlfriend, could you share with me what, you are thinking about and especially why, you have been fixing your eyes on me, like that?"

"Nothing," replied Juan stubbornly, as if she were a pupil that was found cheating in a test, "Ader, you are very unique and different. I have never met, a widow like you. You have the courage of a lioness, to face your miserable life."

"Stop being silly, beautiful girl, you, too, are a strong woman," Ader told her friend, as they both began to laugh. "Don't be unkind to yourself by, always underrating your ability to do things. Look at how, you have been managing everything in your home efficiently since, your husband had passed away. Juan, you need to have confidence in yourself because that is the only thing that you seem to lack so much."

"Ader, I really admire your courage," said Juan softly and admiringly, "and I hope that I will learn from you and build up my self confidence."

"That I know that you will definitely," Ader told her friend, as they were beginning the carry on their heads the heavy bundles of the firewood, once again

After the rest, Ader and Juan walked hard and got home at about 2:00 PM, while they were feeling very, very exhausted. Ader and Juan had left home at 5:00 AM that morning with the hope that they would return home, by midday. However that day, the women, with whom they had gone for the firewood, decided to go far away into the bushes. After Juan got home, she found that her baby had cried a lot, while she was away. She, therefore, felt sorry for her baby and began nursing her immediately. Jore had cooked some food while, Juan was away and therefore, as soon as Juan had finished nursing her baby, Jore gave her the food. Juan enjoyed, her mother-in-law's food with such an appetite because she was very hungry when she got home.

On Ader's side, she rested, for a while before she went to bring her boys from Nyarata. When Ader got to Nyarata's house, she found that Nyarata had cooked food for her. Ader, like Juan, was very hungry and so ate with such an appetite. When she was done eating therefore, she thanked Nyarata gratefully, "I would have died of hunger today, had you not cooked for me. How can I thank you enough, for your thoughtfulness and generosity?"

"You are more generous than me, my dear child," Nyarata assured Ader. "Ader, can't you remember, all the wonderful things that you have been doing for me, all these years. Cooking food for you today, was fun."

"You are an angel," Ader told Nyarata. "I pray that you may live a long, long life."

"Thank you for your wishes, my dear," said Nyarata with a big smile on her face. "I have lived a long life but it is rather you, whom God should bless with long life so that you could raise up your boys to maturity and be able to see your grand and great grandchildren."

Ader stayed with Nyarata until evening. She gave Nyarata some of the firewood that she had brought that day because Nyarata was old and could not walk, the long distance that the people had been going to bring firewood.

After Ader had put her children to bed that evening, she began to think a lot about her cousins and wondered how far they might have already traveled. She wished that she were the one going home, instead of, her cousins and imagined joyfully how, she would have embraced and held lovingly, her dear mother. Ader felt so lonely and the thoughts for missing her mother overwhelmed her so much that tears began to run down her cheeks. 'I cannot keep breaking down like this forever,' she thought painfully. 'I have to be strong and accept my life, the way it is. Someday in the future, God will help me to meet my mother once again hopefully. Mom, may my guardian angel tell you tonight that I love and miss you a lot.' Ader then began wiping off her tears and felt a lot better. Therefore, since Ader was very tired that day, she decided to go to bed early and had a good night sleep.

Chapter Thirty-Five
Ader Got Stung by Gossips

After Ader had worked with the CART organization for three years, she was called back to her old ministry and assigned to work in the office of the director general. Ader's hard work won the heart of her new boss, who became very kind to her. After Ader had returned to her old ministry, she began to remember the good old time when, she was still dating her late husband and how then, her life seemed so sweet and full of beautiful dreams for wonderful future. She avoided, most of the time to look at the door of the office where, her late husband used to work but that did not help her in any way because the memories kept flooding back into her mind. Hinda had returned to the old ministry before Ader and her friendship and good sense of humour helped Ader coped relatively well. Ader and Hinda spent a lot of time together, especially, during lunch. The women talked about, the wonderful time that they had had, while they were working with the CART and therefore, missed very much, the good friends they had left behind there. However, before the CART could send both Hinda and Ader back to their old place of work with the government, they first registered their names in the list of the displaced people in the camp, so that they could receive the relief food.

As the time was going by, Hinda began to date a certain man but kept secret, her new romance, from Ader because she was thinking that Ader might despise her. However, one day when they were going out for lunch, the man followed them and the way in which, he was looking at Hinda, convinced Ader that something extraordinary was going on between the two. A short while, after the man had left, Hinda then decided to disclose to Ader, her long kept secret.

"I am aware that you have noticed the way that, that man and I were looking at each other," Hinda said quite humbly. "However, I am sorry that I have not told you, about my new life. Ader, my dear friend, that man is my new boyfriend and we have been courting each other for, quite sometime now."

"Why did you not, tell me about the man, girlfriend?" Ader asked her friend puzzlingly.

"I have been quite ashamed of myself and was thinking that you might despise me," replied Hinda, with such a subdued spirit.

"You know very well that I would not," refuted Ader because she was feeling quite disappointed in Hinda and did not like the way that she had been thinking about her. "Hinda, I have been holding you tenderly in my heart, as if, you were my biological sister, all these years because I love you deeply and your friendship has been such a treasure for me but I do not why, all of a sudden, you have been thinking that I could despise you for falling in love again. However, I am happy to know that you have met someone who would, bring some meaning back into your life."

Hinda was quite puzzled by her friend's remarks that she broke down, out of shame and started shedding tears. Ader did not understand, what the tears were meant for and therefore, she asked Hinda quite surprisingly, "Could you please kindly explain to me, why you are crying?"

"I am crying because I am so ashamed of myself, for keeping secret, my new relationship from you, Ader, my very dear and long time best friend and right now I am feeling so terrible. Ader, I know how you love and care about me so dearly and I hope that you will find it in your heart to forgive me, for being so stupid," concluded Hinda, while her tears were still streaming down.

Ader therefore, hugged Hinda tenderly and told her that "Hinda, I love you, my dear girl, and will never hate you for any reason. I am very happy and proud of you, for being able to fall in love once again. Please, don't you ever feel bad about yourself, anymore because you deserve love and I am going to support you, one hundred percent."

"Ader, thank you, for being so understanding," said Hinda, as she was feeling quite relieved to know that Ader was still loving her as usual. "My dear Ader, I promise you that I will never hide anything from you again, in the future."

"I sure hope that you will keep your promise," said Ader as she was hugging her friend. "God bless you, Hinda."

Some of the men, from the ministry, who had tried in the past, to have relationship with Ader, before she was married but failed, started attempting to date her again. Some of them were quite hopeful to win Ader's heart because they were thinking, that since she was then a widow, she might be in need for a new husband desperately. Oh boy, did they all get it wrong! To their dismay, Ader rejected them all and stated that she did not need any man anymore in her life. However, one haughty and tawdry man, called Juma, who was already married but had sent his wife and children to Khartoum, as most of the men had done, due to the insecurity in Juba, insisted that he would like to marry Ader. He even attempted, to lie to Ader that he was not yet married but Ader was quite aware that the man was such a pathological liar and therefore, she tried to reject him politely but he would not heed. One day, out of frustration, Ader admonished Juma quite sternly, "Hey Juma, it is very erroneous for you to think that my vulnerable situation as a widow, has made me so desperate for a man. Let me tell you the truth, no man, under the sun, could ever give me the kind of love and affection that my beloved late husband had pampered me with, when he was alive. His wonderful love for me was strong, faithful committed, understanding and very trustworthy. I thank God, for having enabling me to experience and enjoy the deepest true love from my late husband, the kind of love that not many women in this world have had the chance to feel. Therefore, his genuine love, will continue to guide and guard me, throughout the remaining days of my life because I am just not interested, in the kind of cheap love that most of the women are enduring from their cruel husbands. I just cannot love another man again. So, leave me alone."

Juma rascally ignored Ader's rejection for him and persisted on his libidinous pursuit of her until, one day he went up to Ader's house. Ader was so overcome with rage, as soon as she saw Juma that she entered into her house, grabbed a folded chair and began swinging it towards him that she almost hit him on the head, as he was trying to enter her house. The short and ugly-looking man sprinted for his life, without looking back. Many of Ader's neighbours, who had seen Juma, as he was running briskly, away from Ader's door, laughed at him with tears. Therefore, from that moment onward, Juma never bothered Ader anymore. Most of the people, praised Ader for what she had done that day because they were quite aware that Juma was only trying to make a joke out of her because he was such a womanizer. After the incident, no man attempted to approach Ader for a relationship anymore. They were scared that she might beat the hell out of them.

The incident between Ader and Juma spread like wild fire and soon even in the place of work, some workers were referring to Ader as the monster. Every morning, as Ader was going to her office, her tormentors would gawp, leer and mockingly laugh at her. Ader did not care about the situation initially but as the ugly situation was getting worse, it took a big painful bite into Ader's heart, began crushing her spirit relentlessly and she did no longer feel like going to work anymore. Ader battled with the nerve-wrecking situation that she was facing, alone for a long time but decided eventually to share it with old Nyarata. However, humourous Nyarata looked at Ader in such dismay and then told her, "I have been thinking mistakenly that you were mature enough to withstand such, foolish and idiotic insults. You know what, if I were you, I would have boasted even more to those silly men, who are calling you a monster. How could a beautiful young woman, like you, be a monster, anyway? Those men's main problems with you, are jealousy and envy because you are not some cheap kind of woman that they could play around with. Besides, you have already decided that you will not marry anymore and therefore, why are you letting such silly name-calling crushing you down? Ader, my child, you are a strong, beautiful, intelligent, wise, kind, compassionate, gracious, wonderful and courageous woman and I think that those men envy your outstanding qualities and are wishing that you were a wife to any one of them. All I would tell you, my dear child, is that stand up for what you believe in and don't allow anyone to crush your indomitable spirit."

"Thank you very much, Nyarata, for your insight," gratefully said Ader because of the wise things that the old woman had told her, "I wonder what my life would be like if, you had not been available, to always give me your invaluable advice and support in my time of desperation. I will therefore never, allow those flibbertigibbets to get to me, anymore and should any one of them bother me once again, I will roar on him like a horrible thunderstorm."

"That is my girl!" exclaimed Nyarata quite proudly, as she was rejoicing in Ader's rejuvenated spirit. "My dear child, next time try to tell me anything that that is bothering you before, it could almost break you down."

"Definitely, I will surely do that," said Ader with such a grateful heart, as she was sweet smiling. "I have tortured myself, all this time for nothing when, I should have told you about my situation, earlier." Ader then hugged Nyarata and felt so happy, for the first time in a long time.

Nyarata's wonderful advice boosted Ader's morale a lot, and therefore, she begun going to work each day, with the determination of a lioness and faced her stupid adversaries squarely because she was no longer caring about, whatever they were tattling about her. Ader's tormentors realized eventually that their smudges against her character, was not bothering her at all and so they discontinued with their malodorous exercise because there was nothing else that they were able to come up with, in order to break her daring spirit.

Ader used effectively, the new ammunition of power that old Nyarata had given to her to withstand her enemies and from that time onwards, each morning when she was going to work, she would dressed up professionally and walked with such confidence and dignity that evidently showed everyone that she was in full control of her life. Therefore, it was quite hard then for anyone to tell that Ader was indeed a grieving widow.

On the other hand, Hinda decided eventually, to tell her new boyfriend, more about Ader and one day she told him delightfully that "My dear , Ader, is my best friend and I regard her more as if she were my real sister. Ader and I have been friends since we were young girls at school and throughout our marriages that were cut short by the monstrous hands of the rebels. I have been through thick and thin with Ader and I love her a lot because she means so much to me. I would really like you to meet her formally, one of these days. She already, knows about you and I and has given me, her full support."

The boyfriend of Hinda was called, Lotombe. He was not that good-looking but quite arrogant in the way that he talked to everyone, including Hinda. He liked assuming false things about others a lot and thought very high of himself. Therefore, he listened attentively to whatever, his girlfriend was telling him about Ader and said eventually, "I hope that Ader has truly accepted me, as your boyfriend since, you are best of friends, according to what, you have just told me."

Hinda did not understand why, Lotombe was a little sarcastic in his reply to her because she had not yet heard about, the incident that had happened between Juma and Ader but Lotombe had already heard about it. "Don't be silly, I am very sure that Ader has accepted you," Hinda told her arrogant boyfriend. "You really do not know my friend at all, she is such a wonderful person because she is very loving, peaceful, thoughtful, compassionate, trustful, faithful, kind, tolerant and understanding. Furthermore, it is always very easy, to get along with her."

"Well, well, I am very happy, to hear what you have said about your friend," Lotombe told his girlfriend rather doubtfully. "Therefore, I look forward to visiting and knowing her a little better, if that would be ok with you."

Hinda wanted so much that her boyfriend should meet and get to know her best friend better and therefore, she approached Ader one day and told her that "Ader, My boyfriend and I would like to visit you this weekend but what do you think about our intention?"

"I would be delighted to have both of you for my visitors on Saturday," said Ader because she had been waiting for an opportunity, so as to get to know, what kind of a man, Lotombe truly was.

"Therefore, I will then tell Lotombe that it is ok for us to visit you," said Hinda, as she was feeling quite excited.

"See you all, when you see me," said Ader quite delightfully.

On the day that Hinda and her boyfriend had visited Ader, she cooked very delicious meal and warmly welcomed them into her house. The two old friends then confabulated about a lot of things, as they were having such a wonderful time together. However, Lotombe did not say much because he had already developed an impression of Ader in his mind that she was a fastidious and violent woman against men. As a result therefore, when he and Hinda were returning home, Lotombe bluntly told Hinda, "Sweetheart, I am rather sorry, to tell you this, I am kind of scared of your friend because she seemed like a woman who, does not enjoy the company of any man at all."

Hinda was so terribly offended by her boyfriend's negative remarks against Ader that she did not say anything to him until they got to her house and then she told him disappointingly, "Could you please go to your house because I want to be alone tonight."

"Why the change for the worse, in your mood all of a sudden?" Lotombe asked Hinda curiously because he was not aware that he had offended Hinda quite seriously, by his negative remarks against Ader.

"If you really want to be my boyfriend, then you must stop talking disrespectfully about my dearest friend, Ader," Hinda gave an ultimatum to her boyfriend. "Your demeaning remarks against her, on our way home, was very judgmental. You really do not know Ader at all, to say such insulting statement about her."

Lotombe apologized and contritely said, "I truly didn't mean to judge your friend, as I have sounded to you, my dear because I was telling honestly to you, my impression of her. However, I am very sorry, that I have hurt your feelings and I promise you that I will never say anything derogative about your friend, again." Lotombe did love Hinda a lot and therefore, he controlled his dislike for Ader, so as to be with her.

Ader's friendship with Hinda started eventually to drift apart for Lotombe was not allowing Hinda to be alone with Ader because he was afraid that Ader might advice his girlfriend to leave him. Ader read the negative expressions on Lotombe's face, whenever she was with them and meticulously concluded that he did not like her. Therefore, Ader began to avoid Hinda all the time. However, one day Hinda got a chance to talk to Ader alone, when her boyfriend had gone somewhere and humbly asked her, "Ader, my dear, why are you avoiding me so much, these days?"

"It is not you, that I am avoiding but your boyfriend," replied Ader honestly. "He does not like me for some reason and I have been noticing the negative expressions on his face against me, whenever I am talking with you. Hinda, you must understand that I don't want to come between the two of you because I love you dearly but I think that it would be wise for us not to be close with each other, at the moment. Remember, when it comes to romance, three is a crowd, as you once upon a time told me, while I was still dating, my late husband."

"Ader, I hate deeply that my love for Lotombe has to separate us this way," said Hinda because she was feeling quite torn between, her love for Ader and that for her boyfriend. "Anyway, I will respect, the step that you have decided to take but remember I will always love you, Ader."

From then onward, Hinda and Ader occasionally spoke to each other and that was how they kept their friendship.

At home, Juan wondered so much, as to why Ader was dressing up very elegantly each day, while she was going to work. One weekend therefore, she decided to ask Ader and find out from her, as to what was new in her life. "Hey, girlfriend, you seemed to be in high spirit these days. Have you found someone, you know what I mean, don't you?" Juan inquired quite curiously.

"Absolutely not," said Ader very honestly and then she burst into an amusing laughter. "Juan, my dearest friend, if there was someone new in my life, you would have been the first one to know about him."

"Ader, these days, the way that you have been dressing up each working day, has been quite unique, as if you are up to something, I mean, something like a new relationship with a man," Juan explained to Ader. "However, what has been really going on in your life?"

Tears formed into Ader's eyes, as she was remembering vividly all the evil things that many people have been saying about her and she paused for a little while, as she was controlling her emotion. "Some people at work have been calling me terrible names since, I almost beat up that fatuous guy, who had once came here," disclosed Ader quite sadly, as she was wiping off her tears. "I had almost quit my work because of the anguish and frustration that I have been experiencing but Nyarata gave me a good advice that have given me concrete power for withstanding all those ruthless people. Therefore, I am dressing up in the way that I have doing these days because I would like to show all those stupid men that they are not better than me and that there is nothing that they could do that would crush my new indomitable spirit, anymore."

"Go for it, girl!" said Juan delightfully. "Oh, my loving Ader, I did not know that you were suffering that much when, I have been seeing you feeling quite moody, in the past few weeks. I am very proud of you and I think that those men are just envious about you. However, I do not think that any of them could, compare to your handsome late husband."

"I have already defeated those losers," said Ader quite triumphantly because she was feeling like a conqueror. "I am very happy to tell you that none of those agents from hell are bothering me anymore."

Juan then hugged Ader compassionately and whispered into her ears softly, "I delight in your strength, may God continue to strengthen and give you courage, so that you may continue to overcome the difficulties in your life."

"Thank you very much," said Ader, in appreciation for her friend's concern for her. "Juan, my dear girlfriend, you mean such a world to me and your kindness and understanding, has made my miserable life, worth living. I thank God everyday, for permitting our paths to cross in life."

From then onwards, Ader continued to lead her life with such confidence and courage that no one, not even the cruel men at her work, were able to dare her anymore.

Chapter Thirty-Six
Ader in the Desolate Home

Ader and Juan went on living together quite peacefully. The deep love and understanding that they had for each other, made them to encourage one another whenever, any one of them was feeling down because of the harsh realities that they were facing as widows. They took the advantage of the relative cease-fire and continued to go for firewood every other Saturday. Soon, they accumulated a lot of bundles of firewood at home and were very proud about their accomplishment. Unfortunately, the peaceful situation did not last long because the government could not reach any compromise with the rebels, on any issue. The Islamic government in Khartoum insisted that the Sharia Law would always be, the state law in the Sudan. They also stated that no one from the southern Sudan would ever become the President of the country, even if, he/she was Moslem. Furthermore, they said rigidly that the southern Sudan would never be separated from the North, not even in the event that a referendum was held and the southern Sudanese voted unanimously for separation from the north. Therefore, the people from the southern Sudan got quite angry with the Islamic Government in Khartoum over the issue and began wishing that the rebels could behave humanely to the people from the south, so that every young and old men would have join the movement and fight the enemies in Khartoum courageously until, the southern Sudan was liberated from the north. Furthermore, they were also wishing that the rebels should moved their frontline to the northern Sudan, so that the government in Khartoum and the people there, could also feel the sting of the devastating war.

Once upon a time, the wishes of the people from the southern Sudan came true because the rebels, for the first time, moved their frontline to the north and attacked a town called Kurmuk in the Blue Nile Region, after the tentative cease-fire. The southern Sudanese rejoiced at the news about, the capture of Kurmuk and prayed that the rebels should take more towns in the northern Sudan so that the civil war might represent its real name, *Sudan People's Liberation Army*. However, after the fall of Kurmuk to the rebels, the Sudan Government, assisted by some Islamic countries, mobilised a great number of soldiers and fiercely attacked the rebels until, they had recaptured Kurmuk. Multitude, of the southern Sudanese young men, who were in the movement, lost their lives in the battle of Kurmuk. The government's action shocked, most of the people in both northern and southern Sudan because when Kapoeta and Torit towns, being in the southern Sudan, fell into the hands of the rebels, the government did nothing to recapture the towns but Kurmuk, being in the northern Sudan, the Government did all it could, within its power, to immediately recapture the town.

The insecurity in Juba worsened, so bad after the government had recaptured Kurmuk from the rebels. Therefore, the military government went on offences and started bombing randomly, various places in the southern Sudan. The bomb killed many civilians and some of the villages were completely wiped off the map. In retaliation, the rebels started shelling Juba relentlessly and also killed civilians. Amidst the horrible and deadly situation, the government's security personnel began arresting some people, who were falsely accused of collaborating with the rebels, by either their neighbours or co-workers, who hated them. A few of the people who were arrested, were tortured but released eventually, whereas some of them, who had refused completely to answer any of the questions from their interrogators, were tortured to death in a location at the military barrack, locally known as the White House and the rest of them, who were deemed to be the worst enemy of the military government, were put into the fighter planes and dropped to their deaths. The horrible situations that were taking place in Juba then, made the civilians started living in utter despair and fear from, both the government and the rebels.

The rebels continued to shell Juba relentlessly and the people became so terrified and devastated that they were cooking at home only during the night but spending their days by the banks of the river Nile, as they were taking refuge from the deadly shelling. In desperation, some of the people moved to live with the displaced people at the outskirts of the town. However, the refuge that the people were trying to take never helped that much because quite a number of them were killed, when the shelling fell on them, while they were taking refuge by the river Nile. Many people from Juba then decided consequently, to go away to the northern Sudan, although they were quite aware that most of the southern Sudanese there, were having very hard time.

A good number of the people who had gone to the northern Sudan and specifically, those who did not have any proper relatives there, were taken into a place in the desert where, even the water that was being given to them, was rationed. Therefore, the people from the northern Sudan, who were working in the camp for the displaced people, started using food and water as a weapon, to tantalise the displaced people, for their amusement. In desperation therefore, most of the people, especially those, who were having little children, the horrendous situation that they were facing, compelled most of them, to embrace Islam and change their names to Moslem names, so that they could be treated well and receive enough food for their families.

At the camp, the people who had run away from Juba asked, those who had come from Wau and Malakal towns, "Are the rebels shelling your towns, like they are shelling Juba?"

"There is no shelling at all in Malakal," said one of the men from Malakal.

"We also have not experienced any shelling at all in Wau," said the people from Wau.

"What had chased us this far is, the horrendous shelling of Juba, by the rebels," said one of the displaced men from Juba. "Many people in our town have lost their lives because of the terrible shelling by the rebels. I wondered, what motives the rebels have against us, which have angered them so bad that they have decided to shell only Juba, out of the three major towns in the southern Sudan."

"What had driven us, to come to this ugly place," said the people from Bahr-el-Ghazal and Upper Nile Regions, "is the way that we were being mistreated while at home, by the Arab raiders and militiamen form the north. They have been looting frequently our properties and raping our women and the young girls quite brutally and also have been burning down our houses, taking away our cattle and some of our women and children, as slaves. Sometimes, the rebels would help fight the Arab raiders but at other times, they were also mistreating us. Therefore, we have been fed up of the pains, tortures, anguish and uncertainties and that is why, we have decided to run here for refuge. We were thinking that when get here, our lives would be safer and meaningful but look at how we are languishing in this hot and Godforsaken desert."

"I do not blame anyone other than, the leader of the rebels," said one elderly man. "The man has never had any idea at all, on how to structure his war. My impression about, the leader of the rebels is that he is like a father, who has been having a bitter quarrel with his worst enemy, for a long time and instead of fighting with his enemy, has decided to take his anger on his own children and started beating them horrendously and even killing others."

"Could you explain to us exactly, what you mean?" asked one of his audients, who did not understand clearly what the elder had said.

"Was my explanation about, my impression about the leader of the rebels really ambiguous?" replied the elderly man in surprise, as he was laughing amusingly. "I was thinking that you have all clearly understood me. Anyway, my dear children, let me explain to you precisely what, I was meaning to say. Had it not been for the devastating ongoing war in the south would any of you think that any of us could have come to live in this desert place? I do not think so. Look, we all have come here because the frontline of the so-called Sudan People's Liberation Army has been all these years, in southern Sudan. The war has been displacing and killing many of our people, meanwhile in the northern Sudan, the people are enjoying life and getting developed day by day. To me in a way, the leader of the rebels is executing what, the northern Sudanese have been wanting to do for a long time, that is, to displace the southern Sudanese from their lands, so that the northern Sudanese and some other Arabs from the Middle East, who do not have lands and proper homes to live in, could come and some day occupy south, without even having to fight for it."

"That is what is called wisdom," his listeners assured him excitedly, "but what could we do in order to avert the pain and destructions that the war has been continuing to cost the people in southern Sudan?"

"We need to negotiate seriously and indefatigably, for our rights and freedom from the northern Sudanese but with the help of some people from the international community, of course," said the old man intelligently. "Sudan is our land, *the land for the black,* as the meaning of the name is and not for the Arabs, who are thinking that they could own any place in the world, wherever they have gone. Arms struggle could never solve the problem between the south and the north. Do you, most of the young people, remember, how long it had taken us to fight, during the first civil war, seventeen years and yet the peace did last long enough, only twelve years because of the stupidity of some of our southern leaders. The thoughtless things that the leader for our first movement had done during the Addis Ababa agreement, have utterly deprived us of the opportunity for a peaceful southern Sudan, with power in our hands and therefore, has caused us this second war. I wonder how long, this present war would continue, moreover, it has gone on longer than the first one already. Therefore, I think that we lack proper leadership in the southern Sudan because most of our politicians are too greedy, corrupt, lack reasoning and planning for a better future for the southern Sudanese by; abusing the power that they are given, advancing only their selfish ambitions and being always quite scared to withstand the arrogant politicians in Khartoum whenever, they are debating any issue, pertaining to the welfare of the southern Sudanese. I do not think that the present leader of the rebels, is any different from the other politicians from the south because once he is tired of fighting, some day in the future, he is going to sign surely for a peace pact with the government in Khartoum, regardless of what the southern Sudanese would gain from it, so that we should live together with the Arabs in the north, once again. Therefore, all the blood that has been pouring out, from our people in the struggle for our liberation from the Moslem's oppression, would be in vain and we would be once again thrown backward consequently, without any hope for a better future and peaceful existence."

The displaced people, who had been listening to the elderly man, thanked him so much and began thinking about him from then onward as, a very wise old man.

The Moslems, from different parts of the world, who were living in the northern Sudan then, were treated with respect and dignity than, the people from the southern Sudan and were living their life quite joyfully, meanwhile working and earning decent pay simply because they were Moslems. In absolute desperation consequently, some of the people from the southern Sudan, decided to change their names to Arab names, so that they could fit in. However, whatever that they were doing did not help them much because at that time, anywhere in the north, being a Christian and a southern Sudanese, was the same as being a criminal, in that the people from the south were suspected all the times and thrown into prisons, for no apparent reasons. Therefore, most of the displaced people, regretted their decision for going to the northern Sudan to take refuge from the bloody war and wished that they had remained in the southern Sudan where, they could have live and died eventually with their dignity intact.

The few of the displaced people, who were lucky and managed to get some employment, could not afford the rents in the residential areas because the landlords charged them very expensively. Some of them were told, to pay for their rents, three months in advance, which was really impossible because the displaced people did not have any savings at all. Some of them began consequently, to build mud huts, on some pieces of lands that were not inhabited at the outskirts of Khartoum city so that they could survive in their own shelters. However, the Moslems did not want the displaced people from the southern Sudan to have any of peace of mind and therefore, they started accusing them, for breaking the Sharia law. They informed the authorities that the displaced people were brewing beer and living very immoral lives and therefore, they demanded that all their mud houses should be torn down immediately, so that the diabolical activities of the displaced people might be eradicated from their land. The authorities, turned deaf ears initially to the accusers but due to their persistence, eventually issued a decree that all the mud huts in the shantytowns, should be torn down in two weeks. The poor, displaced people from southern Sudan, panicked and did not know what to do anymore. After the two weeks indeed, the authorities in Khartoum sent the bulldozers and all the mud huts were torn down. Most of the displaced people then, quit their jobs and went to live in the camps for the displaced in the harsh desert. The few of them, who had decided to keep their jobs, shared rents and crowded together in one place and therefore, there were a lot of diseases and deaths, especially among the children.

On the other hand, in Juba, the rebels, continued to shell the town relentlessly and in Kator area, at a place called Kassava, the shelling fell and killed a woman with her five children, as they were preparing, to run to the bank of the river Nile, so that they could take refuge from the deadly shelling. The woman's house was burnt down with everything in it. Therefore, most of the people, gave up their idea for going to work during the week because of their fear for the shelling. However, one Sunday afternoon, a watchman, who was working for the Norwegian Church Aid, felt thirsty while on duty and therefore, decided to go to a nearby house to ask for a cup of water. As soon as he had left, the shelling fell exactly, at the very spot that he had been sitting before, he had gone to ask for some water. Therefore, the chair that he had used was burnt into ashes and even the guava tree, nearby, was completely burnt into ashes. The watchman praised and thanked God, for saving him by, making him thirsty at that deadly moment.

When the shelling reached its climax, for the first time, Ader began to wish that her brother, Otim, had not gone to work in Dubai, so that she could have gone to live with him in Khartoum until, the horrible and deadly situation in Juba had improved. Most of the government officials, including doctors, lawyers and directors from the various ministries, relocated their wives and children to Khartoum and therefore, were living alone in Juba. However, Nyarata kept on advising Ader not to worry too much because there would always be an end, to everything that happened in this world and therefore, even the shelling would one day stop but Ader did not see any hope for them to live for a long time because the shelling had been hitting almost, all the areas in Juba but the army barracks. Therefore, she prayed a lot but it seemed then as if, even God had abandoned the people in Juba.

As the situation further deteriorated, Juan's parents sent a message to Jore asking her that they would like to return their daughter home for a while, until the insecurity due to the deadly shelling had stopped. Jore, who was so used, to living with her granddaughters and daughter-in-law, did not know what to say and therefore, she began consequently, to hitting her head hopelessly, most of the time, against the wall in anguish, as she was wishing that the shelling should fall on her so that she would not live to see her grandchildren being taken away from her. Therefore, Jore refused to run for refuge by the bank of the Nile like, most of the people were doing but no shelling fell in her place. Ader, who was also fed up of running every morning with her children to the bank of the Nile, decided to stay home with Jore. They would cook and eat normally as if, nothing terrible was happening. However, many people were thinking that one day, Ader and Jore's luck would run out but it never did. Therefore, after Juan had realised that there was no difference at all whether, she ran for refuge by the river Nile or stay at home, she also joined her mother-in-law and Ader.

When Juan's parents heard that their daughter and grandchildren were not taking refuge by the river Nile, like most of the people were doing, they became aghast and immediately went to bring her home. Therefore, as soon as Juan's parent got into her courtyard, her mother inquired quite angrily that" How could you be so silly and refuse to run and take refuge, by the bank of the river Nile, like most of the people in Juba are doing? Juan, my dear daughter, I think that this sorrowful home of yours has made you insane, just like everyone else living in it. You are coming home with us, this very minute."

"There is death everywhere," answered Juan rather arrogantly because she was quite disgusted by, what her mother had just said. "Mother, even if I were to go with you today, if God chooses that I die, I will die, anyway. Not only that even if I were to take refuge, from the deadly shelling, by the bank of the river Nile, if that were my day to die, I would be hit by the shelling nevertheless. Please, Mom, give me some time to package my belongings in order, before I could return home."

"I am glad, at least to know that you have seen some sense in the importance that you should return to live with us," said the rude Juan's mother, with a body language that made her seemed like she had got, the power over life and death. "This home of yours, is no longer fit for human habitation and I wonder very much how, you are managing to continue to living here."

"Hey, hey, hey, ah, Mother. Are you implying that because there is no man in this home, therefore, it is now a useless place for us live in?" Juan interrogated her arrogant mother quite angrily because she was quite disappointed, by the terrible statement that her mother had just said. "Mother, why can't you thank God, for allowing my dad to live with you joyfully, for such a long time and do you think that every woman is as lucky as you are?"

"Juan, my daughter, I did not mean, to sound that rude," answered her mother shamelessly. "However, I am sorry, for the way that I have sounded to you but I really want you to come home with us."

"I have already told you that I would," said Juan quite disgustingly and she began to walk arrogantly away from her parents.

Juan's father, who had been watching his daughter and wife, without saying a word, while they were having an altercation, rebuked disciplinarily his wife later, on their way home, for being senseless to Juan, Ader and Jore's, feelings.

Ader helped her friend a lot, while she was sorting out and packaging her belongings before she could return to her parents' home. Jore watched frustratingly in silence, as her daughter-in-law was doing everything. However, she was wishing then that she could have had some power, so as to stop Juan from going back to her parents. Jore sighed deeply from time to time, as she was trying to clear the thick stuff that had been building on her throat because of the stress that she was going through. However, Jore began to spend, most of her time with her granddaughters, while they were laughing and playing joyfully together because she was aware that those were the only moments that she was having to spending with them, before they could go away. Juan felt quite sorry for her mother-in-law but there was nothing that she was able to do in order to help, alleviate her mother-in-law's anguish. Therefore, Juan began to cook very delicious meals and tried to joke with her mother-in-law most of the time but the air was too thick with sorrow for poor old Jore.

A week, after, Juan had packaged everything in her house in order; she and Ader jointly cooked a big meal which they knew that they were going to eat together for the last time, in that grief-stricken home and Ader called it "*The Last Supper*." Ader and Juan invited, Juan's parents and old Nyarata, to come and share with them, their last meal together. The young women cleaned the courtyard and erected a shade outside for eating. They acted like, they were very happy and celebrating a big occasion by playing the Christian songs on the radio cassette, which made everything seemed quite festive, as though, there was no war going on. Jore was quit happy, for what the young widows had done by inviting Juan's parents over because she would then able to use the opportunity, to talk to Juan's parents, for one last time. Juan's parents arrived at about 4:00 PM and Nyarata joined them, shortly after. Jore warmly welcomed her in-laws but deep in her heart, she was torn to pieces because she could not imagine her life in that home, without her beloved granddaughters and daughter-in-law in it. Therefore, Ader and Juan served the meal but everyone ate in silence. While they were eating, Ader controlled her tears with such difficulty and avoided to look at Juan completely because according to her, Juan was like the sister that she did not have in Juba and the very knowledge that Juan was going finally away from that home that day, shattered Ader's heart into dust.

After the meal, old and frail-looking Jore courageously said to Juan's parents, "I would like to thank you first, for having allowed your beloved daughter, Juan, to live with me for such a long time, after the death of my son. I have known all along that one day Juan was going to leave me alone but I have never expected that it would be this soon. However, I am blaming, whoever had started the bloody war that has claimed the lives of so many young men, women and children and especially, my only dearly beloved son, Mori. Therefore, there is one thing that I would like to ask of you, my dear in-laws and that is, for you to allow your daughter and my grandchildren to visit me quite frequently because I would like my grandchildren, to grow up knowing me very well as, the mother of their late father. It is very important that we keep in touch because I love my grandchildren very much and I see a lot of my late son on their faces. My grandchildren are the reason why, I am going on living and the fact that they are going away today from this home, is making me feeling like, a hot iron bar is being driven through my heart. I just cannot describe to you in words how, I am feeling right now but yet, I have no one to blame for my miseries in life."

"Had it not been because of the shelling and the general uncertainties that everyone is facing in Juba at the moment," said Juan's mother, "we would have allowed our daughter to live with you a little longer, otherwise, with the security situation worsening everyday, we could not help but return our dear daughter home. We are afraid that some day, some bad men might come at night to rape or even kill our daughter since, there is no man in this home to protect her."

"Everything that you have said is quite true," Jore told Juan's mother quite humbly, "and I would like to assure you that I am not bitter at all about, you taking away my daughter-in-law and my grandchildren. I wish all of them and as well as you and the rest of the members of your family, a good and safe life. May God watch over us all until that day, when peace shall prevail again in the southern Sudan, especially, here in Juba."

Ader listened, quietly to whatever was being said and wished that she had parents like that of Juan in Juba, so that she would have also gone away from the sorrowful home that was going to be so desolate for her, without Juan around.

To support the statement that Juan's mother had made about raping and killing of women, there were indeed such cases in Juba. Some of the northern Sudanese soldiers and merchants, were opening randomly people's houses at night in desperate search for women to have sex with because they were erroneously thinking that since, the southern Sudanese women were not covering their heads with veils, like the Moslem women would, therefore, they could easily give in to any man, who would approached them for sex. Good heavens were they so much mistaken! Everyone in Juba was so much offended by the diabolical activities of the lunatics, especially the women that they began to properly arm up themselves at night, just in case, any of the stupid northerners would venture to break into their houses. Therefore, one night, some of the idiots tried to rape some widows, who were living together in a big home so that they could protect each other. However, the women beat up their attackers viciously and injured a number of them quite seriously while, the rest of them fled for their lives. The ones who were injured, were left lying in the courtyard until, some of the kind people informed the authorities about them then, they were collected and flown immediately to Khartoum because the authorities were afraid that if they were treated in the hospital in Juba, some people might attack them. The southern Sudanese women are very strong, when it comes to self-defense and would not tolerate any abuse, especially from the shameless and heartless northern Sudanese men.

The story about the women, who had beaten up the northern Sudanese men at night, spread like wild fire all over Juba and therefore, most of the people were quite delighted to hear about it. However, the news angered so much, most of the northern Sudanese, who were living in Juba then. They began, to demand seriously from the security officers that they were in need for protection from, the people in Juba who were perpetrating violence against them. Consequently, the Security Personnel began to stoop so low that they started monitoring frequently the ways in which the Christian denominations were preaching in their churches. Therefore, some of the Catholic priests became consequently their main targets because the Security Personnel had then deemed that the ways in which, some of the priests had been preaching, were quite unrealistic, out of context, instigative and against the government's policies and so,they arrested some of them. To make their cases more credible against the priests that they had arrested, the Security Personnel implicated them falsely that they were collaborating with the rebels. They blindfolded consequently the priests and beat them up quite ruthlessly before they could send them eventually, for further interrogations in Khartoum where, they were heinously tortured and locked up in murky underground detention centres. The horrendous way in which, the priest were mistreated, was kept totally secret by the government in Khartoum, from the international press because they were afraid that the heart-wrenching truth might spark, demonstrations and outcries from the international community, for the immediate release of the priests.

After Jore and Juan's mother had finished talking, the dreaded moment for saying goodbye and separation arrived. Juan hugged Ader tenderly for a long time and began sobbing. However, her mother, who did not want her daughter to cry, stared at her meanly and therefore, Juan stopped crying and wiped off her tears immediately. Jore then held tenderly, her beloved grandchildren, each at a time, as she was blowing her blessings on their head and then wished them, a good health and safe stay at their new home. Thereafter, Jore hugged her daughter-in-law lovingly and said, "Juan, you will always be my daughter-in-law forever. It doesn't matter whether you are married to another man, some day because remember, it is only the terrible hands of death and the cruel civil war that are now separating us today. My dear daughter, you have been very loving, kind, compassionate and respectful to me, as if, I were your real mother and therefore, my relationship with you, will not be lost until, I die."

"I will not forget you too because you are such a wonderful person and full of wisdom," the quite sad-looking Juan told her mother-in-law. "I will always be visiting you, if the shelling spare us."

"Nothing bad will happen to you, my dear," Jore assured confidently her daughter-in-law. "You have enormous responsibilities for raising my orphaned grandchildren and I believe that God, in his kindness, will watch over all of you everyday and nothing bad will ever cross our paths."

"Thanks, Mom," said Juan, in despair. "May God watch over you, Ader and her children until peace shall prevail again here in Juba, so that I could return and live with you, my beloved friends. I love you, very much and will be missing you a lot.

After the final goodbyes, Juan, her children and parents, began to walk away, on their way home. Ader escorted them, as far as the gate to the courtyard only because she was emotionally torn inside and could not imagine her life, in that miserable home without Juan, as she was greatly missing her already. Therefore, Ader began to think deeply, as she was searching her soul about, what wrong she might have done against God or anyone at all which, she had not confess to God, that has caused her life to be so miserable, sorrowful and lonely. She began wishing for the first time that she had never been married, while fear was gripping and pounding at her broken heart and soul relentlessly. Murk and despair engulfed automatically, the once upon a time, so joyful, happy, wonderful and lovely home, while Ader was standing at the gate, as she was watching Juan, her children and parents, as they were going away until, they were out of sight. Ader then turned and looked sorrowfully at Jore, who was standing in the courtyard with, both of her hands over her head and seemed very miserable. Ader's heart was completely crushed, as she was looking at the old woman, who was standing feebly in despair like, the tiniest island in the ocean or a tiny tree in the middle of the desert. Therefore, she began to wonder hopelessly what, the future was really holding for herself, her little boys and poor old Jore, who was so dear to her in that desolate home, for as long as the unknown to the rest of the world but devastating war in the southern Sudan was going on.

Ader then sighed deeply and began spontaneously to gaze eventually towards the sky, as if, she had seen something very mysterious up there and said thoughtfully to herself, as she was continuing to gaze towards heaven, *My children, Jore and I are the righteousness of God in Christ Jesus, and despite our heart-wrenching losses, God still loves us dearly and will always watch over us in this forlorn home. Isn't it amazing how lately we have completely trusted in God's protection and defied the fear of death by staying here and refusing to take refuge by the River Nile, from the deadly shelling and yet nothing bad has happened to us? We are more than conquerors in Christ Jesus, who loves us selflessly. Furthermore, who could have thought that I, who love indelibly and deeply my dearly beloved late husband, would live this long after his death? Yet here I am, dragging on, despite all the odds against my children and me. Therefore, I do not want to indwell despair in my heart anymore because if heaven and earth would, some day, pass away, how about this lousy ongoing civil war that has lost its original intention. I, Ader, believe consequently and trust that God, in his loving kindness, will let us live securely in this desolate home until He would make it possible some day in the future for a lasting peace to prevail in the southern Sudan for all to enjoy.*

Printed in the United States
80425LV00003B/109-156

9 781424 163724